About

Amanda Stevens is an ~~...~~
fifty novels. Born and ra~~...~~
resides in Houston, Tex~~...~~

Debra Webb is the award-winning, USA Today
bestselling author of more than 150 novels, including
reader favourites the *Faces of Evil*, the *Colby Agency,*
and the *Shades of Death* series. With more than four
million books sold in numerous languages and
countries, Debra's love of storytelling goes back to
her childhood on a farm in Alabama. Visit Debra at
www.DebraWebb.com or write to her at PO Box 176,
Madison, AL 35758.

Jennifer D. Bokal penned her first book at age eight. An
early lover of the written word, she followed her passion,
becoming a full-time writer. From there, she never
looked back. She earned a master of arts in creative
writing from Wilkes University and joined the Romance
Writers of America. Happily married to her own alpha
male hero, Jennifer and her husband live in upstate New
York with their three beautiful daughters, two spoiled
dogs and a kitten who aspires to be a Chihuahua.

Love Under Fire

Love Under Fire: Past Wrongs

AMANDA STEVENS

DEBRA WEBB

JENNIFER D. BOKAL

MILLS & BOON

First Published in Great Britain 2022
By Mills & Boon, an imprint of HarperCollins*Publishers,* Ltd
1 London Bridge Street, London, SE1 9GF

www.harpercollins.co.uk

HarperCollins*Publishers*
1st Floor, Watermarque Building,
Ringsend Road, Dublin 4, Ireland

LOVE UNDER FIRE: PAST WRONGS © 2022 Harlequin Books S.A.

Killer Investigation © 2019 Marilyn Medlock Amann
The Dark Woods © 2019 Debra Webb
Under the Agent's Protection © 2019 Jennifer D. Bokal

ISBN: 978-0-263-30402-2

MIX
Paper from
responsible sources
FSC® C007454

This book is produced from independently certified FSC™ paper
to ensure responsible forest management.

For more information visit: www.harpercollins.co.uk/green

Printed and Bound in Spain using 100% Renewable electricity at
CPI Black Print, Barcelona

KILLER
INVESTIGATION

AMANDA STEVENS

Chapter One

The house on Tradd Street hadn't changed much since Arden Mayfair had left home fourteen years ago. The beautiful grand piano still gathered dust at one end of the parlor while a long-dead ancestor remained on guard above the marble fireplace. Plantation shutters at all the long windows dimmed the late-afternoon sunlight that poured down through the live oaks, casting a pall over the once stately room. The echo of Arden's footfalls followed her through the double doors as the oppressive weight of memories and dark tragedy settled heavily upon her shoulders.

Her gaze went to the garden and then darted away. She wouldn't go out there just yet. If she left tomorrow, she could avoid the lush grounds altogether, but already the interior walls were closing in on her. She drew a breath and stared back at her ancestor, unfazed by the flared nostrils and pious expression. She'd never been afraid of the dead. It was the living that haunted her dreams.

She wrinkled her nose as she turned away from the portrait. The house smelled musty from time and neglect, and she would have liked nothing more than to throw open the windows to the breeze. The whole place needed a good airing, but the patio doors were kept closed for a reason.

Berdeaux Place hadn't always been a shuttered mausoleum. The gleaming Greek Revival with its elegant arches and shady piazzas had once been her grandmother's pride and joy, an ancestral treasure box filled with flowers and friends and delectable aromas wafting from the kitchen. When Arden thought back to her early childhood days, before the murder, she conjured up misty images of garden parties and elegant soirees. Of leisurely mornings in the playroom and long afternoons in the pool. Sometimes when it rained, her mother would devise elaborate scavenger hunts or endless games of hide-and-seek. Arden had once sequestered herself so well in the secret hidey-hole beneath the back staircase that the staff had spent hours frantically searching the house from top to bottom while she lay curled up asleep.

After a half-hearted scolding from her mother, Arden had been allowed to accompany her into the parlor for afternoon tea. The women gathered that day had chuckled affectionately at the incident as they spooned sugar cubes into their Earl Grey and nibbled on cucumber sandwiches. Basking in the limelight of their indulgence, Arden had gorged herself on shortbread cookies while stuffing her pockets with macaroons to later share with her best friend. When twilight fell, wrapping the city in shadows and sweet-scented mystery, she'd slipped out to the garden to watch the bats.

It was there in the garden that Arden had stumbled upon her mother's body. Camille Mayfair lay on her back, eyes lifted to the sky as if waiting for the moon to rise over the treetops. Something had been placed upon her lips—a crimson magnolia petal, Arden would later learn. But in that moment of breathless terror, she'd been aware of only one thing: the excited thumping of a human heart.

As Arden grew older, she told herself the sound had been her imagination or the throb of her own pulse. Yet, when she allowed herself to travel back to that twilight, the pulsation seemed to grow and swell until the cacophony filled the whole garden.

It was the sound of a beating heart that had lured her from her mother's prone body to the summerhouse, where a milky magnolia blossom had been left on the steps. The throbbing grew louder as Arden stood in the garden peering up into the ornate windows. Someone stared back at her. She was certain of it. She remained frozen—in fear and in fascination—until a bloodcurdling scream erupted from her throat.

As young as she was, Arden believed that bloom had been left for her to find. The killer had wanted her to know that he would one day come back for her.

Camille Mayfair had been the first known victim of Orson Lee Finch, the Twilight Killer. As the lives of other young, single mothers had been claimed that terrible summer, the offspring left behind had become known as Twilight's Children, a moniker that was still trotted out every year on the anniversary of Finch's arrest. New revelations about the case had recently propelled him back into the headlines, and Arden worried it was only a matter of time before some intrepid reporter came knocking on her door.

So why had she come back now? Why not wait until the publicity and curiosity had died down once again? She had business to attend to, but nothing urgent. After all, months had gone by since her grandmother's passing. She'd certainly been in no hurry to wrap up loose ends. She'd come in for the service, left the same day, and the hell of it was, no one had cared. No one had asked her to stay. Not her estranged grandfather, not her uncle, not the friends and distant relatives she'd left behind long ago.

Her invisibility had been a painful reminder that she didn't belong here anymore. Although Berdeaux Place was hers now, she had no intention of staying on in the city, much less in this house. Her grandmother's attorney was more than capable of settling the estate once Arden had signed all the necessary paperwork. The house would be privately listed, but, with all the inherent rules and regulations that bound historic properties, finding the right buyer could take some time.

So why *had* she come back?

Maybe a question best not answered, she decided.

As she turned back to the foyer to collect her bags, she caught a movement in the garden out of the corner of her eye. She swung around, pulse thudding as she searched the terrace. Someone was coming along one of the pathways. The setting sun was at his back, and the trees cast such long shadows across the flagstones that Arden could make out little more than a silhouette.

Reason told her he was just one of the yard crew hired by the attorney to take care of the grounds. No cause for panic. But being back in this house, wallowing in all those old memories had left her unnerved. She reached for the antique katana that her grandmother had kept at the ready atop her desk. Slipping off the sheath, Arden held the blade flat against the side of her leg as she turned back to the garden.

The man walked boldly up to one of the French doors and banged on the frame. Then he cupped his face as he peered in through one of the panes. "I see you in there," he called. "Open up!"

Arden's grip tightened around the gilded handle. "Who are you? What do you want?"

"Who am I? What the…?" He paused in his incredulity. "Cut it out, Arden. Would you just open the damn door?"

The familiarity of his voice raised goose bumps as she walked across the room to peer back out at him. Her heart tumbled in recognition. The eyes...the nose...that full, sensuous mouth... "Reid?"

His gaze dropped to the weapon in her hand. "Just who the hell were you expecting?"

She squared her shoulders, but her tone sounded more defensive than defiant. "I certainly wasn't expecting you."

"Are you going to let me in or should we just yell through the glass all night?"

She fumbled with the latch and then drew back the door. "What are you doing here anyway? You scared me half to death banging on the door like that."

He nodded toward the blade. "Were you really going to run me through with that thing?"

"I hadn't decided yet."

"In that case..." He took the sword from her hand and brushed past her into the parlor.

"By all means, come on in," she muttered as she followed him back into the room. She clenched her fists as if she could somehow control her racing pulse. He had startled her, was all. Gave her a bad fright leering in through the windows like a Peeping Tom. Her reaction had everything to do with the situation and nothing at all to do with the man. She was over Reid Sutton. He'd been nothing more than a memory ever since she'd left for college at eighteen, determined to put him and Charleston in her rearview mirror. They'd had a grand go of it. Given both families plenty of gray hairs and sleepless nights, and then the adventure had run its course. Arden had needed to get serious about her future and, at eighteen, Reid Sutton had been anything but serious. They'd both had a lot of growing up to do. At least Arden had been mature enough to realize she needed to break away before she made an irrevocable mistake.

She wondered if Reid had ever learned that lesson. She

took in his faded jeans, flip-flops and the wavy hair that needed a trim. He was still devastatingly handsome with a smile that could melt the polar ice caps, but she knew better than to succumb to his particular allure. He was still big-time trouble from everything she'd heard, and he still had too much of the rebel in him even at the age of thirty-two. Which was, she suspected, only one of many reasons he'd recently left his family's prestigious but stodgy law firm.

Arden watched him put away the weapon. She had to tear her gaze away from his backside, and that annoyed her to no end. "How did you get into the garden anyway? The side gate is always kept locked." Her grandmother had made certain of that ever since the murder.

He turned with a grin, flashing dimples and white teeth. "The same way you used to sneak out. I climbed up a tree and jumped down over the wall."

She sighed. "You couldn't just ring the doorbell like any normal person?"

"What fun would that be?" he teased. "Besides..." He glanced around. "I wasn't sure you'd be alone."

"So you decided to spy on me instead?"

"Arden, Arden." He shook his head sadly. "Since when did you become so pedestrian? You sound like an old lady. Though you certainly don't present as one." His gaze lingered, making Arden secretly relieved for the Pilates classes and the sleeveless white dress she'd worn to meet her grandmother's attorney. "Just look at you. Thirty-two and all grown-up."

"Which is more than I can say for you." She returned his perusal, taking in the faded jeans and flip-flops.

"It's after-hours, in case you hadn't noticed the time."

"Fair enough. But don't pretend this is our first meeting since I left Charleston. I saw you just six months ago at my grandmother's funeral."

"Yes, but that was from a distance and you were dressed all in black. The hat and veil were sexy as hell, but I barely caught a glimpse of you."

"You could have come by the house after the service."

"I did."

She lifted a brow. "When? I never saw you."

"I didn't come in," he admitted. "I sat out on the veranda for a while."

"Why?"

For a moment, he seemed uncharacteristically subdued. He tapped out a few notes on the piano as Arden waited for his response. The strains of an old love song swirled in her head, tugging loose an unwelcome nostalgia.

"Why didn't you come in?" she pressed.

He hit a sour note. "I guess I wasn't sure you'd want to see me after the way we ended things."

"That was a long time ago."

"I know. But it got pretty heated that last night. I always regretted some of the things I said before you drove off. I didn't even mean most of it."

"Sure you did, but your reaction was understandable. You were angry. We both were. I said some things, too." She shrugged, but inside she was far from cavalier about their current discussion. "I guess it made leaving easier."

"For you maybe."

She cut him a look. "Don't even try to put it all on me. You left, too, remember? That was the agreement. We'd both go off to separate colleges. Do our own thing for a while. Have our own friends. We needed some space. It was all for the best."

"But you never came back."

"That's not true. I came back on holidays and every summer break."

"You never came back to me," he said quietly.

Arden stared at him for a moment and then took a quick glance around. "Are we seriously having this conversation? I feel like I'm being pranked or something."

He didn't bat an eye as he continued to regard her. "You're not being pranked. We're just being honest for once. Airing our grievances, so to speak. Best way to move on."

Arden lifted her chin. "I don't have any grievances, and I moved on a long time ago."

"Everyone has grievances. Without them, there'd be no need for people like me."

"Lawyers, you mean." Her tone sounded more withering than she'd meant it.

He grinned, disarming her yet again. "Grievances are our lifeblood. But to get back on point… Yes, you're right, we did agree to separate colleges. We were supposed to go off and sow our wild oats and then come back to Charleston, settle down, marry and have a few kids, number negotiable."

She gave a quick shake of her head, unable to believe what she was hearing. "When did we ever talk about anything remotely like that?"

"I thought it was understood. In my mind, that was the way it was always supposed to end."

"Is this the part where you tell me you've been pining for me all these years? That I'm the reason you never married?"

"You never married, either," he said. "Have you been pining for me?"

"No, I have not." She planted a hand on one hip as she stared him down. "As fascinating as I'm finding this conversation, I really don't have time for a trip down memory lane. I have a lot of things to do and not much time to do

them. So if you'd like to tell me why you're really here…"
She tapped a toe impatiently.

"I was hoping we could have dinner some night and
catch up."

The suggestion hit her like a physical blow. Dinner?
With Reid Sutton? No, not a good idea, ever. The last thing
she needed was more drama in her life. All she wanted
these days was a little peace and quiet. A safe place where
she could reflect and regroup. Her life in Atlanta hadn't
turned out as she'd hoped. Not her career, not her personal relationships, not even her friendships. There had
been good times, of course, but not enough to overcome
the disappointment and humiliation of failure. Not enough
to ward off a dangerous discontent that had been gathering for months. None of that needed to be shared with
Reid Sutton.

She wandered over to the fireplace, running a finger
along the dusty mantel before turning back to him. "What
do you call this discussion if it's not catching up?"

"Airing grievances and catching up are two different
things." He followed her across the room. "The latter usually goes down better with a cocktail or two. The former
sometimes requires a whole bottle."

"The liquor has all been put away," she said. "And as
tempting as you make it sound, I'm leaving tomorrow so
there's no time for dinner."

He turned to glance back at the foyer where she'd
dropped her luggage. "That many suitcases for just one
night?"

She shrugged. "I like to be prepared. Besides, I may be
going somewhere else after I leave here."

"Where?"

"I haven't decided yet."

He cocked his head and narrowed his gaze. "Is that the

best you can do? Disappointing, Arden. You used to be a much better liar."

"I don't have as much practice these days without you egging me on."

His demeanor remained casual, but something dark flashed in his eyes. "As if I ever had to egg you on. About anything."

She felt the heat of an uncharacteristic blush and turned away. "Funny. I don't recall it that way."

"No? I could refresh your memory with any number of specifics, but suffice to say, you were always very good at deception and subterfuge. Better than me, in fact."

"No one was a better liar than you, Reid Sutton."

"It's good to excel at something, I guess. Seriously, though. How long are you really here for? The truth, this time."

She sighed. She could string him along until they both tired of the game, but what would be the point? "I haven't decided that, either." She brushed off her dusty fingers. "The house needs work before I can list it and I'm not sure I trust Grandmother's attorney to oversee even minor renovations. He's getting on in years and wants to retire." There. She'd owned up to Reid Sutton what she hadn't dared to admit to herself—that she'd come back to Charleston indefinitely.

"Ambrose Foucault still handling her affairs?"

"Yes."

"He's no spring chicken," Reid agreed. "First I'd heard of his retirement, though."

"It's not official. Please don't go chasing after his clients."

He smiled slyly. "Wouldn't dream of it. What about your job? Last I heard you were the director of some fancy art gallery in Atlanta."

"Not an art gallery, a private museum. And not the director, just a lowly archivist."

His eyes glinted. "I bet you ran things, though."

"I tried to, which is why I'm no longer employed there."

"You were fired?"

"Not fired," she said with a frown. "It was a mutual parting of the ways. And anyway, I was ready for a change. You should understand that. Didn't you just leave your father's law practice?"

"Yes, but I *was* fired. Disowned, too, in fact. I'm poor now in case you hadn't heard."

She was unmoved by his predicament. "By Sutton standards maybe. Seems as though I recall a fairly substantial trust fund from your grandfather. Or have you blown through that already?"

"Oh, I've had a good time and then some. But no worries. Provisions have been made for our old age. Nothing on this level, of course." He glanced around the gloomy room with the gilded portraits and priceless antiques. "But we'll have enough for a little place on the beach or a cabin in the mountains. Which do you prefer?"

Arden wasn't amused. The idea that they would grow old together was ludicrous and yet, if she were honest, somehow poignant. "Go away, Reid. I have things to do."

"I could help you unpack," he offered. "At least let me carry your bags upstairs."

"I can manage, thanks."

"Are you sure you want to be alone in this house tonight?"

His tone altered subtly, sending a prickle of alarm down Arden's spine. "Why? What aren't you telling me?" When he didn't answer immediately, she moved closer, peering into his eyes until he glanced away. "You didn't come over here to clear the air, did you? What's going on, Reid? For the last time, why are you really here?"

He peered past her shoulder into the garden. "You haven't heard, then."

"Heard what?"

His troubled gaze came back to her. "There's been a murder."

Chapter Two

"The victim was a young female Caucasian," Reid added as he studied Arden's expression.

She looked suddenly pale in the waning light from the garden, but her voice remained unnervingly calm. "A single mother?"

The question was only natural considering Orson Lee Finch's MO. He'd preyed on young single mothers from affluent families. It was assumed his predilection had been nurtured by contempt for his own unwed mother and resentment of the people he'd worked for. Some thought his killing spree had been triggered by the rejection of his daughter's mother. All psychobabble, as far as Reid was concerned, in a quest to understand the nightmarish urges of a serial killer.

"I don't know anything about the victim," he said. "But Orson Lee Finch will never see the outside of his prison walls again, so this can't have anything to do with him. At least not directly."

Arden's eyes pierced the distance between them. "Why are you here, then? You didn't just come about any old murder."

"A magnolia blossom was found at the scene."

Her eyes went wide before she quickly retreated back into the protection of her rigid composure.

This was the part where Reid would have once taken her in his arms, letting his strength and steady tone reassure her there was no need for panic. He wouldn't touch her now, of course. That wouldn't be appropriate and, anyway, he was probably overreacting. Homicides happened every day. But, irrational or not, he had a bad feeling about this one. He'd wanted Arden to hear about it from him rather than over the news.

She'd gone very still, her expression frozen so that Reid had a hard time reading her emotions. Her hazel eyes were greener than he remembered, her hair shorter than she'd worn it in her younger days, when the sun-bleached ends had brushed her waist. The tiny freckles across her nose, though. He recalled every single one of those.

If he looked closely, he could see the faintest of shadows beneath her eyes and the tug of what might have been unhappiness at the corners of her mouth. He didn't want to look that closely. He wanted to remember Arden Mayfair as that fearless golden girl—barefoot and tanned—who had captured his heart at the ripe old age of four. He wanted to remember those glorious days of swimming and crabbing and catching raindrops on their tongues. And then as they grew older and the hormones kicked in, all those moonlit nights on the beach. The soft sighs and intimate whispers and the music spilling from his open car doors.

The Arden that stood before him now was much too composed and untouchable in her pristine white dress and power high heels. This Arden was gorgeous and sexy, but too grown-up and far too put together. And here he was still tilting at windmills.

He canted his head as he studied her. "Arden? Did you hear what I said?"

"Yes, I heard you." Her hair shimmered about her shoulders as she tucked it behind her ears. "I'm just not sure what I'm supposed to do with the information."

"You don't have to do anything. I just thought it was something you'd want to know."

"Why?"

"*Why?* Are you really going to make me spell it out?"

"Murder happens all the time, unfortunately, and magnolia blossoms are as common as dirt in Charleston. You said yourself this has nothing to do with Orson Lee Finch."

"I did say that, yes."

"This city has always had a dark side. You know that as well as I do." She glanced toward the garden, her gaze distant and haunted. It wasn't hard to figure out what she was thinking, what she had to be remembering. She'd only been five when she found her mother's body. Reid was a few months older. Even then, he'd wanted to protect her, but they'd been hardly more than babies. Pampered and sheltered in their pretty little world South of Broad Street. The fairy tale had ended that night, but the magic between them had lasted until her car lights disappeared from his view on the night she left town.

No, that wasn't exactly true. If he was honest with himself, their relationship had soured long before that night. The magic had ended when they lost their baby.

But he didn't want to think about that. He'd long since relegated that sad time to the fringes of his memory. Best not to dredge up the fear and the blood and the look on Arden's face when she knew it was over. Best not to remember the panicked trip to the ER or the growing distance between them in the aftermath. The despair, the loneliness. The feeling inside him when he knew it was over.

Reid had learned a long time ago not to dwell on matters he couldn't control. Pick yourself up, dust yourself off and get on with life. Hadn't that been his motto for as long as he could remember? If you pretended long enough and hard enough, you might actually start to believe that you were happy.

In fairness, he hadn't been unhappy. He still knew how to have fun. He could still ferret out an adventure now and then. That was worth something, he reckoned.

With a jolt, he realized that Arden was watching him. She physically started when their gazes collided. Her hand went to her chest as if she could somehow calm her accelerated heartbeat. Or was he merely projecting?

He took a deep breath, but not so deep that she would notice. Instead, he let a note of impatience creep into his voice. "So that's it, then? You're just going to ignore the elephant in the room."

She smoothed a hand down the side of her dress as if to prove her nonchalance. "What would you have me do?"

"I would expect a little emotion. Some kind of reaction. Not this…" He trailed away before he said something he'd regret.

"Not this what?" she challenged.

He struggled to measure his tone. "You don't have to be so impassive, okay? It's me. You can drop the mask. I just told you that a magnolia blossom was found at the crime scene. Only a handful of people in this city would understand the significance. You and I are two of them."

"White or crimson?"

Finally, a spark. "White. A common variety. Nothing exotic or unusual as far as I've heard. It probably doesn't mean anything. It's not like the killer placed a crimson magnolia petal on the victim's lips. Still…" He paused. "I thought you'd want to know."

Arden's expression remained too calm. "Who was the victim?"

"I told you, I don't know anything about her. The name

hasn't been released to the public yet. Nor has the business about the magnolia blossom. We need to keep that to ourselves."

"How do you know about it?"

"I have a detective friend who drops by on occasion to shoot the breeze and drink my whiskey. He sometimes has one too many and let's something slip that he shouldn't."

"What does he think about the murder?" Arden asked. "Do they have any suspects yet?"

"He's not working the case. His information is secondhand. Police department gossip. The best I can tell, Charleston PD is treating it like any other homicide for now."

"For now." She walked over to the French doors and leaned a shoulder against the frame. Her back was to him. He couldn't help admiring the outline of her curves beneath the white dress or the way the high heels emphasized her toned calves. Arden had always been a looker. A real heartbreaker. No one knew that better than Reid.

She traced her reflection in the glass with her fingertip. "When did it happen?"

"The body was found early this morning in an alleyway off Logan." Only half a block from Reid's new place, but for some reason, he didn't see fit to mention that detail. There were a few other things he hadn't shared, either. He wasn't sure why. He told himself he wanted to keep the meeting simple, but when had his feelings for Arden Mayfair ever been simple?

She dropped her hand to her side as she stared out into the gathering dusk. Already, the garden beyond the French doors looked creepy as hell. The statues of angels and cherubs that her grandmother had collected had always been a little too funereal for Reid's tastes. The summerhouse, though. He could see the exotic dome peeking through the tree limbs. The Moroccan structure conjured images of starry nights and secret kisses. He and Arden had made that place their own despite the bad memories.

"Reid?"

He shook himself back to the present. "Sorry. You were saying?"

"The cabdriver had the radio on when I came in from the airport. There wasn't a word of this on the news. No mention of a homicide at all. Ambrose didn't say anything about it, either."

"No reason he would know. As I said, the details haven't yet been released. With all the Twilight Killer publicity recently, the police don't want to incite panic. Keeping certain facts out of the news is smart."

Arden turned away from the garden. "What do you think?"

"About the murder?"

"About the magnolia blossom."

Reid hesitated. "It's too early to speculate. The police are still gathering evidence. The best thing we can do is wait and see what they find out."

The hazel eyes darkened. "Since when have you ever waited for anything?"

I waited fourteen years for you to come back. "I have no choice in the matter. I don't have the connections or the clout I had when I was with Sutton & Associates. All I can do is keep my eyes and ears open. If my friend lets anything else slip, I'll let you know."

She regarded him suspiciously. "You're saying all the right things, but I don't believe you."

"You think I'm making this up?"

"No. I think you came over here for a reason, but it wasn't just to tell me about a murder or to suggest we wait and see what the cops uncover. You're right. Only a handful of people would remember that a white magnolia blossom was left on the summerhouse steps the night my mother was murdered. Everyone else, including the police, focused on the crimson petal placed on her lips—the kiss of death that became the Twilight Killer's signature. The creamy magnolia blossom was never repeated at any of the other murder scenes. Which means it was specific to my mother's death."

"That's speculation, too. We've never known that for certain."

"It's what we always believed," she insisted. "Just like we became convinced that the real killer remained free."

"We were just dumb kids," Reid said. "What were we—all of twelve—when we decided Orson Lee Finch must be innocent? No proof, no evidence, nothing driving our theory but boredom and imagination. We let ourselves get caught up in a mystery of our own making that summer."

"Maybe, but we learned a lot about my mother's case and about how far we were willing to push ourselves to uncover the truth. Don't you remember how dedicated we were? We sat in the summerhouse for hours combing through old newspaper accounts and scribbling in note-books. We even rode our bikes over to police headquarters and demanded to speak with one of the detectives who had worked the Twilight Killer case."

"For all the good that did us," Reid said dryly. "As I re-call, we were not so politely shown the door."

"That didn't stop us though, did it?" For the first time, her eyes began to sparkle as she recalled their ardent pursuit of justice. The polished facade dropped and he glimpsed the girl she'd once been, that scrawny, suntanned dynamo who'd had the ability to wrap him around her little finger with nothing more than a smile.

"No, it didn't stop us," he agreed. "When did anything ever stop us?"

She let that one pass. "We decided the white magnolia blossom represented innocence, the opposite of the bloodred petal placed on my mother and the other victims' lips. Given the Twilight Killer's contempt for single mothers, he would have viewed all of them as tainted and unworthy, hence the crimson kiss of death."

In spite of himself, Reid warmed to the topic. "You were the innocent offspring. The first Child of Twilight."

She nodded. "The white blossom not only represented my virtue, but it was also meant as a warning not to follow in my mother's sullied footsteps."

They shared a moment and then both glanced quickly away. The memory of what they'd created and what they'd lost was as fleeting and bittersweet as the end of a long, hot summer.

"No one knew about the baby," he said softly.

Her gaze darted back to him. "Of course, someone knew. Someone always knows. Secrets rarely stay hidden."

"It never needed to be a secret. Not as far as I was concerned. But..." He closed his eyes briefly. "Water under the bridge. This murder has nothing to do with what happened to us. To you."

"If you believed that, you wouldn't be here."

"Arden—"

"I know why you're here, Reid. I know you. You won't come right out and say it, but you've been dancing around the obvious ever since you got here. Despite what you said earlier, this does involve Orson Lee Finch. The way I see it, there can only be two explanations for why a magnolia blossom was left at that murder scene. Either Finch really is innocent or we're dealing with someone who has been influenced by him. A copycat or a conduit. Maybe even someone with whom he's shared his secrets."

Reid stared at her in astonishment. "You got all that out of what I just told you? That's quite a leap, Arden."

"Is it? Can you honestly say the thought never crossed your mind?"

"You're forgetting one extremely important detail. No red magnolia petal found on the body. No crimson kiss of death placed on the lips. This isn't the work of a copycat and I seriously doubt that a dormant serial killer has suddenly been reawakened after all these years. A jury of Finch's peers found him guilty and none of his appeals has ever gone anywhere. This has to be something else."

Arden refused to back down. "Then I repeat, why are you here?"

He ran fingers through his hair as he tried to formulate the best answer. "Damned if I know at the moment."

She regarded him with another frown. "Just consider the possibility that you and I were right about Orson Lee Finch's innocence. The monster who killed all those women, including my mother, has remained free and well disguised all these years. Maybe I'm the reason he's suddenly reawakened. Maybe the white magnolia blossom left at the crime scene was meant as another warning."

"It's way too early to head down that road," Reid said. "If anything, we may be dealing with a killer who wants to throw the police off his scent."

"So you don't think my coming home has anything to do with this?"

"You just got in today. The murder occurred sometime last night or early this morning."

"A coincidence, then."

"What else could it be?"

She sighed in frustration. "I don't understand you, Reid

Sutton. You berate me when I don't show the proper reaction to your revelation about the magnolia blossom, and now you go out of your way to try and convince me—and yourself—that it has nothing to do with me. You came all the way over here just to tell me about a coincidence."

"I'm just trying to be sensible," Reid said.

"You were never any good at that."

"Maybe not, but someone needs to put on the brakes before we get too carried away."

"Now who's being pedestrian?" She brushed back her hair with a careless shrug. "Something's not right about all this. Something's not adding up. Why do I get the feeling you're still holding out on me?"

Reid glanced away. The proximity of the crime scene to his place niggled. Another coincidence, surely, but ever since he'd heard about the murder, he hadn't been able to shake a dark premonition. For days he'd had the feeling that his house was being watched. He'd caught sight of someone lurking in the shadows across the street. One night he'd heard the knob at the back door rattle.

The incidents had started at about the time Dave Brody had been released from prison. The ex-con had stopped by the office as soon as he'd hit town, strutting like a peacock with his smirks and leers and ominous tattoos. He blamed his incarceration on Sutton & Associates, claiming the attorneys that had represented him pro bono—in particular, Reid's father, Boone Sutton—had suppressed a witness that could have corroborated Brody's alibi.

Why he hadn't gone straight to the source of his resentment, Reid didn't know. He hadn't even been out of law school when Brody had been sent up, had only worked peripherally on the appeals. Yet he was apparently the attorney Dave Brody had decided to target for the simple reason that Reid was now the most vulnerable. Without the money and prestige of the firm backing him, he was the easiest to get to. Knock out the son in order to get to the father. But Brody would find out the hard way that Boone Sutton didn't cave so easily, even when family was involved.

Reid hadn't reported the incidents because police involvement would only provoke a guy like Brody. It wasn't the first time and it wouldn't be the last time an irate client had harassed him. Best just to ignore the creep, but still the location of that murder scene bothered him.

"Look, to be honest, I don't know what any of this means," Reid said. "I just knew that I wanted you to hear about that magnolia blossom from me."

He expected another argument; instead, she nodded. "Okay. Thank you. I mean it. I haven't been gracious about any of this. You caught me off guard. That's my only excuse."

"I understand."

"I'm not usually like this. It's just…" She seemed at a loss. "You and I have a complicated history."

"To put it mildly," he agreed.

She drew a breath. "Fourteen years is a long time and yet here we are, back where it all started."

He smiled. "History repeating."

"God, I hope not."

"I'll try not to take that personally."

"You know what I mean. Everything was so intense back then. So life and death. I don't think I could take all that drama these days."

"That's why we have booze. Adulthood has its perks."

"I don't want to numb myself," Arden said with a reproving glance. "But a little peace and quiet would be nice."

"You'll have that in spades here," he said as his gaze

traveled back into the foyer. "Are you sure I can't help you with those bags?"

"I can manage."

He lingered for a moment longer, letting his senses drink her up as memories flowed. Man, they'd had some good times together. He hadn't realized until that moment how much he'd missed her. Arden Mayfair wasn't just his ex-girlfriend. She'd been his best friend, his soul mate, and a true and enthusiastic partner in crime. He hadn't had anyone like her in his life since she'd left town. Oh, he had plenty of friends, some with benefits, some without. He never lacked for companionship, but there was no one like Arden. Maybe there never would be.

"I guess I'll say good-night then." He wondered if she noticed the hint of regret in his voice.

"Reid?" She crossed the room quickly and stood on tiptoe to kiss his cheek. She was like quicksilver in his arms, airy and elusive. Before he had time to catch his breath, she'd already retreated, leaving the scent of her honeysuckle shampoo to torment his senses.

He caught her arm and drew her back to him, brushing her lips and then deepening the kiss before she could protest. "Welcome home, Arden."

She looked stunned. "Good night, Reid."

Chapter Three

Arden finished unpacking and then took a quick shower, dressing in linen pants and a sleeveless top before going back downstairs to decide about dinner. There was no food in the house, of course. No one had been living in Berdeaux Place since her grandmother's passing. She would need to make a trip to the market, but for now she could walk over to East Bay and have a solitary meal at her favorite seafood place. Or she could unlock the liquor cabinet and skip dinner altogether. She was in no hurry to venture out now that twilight had fallen.

At loose ends and trying to avoid dwelling on Reid's visit, she wandered through the hallways, trailing her fingers along dusty tabletops and peering up into the faces of forgotten ancestors. Eventually she returned to the front parlor, where her grandmother had once held court. Arden had a vision of her now, sitting ramrod straight in her favorite chair, teacup in one hand and an ornate fan in the other as she surveyed her province with quiet satisfaction. No matter the season or temperature, Evelyn Mayfair always dressed in sophisticated black. Maybe that was the reason Arden's mother had been drawn to vivid hues, in particular the color red. Arden supposed there was irony—or was it symmetry?—in the killer's final act of placing a crimson petal upon her lips.

Enough reminiscing.

If she wasn't careful, she could drown in all those old memories.

Crossing over to the French doors, she took a peek out into the gardens. The subtle glow from the landscape lighting shimmered off the alabaster faces of the statues. She could hear the faint splash of the fountain and the lonely trill of a night bird high up in one of magnolia trees. Summer sounds that took her back to her early childhood days before tragedy and loss had cast a perpetual shroud over Berdeaux Place.

Checking the lock on the door, she turned away and then swung back. Another sound intruded. Rhythmic and distant.

The pound of a heartbeat was her first thought as her own pulse beat an uneasy tattoo against her throat.

No, not a heartbeat, she realized. Something far less sinister, but invasive nonetheless. *A loose shutter thumping in the breeze most likely. Nothing to worry about. No reason to panic.*

She took another glance into the garden as she reminded herself that her mother had been murdered more than twenty-five years ago. It was unreasonable and perhaps paranoid to think that the real killer had waited all these years to strike again. Reid was right. The magnolia blossom found at the murder scene couldn't be anything more than a coincidence.

Arden stood there for the longest time recounting his argument as she tried to reassure herself that everything was fine. A jury of Finch's peers had found him guilty beyond a reasonable doubt. He would never again be a free man. And even if another killer did prowl the streets, Arden was as safe here as she was anywhere. The property was sequestered behind brick walls and wrought-iron gates.

The house had good locks and, ever since the murder, a state-of-the-art security system that had been periodically updated for as long as she could remember. She was safe.

As if to prove to herself that she had nothing to fear, she turned the dead bolt and pushed open the French doors. The evening breeze swept in, fluttering the curtains and scenting the air with the perfume of the garden—jasmine, rose and magnolia from the tree that shaded the summerhouse. She'd smelled those same fragrances the night she'd found her mother's body.

She wouldn't think about that now. She wouldn't spoil her homecoming with old nightmares and lingering fears. If she played her cards right, this could be a new beginning for her. A bolder and more exciting chapter if she didn't let the past hold her back.

Bolstering her resolve, she walked down the flagstone path toward the summerhouse. The garden had been neglected since her grandmother was no longer around to browbeat the yard crew. In six months of Charleston heat and humidity the beds and hedges had exploded. Through the untrimmed canopy of the magnolias, the summerhouse dome rose majestically, and to the left Arden could see the slanted glass roof of the greenhouse.

The rhythmic thud was coming from that direction. The greenhouse door had undoubtedly been left unsecured and was bumping in the breeze.

Before Arden lost her nerve, she changed course, veering away from the summerhouse and heading straight into the heart of the jungle. It was a warm, lovely night and the garden lights guided her along the pathway. She detected a hint of brine in the breeze. The scent took her back to all those nights when she'd shimmied down the trellis outside her bedroom window to meet Reid. Back to the innocent kisses in the summerhouse and to those not so innocent nights spent together at the beach. Then hurrying home before sunup. Lying in bed and smiling to herself as the light turned golden on her ceiling.

Despite the dark shadow that had loomed over the house since her mother's murder, Arden had been happy at Berdeaux Place, thanks mostly to Reid. He'd given her a way out of the gloom, an escape from the despair that her grandmother had sunk more deeply into year after year. Evelyn Berdeaux Mayfair had never gotten over the death of her only daughter and sometimes Arden had wondered if her presence had been more of a curse than a blessing, a constant reminder of what she'd lost.

Her grandmother's desolation had worn on Arden, but Reid had always been there to lift her up. He'd been her best friend, her confidant, and for a time she'd thought him the love her life. Everything had changed that last summer.

Too soon, Arden. Don't go there.

There would be time enough later to reflect on what might have been.

But already wistfulness tugged. She paused on the flagstones and inhaled sharply, letting the perfume of the night lull her. A moth flitted past her cheek as loneliness descended. It had been a long time since she'd felt so unmoored. She blamed her longing on Reid's unexpected visit. Seeing him again had stirred powerful memories.

Something darted through the trees and she whirled toward the movement. She'd been so lost in thought she hadn't kept track of her surroundings, of the danger that had entered the garden.

She stood frozen, her senses on full alert as she tried to pinpoint the source of her unease. The thumping had stopped, and now it wasn't so much a sound or a smell that alarmed her but a dreaded certainty that she was no longer alone.

Her heart started to pound in fear as she peered through the darkness. The reflection of the rising moon in the glass ceiling of the greenhouse cast a strange glow directly over the path where someone stood watching her.

In that moment of terror, Arden wanted nothing so much as to turn and run from the garden, to lock herself away in Berdeaux Place as her grandmother had done for decades. She could grow old in that house, withering away with each passing year, lonely and desolate yet safe from the outside world. Safe from the monster who had murdered her mother and would someday return for her.

She didn't run, though. She braced her shoulders and clenched her fists even as she conjured an image of her own prone body on the walkway, with blood on the flag-stones and a crimson magnolia petal adorning her cold lips.

"Arden?"

The voice was at once familiar and strangely unsettling, the accent unmistakably Charleston. A thrill rippled along her backbone. She had lots of videos from her child-hood. Her mother had pronounced her name in that same dreamy drawl. *Ah-den.*

He moved out of the shadows and started down the path toward her. Arden stood her ground even as her heart continued to flail. The man was almost upon her before recognition finally clicked. "Uncle Calvin?"

"I'm sorry. I didn't mean to frighten you," he said in his elegant drawl.

"No, it's okay. I just… I wasn't expecting anyone to be out here."

"Nor was I. You gave me quite the start, too, seeing you there in the moonlight. You look so much like your mother I thought for a moment I was seeing her ghost."

For some reason, his observation sent another shiver down Arden's spine.

As he continued toward her, she could pick out the familiar Mayfair features—the dimpled chin and piercing blue eyes melding seamlessly with the Berdeaux cheekbones and nose. Arden had the cheekbones and nose, but her hair wasn't quite so golden and her complexion was far from porcelain. Her hazel eyes had come from her father, she'd long ago decided. A frivolous charmer who'd skipped town the moment he'd learned she was on the way, according to her grandmother. Still, the resemblance was undeniable.

"Ambrose told me a few days ago that you were coming, but somehow it slipped my mind," her uncle said. "I'm so used to letting myself in through the garden gate I never even thought to stop by the house first." He came to a halt on the path, keeping distance between them as if he were worried he might startle her away. "I hope I didn't frighten you too badly."

"It's not you." She let out a breath as she cast a glance into the shadows. "It's this place. After all these years, the garden still unnerves me."

"I'm not surprised." His hair looked nearly white in the fragile light as he thrust it back from his forehead. He was tall, slender and somehow stylish even in his casual attire. In her younger years, Arden had thought her uncle quite dashing with his sophisticated demeanor and mysterious ways. She had always wanted to know him better, but his remoteness had helped foster his mystique. "Even after all these years, the ghosts linger," he murmured.

"You feel it, too," Arden said with a shudder.

"No matter the time of day or year." He paused with a wan smile. "You were so young when it happened. I'm surprised you still feel it so strongly."

"It's not something you ever get over."

"No, I suppose not. I was away at the time. Father and

I had had a falling out so I didn't find out until after the funeral. Maybe that's why the impact only hit me later. I'm sorry I wasn't around to at least offer some comfort."

"I had Grandmother."

"Yes. I remember hearing how she clung to you at the funeral. You were her strength."

"And she, mine, although I don't remember much about that day. It passed in a haze."

"Probably for the best." He gave her another sad smile. "So here you are. Back after all these years."

"Yes."

"It's been a long time. Everyone had begun to think that we'd lost you for good."

Arden wondered whom he included in that "everyone." Not her grandfather, surely. Clement Mayfair had never shown anything but a cursory concern for her welfare. "I've returned periodically for visits. I spent almost every Christmas with Grandmother."

"And now you've come home to any empty house and me looking like something the cat dragged in. I apologize for my appearance," he said as he held up his gloved hands. "I've been working in the greenhouse."

He looked nothing short of pristine. "At this hour?" Arden asked in surprise.

"Maybe you'd like to see what I've been up to. That is, if you don't mind the general disrepair. The greenhouse is in rather a dismal state so mind your step."

"What have you been working on?"

His eyes gleamed in the moonlight. "You'll see."

He turned and she fell into step behind him on the flagstone pathway, following his graceful gait through borders of silvery artemisia and pale pink dianthus. She felt safe enough in the company of her uncle. She didn't know him well, but he'd always been kind. Still, she couldn't help glancing over her shoulder. She couldn't help remembering that her mother had been murdered on an evening such as this.

The greenhouse door opened with a squeal.

"The hinges have rusted and the latch doesn't catch like it should," he said. "Not that there's anything of value inside. The tools, what's left of them, are secured in the shed around back. The lock needs to be replaced, regardless. No one needs to be traipsing about inside. Could be a lawsuit waiting to happen."

"Ambrose should have had that taken care of," Arden said. "At any rate, I'll have someone come out as soon as possible."

Her uncle glanced over his shoulder. "You're here to stay then."

"I don't know. I haven't made any plans yet."

He looked as if he were on the verge of saying something else, but he shrugged. "You've plenty of time. There's no need to rush any decisions."

She stepped through the door and glanced around. The tables and racks were nearly empty except for a few chipped pots.

"Straight ahead," he said as he peeled off his gloves and tossed them aside.

"I'd nearly forgotten about this place." Arden glanced up in wonder through the glass panels where a few stars had begun to twinkle. "Grandmother never talked about it anymore and we didn't come out here on any of my visits. She gave up her orchids long ago. I'm surprised she didn't have the structure torn down."

"It served a purpose," Calvin said.

"You're being very mysterious," Arden observed.

"Just you wait."

Arden hugged her arms around her middle. "When I

was little, Grandmother used to let me come in here with her while she mixed her potions and boosters. Her orchids were the showstoppers at every exhibit, but secretly I always thought they were the strangest flowers with the spookiest names. Ghost orchid, fairy slipper, Dracula benedictii. They were too fussy for my taste. Required too much time and effort. I adored Mother's cacti and succulents. So hardy and yet so exotic. When they bloomed, the greenhouse was like a desert oasis."

"I can imagine."

Arden sighed. "The three of us spent hours in here together, but Grandmother lost interest after the—after Mother was gone. She hired someone to take care of the plants for a while… Eventually everything died."

"Not everything." Her uncle's blue eyes glinted in reflected moonlight. He stepped aside, leaning an arm on one of the tables as he waved her forward. "Take a look."

Arden moved around him and then glanced back. "Is that…it can't be Mother's cereus? It's nearly to the ceiling!" She trailed her gaze up the exotic cactus. "You kept it all this time?"

"Evelyn kept it," he said, referring to his mother and Arden's grandmother by her given name. "After you moved away, it was the only thing of Camille's she had left. She spent most of her time out here, trimming and propagating. As you said, mixing her potions and boosters. She may have lost interest in the orchids, but she never lost her touch."

Arden felt a twinge of guilt. She could too easily picture her grandmother bent to her work, a slight figure, wizened and withered in her solitude and grief. "I see lots of buds. How long until they open?"

"Another few nights. You're lucky. It's promising to be quite a show this year."

"That's why you're here," Arden said. "You've been coming by to take care of the cereus."

"I couldn't let it die. Not after Evelyn had nurtured it all those years. A Queen of the Night this size is rare in these parts and much too large to move. Besides, this is its home."

He spoke in a reverent tone as if concerned for the plant's sensibilities. That was nonsense, of course, nothing but Arden's overstimulated imagination; yet she couldn't help sneaking a glance at her uncle, marveling that she could look so much like him and know so little about him.

Arden's grandparents had divorced when their children were still young. Calvin had remained in the grand old mansion on East Bay Street with Clement Mayfair while his older sister, Camille—Arden's mother—had gone to live with Evelyn at Berdeaux Place. Outwardly, the divorce had been amicable; in reality, a simmering bitterness had kept the siblings apart.

Growing up, Arden could remember only a handful of visits from her uncle and she knew even less about her grandfather, a cold, taciturn man who disapproved of little girls with dirty fingernails and a sense of adventure. On the rare occasions when she'd been summoned to Mayfair House, she'd been expected to dress appropriately and mind her manners, which meant no fidgeting at the dinner table, no speaking unless spoken to.

Clement Mayfair was a tall, swarthy man who had inherited a fortune and doubled it by the time he was thirty. He was in shipping, although to this day, Arden had only a vague idea of what his enterprises entailed. His children had taken after their mother. In her heyday, Evelyn Berdeaux had been a blonde bombshell. Capricious and flirtatious, she must have driven a reclusive man like Clement mad at times. No wonder the marriage had ended so acrimoniously. Opposites might attract, but that didn't make for an easy relationship. On the other hand, Arden and Reid had been so much alike there'd been no one to restrain their impulses.

Her uncle watched her in the moonlight. He had the strangest expression on his face. "Is something wrong?" Arden asked.

Her voice seemed to startle him out of a deep reverie. "No, of course not. I just can't get over how much you look like your mother. Sometimes when you turn your head a certain way..." He trailed off on a note of wonder. "And it's not just your appearance. Your mannerisms, the way you pronounce certain words. It's really remarkable considering Camille died when you were so young."

"That's interesting to know."

He seemed not to hear her. "My sister was full of sunshine and life. She considered each day a new adventure. I was in awe of her when we were children. I sense that quality in you, too, although I think you view each day as something to be conquered," he said with a smile. "Evelyn always said you were a handful."

Arden trailed her finger across one of the scalloped leaves of the cereus. "I suppose I did give her a few gray hairs, although I'm sure she had her moments, too. She became almost a shut-in after Mother died, but I remember a time when she loved to entertain. She kept the house filled with fascinating people who'd traveled to all sorts of glamorous places. It was a bit like living in a fairy tale."

Her uncle remained silent, gazing down at her in the moonlight as if he were hanging on her every word.

"Did you know that she used to organize blooming socials for Mother's cereus? The buds would never open until well past my bedtime, but I was allowed to stay up on the first night to watch the first blossom. The unfurling was magical. And that heavenly scent." Arden closed her eyes and drew a deep breath. "I remember it so well. Not too sweet or cloying, more like a dark, lush jungle."

"I have cuttings at my place and I still do the same," Calvin said. "My friends and I sit out on the balcony with cameras and mint juleps. There's something to be said for Southern traditions. You should join us this year." His voice sounded strained and yet oddly excited.

"At Mayfair House?" Somehow Arden couldn't imagine her prim and proper grandfather being a party to such a frivolous gathering.

"I haven't lived at Mayfair House in years. I have a place near my studio."

"Your studio?"

His smile turned deprecating. "I paint and sculpt. I dabble a bit in pottery. I even manage to sell a piece now and then."

She put a hand to her forehead. "Of course. You're an artist. I don't know how I let that slip my mind. I'm afraid I haven't been very good at keeping in touch."

"None of us has. We're a very strange family in that regard. I suppose we all like our secrets too much."

Arden couldn't help wondering about his secrets. He was a handsome man, still young at forty-six and ever so charming in manner and speech. Yet now that she was older, the drawl seemed a little too affected and his elegance had a hint of decadence that hadn't aged well. Maybe she was being too critical. Looking for flaws to assuage her conscience. No one on either side of the family had been more distant or secretive than she. Her grandmother had given her a home and every advantage, and Arden had repaid that kindness with bimonthly phone calls and Christmas visits.

As unsatisfied as she'd been with her professional life

in Atlanta, she was even more discontent with her personal growth. She'd been selfish and entitled for as long as she could remember. Maybe that assessment was also too critical, but Arden had reached the stage of her life, a turning point, where hard truths needed to be faced. Maybe that was the real reason she'd come back to Charleston. Not to put old ghosts to rest, but to take stock and regroup.

Her uncle picked up a pair of clippers and busied himself cleaning the blades with a tattered rag and some rubbing alcohol. "You know the story of your grandparents' divorce," he said. "I stayed with Father and Camille came here with Evelyn. We lived only blocks apart, yet we became strangers. She blamed Father for the estrangement, but Evelyn could be just as contentious. She had her secrets, too," he added slyly as he tested the clippers by running his finger along the curved blades. Then he hung them on the wall and put away the alcohol.

Arden watched him work. His hands were graceful, his fingers long and tapered, but his movements were crisp and efficient. She marveled at the dichotomy. "No matter who was at fault, it was wrong to keep you and my mother apart. To force you to choose sides. She never wanted that. She used to tell me stories of how close the two of you were when you were little. I know she missed you."

"And yet she never reached out."

"Did you?"

He shrugged good-naturedly. "That's a fair point. Fear of rejection is a powerful deterrent. After the divorce, I'd sneak away from my father's house and come here every chance I got. Sometimes I would just sit in the garden and watch my mother and sister through the windows. Or I'd lie in the summerhouse and stare up at the clouds. Berdeaux Place was like a haven to me back then. A secret sanctuary. Even though Mayfair House has a multitude of sunlit piazzas with breathtaking views of the sea, it seemed a gloomy place after the divorce. It was like all the joy had been stolen and brought here to this house."

"You must have been lonely after they left." Arden knew loneliness, the kind of killing emptiness that was like a physical ache. She'd felt it often in this house and even more so in Atlanta. She felt it now thinking about Reid Sutton.

She brushed back her hair as she glanced up at the sky, trailing her gaze along the same twinkling stars that she and Reid had once counted together as children.

You see that falling star, Arden? You have to make a wish. It's a rule.

I already made a wish. But if I tell you, it won't come true.

That's dumb. Of course, it'll come true.

All right, then. I wish that you and I could be together forever.

That's a stupid thing to wish for because we will be. Promise?

Promise. Now hurry up and make another wish. Something important this time. Like a new bike or a pair of Rollerblades.

"Arden?"

She closed her eyes and drew another breath. "Yes?"

"Where did you go just now? You seemed a million miles away."

"Just lost in thought. This place takes me back."

"That's not a bad thing. Memories are how we keep those we've lost with us always. I made my peace with Evelyn before she passed. I'm thankful for that. And I'm thankful that you're back home where you belong. Perhaps I'm overstepping my bounds, but I can't help wondering..." He trailed away on a note of uncertainty.

"What is it?"

"You said you haven't made any definitive plans, but Ambrose tells me you're thinking of selling the house."

"When did he tell you that?" Arden asked with a frown. She didn't like the idea of her grandmother's attorney repeating a conversation that Arden had considered private.

"Don't blame Ambrose. He let it slip in passing. It's none of my business, of course, but I would hate to see you sell. This house has been in the Berdeaux family for generations."

Was that a hint of bitterness in her uncle's voice? He would have every right to resent her inheritance. He was Evelyn's only living offspring. Why she hadn't left the property to him, Arden could only guess. In the not-too-distant future, her uncle would be the soul beneficiary of Clement Mayfair's estate, which would dwarf the worth of Berdeaux Place.

She rested her hand on one of the wooden tables. "It's not like I want to sell. Though I can't see myself living here. The upkeep on a place like this is financially and emotionally draining. I don't want to be tied to a house for the rest of my life."

"I understand. Still, it would be nice to keep it in the family. Perhaps I could have a word with Father. He's always had an interest in historic properties and a keen eye for real estate. And I imagine the idea of Evelyn rolling over in her grave would have some appeal."

Hardly a convincing argument, Arden thought in distaste.

"A word of warning, though. Keep everything close to the vest. Father is a master at sniffing out weakness."

Arden detested the idea of her grandmother's beloved Berdeaux Place being used as a final weapon against her. She'd have Ambrose Foucault put out feelers in other directions, although she was no longer certain she could trust his discretion. Maybe it was time to look for a new attorney.

She glanced at her uncle. "Please don't say anything to anyone just yet. As I said, my plans are still up in the air."

"Mum's the word, then. I should get going. I'm sure you'd like to get settled."

"It's been a long day," she said.

"Don't forget about the blooming party. And do stop by the studio when you get a chance. I'll give you the grand tour."

"Thank you. I would like that."

"You should probably also know that the Mayor's Ball is coming up. It's being held at Mayfair House this year, all proceeds to go to the construction of a new arboretum. You know how political those things are. Everything revolves around optics. If Father gets wind that you're home, he'll expect an appearance."

"Balls are not really my thing," Arden said with a shrug. She could hardly imagine Clement Mayfair hosting an intimate dinner, much less a grand ball, but as her uncle said, those things were political. She doubted her grandfather had agreed to throw open his doors and his wallet without getting something very valuable in return.

"He can be relentless when he wants something," her uncle cautioned. "It's never a good idea to cross him."

Arden lifted her chin. "I'm pretty stubborn, too. I guess that's the Mayfair gene."

Calvin's expression froze for an instant before a smile flitted. "Yes, we are a hardheaded lot. Maybe Father will have finally met his match in you. At any rate, your presence at the ball would certainly make things more interesting."

They stepped out of the steamy greenhouse into the

cool evening air. He turned to her on the shadowy pathway. "Whether you come to the ball or not, Arden, I'm glad you're home. It's good to have someone in the house again."

"It's good to be here." *For now.*

"Good night, Niece."

"Good night, Uncle."

He strode down the flagstones toward the gate, pausing at the entrance to pluck a magnolia petal from a branch that draped over the wall. Lifting the blossom to his nose, he tilted his head to the moon as he closed his eyes and savored the fragrance.

Then he dropped the flower to the ground and walked through the gate without a backward glance.

Chapter Four

Reid pulled his car to the rear of the house and cut the engine. The bulb at the top of the back stairs was out. He'd been meaning to replace it, and now he decided that adding a couple of floodlights and cameras at the corners of the house might not be a bad idea. The neighborhood was normally a safe place, but a murder half a block from where he sat tended to make one reevaluate security. He scanned the shadows at the back of the house before he got out of the car. Then he stood for a moment listening to the night.

Somewhere down the block, two tomcats sized each other up, the guttural yowls unnerving in the dark. He was on edge tonight. He rubbed a hand over his tired eyes, feeling weary from too little sleep and too many conflicting emotions. Seeing Arden had affected him far more deeply than he cared to admit. Maybe that was why he'd remained on the veranda after Evelyn Mayfair's funeral rather than going inside to offer Arden his condolences. He'd sensed even then that a face-to-face would awaken all those old memories.

Too late now to put that genie back in the bottle. Already he could feel himself tumbling down the rabbit hole of their past.

He should have left well enough alone. There was no real reason she'd needed to hear about that magnolia blossom from him. She wasn't a little girl anymore. She could take care of herself. Truth be told, she'd never needed his protection, but there was a time when Reid had liked to think that she did.

Okay, so, big mistake. Miscalculated his feelings. Now he would have to make sure that he stayed on guard, stayed on his side of town, but why did she have to be one of those women who grew more attractive and interesting as she settled into her thirties? More desirable as the years went by with her sunlit hair and secretive smile?

A part of Reid wanted nothing more than to pick back up where they'd left off, while another part—the more distant and less-listened-to part—reminded him of the hurt she'd once inflicted. Maybe that assessment was overblown and unfair, but she'd turned her back on him when he needed her the most. When he'd been drowning in pain and confusion and desperately needed a lifeline. That she had been just as hurt and confused did little to soften the betrayal.

That was all water under the bridge. Reid had made peace with their estrangement years ago. He hadn't exactly been pining away. He'd sowed his wild oats and then some. No regrets. Still, no matter how much he wished otherwise, her homecoming wasn't something he could take in stride.

The back of his neck prickled as he scoured his surroundings. An indefinable worry blew a chill wind across his nerve endings, and he frowned as he tried to clear the cobwebs from his memory. Arden's return wasn't the only thing that had thrown him off his game tonight. The proximity of the murder disturbed him on a level that he didn't yet understand.

He'd come home last night, having called a cab from the bar where he'd spent the evening with friends. Vaguely he remembered paying the driver and watching the taillights disappear around the corner. As the sound of the engine faded, he'd heard the tomcats fighting. Or had the sound been something else entirely?

He told himself he'd been sober enough to discern caterwauling felines from a human scream. But he couldn't shake the feeling that he'd seen something, heard something that had gotten lost in his muddled dreams.

He thought about walking down to the alley where the body had been found to see if anything jarred loose. He discarded the notion at once. The entrance was still cordoned off, and, for all he knew, the cops might have the street staked out in hopes the killer would return to the scene of the crime. Best not to get involved. He had enough on his plate at the moment. This was make-or-break time for the new firm, and he couldn't afford to get sidetracked by a murder or by Arden Mayfair or by an ex-con with an ax to grind against his family. *Keep your head down and stay focused.*

After locking the car door with the key fob, he climbed the back stairs and let himself into the apartment, flipping on lights as he walked through the rooms. The house was old and creaky, his living quarters in bad need of remodeling. But for now the space suited his needs. He didn't mind the peeling paint or the sagging doors or even the ceiling stains from a leaky roof. What he cared about were the long windows that let in plenty of natural light and the oak floors that had been worn to a beautiful patina. The house on Logan Street felt more like home to Reid than his sleek waterfront condo ever had. He'd never liked that place or the position at Sutton & Associates that had paid for it.

He poured himself a drink and then leaned against the counter to glance through the paper. The murder received only a scant mention. The victim's name was still being withheld, along with any details about the crime scene. Nothing about the magnolia blossom or any suspects. Nothing at all to explain that warning tingle at the back of Reid's neck.

He scanned the rest of the paper as he finished his whiskey and then poured another, telling himself he needed to relax, just needed to take the edge off that meeting with Arden. He still had a bit of a hangover from the night before so hair of the dog and all that. Booze had flowed freely at Sutton & Associates. The competitive nature of the firm had worn on the associates and junior partners, and Reid, like the others, had fallen into the habit of happy hour cocktails with clients and colleagues, wine with dinner, liqueur with coffee and then a nightcap to finish off the evening. Sometimes two or three nightcaps just so he could shut down and get to sleep.

Now that he was out of the pressure cooker environment of his father's firm, he needed to start taking better care of himself. Lay off the hooch. Hit the gym. Add a few miles to his morning run. Get back in shape mentally and physically. Turn over a new leaf, so to speak.

Resolved for at least the rest of the evening, he poured the remainder of his drink down the sink and then stuffed the newspaper in the trash can. Out of sight, out of mind.

It was too early to turn in so he went out to the balcony to enjoy the evening breeze. The house was built in the Charleston style—narrow and deep with the windows and balconies overlooking the side garden. If he turned his chair just so, he could glimpse the street through the lush vegetation. A ceiling fan whirled sluggishly overhead, stirring the scent of jasmine from his neighbor's fence. He propped his feet on the rail and clasped his hands behind his head.

This had become his favorite spot. Hidden from view, he could sit out in the cooling air and watch the comings and goings in the neighborhood while his mind wound down from the daily grind. Not that his schedule was all that packed these days, but he'd just taken on a couple of promising cases, and the stress of any new venture took a toll.

He'd been rocking gently as he let his mind drift, but now he stopped the motion and sat up straight as he listened to the night. The tomcats had long since called a truce and moved on. There was no traffic to speak of, no music or laughter from any of the nearby houses. Everything had gone deadly still. It was as if something dark had crept once more into the neighborhood. A shadowy menace that prowled the streets, luring young women into alleyways and leaving the kiss of death upon their lips.

Or white magnolia blossoms beside their dead bodies.

Reid chided himself for letting his imagination get the better of him. But the longer he stared into the darkness, the more certain he became that his house was being watched. Across the street, someone hunkered in the shadows.

It's nothing. Just a tree or a bush. No one is there.

But he was already up, leaning far over the balcony railing to peer through the oak leaves, zeroing in on a dark figure that didn't belong in the neighborhood.

The silhouette took on definition. Slumped shoulders. Tilted head. Reid could imagine the sneer.

Dave Brody.

Keeping to the shadows, Reid slipped back into the apartment, and then raced down the stairs and out the front door. But Brody had vanished by the time he crossed the street.

Probably not a good idea to go traipsing about his neighbor's yard, Reid decided. Good way to get shot. Instead, he circled the block, eyeing fences and garden gates until he found himself back on his street, standing at the alley-way where the young woman's body had been found early that morning. Police tape barricaded the entrance, but no one was about. No one that he could detect.

He lifted his gaze, searching along the buildings that walled in the alley. Apartment windows looked down on the narrow street. Someone must have seen something, *heard* something. Had the police done a thorough job canvassing the area? Were they even now zeroing in on a suspect?

Reid turned to scour the street behind him, and he cocked his ear to the night sounds. The screech of a gate hinge. The scratch of a tree limb against glass. Somewhere at the back of the alley, a foot connected with an empty can. Or was that just the wind?

The sound jarred Reid and he told himself to go home. Leave the investigation to the police. He would be a fool to breach the police barricade and an even bigger idiot to pursue Dave Brody down a dark, deserted alley.

But when had he ever taken the prudent way out?

Ducking under the tape, he paused once more to glance over his shoulder. He could just make out his house through the lush foliage. He hadn't taken the time to lock up on his way out. If he was bound and determined to do this, he needed to be quick about it. For all he knew, Dave Brody could already be inside his house, hiding in a closet or underneath the bed.

Disturbing thought. Chilling image.

Almost as unnerving as exploring the scene of a violent murder.

He shook off his disquiet as he entered the alley, hugging the side of the building to avoid the glow from the streetlights. He came upon the bloodstains. There were a lot of them. Whoever the young woman had been, she'd met with a violent end.

Crouching beside the stains, he lifted his gaze to the buildings. The night was very still except for the quick dart of a shadow on one the balconies. Reid's pulse quickened as he strained to make out a silhouette. No one was there. Just his imagination.

He rubbed the gooseflesh at the back of his neck as he scoured his surroundings. A dog barked from behind a garden gate, and a fluffy yellow cat eyed him from atop a brick wall before leaping headlong into darkness. Night creatures stirred. Bats circled overhead. And somewhere in the alley, a two-legged predator watched from the shadows.

"Evening, Counselor," a voice drawled.

It took everything Reid had not to react to that whiny twang. Instead, he rose slowly, peering back into the alley as he said in a matter-of-fact tone, "That you, Brody?" As Reid's eyes adjusted to the gloom, the man's form took shape. He lounged against the wall of the building, one foot propped against the brick facade as he regarded Reid in the filtered moonlight. Reid couldn't see his features clearly, but he had no trouble imagining the tattoos, the buzzed head, the perpetual smirk. He hardened his voice. "What the hell are you doing back there?"

"I could ask you the same thing. Me? I'm just enjoying the night air while I check out the neighborhood. I always liked this area. Quiet streets. Friendly people. Maybe I should start looking for a place around here. Put down some roots. What you think about that?"

Having Dave Brody for a neighbor was the last thing Reid wanted to contemplate. And the irony of waxing poetically about the quiet streets while standing at the scene of a brutal murder seemed particularly creepy, but Reid knew better than to allow the man to goad him. "I saw you watching my house just now. You weren't out for a stroll. You were hiding in the bushes staring up at my balcony."

Brody turned his head and spit into the alley. "If I meant to hide, you wouldn't have seen me. I did tell you I aimed to keep an eye on you, didn't I?"

Reid clenched and unclenched his fists as he worked to keep his voice even. "We have more stringent stalker laws these days. You cross a line, I'll have your hide back in jail."

He could hear the amusement in Brody's voice. "I'm not too worried about that, Counselor. See, I had a lot of time on my hands in prison. Did a lot of reading. I know my rights and I know the law. I won't be crossing any lines. Just nudging up against them a little."

"You already crossed a police barricade. I could call the cops on you right now."

"But then you'd have to turn yourself in, and I don't think you want to get all jammed up with the Charleston PD right now."

Reid scowled. "What's that supposed to mean?"

Brody's gaze sliced through the darkness. "A good detective might start to wonder what *you're* doing in this alley, standing in the exact spot where a woman was stabbed last night. A good detective might start to dig a little deeper and find out you have a connection to the victim."

Reid's heart jumped in spite of himself. "Nothing about the victim has been released to the public. No name, no description, no cause of death. There's no way you could know anything about her unless you—"

"I didn't lay a hand on her. Didn't have to. I just happened to be at the right place at the right time." Brody pushed himself away from the wall and came toward Reid. Despite the heat, he wore steel-toed work boots and an army jacket with crude lettering down the sleeves. It was dark in the alley, but enough light filtered in to emphasize the spiderweb tattoo on his neck and the three dots at the corner of his right eye. Common enough prison ink, but the images seemed even more ominous on Brody.

"Don't come any closer," Reid warned.

Brody laughed, displaying unnaturally white teeth in the moonlight. "See, I was in a bar on Upper King Street last night. Yeah, *that* bar. I saw you and your friends having a grand old time, not a care in the world. You were attracting plenty of female action, too, the way you were throwing around all that money. One gal in particular seemed mighty taken with you, Counselor. Kept trying to cozy up to you at the bar, touching your arm, whispering sweet nothings in your ear. She even passed you a note. Don't tell me you don't remember her. About yay-high, bleached blond hair?"

Something niggled at the back of Reid's mind. Although he tried to swat it away, a nebulous worry kept creeping back into his consciousness. "There were a lot of people in that bar last night. I didn't see you, though."

"Like I said, you won't see me unless I want to be seen. I found myself a quiet corner just so I could take it all in." Brody reached inside his jacket and Reid reflexively stepped back. "Relax. I'm just trying to help jar your memory." He flung a photograph in the air and Reid flinched. The snapshot hung on the breeze for a moment before fluttering to the ground at Reid's feet. "Pick it up."

Reluctantly, Reid retrieved the picture, positioning himself so that he could use the light on his phone while keeping Brody in his periphery. He could make out a few faces in the photograph. His own, some of his friends. A woman he'd never seen before stood gazing up at him at the bar. Reid didn't recognize her, had only a hazy memory of someone coming onto him as he waited for a drink.

"Now do you remember?" Brody pressed.

"Who is she?"

"Who *was* she, you mean."

Dread rolled around in Reid's stomach as he glanced up. "What did you do?"

"I told you, I didn't lay a hand on her. See, I was out for a walk this morning when a bunch of police cars go roaring by. A guy in my position tends to notice that sort of thing. So I walk down here to see if I can figure out what's what. Got a look at the body before they bagged her up. Imagine my surprise when I recognized the blonde from the bar, dead in an alley not even a block from your place. Pretty little thing, too, but nothing like that blonde you went to see earlier this evening. Now she's a real looker."

Reid's head came up. "You stay away from her. Whatever your beef is with me, she has nothing to do with it. You go near her place again, you even so much as glance down her street, I will personally see you back behind bars or in your own body bag."

"Mighty big words for a guy who's spent his whole life riding his daddy's coattails." Brody wiped his mouth with the back of his hand. "But no call to get all riled up, Counselor. I don't have any interest in your girlfriend so long as you help me get what I want."

"And what is it you want, Brody?"

"Justice."

"That's rich coming from you. What makes you think I'd ever want to help the likes of you? You haven't exactly been the poster child for rehabilitation since you hit town."

"Well, that's all in the past. Things have changed since last night. Now I'm in a position to help you out, too, Counselor. I'm hoping we can come to an understanding that will be mutually beneficial. See, that gal didn't just slip you a note last night. She put something in your drink."

Reid stared at him blankly. "What?"

"You wake up with a headache this morning? Have trouble remembering what you did and who you did it with?"

Reid's mind reeled back to the bar, to the cab ride home, to the cats fighting in the alley. When he'd finally tumbled into bed, he'd slept the sleep of the dead, awakening that morning to the sound of sirens outside his window. He'd had a dry mouth, a splitting headache and the sense that things had happened he couldn't remember.

All that flitted through his head in the blink of an eye.

Outwardly he remained calm as he casually glanced back at the street, telling himself to get the hell out of that alley. Whatever game Brody was playing, Reid wanted no part of it. Still, he lingered.

He turned back to Brody, dipping his head slightly as he peered into the shadows. "You just happened to be in a bar taking photographs when someone drugged my drink. That sounds totally believable."

"I didn't just *happen* to be anywhere," Brody said. "I followed you to that bar. I told you, I aim to keep an eye on you. As for the blonde, I never saw her before last night. She could have been working alone for all I know. Slipped you a roofie so she could roll you in the alley. You looked like an easy enough mark. My guess, though, is that someone paid her. Now you think about that for a minute. A woman comes on to you in a crowded bar and then she's later found dead half a block from your house. If the police start asking questions, someone will likely remember seeing the two of you leave together."

"I left the bar alone," Reid said. "I caught a cab and came straight home."

"Maybe you did, maybe you didn't. People tend to remember all sorts of things when an idea is put in their head.

It's called the power of suggestion. The point is, you were seen with a woman who later ended up dead. If I was a betting man, I'd say someone is setting you up, Counselor."

Reid was getting queasier by the minute. He told himself again to end the conversation. *Go home. Forget Brody. He's working a con on you.* "How do I know you're not making all this up? Or that you weren't the one who drugged me?"

"Plenty more photographs where that came from, and they tell a story. Two stories really. The blonde getting all touchy-feely—those photographs make you at the very least a person of interest if not an outright suspect. But the photographs of her slipping you a Mickey kind of make you look like a victim. Kind of proves someone is trying to set you up. See how that works? One set convicts, the other set clears. Now if the police were to get their hands on the wrong set, they might show up at your place of business, put you in cuffs, read you your rights and make a great big spectacle out of a Sutton arrest. Don't think they wouldn't get a charge out of that."

Oh, they would. Reid could see the headlines now. A famous defense attorney's son hauled in for questioning in a brutal homicide.

"Course, then your old man gets to swoop in and save the day," Brody continued. "But imagine his surprise when the one person who can clear his only son turns out to be yours truly." He gave a low, ugly laugh.

"You've given this a lot of thought," Reid said.

"Nah. The script practically wrote itself last night."

Dread was no longer tumbling around in Reid's stomach. It had settled like a red-hot coal in the pit. "You say you want justice, but what specifically do you want from me?"

"Now we're getting somewhere," Brody said with an

appreciative nod. "You worked for your old man's firm up until a couple of months ago. You know where they keep the files, the pass codes, where they bury the bodies, so to speak. I want you to find out what they did with a witness that could have corroborated my alibi. Her name was Ginger Vreeland, but I doubt she goes by that name anymore. She disappeared the night before she was to take the witness stand on my behalf."

"Maybe she got cold feet and left town," Reid said. "It happens more often than you think."

"Not Ginger. She was hard as nails, but she was loyal. We grew up together. She wouldn't have turned her back on me unless someone made her an offer she couldn't refuse. I've tried to find her over the years, but none of her kin is talking. I even hired a PI, someone I knew in the joint. He said it was like she fell off the face of the earth. Now, you don't vanish without a trace in this day and age unless deep pockets have funded your disappearance."

"You think someone paid her off," Reid said. "Why would they do that?"

"Not someone. Boone Sutton."

Reid stared at the man for a moment. "If you think my father would have intentionally thrown a case, you know nothing about him. Winning is everything in his book. Guilt or innocence is a distant second."

"Oh, I know him all right," Brody said. "I've studied up on all his cases. I know him inside and out and, yeah, you're right. He wouldn't have thrown a case unless he had a personal reason for doing so."

"And you think you know what that personal reason is?"

"I have a pretty good idea. Ginger was a working girl. The old-school type who kept track of her johns and their peculiarities in a little black book. If Boone Sutton's name was in that book, he might have been afraid of what she'd let slip on the witness stand. You say winning is everything to your daddy? I'd say reputation is right up there."

Reid wanted to deny the accusation, but he couldn't help thinking of all those nights his father never made it home. All the screaming matches between his parents that had eventually settled into contempt and then indifference. Their marriage had been one only in name for as long as Reid could remember. It was certainly possible his father had had a relationship with this Ginger Vreeland. If anyone could have helped her disappear without a trace it was Boone Sutton. He had contacts everywhere.

"There's no guarantee that Miss Vreeland's testimony would have cleared you," he said. "The evidence against you was overwhelming and the DA would have done everything in his power to discredit her as a witness. The outcome would probably have been the same."

Brody was quiet for a moment, and then he said with barely controlled rage, "That's not the point, Counselor. The point is, I deserved a fair hearing. I deserved an attorney who didn't sell me down the river. My rights should have been protected the same as anyone else's."

Reid steadied his voice. "In theory, I agree with you, but I don't know what you think I can do. How do you expect me to find someone who disappeared a decade ago when this person likely doesn't want to be found? I no longer work for my father. We barely even speak. The day I got fired, they took away my keys and changed the passwords and security codes after they escorted me out of the building. Even if I could manage to finagle my way through the front door, I wouldn't get near a computer, much less the file room."

Brody shrugged. "You'll figure something out. I'd start with your old man's home office. He's careful, but he's old-school like Ginger. He likes records. A paper trail even if it incriminates. You've got a lot riding on this, Counselor, so don't you go trying to sell me down the river, too."

"This is insane," Reid muttered.

"It's a little crazy, but play your cards right and we can both get what we want. Don't tell me you wouldn't like to take your old man down a peg or two. Think about it. You have until morning to give me your answer. Best you keep that photograph for incentive."

Reid glanced down at the dead woman's face.

"If I were you," Brody drawled, "I'd get back on home and find that gal's note before someone else does."

Chapter Five

It was after nine by the time Reid dragged himself downstairs the next morning. He hated getting such a late start. Made him feel as if he'd already wasted half his day. His only excuse was that he'd had a rough night. He'd gone home from the confrontation with Dave Brody and torn his house apart searching for the note the dead woman had allegedly slipped him in the bar. Then he'd poured himself a drink and searched again.

One drink had turned into a double and the next thing he knew, he'd been sprawled across his bed with a pillow over his head to drown out the street noises. He got up at some point to check the doors, drank a bottle of water, showered and then dropped back into bed. Sunlight streaming across his face had awakened him the second time. He drank more water, went for a run and then, after another shower, some ibuprofen and two cups of black coffee, he was finally starting to feel human again.

He'd just finished cleaning up the kitchen when a sharp rap sounded at the front door. He hadn't opened up the office yet, so he took a quick glance through the blinds. A tall man with a detective shield clipped to his belt stood on the front porch. His slicked-back hair and hawkish nose gave him an ominous air as he rested his hands on his hips, parting his suit jacket so that Reid could glimpse the shoulder holster beneath.

He turned the dead bolt and drew back the door. "Can I help you?"

The detective pointed to the plaque attached to the wall, which read Sutton Law Group. Then he glanced at Reid. "You Sutton?"

"Yes, I'm Reid Sutton. How can I help you?"

"I'm Detective Graham with the Charleston PD." He flashed his credentials. "I'm investigating a homicide that occurred in the area night before last."

"I heard about that." Reid kept his tone one of mild concern while, on the inside, he braced himself. Had Brody turned over the photographs to the authorities already?

After searching every square inch of the house, Reid had convinced himself the man had made up the whole thing. Brody had no other photographs; nor had he witnessed anyone drugging Reid's drink. No one was setting him up unless it was Brody himself.

But what if he was wrong? Reid found himself in a tricky situation, and on the slim chance that Brody could do real harm, he had to watch his step. He was an officer of the court and he believed absolutely in the rule of law. He didn't want to mislead, much less outright lie to a police detective, but he also didn't want to volunteer unnecessary information. The less said, the better. Inviting scrutiny was never a good idea.

"Do you mind if I ask you a few questions?"

Reid nodded. "Whatever I can do to help, Detective."

"Can we talk inside? It's a real scorcher out here today."

"Sure. Come in." Reid pushed back the door to allow the detective to enter.

Graham stepped across the threshold and moved into the small foyer, glancing into what had once been the front parlor but now served as the reception area. On the other side of the entrance, the once formal dining room was now Reid's office, every inch of workable space piled high with file folders, contracts and briefs.

"Excuse the chaos," he said as he closed the front door. "I'm still getting settled."

"Just move in?"

"I've been here a couple of months."

The detective's gaze climbed the stairs. "What's up there?"

"My apartment."

"Just you here?"

"For the time being."

"Not much of a law group."

"Not yet, but I have big plans."

"I'm sure you do." Graham propped his hand on the banister as he scoured his surroundings. "Nice place."

"Thanks."

"An old house like this can be a real money pit, but the renovated buildings in the area are going for a mint. Good investment potential."

Reid could practically see dollar signs flashing in the detective's eyes. "Time will tell, I guess."

Graham dropped his hand to his side and turned with an apologetic smile. "Sorry. My wife's in real estate. I can't help noticing these things."

Reid brushed past him and stepped into his office. "Can I get you something to drink? Water, coffee…?"

"Water would be great if it's not too much trouble."

"No trouble." Reid walked back into the kitchen, where he grabbed a bottle of water from the fridge. When he returned to his office, Graham stood at one of the bookshelves perusing the contents. Reid placed the water bottle on the edge of his desk and then went around to take his seat, purposely drawing the detective away from any potential hiding spots he may have missed in his search for that note.

Graham took a seat across from Reid and uncapped the bottle. "I don't mean to stare, but you look familiar. Have we met? I'm not so good with names, but I rarely forget a face."

"It's possible," Reid said with a shrug. "Except for law school and college, I've lived in Charleston my whole life. I've practiced law here for the past five."

"You wouldn't be related to Boone Sutton, by any chance?"

Something in the detective's voice put Reid on guard. "He's my father."

Contempt flashed across the detective's face before he could hide his true feelings.

"I take it you're familiar with his work," Reid said.

"He's a legal legend in these parts. Not too popular at police headquarters, though."

"No, I don't imagine he would be. But you know what they say. No one likes defense attorneys until they need one."

"That is what they say." Graham glanced around the room. He still seemed fixated on the house. "Long way from Sutton & Associates on Broad Street. Talk about your prime real estate. That building must be two hundred years old if it's a day."

"It's a beautiful place," Reid agreed. "But I like it just fine where I am."

Graham canted his head as he regarded Reid across the desk. "Now I remember where we met."

"Oh?"

"I pulled you over once when I was still on patrol. You were maybe eighteen, nineteen years old, hauling ass down

the I-26 in some fancy sports car. You failed the field so-
briety test so I took you in. You're lucky you didn't kill
someone that night."

"That was you?" Reid shifted uncomfortably. There
were a lot of things in his past that he didn't much care to
revisit. He'd gone through a reckless stage that could have
ended badly for a lot of innocent people. Those days were
long behind him, but some of his antics still haunted him.

"A kid like you needed a firm hand," Graham said.
"But I guess your old man thought differently. He called in
some favors and got you released without a mark on your
record. And I was read the riot act for doing my job. Took
me another five years to make detective because I pissed
off some rich attorney with connections."

"I remember that night." Reid particularly recalled the
part where he'd been used as a punching bag by a couple
of thugs who'd joined him in the drunk tank. That experience had left a mark. "You had every right to take me in.
I was a stupid kid back then and, yes, I am lucky I didn't
kill someone. But if it makes you feel any better, I did
learn my lesson. I don't get behind the wheel of a car if
I've had so much as a glass of wine with dinner. I walk or
I use a car service. So thank you. As for my father's inter-
ference, I can't do much about that except apologize. Your
actions that night likely saved my life or someone else's.
I was on a bad path."

The detective seemed unimpressed. "Guys like you always get second, third and fourth chances. Influence and
money still go a long way in this town. Rules for me but
not for thee, as they say. But if you really did turn over a
new leaf, then more power to you." He sounded doubtful.

"I appreciate that." Reid sat back in his chair, discom-
fited by the detective's hostility. "I don't want to take up

any more of your time. I'm sure you have a lot of people you need to talk to."

Graham took out his phone and glanced at the screen, leisurely scrolling through a series of text messages. He seemed in no hurry to get on with the interview.

"There hasn't been much about the case in the news," Reid prompted. "I understand the victim was a young female Caucasian."

Graham glanced up. "Where did you hear that?"

"People in the neighborhood talk," Reid said. "Did she live around here?"

"I think it would be best if I ask the questions."

"Of course. Force of habit." Reid smiled.

"Where were you on Sunday night?"

Right to the chase. Reid took a quick breath. "I went out to a bar to meet some friends. We were there for most of the evening. We had a few drinks, played some darts. It must have been just past midnight when I got home."

"You're sure about the time?"

"As sure as I can be. I didn't look at my watch or phone. The others weren't ready to leave so I hailed a cab. You can probably check the dispatcher's logs if you need the exact time…"

Graham didn't take notes. Reid wasn't sure if that was a good thing or not.

"You didn't see or hear anything unusual on the street?"

Reid paused. "I heard two tomcats fighting, but that's not unusual. They've been going at it for weeks."

Graham extracted a photo from his inside jacket pocket and slid it across the desk. "Do you recognize this woman?"

Reid braced himself yet again. He didn't want to give anything away with his reaction, but on the other hand, he had nothing to hide and he only had Brody's word for what had gone down in the bar. Best to be as straightforward as he could while taking care to protect himself.

He picked up the photo, turning his chair slightly so that he could catch the morning light streaming through the blinds. He studied the dead woman's features. Blond hair, blue eyes. A wide smile. She was attractive, but not memorable. And yet there was something about her—

Was she the woman in Brody's photo? Hard to tell. His snapshot had caught her in profile in a dimly lit bar while this image was straight on.

Graham sat forward. "Do you recognize her?"

"I don't know her," Reid said definitively. "But there is something vaguely familiar about her. It's possible I've seen her before, especially if she lives in the neighborhood. Has her name been released yet?"

"Haley Cooper. Ring any bells?"

"No, I'm afraid not."

"She worked at one of the clothing shops on King Street. Roommate says she left their apartment around nine on Sunday night to meet up with a friend at a local bar. That's the last anyone heard of her until her body was found early Monday morning." The detective gave Reid a shrewd look. "You do any shopping on King Street recently? Maybe that's where you know her from."

"Or maybe she just has one of those faces," Reid said.

"That could be it." Graham tucked away the photograph. "I expect the chief will put out a full statement later today, but until her name is released to the public, I'd appreciate you keeping this conversation on the down low. If you think of anything…" He placed a business card on the desk.

"I'll call you," Reid said.

He got up to walk the detective out, trailing him onto the porch and then stopping short when he saw Arden lounging in one of the wicker chairs. She looked the embodiment of a Charleston summer morning in a yellow cotton dress and sandals. Her hair was pulled back in a loose bun and she wore only the barest hint of lipstick. The sprinkling of freckles across her nose gave her a youthful vibrancy that took Reid straight back to the old days. She looked at once wholesome and seductive, a suntanned temptation that smelled of raindrops and honeysuckle.

"What are you doing here?" he asked in surprise.

"Just dropping by to say hello. I hope I didn't come at a bad time." She rose and turned to the detective expectantly.

"Arden, this is Detective Graham. He's investigating a homicide in the neighborhood. Detective, this is Arden Mayfair, an old friend of mine."

She shot Reid a glance before turning back to Graham. "A homicide? That's alarming."

"Yes, ma'am, it is." The detective's attention lingered a shade too long on her slender form.

"Do you have any suspects?"

"That's not something I can discuss at the present."

"Of course. I should have realized that you're not allowed to talk about an ongoing investigation." She sounded contrite, but Reid detected a shrewd gleam at the back of her eyes. That was Arden. Wheels already turning ninety to nothing.

Graham continued to size her up. "Do you live in the area?"

"No, I live back that way." She gave a vague nod toward the tip of the peninsula. "I was just out for a stroll and decided to stop by and check out Reid's new place."

"You say your last name is Mayfair. As in Mayfair House on East Bay?"

"I don't live there, but Clement Mayfair is my grandfather. Do you know him?"

"Oh, sure. I was over there just last Sunday for dinner."

Arden blew off the detective's sarcasm with a smile and a shrug. "I find that hard to believe. I don't see any sign of frostbite."

"I beg your pardon?"

She exchanged another glance with Reid. "Mayfair House has a tendency to be bone cold even in the dead of summer."

"I see. Well, I'll have to take your word for that." Graham turned back to Reid. "You didn't mention the cab company you used."

"It was Green Taxi," Reid said. "I remember the driver's name. It was Louis."

"Shouldn't be too hard to track down. Maybe he saw something after he dropped you off."

"It's certainly possible."

Graham gave Arden a brisk nod. "Miss Mayfair."

"Detective."

She moved back beside Reid as they watched Graham depart. Once he was out of earshot, she said, "Not exactly the friendly sort, is he?"

"I get the distinct impression he doesn't like our kind."

"Our kind?"

"People who grew up South of Broad. Trust fund babies."

She wrinkled her nose. "Who does? Half the time, we can't even stand ourselves. Not that my trust fund is anything to write home about these days. Once work begins on Berdeaux Place, I'll be lucky to have two nickels to rub together."

"And I've been disowned so..."

They shared a knowing look before she turned back to the street. "What was he doing here anyway?"

"Graham? Just what I said. He's investigating a homicide in the area."

"*The* homicide?"

"Yes."

Her eyes widened. They looked very green in the morning light. "You never said anything last night about the murder being in your neighborhood."

"I didn't think it relevant."

She said incredulously, "Not relevant? Are you kidding me? After all our talk about the magnolia blossom found at the crime scene?"

Reid tried to downplay his omission. "I figured I'd already dropped enough bombshells on you for one night. I was going to tell you, just not right away."

Her gaze narrowed before she turned back to the street. "What did you tell the detective?"

"There wasn't much I could tell him. I don't know anything."

"Why did he come to see you?"

"He's talking to everyone on the street, apparently."

"Then why did he get in his car and drive off just now?"

"What is this, an inquisition? I don't know why he drove off. Maybe I was his last stop. I didn't ask for his schedule." Reid watched her for a moment as she watched the street. "Why are *you* here? Something tells me you didn't just drop by."

"No, I came for a reason," she admitted. "I have a proposition for you."

"A proposition? For me?" He ran fingers through his hair as he gave her a skeptical look. "The guy you couldn't get rid of fast enough last night?"

"That's not true. Things started out a bit rocky. You did catch me by surprise, after all. I wasn't expecting to see anyone in the garden, least of all you, and then you dropped your bombshells. Was I supposed to welcome you with open arms after that? I was a little preoccupied in case you didn't notice." She paused, slipping her hands into the pockets of her dress as she gave him a tentative smile. "The evening ended well enough, didn't it?"

He had been trying not to think about that kiss. The way she'd instantly parted her lips in response. The way, for just a split second, she'd melted into him. No one could melt like Arden. No one had ever made him feel as strong and protective and at the same time as vulnerable. "I guess that depends on one's perspective," he said.

Her smile faded and she grew tense. "I didn't come over here to pick a fight."

"Okay."

"I just…" She seemed at a loss as she closed her eyes and drew in a long breath. "Do you smell that?"

"You mean the jasmine? It's all over my neighbor's fence. Gets a little potent when the sun heats up."

"No, Reid. That's the scent of home."

Something in her voice—or maybe it was the dreamy look on her face—made it hard for him to keep up the pretense that her presence had no effect on him. He said almost sharply, "You didn't have jasmine in Atlanta?"

"Of course we did, but not like this. Not the kind of fragrance that sinks all the way down into your soul. There's no perfume in the world that can touch a Charleston summer morning." She hugged her arms around her middle as she drew in the scent. "I've missed this city. The gardens, the people, the history."

"Since when did you become so sentimental?"

"I get that way now and then. Comes with age, I guess. I even have my maudlin moments." She turned with her perfect Arden smile. "Would it be forward of me to admit that I missed you, too?"

Now it was Reid who had to take a deep breath. "Forward, no. Suspicious, yes. What are you up to, Arden?"

"Let's go inside and I'll tell you all about it."

He nodded and had started to turn back to the door when he spotted a familiar figure across the street. Dave Brody stood on the sidewalk, one shoulder propped against a signpost as he picked at his nails with a pocketknife. He dipped his head when he caught Reid's eye and gave him an unctuous grin.

"Go on in," Reid said. "I'll be right back."

Arden followed him to the edge of the porch. "Where are you going?"

"Wait for me inside. This won't take a minute."

He hurried down the steps and across the street. This time Brody didn't run away. He waited with that same oily smile as Reid approached.

"Morning, Counselor. Mighty fine company you've got waiting for you over there on your front porch." He nodded in the direction of Reid's house and then lifted the hand with the knife to wave at Arden.

Reid glanced over his shoulder. Instead of going inside, she lingered on the porch, watching them from the shade. He could almost hear the wheels spinning inside her head. He turned back to Brody. "I told you last night, she's off-limits. That means don't wave at her. Don't talk about her. Don't so much as glance in her direction."

"Touchy, aren't we?" Brody pushed himself away from the post. "And I told you I have no interest in your girlfriend so long as you help me get what I want. I gave you the night to make your decision so here I am." He spread his arms wide as he moved toward Reid, displaying his ominous tattoos. "What's it going to be, Counselor?"

Reid frowned. "Not so fast. Did you have anything to do with a police detective showing up at my door this morning?"

"No, I did not, but I'm flattered you think I have that kind of sway, considering my background and all. I couldn't help noticing the good detective—Graham, was it?—didn't look too happy when he drove away just now."

"How do you know his name?"

Brody gestured with the knife. The action seemed innocent enough, but Reid had no doubt it was meant as subtle intimidation. "He's been hanging around the neighborhood ever since the body was found. Surprised you didn't know that. Been preoccupied, have you?"

Reid wasn't buying any of it. "Are you sure you didn't say something to him? Maybe put a bug in his ear that caused him to come sniffing around my place?"

"Now that sounds downright paranoid. You're the lawyer. Don't it stand to reason he'd be talking to everyone in the neighborhood? Of course, it could be that word has already gotten out about your activities on the night in question. Or…" Brody shaded his eyes as he peered across the street. "Maybe someone else put that bug in the detective's ear. The same someone who's trying to set you up. Seems to me like you've made a powerful enemy in this town."

"And just who is this enemy?" Reid demanded. "Does he or she have a name?"

Brody dropped his hand to his side and shrugged. "How would I know? I'm just a guy who happened to be in the right place at the right time."

Reid thought about that for a moment. "Okay, let's say I do have an enemy. If this person is already talking to the police, then how does it benefit me to help you?"

"A fair question, but you're forgetting something, aren't you? I have photographs that prove someone drugged you. I believe that's called exculpatory evidence? And then there's the matter of some video footage that happened to come my way."

Reid's pulse quickened even though he wasn't about to let Brody prod him into a reaction. "What footage?"

"I'll be happy to email you a copy for your edification, but for now a little preview will have to do." Brody took out his phone. "Amazing what they can do these days. Sure is a lot fancier than the one I had when I got sent up." He scrolled until he found what he wanted. Then he moved into the shade and held up the phone so that Reid could view the screen.

The video was grainy and greenish, like the feed from an outdoor security camera. Reid appeared in the frame and stood silhouetted at the entrance of the alley. Then he ducked under the crime scene tape and walked quickly to the spot where the body had been found, crouching beside the bloodstains as he glanced up to scour the windows and balconies that overlooked the alley. In actuality, he had been wondering if anyone had heard the victim's screams, but to the police, it might appear that he had come back to the scene of the crime to determine whether or not he'd been seen.

"I'm not a cop, but that looks mighty incriminating to me," Brody said.

Reid glanced up. "Where did you get this?"

"Like I said, it just happened to come my way and I'm not one to look a gift horse in the mouth."

"That video doesn't prove anything."

"Maybe, maybe not, but people get convicted on circumstantial evidence every day of the week. No one knows that better than me."

"Your situation was completely different," Reid said. "The evidence against you was overwhelming."

Brody looked as if he wanted to dispute that fact, but he let it pass with a shrug. "You're right. The video and those photographs won't send a guy like you to prison, but at the very least they can instigate an uncomfortable conversation with the cops. A perp walk is all it would take to scare off a sizable portion of your clientele. But there's no need for it to come to that. You help me find Ginger Vreeland and nobody sees any of this but us."

Reid glanced over his shoulder. Arden was still on the front porch waiting for him. He could imagine the questions going through her head. He nodded and gave a brief wave to let her know he'd be right there. "Even if I could find Ginger Vreeland after all these years, do you think I'd give you her name and address so that you can terrorize the poor woman?"

"You've got me all wrong, Counselor. I've got no beef with Ginger. She had to claw and scratch for everything she got just like I did. If somebody made her an offer she couldn't refuse, I can't fault her for taking it. I would have done the same thing in her place. All I want to know is who paid her to leave town and why. If it was Boone Sutton, then I want to know what she wrote in that little black book of hers every time he came calling. I bet, deep down, you'd like to know that, too."

"You'll never touch him," Reid warned.

"We'll have to see about that, won't we? Like I said last night, the best place to go looking is in his personal papers. A little birdie tells me that your mama spends a whole lot of time all by her lonesome in that fancy house on Water Street. I bet she'd dearly love a visit from her one and only son."

"Leave my mother out of this."

"That's up to you. If you can't or won't finish the job, then I'll have no recourse but to have a little chat with Mrs. Sutton. Find out what she knows about her husband's affairs. No pun intended." He went back to work on his nails with the pocketknife.

"All right, you win," Reid said. "I'll do what I can to find Ginger Vreeland, but she's been gone for ten years. The trail is ice-cold by now. I'll need some time."

"I'll give you till Friday. If you haven't made what I deem as sufficient headway, we'll have to reevaluate our arrangement. But fair warning, Counselor."

Reid waited.

Brody's gaze hardened as he moved out of the shade and stood peering across the street at Arden, running his thumb along the sharp edge of the knife blade. "I wouldn't go getting any ideas about trying to double-cross me. I have friends in low places. You know the kind I mean. Hardscrabble guys that would slit a man's throat—or a woman's—for not much more than the loose change in your pocket."

Chapter Six

"Who is that man?" Arden asked as Reid came up the porch steps.

"No one." He pushed past her and opened the front door.

"Didn't seem like no one to me. From where I stood, it appeared the two of you were in a pretty heated exchange."

"He's an ex-client," Reid said. "No one you need to worry about."

She gave him a long scrutiny. "Really? Because *you* sure look worried."

"Didn't you say you have a proposition for me?" He stepped back and motioned for her to enter, catching a whiff of her fragrance as she glided by him. The top note was honeysuckle, but he'd never been able to place the softer notes. He thought again of raindrops. And sunshine. Darkness and light. That was Arden. She'd always been a walking contradiction. An irresistible riddle with a killer smile.

Her timing was lousy, though. He considered making some excuse to send her on her way, but he didn't like the idea of her being out on the street even in broad daylight with Dave Brody lurking nearby. Smarter to keep her inside until Brody had had time to move on.

She hovered in the foyer, suspended in a sunbeam as her

gaze traveled from the front parlor into his office and then up the stairs, just as Detective Graham had done before her.

"So this is your new place."

He checked across the street and glanced both ways before he closed the door. Despite Brody being nowhere in sight, Reid had a feeling he hadn't gone far. "What do you think?"

Arden shot him a look over her shoulder. "You want my honest opinion?"

"I would expect nothing less from you."

"You've got your work cut out for you. I would advise a gut job, but at the very least, the floors will need to be refinished and the windows replaced. The electrical and plumbing will undoubtedly cost a small fortune to bring up to code, and then you still have the less costly but time-consuming tasks of scraping wallpaper and painting drywall. But…" She turned with gleaming eyes. "I love it, Reid. I really do. The millwork is beautiful and the location is perfect. And all this natural light." She stepped into his office and went straight for one of the long windows that opened into the side garden. "This is my favorite style of architecture. I used to dream of owning a house like this. Do you remember? Berdeaux Place always seemed so oppressive to me."

"I remember."

Her gaze turned playful. "You always wanted something sleek and glamorous on the waterfront."

"I had that for a while. I discovered it didn't suit me at all."

She gave him an inquisitive look before turning back to the window. The yellow dress left her tanned back and shoulders bare. Reid had to tear his gaze from her slender form. Too many memories floated between them and his mind had a tendency to linger in dark places when he thought too much about the past. He needed a clear head to deal with Dave Brody. Needed to remain focused if he wanted to stay a step ahead of the police. And to think his life had been relatively uncomplicated just two short days ago.

"Do you want something to drink?" he asked. "I have some iced tea in the fridge."

"That sounds divine. The walk over was longer than I anticipated."

"You're not likely to cool off in here," he warned. "I've been meaning to get someone in to check the AC, but I'm spread a little thin these days." He picked up the detective's water bottle and carried it into the kitchen. Then he got down two tall glasses and poured the tea, taking his time until he had his mask back in place. "I have a couple of cases that have been consuming most of my time," he said in a conversational tone as he came back into his office and placed the drinks on his desk. Arden had already taken a seat, looking as comfortable as could be with her legs crossed and hands folded in her lap. One of the straps of her sundress had fallen down her arm. Reid had the urge to slide it back into place with his fingertip. Or to tug it all the way down with his teeth.

Yes, way to stay focused.

Arden seemed oblivious of his attention. Swiveling her chair around, she gestured to the file boxes strewn across the floor. "All that for just two cases?"

"One of them could be a class action."

"That's exciting." She leaned in to claim her glass and the strap slipped lower, revealing more than a hint of cleavage. Reid tried not to stare, but *damn*.

"What is it?"

"Nothing."

"You seem distracted."

"No, I'm all yours."

She looked doubtful. "I suppose we should get down to it then. I don't want to take up too much of your time."

He nodded. "Whenever you're ready."

She settled back against her chair. "My uncle Calvin was at Berdeaux Place last night. I ran into him in the garden. He said he'd been working in the greenhouse."

Reid frowned. "At night?"

"That's what I said, too. It just seemed odd. But considering his strained relationship with Grandmother, I would have been surprised to see him there at any hour."

"How did he get in?"

"He said he'd been letting himself in through the side gate so someone must have given him a key. Maybe Grandmother made arrangements before she died. I don't know. But, evidently, he's been coming by every evening to take care of Mother's cereus."

"Her what?"

Arden made a dismissive gesture with her hand. "It's a night-blooming cactus. Some call it a Queen of the Night. When it blooms, the scent is out of this world."

"You people and your flowers," Reid muttered.

"I know. We were all thwarted horticulturists, I think. Anyway, Calvin told me that Ambrose Foucault had mentioned my plans to sell Berdeaux Place. As you can imagine, I was pretty upset to learn that a conversation with my grandmother's attorney, one that I considered confidential, had been shared with my uncle."

Reid folded his arms on his desk. "Have you talked to Ambrose about it?"

"Not yet, but I intend to. As you can also imagine, Calvin wasn't too happy with the idea of my selling the house. He reminded me that Berdeaux Place has been in Grandmother's family for generations. I understand his position.

Even though he never lived there, the house is his legacy, too. I don't want to be insensitive to his feelings, and at the same time—"

"Your grandmother left the property to you. You have the final decision."

"Exactly. And I don't take that responsibility lightly. Berdeaux Place was her pride and joy. Whatever I do, I want to make certain that the house and her memory are honored. But I have to be realistic about my prospects. Historic properties of that age and size come with a ton of legalities, so the pool of prospective buyers is limited. Grandmother left a contingency account and I still have money in the trust fund, but neither will last forever. I don't want to rush a decision, but I also can't afford to wait until I'm desperate and out of options."

"So put the place on the market as is," Reid suggested. "Get the ball rolling. You may be pleasantly surprised by the amount of interest the listing generates."

She idly twirled a loose strand of hair around her fingertip. "I've considered that, but now may not be the best time. I've reason to believe vultures are circling."

That got Reid's attention. He lifted a brow. "Are you worried about anyone in particular?"

"Yes." A shadow flitted through her eyes. She turned to stare out the front window as she gathered her thoughts. When she glanced back at Reid, the shadow had resettled into the hard gleam of determination. "Calvin told me that Grandfather might be interested in acquiring the house. He's always had an appreciation for historic properties."

"Well, there you go," Reid said. "Wouldn't that solve all your problems? The house stays in the family, and the burden is lifted from your shoulders."

"You're presuming his intentions are honorable, but I've never known Clement Mayfair to have an altruistic bone in his body. He's up to something. I just know it. His own son made the offhand comment that he might be interested in buying the house for no other reason than to imagine my grandmother rolling over in her grave."

"I'm sure Calvin was joking," Reid said.

"A joke based on an ugly truth," Arden insisted.

Reid canted his head as he studied her. "What are you really worried about?"

She took her time answering. "You'll think I'm paranoid, but I have a bad feeling that Grandfather is planning to take Berdeaux Place away from me somehow. He may even try to convince Calvin to challenge Grandmother's will. All I know for certain is that he has no sentimental interest in that house. He wants it out of pure spite."

"You really think he'd go to that much trouble and expense just to get back at a dead woman?"

"You have no idea the animosity that festered between them," Arden said. "They despised each other so much that they raised their children as strangers. Grandmother took my mother when she left and my uncle stayed behind with Grandfather. They barely ever saw each other even though they lived only blocks apart. I ask you, who does that kind of thing?"

"Relationships can be complicated, but that does seem a bit extreme." Reid thought about his mother spending so much time alone in the stately old mansion on Water Street. He felt a pang of guilt that he hadn't gone to see her in weeks, but they'd never been close. Her emotional distance had kept the two of them almost strangers. Why she stayed with Reid's father after so many years of contempt and neglect, he could only guess; undoubtedly, money played a role. She was a woman who appreciated her creature comforts. Now that Dave Brody had brought her into his machinations, Reid resolved to keep a closer eye on her.

He put that thought away for the time being and re-focused on Arden. "You don't know what happened between them?"

Arden lifted a shoulder. "Grandmother would never talk about it, but I think it was something really bad. If Grandfather manages to get his hands on Berdeaux Place, I can only imagine the pleasure he would take in destroying it."

"You said yourself, there are rules and regulations that protect historic properties."

"He could burn it to the ground before anyone could stop him."

She'd worked herself into a state. Color tinged her cheeks and anger flared in her eyes, reminding Reid that Arden Mayfair had always been a woman of passion. In love, in anger, in hate. She gave it her all. Watching that fire burn out had pained him more than he wanted to remember.

"What can I do to help?" he asked quietly.

She glanced up gratefully. "If Ambrose can so easily be manipulated into revealing the details of our private conversation, then I can no longer trust him to have my best interests at heart. I'd like to hire you as my attorney."

That took him aback. "You want me to represent you?"

"Why not? Unless you don't want my business."

"It's not that. I think you'd be better served with someone who has expertise in probate and real estate law."

She waved off his argument with another dismissive gesture. "How do I know another attorney couldn't be bought off by my grandfather? You're the only one I trust, Reid. I know you can't be bribed or intimidated. Not by Clement Mayfair, not by anyone. Quite the contrary, in fact."

She was just full of surprises today. He was the only one she trusted? A man she'd barely clapped eyes on in over a decade? A man whose heart she'd once broken and scattered to the wind without a hint of remorse?

Anger niggled and he gave it free rein for a moment even though he knew the emotion was irrational and unproductive. He sat in silence, observing her through his passive mask until he trusted himself to speak.

"I have to say, that's a pretty bold statement, Arden."

"It's true. I do trust you. I always have." She leaned in. "Will you do this for me? Will you take my case?"

"We don't know yet that there is a case. First things first, okay? I'll need to see a copy of your grandmother's will."

"I can get you one. Does this mean—"

"It means I'll take a look at the will. But the minute you start requesting documents from Ambrose, he'll know something is up."

"I know. I plan to talk to him as soon as I can arrange a meeting. I doubt he'll be upset. If anything, he'll probably be relieved not to be caught in the middle of a Mayfair war."

"If you're right about your grandfather's intentions, the dispute could get ugly," Reid warned. "He has the resources to drag this out for years. Are you sure you don't want to sell him the house and be done with it?"

"Oh, I'm sure." She had that look on her face, the one that signaled to Reid she'd already dug in her heels. "Clement Mayfair needs to know that I'm not afraid of him."

Reid nodded. "Okay. I'll make some discreet calls and see if I can get wind of his plans."

"Thank you, Reid."

"Don't thank me yet. Let's just wait and see what happens." When she made no move to end the conversation, he shuffled a few papers on his desk. He would have liked to check the street, but she was already suspicious. The last thing he wanted was to put Dave Brody on her radar. "If that's all, I have a meeting to get to soon..."

She settled more deeply into her chair.

He sighed. "Something else on your mind, Arden?"

"I couldn't help noticing all the clutter here and in the other room. Books and files stacked every which way. It's the first thing you notice when you walk in the door and it hardly inspires confidence."

"That's blunt, but you're right. I haven't had a chance to put everything away yet. As I said, I'm spread a little thin these days."

She swiveled her chair back around to face him. "I could do it for you."

He stared at her blankly. "Why would you want to do that?"

"You need help and I need work."

He said in astonishment, "Are you asking me for a job?"

Her own mask slipped, revealing a rare vulnerability, but she tugged it back into place and lifted her chin. "Don't look so shocked. I'm not exactly a slacker, you know. I've been gainfully employed since college."

"My surprise has nothing to do with your work ethic."

She continued on as if he hadn't spoken. "What do you think I did at the museum all those years? I researched, appraised, processed and cataloged. Seems to me that is the kind of experience you need around here. I may not have a law degree, but I'm a fast learner and a hard worker. And you know you can trust me."

Did he know that? Fourteen years was a long time. People changed. Reid knew very little about her life in Atlanta or why she'd decided to come back to Charleston at this particular time. He had a feeling there was more to her story than settling her grandmother's estate.

But then, he was hardly in a position to cast stones. He hadn't been altogether forthcoming with her, either.

"Even if I thought this was a good idea, which I don't," he stressed "take a look around. Do you see a receptionist? A paralegal? Any associates? I haven't staffed up because I can't afford to. I used most of my cash to buy this house, and I promised myself I wouldn't dig any deeper until I was certain I could make a go of it on my own."

She tucked back the loose strand of hair as she gave him her most earnest, Arden appeal. "But wouldn't that be a lot easier with help? Just think about it, okay? I could file briefs, track down witnesses, do all the research and legwork that eats up so much your time. You don't even have to pay me at first. Maybe we can work something out with your legal fees. Give me a month, and I know I can prove myself."

"A month is a long time," he said.

"Two weeks, then, but you have to give me a fighting chance."

"I don't have to do anything."

The edge in his voice stopped her cold. Now she was the one who looked stunned. Rejection wasn't something Arden Mayfair would have ever gotten used to, he reckoned. The more things changed, the more they stayed the same.

"We were a good team once," she said. "Always a step ahead of everyone else, always in sync with each other. Together, we were formidable."

"That was a long time ago."

The furrows deepened as she gave him a long scrutiny. "Be honest, Reid. Are you letting our past color your decision?"

"I don't know what you mean."

"I'll be frank then. Are you still holding a grudge for

the way I left town? What was all that business last night about airing our grievances? Were you just paying lip service to moving on?"

"We can move on without being in each other's face ten to twelve hours a day." He regretted the sharpness of his words the moment they left his mouth. He regretted even more the hurt that flashed in her eyes before she dropped her gaze to her hands.

"Point taken."

"Arden—"

"No, that's fine. It was a crazy idea. I mean, how could we ever work together after everything that happened between us, right?"

"Arden—"

"Don't say anything else. Please. Just let me walk out of here with as much dignity as I can muster." She rose. "I'll send over a copy of Grandmother's will as soon as I can make the arrangements. Unless you've changed your mind."

"No. I said I'd take a look and I will."

She turned toward the door.

"Wait." He winced inwardly, berating himself for succumbing to her emotional manipulation. He didn't think she was maliciously playing him, but she'd always known how to push his buttons.

She sat back down.

"We'll probably both live to regret this, but I may have something for you." He paused, deciding how far he wanted to take this. He could give her an errand or two, something that would occupy her time while he figured things out with Brody. Or he could just send her home where she would be protected behind the high walls of Berdeaux Place. Still, she was alone there and Reid had no way of knowing if the security system had been sufficiently updated. She might be safer here, with a police presence on the street and neighbors who were on guard for anyone suspicious.

"Reid?"

"Sorry. I was just thinking. I have outside meetings for the rest of the day. I won't be back here until late this afternoon, so you'll have the place to yourself. Take a look around, get acquainted with the house and help me figure out how I can best utilize the space. Long term, we can talk about tearing down walls and a possible expansion. For now, we work with what we've got. Upstairs is off-limits. That's my personal space and I don't want to be surrounded by work."

She nodded. "I can do that."

"You say you're good at research? See what you can do with this." He scribbled a name on a piece of paper and slid it across the desk to her.

She scanned the note. "Who is Ginger Vreeland?"

"Ten years ago my father represented a man named Dave Brody on a second-degree murder charge. The evidence against him was overwhelming, but Ginger Vreeland claimed she could corroborate Brody's alibi. She disappeared the night before she was to take the witness stand on his behalf. Brody was found guilty and sent to the state penitentiary."

Arden glanced up. "You suspected foul play?"

"No, more than likely someone bought her off."

"I don't understand. If this was your father's case, why are you getting involved?"

"Let's just say, Dave Brody has become my problem. He's out of prison and looking for answers."

"And you've agreed to represent him?"

"It's a complicated matter," Reid hedged as he opened a desk drawer and extracted a file folder. "There's more where this came from, but the information inside is a good place to start. It includes notes from the attorney that interviewed and prepped Ginger Vreeland for her testimony. Read through the whole thing and see if you can pick up any threads. It won't be easy," he said. "Ten years is a long time and she's likely changed her name at least once. She was a call girl back then so there's no trail of W-2s to follow. I'm not expecting miracles, but at the very least, you can go through all the public databases in case something may have slipped through the cracks."

Arden looked intrigued. "I'll need my laptop."

"You can use mine. I'll log you on as a guest." He pushed back his chair and stood. "One more thing. As soon as I leave here, make sure you lock the door behind me. Don't let anyone in that you don't know. In fact, don't let anyone in but me."

She rose, too. "What about clients?"

"No one," he said firmly. "If anyone needs to get in touch with me, they can leave a voice mail."

She followed him into the foyer. "What's going on, Reid?"

He resisted the urge to put a hand on her arm. The less physical contact the better for his sanity. "We can't lose sight of what's happened, Arden. A woman's body was found down the street from my house and a magnolia blossom was left at the crime scene. That connects us both to the murder. Until the police make an arrest, you need to be careful. We both do."

Something flashed in her eyes. A touch of fear, Reid thought, but she looked no less dauntless or determined. Her chin came up in that way he remembered so well. "I'll be careful. I'll lock the door behind you and I won't let anyone in until you get back. But you need to understand something, too." Her hazel eyes shimmered in golden sunlight. "No matter what happens, I'm not running away this time."

He drew a long breath and nodded. "That's what worries me the most."

Chapter Seven

Reid noticed the Mercedes as soon as he came out of the courthouse. Given the location, he might have assumed his father had tracked him down. The historical building that housed Sutton & Associates was just down the street from the intersection known as the Four Corners of Law at Broad and Meeting. But the long, sleek car was no longer Boone Sutton's style. He'd given up his limo and driver for a shiny red sports car on his sixtieth birthday. The way he tooled around town in his six-figure convertible was an embarrassing cliché, but that was his business. Reid had enough problems without worrying about his father's perpetual pursuit of his youth.

As he headed down the sidewalk, the driver got out and waited by the rear door.

"Mr. Sutton?"

"Yes." He tried to peer around the driver into the car, but the windows were too darkly tinted.

"Mr. Mayfair would like a word."

"Which Mr. Mayfair?"

"Mr. Clement Mayfair." The driver opened the back door. "Would you mind getting inside the car?"

Reid had never spoken more than a dozen words to Arden's grandfather. Truth be told, Clement Mayfair had intimidated Reid when he was younger, but he was a grown man now and his curiosity had been piqued. He nodded to the driver and climbed in.

The interior of the car smelled of new leather and a scent Reid couldn't pin down. Although the fragrance wasn't unpleasant, the mystery of it bothered him, like a memory that niggled. He drew in a subtle breath as he placed his briefcase at his feet and sank down into the buttery seat.

Clement Mayfair sat stone-faced and ramrod straight. Reid tried to recall the older man's age. He must surely be in his seventies, but time had worn easily on his trim frame. He had the same regal bearing, the same aristocratic profile that Reid remembered so well. His hair was naturally sparse and he wore it slicked back from a wide forehead. His face was suntanned, and his eyes behind wire-rimmed glasses were the same piercing blue that had once stupefied Reid into long, sullen silences.

Reid sat quietly now, only a bit apprehensive as he wondered what business the older man had with him.

"Mr. Mayfair," he finally said. "You wanted to see me, sir?"

"Do you mind if we drive? This is a very busy intersection and I don't like tying up traffic." His rich baritone had thinned only slightly with age.

Reid nodded. "I don't mind. But I have a meeting in half an hour. I'll need to be back at the courthouse by then."

Clement Mayfair responded with a sharp rap on the glass partition. The driver pulled away from the curb and glided into traffic.

Reid watched the elegant neoclassical courthouse recede from his view with a strange, sinking sensation. He couldn't shake the notion that he had just made a serious mistake. Willingly entered the lion's den, so to speak.

He kept his voice neutral as he returned Mayfair's scrutiny. "How did you know where to find me?"

"You're an attorney. Call it an educated guess."

"That was some guess," Reid said.

The older man sat perfectly still, one hand on the armrest, the other on the seat between them. He wore a gold signet ring on his pinkie, which surprised Reid. Bespoke suit notwithstanding, Clement Mayfair didn't seem the type to appreciate embellishments.

He smiled, as if he had intuited Reid's assessment. "It might surprise you to know that I've kept track of you over the years."

"Why?" Reid asked bluntly.

"You were once important to my granddaughter. Therefore, you were of some consequence to me. Enough that I took an interest in your career. You were top of your class at Tulane Law. Passed the bar on your first try."

"I'm flattered you took the trouble," Reid said, though *flattered* was hardly the right word. Intrigued, yes, and certainly suspicious, especially after his conversation with Arden. He thought about her insistence that her grandfather was up to something. Reid was now inclined to agree and he braced himself for whatever attack or trickery might be forthcoming.

"You could have had your pick of any number of top-tier law firms in the country," Mayfair said. "But you came back to Charleston to work for your father's firm. I've had dealings with Boone Sutton in the past. I never liked or trusted the man."

"That makes two of us."

The blue eyes pinned him. "And yet you're very much like him. Overconfident and self-indulgent."

"One man's opinion," Reid said with a careless shrug.

Mayfair's gaze turned withering. "I suppose some might find your glibness charming—I've always considered it a sign of a weak mind. You're educated and reasonably intelligent, but you've never been a deep thinker. You were never a match for my granddaughter."

Reid shrugged again. "On that we can agree."

"Then why did you go see her the moment she got back into town?"

A warning bell sounded in Reid's head, reminding him to watch his step. A lion's den was no place to let down one's guard. "Are you keeping track of her...or me?"

"Charleston is still a small town in all ways that matter. Word gets around."

"Let me guess," Reid said. "Calvin told you I'd been by."

"I haven't spoken to my son in days. This isn't about him. This is about my granddaughter." Clement Mayfair leaned in slightly. "You ruined her life once. Why not leave her alone?"

"That's an interesting perspective considering Arden is the one who left me."

"You got her pregnant when she was barely eighteen years old."

"*I* was barely eighteen years old."

"You were old enough to know that precautions should have been taken."

"We were not the first careless teenagers," Reid said.

"Still so cavalier."

Reid was silent for a moment. "How did you even know about the pregnancy? We didn't tell anyone."

"Did you really think I wouldn't find out?" His expression turned contemptuous. "I doubt my granddaughter would have agreed with me back then, but losing that baby was the best thing that could have happened to her."

Reid's fingers curled into tight fists as images flashed at the back of his mind. Arden's pale face against the hospital bed. Her hand clutching his as tears rolled down her cheeks.

"I can't speak for Arden, but I wouldn't have agreed with you then or now. And frankly, that's a pretty callous way of putting things."

"Doesn't make it any less true." Mayfair took off his glasses and methodically polished them with a handkerchief he had removed from his inner jacket pocket. His fingernails were cut very short and buffed to a subtle sheen. "Where do you think either of you would be if things had turned out differently? Would you have married her? Moved her with you to New Orleans and stuck her in some dismal campus apartment while you completed your degree? What about *her* education? *Her* ambitions?"

"This is the twenty-first century, in case you hadn't noticed. Women can do whatever they want."

"Don't fool yourself, young man. A teenager with a baby has limited options, even one with Arden's advantages. The marriage would never have lasted. You may not even have finished law school. I've little doubt that my granddaughter would have ended up raising the child alone."

"Well, we'll never know for certain, will we?" Reid turned to glance out the window as he pushed old memories back into their dark hiding places. In the close confines of the car, he caught yet another whiff of the mysterious fragrance, elusive and cloying. "I have to say, I'm curious about your sudden interest in Arden's well-being." He decided to go on the offensive. "You barely gave her the time of day when she was younger. Even when you invited her to dinner, she sometimes ended up eating alone."

"Arden told you this?"

"She told me everything."

The hand on the seat twitched as if Reid had struck a nerve. "I sometimes had to attend business even at the dinner hour. That was hardly my fault. A man in my position has obligations. But I'm not surprised Arden's recollection would cast me in a bad light. Her grandmother did everything in her power to poison the girl's mind against me just as she kept my own daughter from me years ago. Now that Evelyn is gone, I finally have the chance for a relationship with my granddaughter and I won't have you getting in the way."

Reid gave a humorless chuckle. "That you think I have influence over Arden shows how little you really know about her."

Clement Mayfair gave a grudging nod. "You have more fire than I remembered. Is that why you left your father's firm? The two of you butted heads? Well, I give you credit for that. It takes guts to strike out on your own, especially after being under Boone Sutton's thumb for so long. But I don't have to tell you the streets of Charleston are littered with failed attorneys."

Reid didn't trust the man's change in tactics. "I'm well aware of the risks."

"Then you must also know that in Charleston, it's more about whom you know than what you know. As for me, I never had much use for the elite, the so-called movers and shakers. I preferred building an empire on my own terms and, for the most part, I've been left alone. But you were raised in that environment. You know how the game is played. One word from the right person can make or break a career."

Reid said impatiently, "Is there a point to all this?"

Clement Mayfair put back on his glasses and tucked away the handkerchief. He blinked a few times as if bringing Reid back into focus. "I'm a quiet man who leads a quiet life. I prefer shadows to limelight. But don't mistake my low profile for impotence. A well-placed word from me will bring you more clients than you ever dared to imagine.

Possibly even some of your father's accounts. A desirable feather in any son's cap. Or…" He leaned toward Reid, eyes gleaming behind the polished lenses. "I can see to it that your doors are permanently closed within six months."

Reid fought back another rush of anger. An emotional rejoinder would play right into Mayfair's hands. The older man was obviously trying to get a rise out of him. Trying to prove that he had all the power.

Reid smiled. "For all the interest you've apparently shown in me over the years, you seem to have missed the fact that I don't respond well to threats or ultimatums."

"I assure you, I've missed nothing, young man."

The car glided to a stop in front of the courthouse.

Reid reached for the door handle. "Thank you for the conversation. It's been illuminating."

Before he could exit the car, Clement Mayfair's hand clamped around his wrist. The man's grip was strong for his age. His fingers were long and bony, and Reid could have sworn he felt a chill where they made contact. He thought about Arden's claim that Mayfair House was bone-deep cold even in the dead of summer.

He resisted the urge to shake off Mayfair's hand. Instead, he lifted his gaze, refusing to back down. "Was there something else?"

"Stay away from my granddaughter."

Reid glanced at the man's hand on his arm and then looked up, straight into Clement Mayfair's glacial stare. "That's up to Arden."

The grip tightened a split second before he released Reid. "Trust me when I tell you that you do not want me for an enemy."

There was a quality in his voice that sent a chill down Reid's backbone. "Seems as if I don't have much choice in the matter."

"I'm giving you fair warning. You've no idea the pain I can cause you." The older man's gaze deepened, and for a moment Reid saw something unpleasant in those icy pools, something that echoed the dark promise of his words.

Images swirled in Reid's head as he recalled Dave Brody's insistence that he had a powerful enemy in this city. He thought about the young woman from the bar who had ended up dead in the alley, her body riddled with stab wounds. Then he thought about Camille Mayfair, who had met the same fate, and Arden, only five years old and frozen in fear as her gaze locked onto the killer's through the summerhouse window.

It came to Reid in a flash, as his gaze locked onto Clement Mayfair's, that the elusive fragrance inside the car was magnolia. The scent seemed to emanate from the older man's clothing. Or did it come from the deep, dark depths of his soul?

That smell was surely a fantasy, Reid told himself. The sense of evil that suddenly permeated the car was nothing more than his imagination. Clement Mayfair was just a blustery old man. Powerful, yes, but not malevolent.

Even so, when the driver opened the door, Reid climbed out more shaken than he would have ever dared to admit.

ARDEN SPENT THE rest of the morning sketching floor plans as she went from room to room. She would bring a measuring tape the next day so that she could work to scale, but for now the exploration kept her highly entertained.

Curious about Reid's apartment, she took a peek upstairs. He'd been adamant that his private domain should remain off-limits, but only in so far as using it for an expanded work space. At least that's how Arden interpreted his instructions. Surely, he wouldn't mind if she had a look around. And, anyway, he wasn't here, so…

She climbed the stairs slowly, pausing at the top to glance around. The living area was sparsely furnished with a sleek sofa and an iconic leather lounger that had undoubtedly been transported from his modern apartment. A short hallway led back to the bedroom, a spacious and airy space with a high-coved ceiling and French doors that opened onto a balcony. A pair of old-fashioned rockers faced the street. Holdovers from the previous owner, Arden decided. She pictured Reid out there in the evenings, breeze in the trees, crickets serenading from the garden. She could see herself rocking beside him, head back, eyes closed as the night deepened around them.

Thinking about Reid in such an intimate setting evoked too many memories. He'd once been the most important person in her life. Her soul mate and lifeline. Sad to contemplate how far they'd drifted apart. Sadder still that pride and willfulness had kept her away for so long. She wondered what his reaction would be if he discovered the real reason she'd come back to Charleston, tail between her legs, looking to start anew from the unpleasantness she'd left behind in Atlanta. No use dwelling on bad memories. No sense conjuring up the pain and humiliation that had hung like a bad smell over her abrupt departure. She had a mission now. A purpose. No more spinning her wheels.

She closed the French doors and went back downstairs. Taking a seat behind Reid's desk, she set to work, scribbling notes on a yellow legal pad she'd found in one of the boxes before turning her attention to the name she'd been tasked to research. Ginger Vreeland.

Taking his suggestion, she read through the file, quickly the first time and then more slowly the second, making more notes on the same legal pad. The hours flew by, and before she knew it her stomach reminded her that she'd worked through lunchtime. She went into the kitchen to check the refrigerator, helping herself to the last container of blueberry yogurt before returning to her assignment.

Research could be tedious, and she knew enough to pause now and then to stretch her legs and work out the kinks in her neck and shoulders. She'd just settled back down from a brief respite when she heard someone at the back door. She assumed Reid had returned and barely gave the intrusion a second thought until she remembered he was supposed to be away until late that afternoon.

Rising slowly, she walked across the room to peer into the kitchen. She could see someone moving about on the porch through the glass panel in the door. The man was about the same height and size as Reid, but she knew instinctively it wasn't him even though she never got a look at his face.

Pressing against the wall, she had started to take another peek when she heard the scrape of a key in the lock. Then the door handle jiggled. Alarmed, Arden glanced around the office, wondering what she should do. Wait and confront the interloper? Let him know she was there before he got inside?

She did neither, opting to heed the little voice in her head that commanded her to hide. She had no idea who else would have a key to Reid's house, but she wasn't about to wait around and find out. Hadn't Reid warned her not to let anyone inside? Hadn't he reminded her that the proximity of his office and the magnolia blossom left at the crime scene connected them both to the murder? And to the murderer?

Hurrying across the office, Arden stepped into the foyer, taking another quick glance around. Slipping off her sandals, she hooked them over her finger as she ran quietly up the stairs, pausing on the landing to peer over the banister. She heard the back door close a split second before she retreated into Reid's apartment. She made for the bedroom, wincing as a floorboard creaked beneath her bare feet. After tiptoeing across the hardwood floor, she opened the closet door and dropped to her knees, pulling the door closed behind her. Then she scrambled into the corner, concealing herself as best she could with Reid's clothing.

The closet wasn't large. If the intruder wanted to find her he could do so without much effort, but Arden had been nearly silent in her escape. He hadn't heard her. He didn't know she was there. She kept telling herself that as she drew her knees to her chest, trying to make herself as small a target as possible. There could be any number of legitimate reasons someone would have a key to Reid's house. Maybe he'd given a spare to a repairman or a neighbor. Maybe he had a cleaning service that he'd neglected to tell her about. Maybe Reid himself had returned and she'd allowed panic to spur her imagination.

She kept telling herself all those things right up until the moment she heard slow, heavy footsteps on the stairs. The intruder approached the second floor with purpose. He knew she was there. Knew there was no escape.

Why hadn't she gone out the front door or even onto the balcony? Maybe she could have shimmied down a tree or a trellis. She wasn't afraid of heights. She could have even climbed up to the roof and waited him out.

She scooted toward the door, thinking she might still have time. She reached for the knob and then dropped her hand to her side. He was in the bedroom already. How had she missed the sound of his footsteps in the other room?

Holding her breath, she flattened her hands on the floor and pushed herself back into the corner, taking care not to disturb the hangers. She pulled her knees back up and waited in the dark.

He walked around the room, taking his time as he opened and closed drawers, checked the balcony and then moved back into the room. Arden clamped a hand over her mouth to silence her breathing. She couldn't see anything in the closet. Could barely detect his footsteps. Had he left already? Did she dare take a peek?

The closet door opened and a stream of light edged up against her. She shrank back, unable to see the intruder. She didn't dare part the clothes to get a look at his face, but she sensed him in the doorway. Waiting. Listening.

An image came to her of a woman's body in a dark alleyway, and of a figure—gloved and hooded—bending over her as he placed a magnolia blossom on the ground beside her. She could almost smell that scent. The headiness took her back to that summer twilight when she'd discovered her mother's lifeless body in the garden with the crimson kiss of death upon her lips. Arden thought of the killer watching her from the summerhouse window, leaving a pristine blossom on the steps as a warning that he would someday return for her.

Adrenaline pumped hard and fast through her veins. She smothered a scream as the wooden hangers clacked together. In another moment, he would part Reid's clothing and discover her cowering in the corner.

He rifled through a few items and then stepped back. A folded paper square fell to the floor. Arden could see it in a patch of sunlight. She didn't know if the note had come from one of Reid's pockets or if the intruder had dropped it. If he bent to pick it up, he would surely see her. He didn't pick it up. Instead, he kicked the note back into the closet, as if he didn't want it to be found. At least not right away.

The closet door closed. The footsteps receded across the bedroom floor, into the living room and then down the stairs. Arden lifted her head, turning her ear to the sound.

She was almost certain she heard the back door close, but she waited for what seemed an eternity before she ventured from her hiding place.

She grabbed the note as she scrambled to her feet and all but lunged from the closet, drawing long breaths as she tried to calm her pounding heart. Then she slipped through the rooms, pausing at the top of the stairs to listen once more before slowly descending. She went through every room checking doors and windows, and only when she was satisfied that she was alone did she go back into Reid's office and open the folded note.

A woman's name and phone number were scrawled in flowery cursive across the paper and sealed with a vivid red lipstick print.

The crimson kiss of death.

Chapter Eight

Arden jumped when she heard footsteps on the front porch. She was seated at Reid's desk trying to concentrate on work, but now she leaped to her feet and hurried over to the window to glance out. She could see Reid through the sidelight. Before he had a chance to insert his key in the lock, she drew back the door, grabbed his arm and all but yanked him inside. She'd never been so relieved to see anyone.

"Hello to you, too," he quipped, and then he saw her face as she closed the door and turned the dead bolt. He tossed his jacket on the banister and removed his sunglasses. "Arden? What's going on?"

"Someone broke into your house after you left."

"What?" He took her arm. "Are you okay? Were you hurt?"

Even as shaken as she was, his concern still gratified her. "I'm fine. I wasn't touched. He never even saw me. When I realized it wasn't you, I went upstairs and hid."

"How did he get in?"

"He came in through the back door."

His hand tightened on her arm as he glanced past her into the kitchen. Then his gaze shot back to her. "Are you sure you're okay?"

"I was scared and I'm still a little wobbly, but I'm fine."

He laid his sunglasses on the entrance table without ever releasing her. "When did all this happen?"

"A little while ago."

"Did you call the police?"

Arden hesitated. She hadn't called the police. She hadn't called anyone. The reason didn't matter at the moment. They would get to that later. "There wasn't time. It happened so quickly..."

He took both her arms and studied her intently as if he needed to prove to himself she wasn't injured. She inhaled sharply. She'd forgotten how dark his eyes were. A deep, rich brown with gold flecks that looked like tiny flares in the sunlight streaming in through the windows. He'd removed his tie and rolled up his shirtsleeves. He was very tanned, Arden noticed. She wondered if he still went to the beach on weekends. She wondered a lot of things about Reid's life, but now was not the appropriate time to ask questions or wallow in memories. An hour ago, she'd been certain an old killer had come to track her down. She could still picture his shadow across the closet floor, could still hear the sound of his breath as he stood in the doorway searching through Reid's clothes. Had he known she was there all along? Had he left her alone in order to prolong his sick game?

"Arden?"

She jumped. "I'm sorry. What did you say?"

Reid canted his head as if trying to figure something out. "Can you tell me what happened?"

She nodded. "I said someone broke in, but that's not entirely accurate. He had a key. He let himself in the back door, and he didn't seem at all worried about being caught. He must have seen you leave and thought the house was empty." She moved away from Reid's touch and turned to glance back out at the street. Everything looked normal, but she could imagine someone out there watching the house, perhaps plucking a magnolia blossom from a nearby tree as he vectored in on the window where she stood.

"Did you get a look at him?" Reid asked. "Can you describe him?"

"Not really. I only glimpsed him through the window. He seemed to be about your general height and build." She scoured a neighbor's yard before turning back to Reid. "Have you given a key to anyone lately? A repairman or a neighbor maybe?"

"I don't give out my keys." He spoke adamantly.

"Did you get the locks changed after you moved in?"

He winced. "I've been meaning to."

"*Reid.* That's the first thing you're supposed to do when you move into a new place."

"I know that, but I've been a little busy lately." Now he was the one who turned to glance out the window. He looked tense as he studied the street. They were both on edge. "This is my fault," he said. "I should never have left you here alone."

She scoffed at his reasoning. "Don't be ridiculous. You couldn't have known something like this would happen. And you did caution me not to let anyone in. That's why I hid. I kept thinking about what you said earlier. We're both connected to that murder. If your warning hadn't been fresh on my mind, I might have confronted him. Who knows what would have happened then?"

"You've always been quick on your feet," Reid said. "So you went upstairs to hide. Could you tell if anything was missing when you came back down?"

"I don't think he took anything. But he may have left something."

Reid frowned at her obliqueness. "What do you mean?"

"He went up to your apartment. By that time, I was hiding in your closet and I couldn't see anything. I heard him walking around in the bedroom, opening dresser drawers and looking out on the balcony. When he came over to the closet, I was certain he knew I was in there. You can't imagine the things that went through my head. I even thought I smelled magnolia..." She rubbed a hand up and down the chill bumps on her arm. "You must think I'm crazy."

He gave her a strange look. "Because you smelled magnolia? No, I don't think you're crazy. Far from it. What happened then?"

"He dropped a note on the floor. Or else it fell out of one of your pockets. He kicked it to the back of the closet as if he didn't want you to find it right away."

Reid had gone very still. Something flickered in his eyes. "Do you have the note?"

She took it from her dress pocket and handed it to him. He unfolded the paper and scanned the contents. Arden watched his expression. The look that came over his face frightened her more than the intruder.

"That's the dead woman's name, isn't it?" she asked quietly.

He glanced up from the note. "How did you know?"

"The police chief had a press conference earlier. I streamed it while I worked."

"Did he say anything about suspects? Or the magnolia blossom?"

"He was pretty vague. They're pursuing several leads, leaving no stone unturned and all that, but he didn't say a word about the magnolia blossom."

"They're still keeping that close to the vest," Reid said.

"Or else they have no idea of the significance."

"I think they know. They don't want to panic the public with premature talk of a copycat killer."

"Maybe," Arden said pensively. "I keep going back to my mother's murder. The magnolia blossom left on the summerhouse steps was all but forgotten because the crimson kiss of death soon became Finch's signature. You said yourself only a handful of people would understand the implication of a *white* magnolia blossom. You and I are two of them. My mother's killer is a third."

"I don't want to get sidetracked with a long conversation about Orson Lee Finch's guilt or innocence," Reid said. "Right now, we need to focus on our immediate situation."

"I agree. First things first. Why would someone break into your home and leave that note? Did you know this woman?" Arden had expected an instant denial; instead, he dropped his gaze to the note, pausing for so long that her heart skipped a beat. "Reid?"

He glanced up. "I didn't know her, but it's possible I may have seen her on the night she was murdered."

Arden caught her breath. "When? Where? Why didn't you say anything?"

"Because I didn't know until last night. I'm still not certain it was her."

"Reid—"

He headed her off. "I'll tell you everything I know, but I need a drink first. It's been a long day."

Arden followed him into the kitchen. When he got a bottle of whiskey from one of the cabinets, she took it from him and poured the contents down the sink.

He didn't try to stop her, though his look was one of annoyance. "Why did you do that?"

"Because a drink is the last thing you need," she said firmly. "Until we figure out what's going on, we both need to keep a clear head."

He looked as if he wanted to argue, and then he shrugged. "Water, then."

She handed him a chilled bottle from the refrigerator. He took a long swig before recapping and setting it aside. "Let's go sit in my office. This could take a while."

Arden led the way this time, taking the position behind his desk where she had been working earlier. Reid didn't seem to notice or care. He plopped down in a chair across from her, his long legs sprawled in front of him as he braced his elbows on the armrests.

"Where should we start?" Arden asked.

"I'm still trying to figure out why you didn't call the police," he said.

"I told you. There wasn't time."

"I mean afterward. Why didn't you at least call me?"

"You said you had meetings all afternoon. I didn't want to leave a voice mail. I thought it better that I tell you in person. As for the police…" She paused. "How long have we known each other? Since we were four years old, right? Has there ever been a time when I couldn't read you like a book?"

He lifted a brow but kept silent.

"I knew the moment you came to Berdeaux Place last evening that you were keeping something from me. I felt it even stronger this morning. I didn't want to involve the police until I could figure out what you might be mixed up in."

Reid looked taken aback by her revelation. "You were trying to protect me?"

"Why does that surprise you? We've always had each other's back."

"Fourteen years, Arden."

"So?"

"That's a long time."

"Some things don't change, Reid." She tried not to think about the loneliness of those fourteen years. "My turn to ask the questions," she said briskly. "Who was that man on the street you talked to this morning?"

He answered without hesitation, as if he'd decided it was pointless to keep things from her any longer. "Dave Brody."

"Your father's ex-client? What did he want?"

Reid sighed. "It's a long story—in a nutshell, he has a bone to pick about his defense. Ever since he got out of prison, he's been coming around making veiled threats. He watches the house, follows me when I leave. That sort of thing."

"But you weren't his attorney. Why is he harassing you?"

"He wants me to help prove that my father was responsible for Ginger Vreeland's disappearance."

Arden stared at him in shock. "Responsible...how? He doesn't think—"

"No, nothing like that. He thinks she was paid to leave town."

"That's still insane. Boone Sutton is one of the best defense attorneys in the state. Why would he get rid of his own witness?"

"Apparently, Ginger kept a little black book with all her clients' names and their preferences. Kinks. Whatever you want to call them. Brody is convinced my father was one of her clients. He was afraid of what might come out during her testimony so he arranged for her to disappear."

"But she was prepped for her testimony. Wouldn't he have known what she would say before he called her to the witness stand?"

"Witnesses have been known to fall apart under cross-examination," Reid said. "Plus, we don't know what went down between them before she left town. Maybe she black-mailed him. Offered to keep quiet in exchange for money."

"Wow." Arden sat back against the chair. "I have to say, this is getting really interesting."

"I'm glad you're entertained."

"Don't tell me you're not. Boone Sutton and a prostitute? Wouldn't that set tongues to wagging!" A dozen questions bubbled, but Arden batted them away so that she could remain focused on the situation at hand. "What happens if we find Ginger Vreeland and her little black book? What does Brody plan to do with the contents?"

"My guess is, he's looking for a big payday. Barring that, he'll settle for my father's public humiliation."

"And you're helping him," Arden said. "So what does he have on you?"

"Are you sure you want to hear this?"

"Yes, I think I'd better."

He told her about the confrontation in the alley and Brody's claim that he had photographs from the bar. He told her about the note, the laced drink and the possibility that someone with a lot of power was setting him up for murder. Arden leaned forward, watching his expression as she hung on his every word.

By the time he finished, she was aghast. "This is unreal. Who would do such a thing?"

"I don't know."

"Are you sure Brody's not the one setting you up? Or maybe he's just making it all up to get you to help him."

"He showed me a photograph from the bar, so he's not making everything up. As to the rest..." Reid shrugged. "I don't put anything past him."

"What are you going to do?"

"For the time being, try to keep a low profile." He massaged his temples with his fingertips.

"What did you tell the detective who came by here this morning?"

"Nothing of what I just told you."

"Why not? If someone is setting you up, the police need to know about it. At the very least, you should tell them about Brody's threats."

Reid dropped his hands back to the armrests. "You saw the way Detective Graham looked at us this morning. He didn't even bother to hide his contempt."

"He did have an attitude," Arden agreed.

"More than an attitude. He came to my front door with a chip on his shoulder. Turns out, our paths have crossed before. He arrested me several years back. Apparently, my father pulled strings to arrange for my release and have my record expunged. Then he made sure Graham wasn't promoted to detective for another five years."

Arden digested that for a moment. "Does your father have that kind of clout with the police department?"

"Yes. But if he interfered with anyone's career, it likely had more to do with my black eye and cracked ribs than it did with the initial arrest."

"Graham beat you up?"

"Not personally, no. Two thugs jumped me in the holding cell, and I'd be willing to bet Graham was behind the attack. I think he wanted to teach me a lesson. Maybe he still does. The point is, if he gets a look at those photographs, he'll zero in on me to the exclusion of any other leads or suspects. If he goes to the bar and asks the right questions, someone may remember that they saw me leave with the victim. I didn't," he added quickly. "But Brody is right. The power of suggestion is a real thing. That's why eye-witness testimony can be so unreliable."

Arden shook her head. "I had no idea all this was going on. No wonder you looked like death warmed over when I got here this morning."

"Felt like it, too."

She said hesitantly, "This is a long shot, but you don't think your father could be behind this, do you? You said you were fired from Sutton & Associates. It must have been a serious falling-out if he also disowned you. Maybe this is *his* way of teaching you a lesson."

"Boone Sutton is a lot of things, but he's no murderer," Reid said.

"Maybe that girl wasn't supposed to die. Maybe Brody was just supposed to harass you so that you would be forced to return to the firm. But he took matters into his own hands because he has his own agenda."

"It's possible, of course, but I don't see my father getting into bed with a guy like Dave Brody. Not with their history."

"Their history is precisely why he would have thought of Brody in the first place. But leaving that aside, is there anyone else who would want to frame you? Do you have any other enemies that you know of?"

He scowled at the window as if he were deep in thought. "There may be someone," he said slowly. "You're not going to like hearing about it, though."

"I take it you don't mean Detective Graham."

Reid's gaze came back to hers. "Your grandfather was waiting for me when I came out of the courthouse earlier. He asked me to take a ride."

"What?" Arden could hardly comprehend such a thing. "Clement Mayfair asked you to take a ride? Why? What did he want?"

"He warned me to stay away from you."

"What?"

Reid nodded. "He thinks now that your grandmother is gone he can have a relationship with you. He doesn't want me standing in the way."

"He said that? I'm...speechless," Arden sputtered.

"I was pretty surprised myself," Reid said.

"Surprised doesn't even begin to cover it. That man... that *insufferable man*...has never once shown the slightest bit of interest in me, and now he's warning you to stay away from me?" She got up and paced to the window. "This just proves I'm right. He's up to something."

"I think so, too," Reid said. "Until we can figure out his agenda, you should stay away from him."

She marched back to the desk and plopped down. "Oh, no. I'm going over there tonight to give him a piece of my mind."

"Arden, don't do that."

"Who does he think he is? He can't bully my friends and get away with it. He can't bully me. I won't let him."

"Calm down, okay? I understand how you feel but listen to me for a minute. Arden? Are you listening?"

She folded her arms. "What?"

"Clement Mayfair is a powerful man with unlimited resources. We have to be careful how we take him on. We have to keep our cool. He said I didn't want him for an enemy and I believe him."

She glanced at Reid in alarm. "Does this mean you don't want to take my case? Maybe you don't want me working here, either. I understand if you don't. I could walk out the door right now, no hard feelings."

"I didn't say any of that."

"I know, but I came here this morning and more or less forced myself on you."

A smile flitted. "I'm not sure I would put it quite that way."

"You know what I mean. I made it nearly impossible for you to say no to me. I'm giving you that chance now. Say the word, Reid."

He gave her an exasperated look. "Did you even hear

what I said? We need to be careful how we take him on. *We.* Us. You and me."

"You don't have to do this."

He entwined his fingers beneath his chin as he gazed at her across the desk. "Weren't you the one who said we make a formidable pair?"

"Yes, but that was before I knew my grandfather had threatened you. You're trying to start your own firm. The last thing you need is Clement Mayfair making trouble for you. And you don't need to protect me. I can take care of myself."

The gold flecks in his eyes suddenly seemed on fire as his gaze intensified. "I told you before, old habits die hard."

"Fourteen years, Reid."

"Some things don't change."

ARDEN HAD A difficult time forgetting that look in Reid's eyes. She thought about it all the way home. She thought about it during an early, solitary dinner, and she was still thinking about those golden flecks when she drifted out to the garden. The sun had dipped below the treetops, but the air had not yet cooled. The breeze that blew through the palmettos was hot and sticky, making her wonder if a storm might be brewing somewhere off the coast.

She started down the walkway, taking note of what needed to be done to the gardens. She wouldn't linger long outside. Once the light started to fade, she would hurry back inside, lock the doors, set the alarm and curl up with a mindless TV program until she grew drowsy. For now, though, she still had plenty of light, and the exotic dome of the summerhouse beckoned.

As tempted as she was by memories, she couldn't bring herself to climb the steps and explore the shadowy interior. She diverted course just as she had last evening, finding herself once again at the greenhouse. She peered through the glass walls, letting her gaze travel along the empty tables and aisles. No one was about. She wondered if her uncle had already been by before she got home. He had been cordial and pleasant, but Arden still didn't feel comfortable with his having the run of the place. Did she dare risk offending him by asking for the key back? Or should she take the advice she'd given to Reid and have all the locks changed?

That wouldn't be a bad idea in any case, she decided. For all she knew, there could be any number of keys floating around. The notion that her grandfather might have gotten his hands on one was distinctly unnerving.

As she stood gazing into the greenhouse, her mind drifted back to her conversation with her uncle and how as a child he'd snuck out of his father's house every chance he got so that he could come here to Berdeaux Place. Arden could imagine him in the garden, peering through the glass walls of the greenhouse to watch his mother and sister as they happily worked among the plants. How lonely he must have been back then. How abandoned he must have felt. What could have happened in her grandparents' marriage to drive Evelyn away, taking her daughter and leaving her son behind to be raised by a cold, loveless man? How could any mother make that choice?

The answer was simple. She hadn't been given a choice.

And now Clement Mayfair wanted a relationship with Arden, his only granddaughter. After all these years, why the sudden interest in her welfare? The answer again was simple. She had something he wanted.

Maybe it was her imagination, but the breeze suddenly grew chilly as the shadows in the garden lengthened. She turned away from the greenhouse, trusting that her mother's cereus wouldn't bloom for another few nights.

She paused again on her way back to the house, her gaze going once more to the summerhouse dome. Did she dare take a closer look? Once the sun went down, the light would fade quickly and she didn't want to be caught out in the garden at twilight. Orson Lee Finch was in prison and would likely remain there for the rest of his natural life, but another killer was out there somewhere. One who knew about the magnolia blossom that had been left on the summerhouse steps.

Arden approached those steps now with a curious blend of excitement and dread. She stood at the bottom, letting her gaze roam over the domed roof and the intricate latticework walls, peering up at the window from which her mother's killer had once stared back at her. Then she drew an unsteady breath as her mind went back to that twilight. She had stood then exactly where she stood now, her heart hammering against her chest. Her mother had lain motionless on the grass, her skin as pale as moonlight.

Even without the bloodstains on her mother's dress, Arden would have known that something truly horrible had happened. She hadn't fully understood that her mother was gone, not at first, but she knew she wanted nothing so much as to turn and run back to the safety of the house and into her grandmother's comforting embrace. A scent, a sound...a strange *knowing*...had held her in thrall until a scream finally bubbled up from her paralyzed throat. Then she hadn't been able to stop screaming even when help arrived, even when she'd been led back inside, away from the body, away from those disembodied eyes in the summerhouse window. She hadn't calmed down until her grandmother had sent for her best friend, Reid.

His father had brought him right over. Back then, he had always come when she needed him. *Some things don't change.*

The breeze was still warm, but Arden felt the deepest of chills. She hugged her arms to herself as she placed a foot on the bottom step. A rustling sound from inside the summerhouse froze her. Was someone in there?

More likely a squirrel or a bird, she told herself.

Still, she retreated back to the garden, rushing along the flagstone path, tripping as she glanced over her shoulder. No one was there, of course. That didn't stop her. She hurried inside and locked the door against the encroaching shadows. Then she unlocked the liquor cabinet and poured herself a shot of her grandmother's best whiskey.

Arden downed the fiery drink and poured another, carrying the glass with her upstairs to her bedroom. She turned on all the lights and searched through her closet until she found her secret stash—the reams of notes she and Reid had compiled during their summer investigation. They had only been children playing at detective, but even then they'd been resourceful and inquisitive. *Formidable.* It wasn't inconceivable that they may have stumbled across something important without realizing it.

Carrying everything back down to the front parlor, she dropped to the floor and spread the notebooks around her on the rug. Imagining her grandmother's irritation at such a mess, she muttered a quick apology before digging in.

Thumbing through the pages, she marveled at how much time and attention a couple of twelve-year-olds had devoted to their endeavor. She finished her drink and poured another. She wasn't used to hard liquor and the whiskey soon went to her head. It was dark out by this time and she turned on a lamp before curling up on the sofa, leaving notebooks and markers strewn across the floor. It was too early to sleep. She would be up at the crack of dawn if she went to bed now. She would rest her eyes just for a few minutes. She would simply lie there very still as the room spun around her.

Sometime later, her eyes flew open, and for a moment she couldn't remember where she was. Then she wondered what had awakened her so abruptly. A sound...a smell... an instinct?

Just a dream, she told herself as she settled back against the couch. Nothing to worry about.

But she could hear something overhead...upstairs. Where exactly was the scrabbling sound coming from?

Bolting upright, she sat in the lamplight listening to the house. Berdeaux Place was over a hundred and fifty years old. Creaks and groans were to be expected. Nothing to worry about.

The sound came again, bringing her to her feet. Squirrels, she told herself. Just squirrels. *Nothing to worry about.*

A family of squirrels had once invaded the attic, wreaking havoc on wiring and insulation until her grandmother had hired an exterminator. He'd trapped mother and babies and transported them to White Point Garden. At least that was the story Arden had been told.

She wasn't afraid of squirrels or mice, but she knew she wouldn't be able to sleep until she made sure nothing had found its way inside the house. Grabbing her grandmother's sword, she followed the sound out into the foyer. She wasn't sure what she hoped to accomplish with the blade. She certainly wouldn't run a poor squirrel through, but she liked to think she had enough grit to protect herself from an intruder. If nothing else, the feel of the curved hilt in her hand brought out her inner warrior woman. She went up the stairs without hesitation, pausing only at the top to listen.

Her grandmother's bedroom was at the front of the

house, a large, airy room with an ancient, opulent en suite. Arden's room was at the back, with long windows that overlooked the garden. Her mother's room was across the hall.

Arden following the rummaging sound down the hallway, pausing only long enough to glance in her room. Everything was as she'd left it that morning. Bed neatly made up, suitcases unpacked, clothing all stored away.

She crossed to her mother's room, hovering in the hallway with her hand on the knob. After the murder, Arden's grandmother had locked the room, allowing only the housekeeper inside once a week to dust and vacuum. The room had become a mausoleum, abandoned and forbidden until Arden had gone to her grandmother and told her how much she hated the locked door. It was as if they were trying to lock their memories away, trying to forget her mother ever existed.

After that, the door had been opened, and Arden had been free to visit her mother's room whenever she desired. She used to spend hours inside, sitting by the windows or playing dress up in front of the long, gilded mirror. Sometimes she would just lie on the bed and stare at the ceiling as she drank in the lingering scent of her mother's candles.

Arden wasn't sure why she hesitated to go inside now. She wasn't afraid of ghosts. She wasn't afraid to remember her mother, whom she had loved with all her heart. She had a strange sense of guilt and displacement. Like she had been gone for so long she had no business violating this sacred place. Her emotions made little sense and felt irrational.

Taking a breath, she opened the door and stepped across the threshold. Moonlight flooded the room, glinting so brilliantly off the mirror that Arden was startled back into the hallway. Then she laughed at herself and reached for the light switch, her gaze roaming the room as she waited for her pulse to settle.

Her mother's domain was just as she'd left it all those years ago. The room was pretty and eclectic, bordering on Bohemian with the silk bed throw and thick floor pillows at all the windows. A suitable space for the mysterious young woman her mother had been. Arden could still smell the scented candles, but how was that possible? Surely the scent would have faded by now. Unless her grandmother had periodically replaced them. She may have even lit them from time to time.

Arden walked over to the dresser and lifted one of the candles to her nose. Sandalwood. The second was patchouli. The third...*magnolia.*

She was so shocked by the scent, she almost dropped the glass holder. Her fingers trembled, her heart pounded. She quickly set the candle aside. It's just a *scent*, she told herself. Nothing to worry about.

Hadn't she been the one who had talked her grandmother out of chopping down the magnificent old magnolia tree that shaded the summerhouse?

It's just a tree, Grandmother.

"It's just a scent," she whispered.

But the notion that someone other than her grandmother had been in her mother's room, burning a magnolia candle...

It *was* just a scent. Just a dream. Just squirrels...

Arden backtracked out of the room and closed the door. She hurried across the hall to her room, locking the door behind her and then shoving a chair up under the knob. She was safe enough at Berdeaux Place. The doors were all locked and the security system activated. No one could get in without her knowing.

She went over to the window to glance down into the

garden. She could see the top of the summerhouse peeking through the trees and the glint of moonlight on the greenhouse. The night was still and calm, and yet she couldn't shake the scary notion that someone was down there hidden among the shadows. She'd once been expert at climbing down the trellis to escape her room. What if someone else had the notion to climb up? Was she really safe here?

She couldn't stand guard at the window all night. Neither could she close her eyes and fall back asleep. She was too keyed up now. Too wary of every night sound, no matter how slight.

Scouring the grounds one last time, she finally left the window and lay down on the bed, her grandmother's sword beside her. She thought again of Orson Lee Finch in prison, but the image of an aging killer behind bars gave her no comfort because another killer had already struck once. If someone wanted to set Reid up for murder, who better than her as his next victim?

She pulled the covers up over her and snuggled her head against the pillow, but she didn't fall asleep until dawn broke over the city and the light in her room turned golden.

Chapter Nine

Reid was already on his second cup of coffee by the time
Arden arrived the next morning. The locksmith had come
and gone and he was seated at his desk glancing through
the paper as he chowed down on a breakfast burrito he'd
bought at the corner store. He'd finally gotten a good
night's sleep and felt better than he had in days. Arden,
on the other hand, looked as if she hadn't slept a wink. The
dark circles under her eyes had deepened and her response
to his greeting had been lukewarm at best.

He gave her a lingering appraisal as she stood in his office doorway. "What's wrong?" he asked in concern. "You
look like something the cat dragged in."

She gave him a pained smile. Then she glanced away
as if she didn't want him to stare too deeply into her eyes.
"I didn't get much sleep last night."

"I can tell." He took a quick sip of his coffee. "Anything
I should know about?"

"Squirrels in the attic," she muttered.

Reid carefully set aside his cup. "Are you sure that's
all it was? Not residual nerves from what happened here
yesterday?"

"I don't think so." Her gaze darted back to him and she
shrugged. "Honestly, I think it's that house. I never imagined it would be so disconcerting to be there alone. Every

time I go out into the garden, I remember what happened. I close my eyes and I picture my mother's body, so cold and still, on the ground. I imagine someone staring back at me from the summerhouse windows."

"You lived in that house for years after your mother died," Reid said. "You never seemed to dwell on it back then."

She brushed back her hair with a careless gesture. "I was a kid. I thought I was invincible. Plus, I had you."

His heart gave a funny little jump. "No one is invincible."

"I've never been more aware of that fact since you came to my house the other evening and told me about the latest murder. And speaking of invincible..." She glanced over her shoulder toward the entrance. "I noticed you had the locks changed. That was fast."

"I have a friend in the business. He sent someone out first thing this morning. I don't want a repeat of what happened yesterday."

"That's smart," she said with a nod. "I've been thinking it would be a good idea to change the locks at Berdeaux Place, as well. If my uncle has a key to the side gate, then he may also have one to the house. And if he has a key to the house—"

"Your grandfather could gain access," Reid finished. "I'll set you up with my friend. You can trust him. I've known him for years. In fact, he was one of my first clients. You should also have him check out your security system, make sure everything is up-to-date. At the very least, you need to change your code."

"I've already done that." She had remained hovering in the doorway of his office all this time; now she came in and dumped the contents of her tote bag on his desk.

He took in the black-and-white notebooks and then glanced up. "What's all this?"

"Don't you recognize them?" Arden sat down in a chair across from his desk. She wore white jeans and a summery top that left her toned arms bare. Her hair was down today and tucked behind her ears. He caught the glitter of tiny diamonds in her lobes, could smell the barest hint of honeysuckle as she settled into her chair. "They're the notebooks from our investigation," she explained.

He picked one out of the pile and opened the cover. "I can't believe you kept these things."

"Why wouldn't I? We worked really hard that summer. I know it's mostly kid stuff, but we actually uncovered some interesting details. For instance, do you remember that Orson Lee Finch once worked down the street from Berdeaux Place?"

"As I recall, he worked for a number of families that resided in the Historic District. He was a well-regarded gardener at one time."

"Yes, but I somehow let all that slip my mind. Deliberately so, perhaps. Grandmother even hired him a few times to do some of the heavy chores that her aging gardener couldn't manage. I vaguely remember Finch. He was a short, thin man with kind eyes and a sweet smile. He once gave me a stick of gum."

"Ted Bundy was a real charmer, too," Reid said as he rifled through a few pages of the notebook. "What's your point?"

"I'm just pointing out that he had ample opportunity to acquaint himself with my mother's circumstances and habits. He had ample opportunity to watch me, too. But then so did a lot of other people. And who's to say the real killer didn't have occasion to observe Finch's circumstances and habits and determine he'd make a good patsy?"

"'The real killer'? 'A patsy'?" Reid gave her a skeptical look.

"If we're working from our old theory that Finch was framed." She reached over and plucked one of the notebooks from Reid's desk. "I went through some of the pages last night and highlighted the entries that caught my eye. When you have time, you might want to take a closer look, too."

"Why?" Reid closed the notebook and set it aside. He had also been doing a lot of thinking since last night. She wasn't going to like what he had to say.

"Why?" She stared him down. "Because a young woman was murdered down the block from where we sit. You said yourself the location of your office and the magnolia blossom left at the crime scene link us to the murder."

"Link *us.* But that doesn't mean there's a connection to your mother's murder. That's a long shot in my opinion."

Arden's expression turned suspicious. "What's going on with you? Why do you keep saying one thing and then five minutes later say the opposite? My head is spinning trying to keep up with you."

He'd be frustrated, too, if he were in her position, but she'd thrown him off his game. He'd said things he shouldn't have and made rash decisions that weren't in either of their best interests. Time to rectify his mistakes. "Unlike you, I got plenty of rest last night. My head is clearer than it's been in days. I'm trying to look at the situation rationally instead of emotionally."

"Okay. But what would be the harm in at least glancing through our notes?" Arden asked. "Who knows? We might find something that would help us with your current predicament."

"By current predicament, I assume you mean Dave Brody. I don't see how."

"If Finch really was framed, maybe the same person is now trying to frame you."

"Arden."

"Don't Arden me. We'll never get to the bottom of anything unless you keep an open mind. But forget about the notebooks for a moment." She sat forward, eyes gleaming. "I think I've figured how we can find Ginger Vreeland."

Reid wrapped up his half-eaten burrito carefully and set it aside.

"Don't you at least want to hear my idea?"

"I don't think so." He folded his arms on the desk and tried to remain resolved. "I've done some thinking, too, and I've decided it's a bad idea to involve you in my problems. We have to be smart about this. If someone is trying to set me up, they wouldn't hesitate to come after you if they thought you were in the way."

"I can take care of myself," she insisted. "Besides that, has it not occurred to you that the killer may come after me whether I'm helping you or not? What better way to frame you for murder than to take out an old girlfriend? Think about that, Reid. There's safety in numbers. We need to stick together. And you need someone you can trust watching your back."

She had a point, but that someone didn't need to be her. *If anything happened to Arden—*

He banished the thought before it could take root.

"I appreciate your enthusiasm. I do. But you need to keep your distance. At least for now."

She rolled her eyes in frustration. "There you go again. Changing your mind on a dime. I don't get you, Reid Sutton. We had all of this resolved yesterday afternoon. What's changed?"

"I'm trying to do what's best for both of us." *Don't back down. And don't get distracted by her I'm-so-disappointed-*

in-you look. The disapproval in her eyes meant nothing to him. This was his house, his business. He had a right to make whatever decisions he deemed necessary. "Why do you want to work here anyway? Don't you have better things to do with your time?"

"Such as?"

"You said you wanted to oversee the renovations to Berdeaux Place because you don't trust anyone else. You even mentioned your plan to take on some of the work yourself. Do you have any idea how time-consuming a project like that can be?"

"Of course I do. I also know I'll go out of my mind if I have to stay in that house twenty-four hours a day."

He picked up a pen and examined the barrel. "Then why not get a job in your field? There are any number of museums and art galleries in this city that would jump at the chance to have someone with your expertise."

"Not a one of them will touch me," she said.

He glanced up. "What?"

She met his gaze boldly. "You heard me. The places you mentioned won't hire me."

"Why not?"

She hesitated, her defiance wilting under cross-examination. "I wasn't altogether truthful with you the other night about the reason I left my job."

"You were fired?"

She sighed. "Try not to gloat? This is hard enough without that smirk."

He didn't think he was gloating or smirking, but he apologized anyway. "Sorry. Go on."

"I wasn't fired. I resigned before it came to that. But just barely," she admitted.

"What happened?"

She entwined her fingers in her lap. "The museum was

sold several months ago. The new owners brought in some of their own staff, including a new director. He was funny, handsome, charismatic. We found we had a lot in common. We liked the same music, read the same books. We became friends. Close friends."

"Is that what they're calling it these days?" Reid had a sudden, inexplicable pain in his chest. He sat up straighter, as if good posture could make the ache go away.

"Call it whatever you like. A friendship. A relationship." She dropped her gaze. "An intense flirtation."

The knife twisted as Reid remained silent.

She fixated on her tangled fingers. "Turns out he was married."

Stab me again, why don't you? "You had an affair with a married man?" He hadn't meant to sound so aghast or judgmental. He hardly had the moral ground here, but still. This was Arden.

She looked up at his tone. "It wasn't an affair. It was never physical. Not *that* physical and I had no idea he was married. Maybe I didn't want to know. But looking back, there were no obvious clues or signs. Nothing that would give him away. He was that good. Or maybe I was just that stupid." Color tinged her cheeks. "Anyway, I later learned that he and his wife had been separated for a time. She followed him to Atlanta and they reconciled. When she got wind of our…"

"Intense flirtation."

Arden's blush deepened. "She stormed into the museum one day and made a scene. She was very upset. Overwrought. You can't even imagine the things she said to me."

"Oh, I bet I can."

"She was under the impression that I was the one who

had come on to her husband. When he rejected my advances, I became aggressive. He told her I *stalked* him."

"Wow."

Arden nodded. "Her accusations blindsided me. I don't consider myself naive, but I was completely fooled."

"Sounds like a real catch, this guy."

She frowned. "It's not funny, Reid."

No, but if he didn't make light of the situation, he might get on the first flight to Atlanta, track this guy down and do something really stupid. "No one who knows you would ever believe such a ridiculous claim."

She gave a weak shrug. "My friends stuck by me, but I was humiliated in front of my coworkers and damaged in the eyes of the new owners. I had no choice but to leave."

"So you came back home to lick your wounds," Reid said.

"Something like that. You see now why I can't apply for a job in my field? The moment anyone calls for a reference, all that ugliness follows me here."

Reid flexed his fingers and tried to relax. "Why didn't you tell me any of this yesterday?"

"It's a hard thing to talk about. It goes against the image I've always had of myself. Strong. Independent. Fearless. The truth of the matter is, I'm none of those things." She glanced out the window before she turned back to Reid. "Do you want to hear something else about me? Another dark truth about Arden Mayfair?"

"Always."

"I'd been spinning my wheels in the same position forever. I only ever became friends with him because I thought he could help advance my career. Turns out, I'm not such a great catch, either."

"I don't know about that," Reid said. "I can name about

a dozen guys right here in Charleston who would disagree with you."

Her gaze burned into his, begging the question: *Are you one of them?*

Reid refused to speak on the grounds he might incriminate himself.

She gave him a tentative smile. The same smile that had held him enthralled since they were four years old. The same smile that had once made him believe he could climb mountains and slay dragons on her behalf.

She broke the silence with another question. "How is it that you always know the right thing to say?" she asked softly.

"It seems to me I've been saying the wrong thing ever since you came back. The one thing I do know is that everyone makes mistakes. Even you. You pick yourself up and you move on. That's all you can do."

"Is that what you did after we split up?"

"Yes, after a while. But we're talking about you right now."

She nodded. "It wasn't my intent to come here yesterday and ask you for a job. I wanted your legal advice. That's all. Then I saw this house..." She glanced around the messy office, lifting her gaze to the stained ceiling before returning her focus to Reid. "I understand your vision for this place. I got it the minute I walked through the door. An unpretentious but respectable neighborhood law firm where ordinary, everyday people in need can come in without fear of rejection or intimidation. In other words, the antithesis of Sutton & Associates."

"And here I thought my vision was just to keep this place afloat."

"You can play it off that way, but I know you have big plans for this firm. Whether you want to admit it or not, I can help you. I'm smart—at least most of the time—and you won't find a harder worker. But you have to get over the antiquated notion that I need to be protected. I'm a big girl, Reid."

"Oh, I know."

"Then what's it to be? Should I leave now, never again to darken your door? Or should I sit right here and tell you how we can smoke Ginger Vreeland out of her hiding place?"

He had already lost the battle and they both knew it. The trick now was to salvage as much of the war as he could. "If we're going to do this, we need to set some ground rules."

"Okay."

He looked her right in the eyes. "This is my house, my firm. I have the final say. If I don't want to take on a particular client, we don't take on that client. If I say something is too dangerous to pursue, that's the end of it."

"Of course."

His gaze narrowed. "That was too easy."

"Maybe," she agreed with a conciliatory smile. "I want this to work, but we have to be realistic. We're both stubborn, impulsive, passionate people. We're bound to clash now and then. But I do agree that when it comes to this firm, you have the final say."

"Then why do I feel like I've just been snookered," he muttered.

"This will work out for both of us. You'll see." She scooted to the edge of her seat. "*Now* do you want to hear about my plan?"

"I'm pretty sure I don't have a choice."

She gave him a brilliant smile, one without arrogance or guile. "It may sound a little convoluted at first, so just hear me out. I studied the file you gave me yesterday, in particular the transcript of Ginger Vreeland's interview. She was once married. Did you know that? She married right out of high school and her husband joined the service a month later. They divorced when he came back from overseas. He died some years back in a motorcycle accident. Her closest living relative is an uncle who lives just outside of town. He practically raised her when her mother would be off on a bender. If anyone knows where she is now, it would be this uncle."

Reid stared at her for a moment. "You got all that from the file I gave you?"

"Yes, didn't you read through it?"

"Not as closely as you did, apparently, but let me see if I can contribute to the conversation. Brody said he'd hired a private detective while he was in prison, someone he'd known in the joint. According to this guy, Ginger's family still wouldn't talk. I'm assuming that includes the uncle."

Arden wasn't the least bit thwarted. If anything, she became more animated. "Then we have to give him an incentive. I thought of something last night when I couldn't sleep."

"Of course you did." Reid couldn't believe this was the same aloof woman he'd confronted on Sunday night. His accusation that she'd become pedestrian over the years suddenly rang hollow. She hadn't changed. Maybe, deep down, he hadn't either. He wasn't sure if that was a good thing or not. But her excitement was infectious and he found himself leaning forward, anticipating her every word.

"A few years ago, I was part of a class action suit against a bank that had opened unauthorized accounts in some of their customers' names. Something like that has been in the news recently with a much larger bank on a much larger scale, but the premise was the same. I was barely even aware of the suit until I was notified that money from the settlement had been deposited into my account. It was only a few hundred dollars, but that's beside the point." She paused to tuck back her hair. "What if we contact Ginger's uncle and tell him that Ginger is still listed as her dead ex-husband's beneficiary? His bank account is considered inactive and unless she acts quickly, she won't be able to claim the money from the settlement. The amount would have to be large enough to tempt her out of hiding, yet not so large as to arouse her suspicions. We'll say our firm specializes in helping people collect forgotten money. For a finder's fee, we'll file all the necessary paperwork to have the funds released to her, but we need to speak with her in person to verify her identity."

"In other words, we lie," Reid said.

"Yes, but would you rather Dave Brody find her first?" Arden asked. "We may be lying but we know we won't hurt her. We can't say the same about him. We'll leave the uncle a business card and tell him time is of the essence."

Reid ran fingers through his hair. "You're right about one thing. This scheme is plenty convoluted."

"It can work, though."

"Maybe, but I see at least one glaring problem. She's bound to recognize my name."

"Then I'll be the contact person. I'll have some business cards printed up with a burner phone number. The name Mayfair might even carry a little weight. I can put up a website, too. Simple but classy. Should only take a couple of days to get everything set up."

"If Ginger suspects a con, it could drive her even deeper underground," he said.

"That's just a chance we'll have to take. And it's still preferable to Brody finding her first."

Reid was silent for a moment as he ran the scenario

through his head. "You say you can get this all set up in just two days' time?"

"Yes, if I put in some overtime, but I'll need a place to work." She glanced in the other room. "I can't sit on the floor all day."

"I'll get you a desk," Reid said. "In the meantime, you can use mine. I'll be out for most of the day anyway. That is, if you're sure you'll be okay here alone."

"I feel safer here than I do at Berdeaux Place. You've had the locks changed and I won't let anyone in while you're gone. I'll be fine."

"You'll need this." He handed her a key.

She looked surprised. "I thought you said you didn't give out keys to anyone."

"Just take it, Arden."

Chapter Ten

Reid had been gone for a few hours when Arden decided to take a lunch break. Since the fridge was pretty much empty, she walked down to a little café on Queen Street that offered a delicious array of wraps and salads. She made her selection and then perused her notes as she ate. She didn't dawdle once she finished and, instead, stuffed everything back into her bag and quickly paid the check. She was just stepping outside when someone across the street caught her attention. Arden recognized him immediately as the man Reid had spoken to the day before. Dave Brody.

Her heart skipped a beat and she started to retreat back into the eatery while she waited for him to pass. But he seemed oblivious to her presence. He had his phone to his ear and appeared agitated by the conversation. He gestured with his free arm and then rubbed a hand across his buzzed head in apparent frustration. Even after he returned the phone to his pocket, he continued to rail at the air and then gestured menacingly at a passerby before he stomped off down the street.

Arden decided he must be heading to Reid's office, and she told herself just to wait inside the café until he'd put plenty of distance between them. Why take a chance on being seen? Hadn't she promised Reid she would be careful?

Still, an opportunity had presented itself. Brody had spent hours watching Reid's place and tailing him around town. Why not turn the tables? She could follow at a discreet distance and observe his behavior and interactions. If he tried to break into the house, she would call the police.

Fishing her sunglasses out of her bag, she slipped them on as she waited underneath the awning to make sure he didn't turn around. But she didn't want him to get too far ahead, so she fell in behind a family of five strolling by. The two adults and tallest child would provide enough cover so that if Brody happened to glance back, he wouldn't be able to see her. That worked for about two blocks and then the family turned a corner, leaving Arden exposed. She hugged the inside edge of the sidewalk, hoping the shade of the buildings would somewhat protect her.

What are you doing, Arden? What on earth are you thinking?

She shoved the voice aside as she hooked her bag over her shoulder and kept walking. Somewhere in the back of her mind, a plan took shape. What if Brody really was working for someone powerful who wanted to frame Reid for murder? What if he was on his way to meet that person right now? It was a long shot and not without risk, but wouldn't it be something if she could solve this whole mystery simply by tailing Brody to his final destination? The trick was to stay out of his periphery. It was broad daylight and traffic was fairly brisk. *Just don't let him get so far ahead of you that he can double back without your knowing.*

They were headed west on Queen Street. If his final destination had been Reid's office, he would have turned right on Logan, but instead he kept going all the way to Rutledge, finally turning left on Wentworth. Then came a series of quick turns onto side streets that left Arden completely disoriented. She didn't know the area well and might have thought Brody was deliberately trying to lose her, but from everything Reid had told her, evasion was hardly Brody's style. He was more likely to turn around and confront her openly.

Still, she widened the distance between them, trying to blend into the scenery as best she could. He made another turn and she finally recognized where they were. The houses along the street had seen better days, but the yards were shady, and every now and then, the breeze carried the scent of jasmine over garden fences.

Traffic dwindled and Arden crossed the street to trail behind a pair of college students, who undoubtedly lived in one of the nearby apartment complexes. Up ahead, Brody stopped in front of a two-story house with a wrought-iron fence encasing the front walkway and garden. Arden broke away from the students and darted into an alley, where she could watch Brody from a safe distance. As he opened the gate and stepped into the garden, a middle-aged woman wearing shorts and a baggy T-shirt came down the porch steps to confront him.

Their raised voices carried across to the alley, but Arden could make out only a word now and then of the argument, something about late rent. The woman, presumably Brody's landlady, gestured toward the outside staircase that led up to a second-story apartment. Brody became so agitated that Arden worried he might actually assault the poor woman.

Although she braced herself to intervene, the disagreement never became physical. Brody headed up the stairs and disappeared inside the door at the top of the landing. He came back out a few minutes later and flung money at the woman. She screamed an oath and then scrambled to grab the bills before the breeze carried them away. Brody watched her for a moment, then turned on his heel and exited the gate, heading back up the street the way he'd come.

Arden pressed herself against the wall, trying to disappear into the shadows until he was safely past the alley. Then she glanced up the street. She could still see him in the distance. She would have left the alley to follow except for the woman across the street, who had once again caught her attention. She plucked the last of the bills from the ground, folded the wad and tucked it into her shorts pocket. Then she came through the gate and stood on the sidewalk, hand shading her eyes as she watched Brody's receding form. Once he rounded a corner, she went back inside the fence and marched up the stairs, pausing on the landing to glance over her shoulder. Satisfied that she was alone, she retrieved a key from a flowerpot and let herself into the apartment.

By this time, Brody was long gone. As much as Arden wanted to try to catch up with him, she was intrigued by the woman's behavior. She waited in the shadows, her gaze fixated on the door at the top of the stairs. The woman reappeared a few minutes later, glanced around once more to make sure no one had seen her and returned the key to the flowerpot. She came down the stairs and rounded the house to the porch. A moment later Arden heard a door slam.

Leaning back against the building, she placed a hand over her pounding heart. The adrenaline pulsating through her veins was a rush she hadn't experienced in years. She was reminded of the time she and Reid had taken his father's boat out for a midnight sail. They'd stayed on the water all night, drunk with freedom and adventure as they contemplated how far they dared go before turning back.

Now, a little voice goaded her. *Now is the time to turn back.*

Arden once again ignored that voice.

Leaving the alley, she glanced both ways before crossing the street. Without hesitation, she made for the garden
gate, rehearsing in her mind what she would say if she were
caught. She wasn't so worried about the landlady. Arden
had always been able to think on her feet. She'd make
up an excuse about having the wrong address or looking for an old friend. Brody was a different story. She'd
glimpsed his temper and had no doubt he was dangerous.
Now, though, she was more convinced than ever that he
had to be working for someone. The area was seedy, but
apartments this close to downtown didn't come cheap no
matter the neighborhood.

How could she pass up this chance? Someone was trying to set Reid up for murder. What if she could determine
the identity of the real killer by searching Brody's possessions? What if she could prove Reid's innocence once and
for all? Wasn't he worth taking that risk?

On and on, the devil on her shoulder goaded her.

Arden knew what Reid would say. He'd tell her to go
back to the office and lock the doors. Hunker down until he
returned later that afternoon. But cowering inside locked
doors wouldn't help him out of his current predicament.
There'd been a time when he would have applauded her
efforts.

In a way, she was doing this as much for herself as for
him, Arden decided. She wanted to be that girl again. The
one who threw caution to the wind and followed her heart.

Let's not get carried away.

She found the key in the flowerpot, unlocked the door
and then returned the key, using her foot to hold open the
door. She slipped inside and took off her sunglasses. The
apartment was dim and overly warm. Or maybe she was
just overly excited. A scene from one of her favorite movies came to mind. A determined young woman risking life

and limb to get the goods on a murderer so she could prove to her adventurous lover she was more than his match.

Focus, Arden. You are not Grace Kelly. And this is not a movie.

She stood with her back against the closed door and drew in air as she tried to quiet her thundering heart. Then her gaze darted about the small space, taking it all in before she began to explore. To the left of the entrance was a tiny bathroom; to the right, a bedroom. The narrow foyer opened directly into a living area and the kitchen was just through an archway. The space was tight but efficient.

Her gaze lit on a wooden table beneath the only window in the living room. An expensive laptop and printer were set up, along with a flat-screen TV. How did someone fresh out of prison afford such expensive devices?

She moved across the room as silently as she could manage on aging floorboards. After taking a quick peek through a stack of papers on the table, she turned her attention to the laptop. It opened to the desktop and she navigated to the Pictures folder, scanning dozens of thumbnails before she found the incriminating photos of Reid. Brody must have been following him for days. He'd captured Reid through his office window, at the courthouse on Broad Street, on the sidewalk in front of Berdeaux Place. When she reached the images from the bar, Arden grew even more agitated. The angle of some of the shots made it look as though Reid and the victim were interacting.

Arden could have spent hours examining every nuance of those photographs, but she'd already spent too much time in Brody's apartment. She'd pressed her luck long enough. Panic had set in so she did the only thing she could think of in the moment. She attached the images to an email and sent them to her account. Then she deleted the message from the Sent folder. *What else? What else?* Grabbing a tissue from her bag, she wiped down the computer and anything else in the vicinity she might have touched.

She was just finishing up when she heard footsteps on the wooden stairs outside the apartment. Quickly she gathered up her bag and took one last look at the table, then hurried to peek out the front widow.

Brody was coming up the stairs. He was almost at the landing.

Arden cast a frantic glance around and then darted inside the tiny bathroom. She flattened herself in the tub and pulled the shower curtain closed.

The door opened and Brody came inside the apartment. She listened as he clomped through the rooms, praying he wouldn't need to use the bathroom or, even worse, decide to take a shower.

A ringtone sounded and he answered with an impatient grunt.

"Yeah, yeah, I know I'm late. Unforeseen circumstances."

Arden heard a drawer slide open. She hadn't left anything on the table, had she? She hadn't moved his laptop enough so that he would notice? She squeezed her eyes closed and waited. Into the silence came the metallic click of what she imagined to be a switchblade. She pictured him testing the vicious blade with his thumb as he glanced toward the bathroom...

"Relax, dude. I'm on my way now. You just make sure you have the money."

He left the apartment and slammed the door behind him. Arden waited to make sure he wasn't coming back, and then she climbed shuddering out of the tub. She went back over to the table to make sure nothing was amiss and quickly exited the apartment.

By the time she got to the street, Brody was well ahead

of her. She accelerated her pace, trying to shorten the distance between them without calling attention to herself. He strode along, a man on a mission, turning here, turning there until they finally reached King Street and she lost him.

Arden came to a stop, glancing up and down the street. The sidewalks were crowded for a weekday, but his appearance would make him stand out among the tourists and shoppers. Maybe he'd gone inside one of the boutiques. That hardly seemed likely, but he couldn't have just vanished.

As she stood there contemplating where he might have gone, a hand fell on her shoulder.

She jumped and turned with a gasp. Her arm went back in self-defense. Instead of swinging her bag at Brody's head, she said incredulously, "Uncle Calvin! What are you doing here?"

A smile flashed, disarming her instantly. "I was just about to ask you the same thing, but then I assumed you'd come for a tour of the studio."

She tried to act natural as she dropped the bag to her side and smoothed back her hair. "Actually, I was just out doing a little shopping. Although if I'd known the address of your studio, I would have stopped by."

He motioned to a building across the street. "I'm on the second floor. Lots of beautiful light. Come up. I'll fix you something cold to drink and give you the grand tour."

"That sounds lovely." Arden shot a glance over her shoulder before she followed her uncle across the street and up to his studio. Despite the heat, he looked cool and collected in khaki chinos and a cotton shirt that complemented his eyes and the white-gold hair that curled at his collar.

Arden marveled at how young he looked for his age. A

stranger would never have guessed that he was well into his forties. It was only when he turned at the top of the stairs and gave her a little smile that she noticed the crinkles at the corners of his eyes and the deeper crevices in his brow. "It's a working studio," he said. "Nothing too fancy and it's a bit of a mess right now. I've been inspired lately and painting like a madman."

"I'm eager to see it."

He stepped back for her to enter, and she stood gazing around. The space was wide open, with an industrial flavor from the original plank flooring, brick walls and long windows that reached to the beamed ceiling. Canvases were stacked at least three deep along the walls and an easel had been set up to take advantage of the morning sunlight.

"It's a wonderful space," Arden said as she moved into the center of the room. "Bigger than I imagined, and the light really is beautiful. So soft and golden. I can see how you'd be inspired here."

"It's not the studio that inspires me, though I do consider myself lucky for having found this place," Calvin said. "It's one of a kind."

"How long have you been here?"

"A while."

"You mentioned that you live nearby?"

"Only a few blocks away. It's very convenient."

Arden walked over to one of the windows that looked down on the street. "If I had this studio, I don't think I'd ever want to leave."

"You haven't seen my apartment," he said with another smile.

"That's true."

"Minuscule compared to Mayfair House, but it suits my needs perfectly."

"I've decided big homes are overrated," Arden said. "Not to mention overwhelming."

"Yes. We tend to take those grand old places and all the accompanying creature comforts for granted when someone else is footing the bill. But there is something to be said for freedom." His gaze darkened before he reclaimed his good humor. "Anyway, you'll have to come to dinner soon. I'm not a bad cook."

"That would be nice. Just let me get settled first."

"Of course. In the meantime, what will you have to drink? I have iced tea, lemonade…"

"Iced tea is perfect."

He disappeared into another room. "Make yourself at home," he called out. "I'll be right back."

"Is it okay if I look at your paintings?"

"Certainly. Nothing in the studio is off-limits."

She wandered around the perimeter of the room, examining the canvases and admiring the iconic landmarks that he had painted. The church towers, the cemeteries, the pastel homes on Rainbow Row. Even Berdeaux Place. The paintings were colorful, the subject matter dear to Arden's heart, and yet an inexplicable melancholy descended. She was home now. She could visit any of these places whenever she liked. But studying her uncle's art was like observing her beloved city through a mist. There was an unsettling disconnection. Was that how Calvin had felt as a child visiting Berdeaux Place? A lonely little boy observing from a distance a happier life that should have been his?

She shrugged, dismissing the thought, deciding it was best to leave the psychoanalysis to the experts.

Circling the room, she finally came to a stop in front of the easel. The unfinished painting jolted her. She blinked and then blinked again. It was like her previous thoughts had suddenly materialized.

"You've painted Mother's cereus." *Through a greenhouse window. From the outside peering in.*

"I've attempted to. It's a rather complicated plant. The texture of the leaves is tricky."

"Are you kidding me? The detail is amazing," Arden said in wonder.

"Thank you for that." He came back into the room and handed her a frosty glass. "I'll paint a companion piece once the blooms have opened. That is, if you have no objection."

"Of course not. Your work is very beautiful and you seem to be quite prolific. I had no idea." She glanced around the room at all the canvases. "Do you paint everything from memory?"

"Not always. I sketch and sometimes I work from photographs."

"This painting almost looks like a photograph. I feel as if I'm gazing through the greenhouse window." She took a sip of tea as she gave him a sidelong glance. "I went out to the garden last night, but I didn't see you working."

"I didn't want to disturb you again. Besides, there's little point in coming every night until the blooms are further along."

"I can't get over the colors," Arden murmured, her attention still on the cereus. "It's almost as if…" She trailed away, shy about her thoughts all of a sudden.

"As if…what?"

"You'll think I'm crazy."

Her uncle smiled. "Artists are by nature crazy. Who am I to judge?"

Still, Arden hesitated. "It's like Grandmother is there in

the greenhouse. Mother, too. You didn't paint them. You can't see them. But I can feel them."

He drew a sharp breath.

"I'm sorry," Arden said. "Did I say something wrong?"

"No, quite the opposite, in fact. It's just so rare to find someone who feels about your work the way you do. You couldn't have known what was in my heart or in my head when I painted that scene and yet…" Now he was the one who broke off. "Forgive me. I'm just… I'm blown away by your insight." He walked over to the easel and picked up the canvas. "I think you must have this."

"Oh, I couldn't. As beautiful as it is, I can't take your work."

"Why not? I'm offering it to you as a gift. Although…" He returned the canvas to the easel. "I have one that you might appreciate more." He set his drink aside and disappeared through another doorway. He returned carrying a small canvas, which he offered to Arden. "My welcome-home gift to you. I hope you like this one as much as I do. And before you say anything, I won't take no for an answer."

Arden went very still as he turned the painting and she got her first glimpse of the subject. Uneasiness crept over her as she took the canvas from his hands and turned toward the light. He had painted her mother in the moonlit garden at Berdeaux Place with the summerhouse dome in the background. Camille Mayfair looked just as Arden remembered her. The mysterious glint in her eyes. The dazzling smile. But there was a feeling of distance again. The perception of admiring her from afar.

The red chiffon gown she wore appeared so soft and airy that Arden could almost imagine the frothy layers floating up from the canvas. Camille's bare arms and shoulders gleamed softly in the moonlight and her blond hair was pulled back and fastened with a creamy magnolia blossom.

A magnolia blossom.

Arden was speechless.

"Do you like it?" her uncle asked softly. "I tried to catch her whimsy and drama, but I'm not that talented."

"No, you are. It's wonderful. I can't stop looking at her." Arden tried to swallow past the sudden knot in her throat.

Calvin seemed overcome, as well. "Now you know why I was so taken aback when I saw you standing in the moonlight the other night."

Arden couldn't tear her gaze from the canvas. "When did you paint this?"

"A few years ago from a photograph that was taken on the night of the Mayor's Ball. It was held at Berdeaux Place that year. I was away at school, but I remember reading about it in the paper."

"I remember it, too," Arden said. "She came into my room before she went downstairs. She looked like a princess in that red dress. I can still remember the way the magnolia blossom smelled in her hair when she leaned over the bed to kiss me good-night. A few days later, she was gone."

Calvin gently took the canvas from her fingers. "I'll wrap this up and have it delivered to the house."

Arden glanced up. "Are you sure?"

"I couldn't bear for anyone but you to have it," he said.

"I don't know what to say. Thank you, Uncle."

"You're welcome, Niece. I have something else for you, too." He placed the canvas on his worktable and took a key from a peg on the wall. "This is the key to the side gate. It was one thing for me to come and go as I pleased when no one was in the house, but the last thing I want to do is intrude on your privacy."

He offered her the key and she took it without argument. "That's very thoughtful of you. Actually, I've been thinking about having all the locks changed. The house has been empty for so long. Who knows how many keys may be floating around?"

Something flashed in his eyes, an emotion that unnerved Arden even more than the painting had. "Probably a good idea," he murmured. "Your safety is paramount."

His mood had changed, though. Arden couldn't figure out what had happened. Maybe he had expected her to refuse the key or to at least offer a token resistance. In any case, it was time for her to leave.

"I should be going. I've taken up enough of your time. Thank you for showing me your studio. As for the painting…" She trailed away. "You have no idea what it means to me."

"I'm glad that it makes you happy." He walked her to the top of the stairs.

"I can see myself down," she said. "Thank you again."

"Come back soon. I've a lot more to show you."

"I'll do that." She went down the stairs without looking back, but when she crossed the street, she couldn't help glancing up at the studio. He stood at one of the long windows staring down at her.

Chapter Eleven

Reid approached the house on Water Street on foot. He'd parked a block over so that his car wouldn't be spotted entering or leaving the driveway. He opened the wrought-iron gate and strode up the walkway to the front door, glancing over his shoulder as he rang the bell. His mother played bridge on Wednesdays and the housekeeper had the day off. He expected the house to be empty, but he still had a key and the security code unless either or both had been changed since his last visit.

He waited a few minutes and then let himself in, disarming the system as he called out to his mother. Then he called out the housekeeper's name. "Anyone home?" He folded his sunglasses and slipped them in his pocket as his gaze traveled up the curving staircase. Nothing stirred. The house was empty except for the ghosts.

Still, he felt uneasy being in his childhood home uninvited. He tried to shake off his disquiet as he headed to the back of the house where his father's office was located, a rich, masculine room that looked out on the pool. The drapes were open and Reid could see the dance of sunlight on blue water as he stepped through the pocket doors. He had no idea what he was looking for. His father's equivalent of a little black book, he supposed. The heavy oak desk was kept locked, but Reid had known since he was a kid that the key rested on a ledge underneath the smooth top.

Plopping down in his father's chair, he felt underneath the desk until he located the key. He was just about to open the top drawer when he heard a car pull up outside. He returned the key to the ledge and got up from the desk, slipping silently into the hallway. He heard the back door close and then someone moving about in the kitchen. Maybe Tess had changed her day off, Reid thought, and he quickly came up with an excuse for his presence as he eased down the corridor.

The kitchen was spacious with gleaming stainless steel appliances and a marble island large enough to accommodate six people. His father stood behind the counter splashing whiskey into a tumbler. Watching him from the doorway, Reid wondered if he was catching a glimpse of his future. The notion was hardly comforting. His father had never been an easy man to know or love. He was brilliant and wildly successful, but he'd never struck Reid as particularly happy, which had not made for a particularly happy household. Yet, despite Boone's failings as a parent and husband, he'd always taken as his due the devotion and respect of those around him.

But credit where credit was due, the man seemed committed to keeping the years at bay. He was as sharp and ruthless as ever, and he kept himself in excellent physical shape. Reid would give him that. He worked out, played tennis twice a week and watched his diet. A cocktail in the middle of the day seemed out of character, but how well did Reid really know his father?

He cleared his throat and Boone looked up in surprise.

"What the hell are you doing here?" he demanded.

"I came to see Mother."

"Your mother has had a standing bridge date every

Wednesday for the past thirty years. You know that as well as I do."

"I guess it slipped my mind," Reid said.

His father frowned at him over the rim of his glass. "How did you get in here anyway?"

Reid sauntered into the kitchen. "I still have a key. You disowned me. Mother didn't."

Boone scoffed as he downed his drink. "Disowned is a little dramatic."

"Is it? Let's recap. You had Security escort me from the building after you fired me, and then you stood on the sidewalk and told me that I was no son of yours, that I would never see a penny of inheritance and that I shouldn't even think about trying to capitalize on the Sutton name. I'd say that's pretty much the dictionary definition of *disowned*, but we can agree to disagree." Reid hadn't realized until that moment how much his father's words still rankled. He'd convinced himself the estrangement was for the best. Time away from the old man suited him just fine. But no son, no matter his age, wanted to be ostracized by his father. A tiny part of Reid still craved a word of encouragement, no matter how fleeting.

"I was angry," Boone said. "And you were insubordinate and disrespectful. I treated you as I would have any other associate."

"I was trying to protect my client. The client you ordered me to drop because one of your cronies had a problem with my representing a man he considered an upstart competitor. Whatever happened to loyalty?"

"Some might say I'm loyal to a fault," his father countered. "That crony, as you call him, has thrown more work my way than you'll ever see in a lifetime. So I made a judgment call. My firm, my decision."

Had he sounded like that much of a pompous ass with

Arden that morning? Reid wondered. The term *like father, like son* had never grated more.

His father glanced up from his drink. "You know what your problem is?"

"No, but I'm sure you're dying to tell me."

"You're too much like your mother. You personalize everything and then you cling to your grudges. Me? I let off steam and then I move on."

"You've moved on?"

"Water under the bridge." His father got down a second glass. "Come have a drink with me."

"It's a little early for me," Reid said as he straddled one of the bar stools.

"What's the saying…? It has to be five o'clock somewhere." Boone poured a whiskey and slid the glass across the island.

Reid cradled the tumbler in both hands, but he didn't drink. "What are you doing home at this time of day anyway?"

Boone shrugged. "I needed a quiet place to work. You know how it gets around the office. So much going on you can't hear yourself think."

"Why not go to the apartment?"

His father had been in the process of lifting his drink, but his hand froze for a split second before he took a sip.

"Yeah," Reid said. "I know about the apartment. So does everyone else in the office. I'm sure Mother knows about it, too."

Something hard glittered in Boone's eyes as he polished off his drink and poured himself another. "I hear you sold your condo. Bought one of those old properties on Logan Street and opened an office. How's that working out for you?"

"It's early days, but I'm staying busy."

"I also hear you had a meeting with Clement Mayfair yesterday. Trying to land yourself a big one, are you?"

Reid frowned. "Where did you hear that?"

"You know how things work in this town. Small circles, big mouths." His father observed him for a moment. "A word of advice?"

"Why not?"

"Think twice before you get into bed with a guy like Clement Mayfair. He's as vicious and vindictive as they come. You cross a line with him, you make an enemy for life."

Reid thought about Clement Mayfair's earlier warning. "He told me he had dealings with you in the past. He called you overconfident and self-indulgent. To be fair, he said the same about me."

Boone smirked. "It's not overconfidence if you can deliver."

"No, I suppose not," Reid said. "You were his attorney?"

"About a hundred years ago."

"What happened?"

Boone made a dismissive gesture with his hand. "Nothing seismic. Your mother and I were good friends with Evelyn. When they separated, it created a conflict of interest."

"So you chose Evelyn."

"It really wasn't much of a choice. I was glad to see the last of Clement Mayfair."

Reid toyed with his glass. "Do you know why they split?"

His father gave him a curious look. "It didn't have anything to do with me if that's what you're implying. I thought the world of Evelyn. She was something back in her day, but I've never gone for older women."

Reid said drily, "Not everything is about you, you know."

"Just most things." Boone grinned.

Reid wasn't amused. "From what Arden has told me, the separation was anything but amicable. Evelyn took the daughter and Clement kept the son. Sounds like a pretty screwed-up arrangement if you ask me."

"The Mayfairs are a pretty screwed-up lot," Boone said. "I don't say that to malign your girlfriend. I've always been fond of Arden."

"She's not my girlfriend."

The denial didn't seem to register. His father leaned an elbow on the marble countertop as he nursed his third drink. "Has Arden ever showed you the family photograph albums?"

"I guess. A long time ago."

"Have her show you again. Take a close look at the faces, the eyes. Arden is the spitting image of her mother, just as Camille was the mirror image of Evelyn. Calvin takes after the old man but with enough Berdeaux blood to soften the hard edges. Ask yourself why Calvin favors both his mother and father, but there is nothing of Clement Mayfair in either of the girls."

Reid stared at him across the counter. "Are you suggesting—"

"I'm not suggesting anything. It's merely an observation." Although Boone sounded sober enough, Reid wondered if his father had been drinking before he ever reached the kitchen door. There was a strange glitter in his eyes, as if he might be enjoying his disparagement of Clement Mayfair a little too much.

Reid thought about the implications of his father's observation. If Clement had found out that Camille wasn't his biological daughter, that would explain the acrimonious separation and the lingering bitterness. That would also explain why Evelyn was allowed to take Camille and forced to leave Calvin behind.

"Why are you so interested in Mayfair ancient history anyway?" his father asked.

"Arden thinks Clement may try to take Berdeaux Place away from her."

His father lifted a brow. "Is that so? Well, I can't say I'm surprised. He's always had a thing about that house. It represents everything he ever desired and could never attain. Legacy. Respectability. Acceptance."

"What are you talking about? Mayfair House is twice the size of Berdeaux Place, and it's been a part of the iconic imagery of Battery Row for generations."

"His grandfather..." Boone frowned. "Or was it his great-grandfather? No matter. Some dead Mayfair lost the house and most of the family money in a series of shady business deals. Another family lived in Mayfair House until Clement made his own fortune. He bought back the property and had money left to burn, but he still wasn't welcome in certain circles. Only his marriage to Evelyn opened those doors and he always resented her for it. After the divorce, he withdrew from society. Sent Calvin away to boarding school, and became reclusive and hostile. Lately, though, I've heard rumbles about efforts to rehabilitate his image. Maybe that has something to do with Arden. He is getting on in years. In any case, she's smart to be on guard."

Reid declined to point out that Clement Mayfair wasn't so much older than Boone. "You haven't heard anything brewing in regards to Berdeaux Place?"

"No, but I'll keep my ear to the ground. If I hear anything I'll let you know."

"Thanks. I appreciate that. Arden will, too."

His father tilted his head, regarding Reid through bloodshot eyes. "This thing with you and Arden. It's just business these days?"

Reid lifted the glass and took his first sip, buying himself a moment. "I told her I'd ask around about her grandfather and, in turn, she's helping me on another case. One of your old clients, as a matter of fact. Dave Brody."

Boone paused just a fraction too long. "Who?"

"Dave Brody. He hasn't tried to contact you?"

"I'm a hard man to reach unless you have my cell number, and I don't give that out to just anybody."

"Brody was sent up on a second-degree murder conviction ten years ago. He got out of prison a few weeks ago and he's been following me around, watching my house. Making a general nuisance of himself."

Boone's face had grown tense and wary. "What does he want with you?"

"He wants me to find Ginger Vreeland." Reid saw the dart of a shadow across his father's expression. "I take it that name rings a bell?"

Boone lifted his drink. "What did he tell you?"

"He thinks you're the reason she left town the night before she was to take the witness stand on his behalf."

"What?"

Reid nodded. "He claims Ginger kept a little black book with all her clients' numbers and—shall we say—preferences? You were afraid of what she might reveal on the witness stand so you paid her to disappear."

"That's ludicrous." Boone slammed his glass to the marble counter so aggressively Reid wondered that the crystal didn't shatter. "Brody was a real piece of work even back then. Guilty as hell, but always wanting to blame his misfortune on someone else. I suggest you keep your distance. Take out a restraining order if you have to."

"I can't do that," Reid said. "He claims someone is trying to set me up for murder and he's the only one who can help clear me."

"Murder?" His father looked stunned. "What are you talking about?"

"You heard about the body that was found Monday morning in an alley down the street from my place? Turns out, the victim and I were in the same bar on the night she was killed. I don't remember her. I don't remember much of anything about that night, but Brody claims he has photographs of the two of us together. He'll take them to the police if I don't help him find Ginger Vreeland. A restraining order wouldn't stop him. It would only egg him on."

"Then just back off. Let me take care of Brody."

That was like him, Reid thought. Always thinking he knew best. Reid couldn't help but remember Brody's taunt about Boone Sutton swooping in to save the day. Or Arden's tentative speculation that his father could be behind everything.

"It's not that simple," Reid said. "One of the detectives on the case is a man named John Graham. He arrested me years ago for driving under the influence. He thinks you not only called in favors to get my record expunged, but you also meddled in his career. So you getting involved will only make things worse all the way around."

"I remember that cop," Boone said. "Bad temper. God complex. Guys like him give all the other police officers a bad name. If he had career setbacks, it was because of his incompetence and attitude. He'd already been suspended once for unreasonable force, by the way. Then he had those two inmates work you over. He should have been fired on the spot. No second chances."

"Why wasn't he?"

"My guess is someone with enough money and clout decided he could be useful. That's how this town works, too."

Was it you? Reid wondered. *Are you the reason John Graham still has a badge?*

"I'll talk to some people," Boone said.

"No, don't do that. All I want from you is Ginger Vreeland's address. Or at least her last known whereabouts."

"So you can try to bargain with Brody?" His father leaned in so close that Reid could follow the roadmap of those tiny red veins in his eyes. "Has it ever occurred to you that Ginger would have had more than one name in her book? More than one name, more than one secret. Her disappearance had nothing to do with me. Maybe she left town because she was afraid."

That stopped Reid cold. "Someone threatened her?"

Boone straightened. "I've said all I can say. You need to let this one go, Reid. Forget you ever heard the name Ginger Vreeland. You have no idea the can of worms you're trying to open."

Chapter Twelve

Arden was seated behind Reid's desk working on her laptop when he got back to the office that afternoon. Despite yesterday's experience, she barely glanced up when he came in the back door, she was that engrossed in the photographs.

"What a day I've had." He glanced in from the kitchen doorway. "You want a drink?"

She answered without looking up. "Thought you'd stopped drinking for now."

"I meant water or a Coke."

"No, I'm fine. I've had a day, too," she said, letting excitement creep into her voice. "You'll never believe what I have to show you."

She heard him close the fridge and then pop the tab on a soda. "So what are you working on?" he asked. "The website?"

"No, not yet. Right now, I'm going through some photographs." She finally glanced up. He stood in the archway leaning a shoulder against the door frame. He'd removed his coat and tie and rolled up his shirtsleeves, revealing his tanned forearms. He looked tall and lean and handsome, the grown-up version of the boy she'd once loved beyond all reason. A thrill raced up her spine in spite of her best efforts. And with those tingles came a memory.

Don't be like that, Reid. Just say it.

Why do I need to say it? You know how I feel.

Because I need to hear it, that's why.

All right, then. I love you, Arden Mayfair. I've loved you from the moment I first laid eyes on you, and I'll love you until the moment I leave this earth. How's that?

"What photographs?" Reid asked.

"What?"

He nodded to the laptop. "You said you were going through some photographs."

"Oh. Right. The photos." She cleared her throat and glanced away. She was letting herself think too much about the past today, falling into the trap of all those old memories. She and Reid had known each other forever, and, yes, she'd once felt closer to him than anyone else on earth. But that was a long time ago. They were adults now with career setbacks and bills and a plethora of other problems that had to be dealt with before she could even think about the future.

"Arden?"

She cleared her throat again. "I want to show you something, but you have to promise you won't get upset."

"I already don't like the sound of that, so no." He pushed away from the door frame and ambled over to the desk, leaning against the edge as he gazed down at her. "I'm not making you any promises."

"Okay. Just keep in mind that I'm perfectly safe. Nothing happened."

"Arden." He drawled out her name. "What have you done?"

The intensity of his gaze...the way he tilted his head as he stared down at her...

She sighed. Even suspicious Reid was suddenly irresistible to her. Maybe it was that death thing she'd read about.

Someone dies and suddenly all you want to do is have sex so that you can feel alive. She'd never personally experienced such a reaction. Maybe it wasn't even a real thing. Maybe she was just—

"What is going on with you?" Reid asked. "I've never seen you so distracted."

"I have a lot on my mind, as I'm sure you do." She brushed back her hair. "Maybe I should just show you the images and then we'll talk. Talk not yell," she added.

"We'll see."

He turned to lean in, placing a hand on the desk and another on the back of her chair. Too close. She couldn't breathe, so she rolled away slightly, hoping he wouldn't notice.

"What? Did my deodorant fail me or something?"

"You smell fine," she said with an inward cringe.

"You're acting really weird today."

"I know. Let's concentrate on the photographs." She clicked on the thumbnails to enlarge the images. "Brody didn't lie. He really did take photos of you and the victim in that bar."

Reid leaned in even closer. "Where did you get these?"

"Someone emailed them to me."

He reached over and clicked another image. "Who?"

"I did," she admitted. "I emailed them to myself."

He turned with a frown. "Where did you get them?"

"They were on Dave Brody's laptop, which I found in his apartment after I broke in." She said it all in a rush.

"You *what*?"

"I didn't actually break in," she clarified. "I used a key that I found in a flowerpot."

He gave a quick shake of his head as if he couldn't keep up with her explanation. "Hold on. What key, what flowerpot?"

She gave him a mostly abbreviated version of events,

but there was no way to sugarcoat her hiding in Brody's bathtub to avoid him.

Reid swiveled her chair around so that she couldn't avoid his gaze. "What were you thinking? Did you even consider what would happen if he caught you in his apartment?"

"But he didn't catch me. I'm perfectly fine. And I kept my head enough to wipe my fingerprints off the laptop before I left. He'll never know I was there."

"Did you wipe down the doorknobs? What about the key? Are you certain the landlady didn't see you enter or leave?" Reid looked to be hanging on to his cool by a thread. "Damn it, Arden. That could have gone wrong in so many ways. I don't even know what to say to you right now."

"How about, good job, Arden. How about, let's take a closer look at these photographs."

He wasn't amused. "How about, you put yourself needlessly at risk and proved that I can't trust you."

Arden was starting to get a little irritated. "You're making too big a deal of this."

"I've barely gotten started. We had an agreement, remember? My office, my firm, my rules."

"I wasn't in the office. I was on my lunch break. I would assume my free time is my own."

"Now you're just being deliberately willful."

"And you're being—what was the word you used the other night—pedestrian," she shot back. "When has either of us ever played by the rules? You actually followed Brody into a dark alley where a woman had been killed the night before. So don't tell me you wouldn't have done the same thing in my place."

"That's different."

"Oh, because you're a man and I'm a woman?"

"No, because this is my problem. I don't want you taking that kind of risk on my behalf."

"It's not just your problem and, for your information, I didn't do it just for you. I want to find out who killed Haley Cooper as much as you do. For all we know, I could be the next victim."

That seemed to take the wind out of his sails. "I won't let that happen."

"Unless we find out what's really going on, you may not be able to stop it. That's why I went up to Brody's apartment. I hoped I could find evidence of the real killer's identity or, at the very least, whether or not someone is paying him to frame you. If you'd settle down for a minute and look at the photographs, I mean, *really look* at the photographs, you might find something interesting."

"Arden..."

"I don't want to fight about this anymore," she said.

"I don't want to fight, either. I was just about to say I'm sorry."

"For what?" she asked suspiciously.

His eyes glinted and a smile flickered. "For being too much like Boone Sutton."

"You're nothing like Boone Sutton. You never were."

His hands were still on the chair arms as he gazed into her eyes. Lips slightly parted. Heart starting to race. Or was that hers?

He leaned in, brushing his lips against hers and Arden's pulse jumped. It was a brief kiss, barely any contact at all, and yet she felt a tremor go straight through her, making her crave a deeper connection. She wanted to feel his tongue in her mouth and his hands on her breasts. She wanted him to whisk her upstairs and undress her slowly with the balcony doors open and the scent of jasmine drifting in on the breeze. She wanted time to melt away, but those fourteen years of estrangement were right there between them, creating obstacles and barriers that she didn't dare breach.

He moved his head away, just a few inches, and smiled down at her. "Sorry again."

"For what?"

"For being too much like the old Reid Sutton."

"Don't ever apologize for that. The old Reid Sutton was pretty wonderful."

"As opposed to the current Reid Sutton?"

"Time will tell," she teased.

For a moment, she thought he might accept the challenge and kiss her again, but he turned back to the laptop and the moment was gone.

Arden scooted back up to the desk and sorted through the photographs until she found the one she wanted, and then she magnified the image.

"What am I looking for?" Reid asked.

"Just study the picture and tell me what you see."

"It's pretty dark, but I recognize a couple of my friends in the background. There I am standing at the bar. The woman next to me is the victim, Haley Cooper. I know because Detective Graham showed me a picture of her. At least I think she's the same woman. It's hard to know for certain."

"Even in the dim lighting, certain faces stand out," Arden said. "Keep looking."

Reid frowned. "Why don't you just tell me who or what I'm looking for?"

"Check out the man at the end of the bar. His head is turned toward you, and he appears to be staring at either you or the victim or both."

Reid concentrated for a moment and slowly turned his head toward Arden. "Is that who I think it is?"

"Sure looks like him to me. What are the chances that Detective Graham would be in that particular bar on that particular night?"

Reid focused on the photograph. "Are you sure it's him?"

"Not one hundred percent. As you said, the photograph is dark, but look at the hair, the way he holds his drink. The expression on his face. You can almost feel the contempt. I don't think his being there was a coincidence. My question is this. Why didn't he tell you that he'd seen you on the night Haley Cooper was murdered?"

"Maybe he wanted to catch me in a lie. Or see if I'd incriminate myself."

"Did you? Lie to him, I mean?"

"I told him she looked vaguely familiar. There was a chance I might have seen her around the neighborhood."

"And he didn't say or do anything to give himself away?"

"No, but I was concentrating pretty hard on not giving myself away. I might not have noticed."

"I did some digging while you were out," Arden said. "There's a lot of information on the internet about cops if you know where to look. Detective Graham has a pretty checkered history with the Charleston PD. Suspensions. Internal Affairs investigations. And that's not all. His personal life is a mess, too. He's going through a second bad divorce. Lots of debt. That kind of guy could be bought off."

Reid gave her an admiring look. "Where did you find all this stuff?"

"Blogs, message boards, news sites. A person's whole life is online." She paused. "Do you think he could be the one who came into your house yesterday?"

"You tell me. You saw him on the porch. Could he have been the intruder?"

She thought about that for a moment. "He's the right size and height, but I never got a look at the man's face. I figured Dave Brody. Regardless, how did the intruder get a key?"

"Maybe he found it in a flowerpot," Reid deadpanned.

She made a face. "Or maybe he got it from the real estate agent who sold you this house. He could have spun any kind of story to get the agent to cooperate. What about motive, though? I get that he doesn't like rich people, but it's hard to believe he'd nurse a grudge against you personally. All because your father got you out of jail?"

"He also thinks Boone meddled in his career. Don't forget that part. And speaking of the devil…" Reid went around the desk and sat down in one of the client chairs. "I saw him today."

"Your father? You went to his office?"

"No, I went by the house. I thought Mother and the housekeeper would be out and I could search his office. See if I could find anything that connects him to Ginger Vreeland."

"Did you?"

"He came home before I had a chance to look around. I told him I was there to see Mother, but I don't think he believed me. Luckily, he was too preoccupied—and possibly inebriated—to press me. Anyway, I brought up Brody's name. He pretended he didn't know who he was until I mentioned Ginger Vreeland. Then he became visibly distressed and implied that she'd left town because one of her clients had threatened her."

"Did he say who?"

"No, but he was pretty adamant that I leave Ginger

alone. He told me in no uncertain terms that I should walk away."

"You're not going to, are you?"

Reid's gaze hardened. "How can I as long as Brody has leverage over me?"

"Then should I move forward with the website and business cards? The sooner we contact her uncle, the closer we are to finding Ginger."

"Yes, go ahead, and make sure you run everything by me before you do anything else. In other words, don't go off on your own trying to track this guy down."

"You have my word." Arden closed the laptop and began gathering up her things. "It's been a long day. I'm heading home now. I've been so distracted by everything that's happened here, I'm behind on the things I need to do at Berdeaux Place."

"Whenever you're ready, I'll drive you," Reid said.

Arden stood and hooked her bag over her shoulder. "That's not necessary. I enjoy the walk. Gives me a chance to get reacquainted with the city."

Reid rose, too. "You'll have plenty of time for that later. It's a long walk and it'll be twilight soon. I don't want you out on the street with Brody lurking around. Before you argue—it has nothing to do with your gender," he said. "It's just common sense."

Hard to disagree with that. Arden nodded. "You're right. We both need to take precautions these days. A ride would be great."

They walked out the back door, pausing on the porch for Reid to lock up. Then they went down the steps together and crossed the yard to the driveway. Arden took a moment to admire the sleek lines of his car before she climbed inside and settled comfortably onto the seat. She ran a hand over the padded leather as Reid started the engine.

"Nice ride. But it kind of stands out in this neighborhood, don't you think?"

He grinned. "Why do you think I park around back? I thought about selling it when I got rid of the condo. I could have used the extra cash, but I'm a Southern boy born and bred. When it comes right down to it, I'd sooner cut off my right arm than get rid of my wheels."

"I sold my car before I left Atlanta," Arden said. "I sold or gave away everything except whatever I could pack in my bags."

Reid shot her a glance. "Clean break."

"Yeah."

They were out on the street now heading toward the tip of the peninsula. Reid checked the rearview mirror and then checked it again.

"What is it?" she asked anxiously.

"Probably nothing. A beige sedan has been behind us for a few blocks. No, don't turn around," he said.

Arden looked in the outside mirror. "Two cars back? Do you think it could be Graham? Looks like an unmarked cop car."

"Let's find out." Reid gave her a warning glance. "You better hold on!"

Chapter Thirteen

Reid jerked the wheel, executing a sharp right turn at the last minute. Then he goosed the accelerator for half a block, threw on the brakes and reversed into an alley.

Through all the maneuvers, Arden clung to the armrest and the edge of her seat. When he finally came to a full stop, she released her held breath. "Are you insane? You nearly gave me a heart attack back there."

"I did warn you to hold on." He focused his gaze on the street in front of them. "Anyway, that's just adrenaline. Don't pretend you didn't like it."

"Maybe I did," she conceded. "That doesn't make you any less crazy."

"No, but it does give me back my partner in crime."

"I don't know if I would go that far." Arden tried not to react to his words. She told herself they meant nothing. It was a slip of the tongue in the heat of the moment. But adrenaline buzzed through her veins. "Where did you learn to drive like that anyway?"

Another grin flashed. "Just a God-given talent. I'm surprised you didn't remember that about me."

"Maybe I tried to forget." Arden faced forward, watching the street. "Do you think we lost him? That is, if anyone was following us in the first place."

"We'll sit here for a minute or two and make sure." Reid

seemed to relax as time ticked away. He rolled down his windows so they could hear the sounds from the street. The smell of barbecue and fresh bread drifted in. "You hungry? We could stop somewhere for a bite to eat."

Arden was starving, as a matter of fact, and it would be so easy to take Reid up on his offer. Drift right back into the comfortable relationship of their youth. Have some wine, some food, some good conversation. She couldn't think of a more pleasant way to spend the evening, but rushing things was a very bad idea. They were still building a work rapport and for now a little personal distance was necessary. *Just wait and see how things play out.* She didn't have the stamina for a broken heart. "I appreciate the offer, but I'm beat. Another time?"

He nodded. "Yeah, no problem. I could use an early night myself." He eased out of the alley and melded into the late-afternoon traffic. Keeping an eye on the rearview mirror, he maneuvered effortlessly through the clogged streets, pulling to the curb in front of Berdeaux Place within a matter of minutes.

Arden reached for the door handle. "You don't need to get out," she said when he killed the engine. "I changed the security code so that even if anyone used a key to get in, they'd set off the alarm. I would have been notified if there'd been a breach." Brave words, but the truth of the matter was that Arden dreaded going inside the empty house. Feared another long night of sounds and shadows and dark memories.

"I'll come in and take a quick look around. For my own peace of mind." He reached across her and removed a small pistol from the glove box.

Arden gasped. "Reid. What are you doing with a gun?"

"I have a license, don't worry."

"That doesn't answer my question."

"Lawyers make enemies," he said as he tucked the gun into the back of his belt.

"You mean like Brody?"

"He or someone else came into my house while you were there alone. I don't intend to be caught off guard again."

Arden started to protest—guns scared her—but who was she to cast stones? Hadn't she slept with her grandmother's katana the night before?

They got out of the car and walked up the veranda steps together. She unlocked the door, turned off the alarm and trailed Reid through the house as he went from room to room. Then she led the way upstairs. She refused to go inside her mother's room. She leaned a shoulder against the wall and waved toward the door. "I'll wait out here for you."

While he was inside, she hollered through the doorway. "See anything?"

"Nope, all clear in here."

"Smell anything?"

There was a significant pause. "Like what?"

"Nothing. I just wondered."

He came out into the hallway and gave her a puzzled look. "What was that about?"

"I heard something last night. I went into my mother's room to check things out and I noticed a magnolia-scented candle on her dresser. For a split second, I had the crazy notion that someone had been inside her room burning that candle."

Reid frowned down at her. "You told me you were kept awake by squirrels."

"A scrabbling sound brought me upstairs, and yes, it probably was just squirrels. Or worse, rats." She shuddered. "I told you this morning. Being in this house is a lot more unnerving than I thought it would be."

"Then move into a hotel for the time being. It would certainly make me feel better."

"I can't afford that right now and, besides, I don't want to. I don't want to become that person who's afraid of her own shadow. I'll take the necessary precautions, but I'm not going to be forced out of my own home. I'm sure that's just what my grandfather would like to happen."

"Stubborn as always."

"I prefer to think of myself as determined."

Reid checked the second-floor bedrooms and took a peek in the attic. Satisfied that everything was as it should be, they went back downstairs. He paused in the doorway of the parlor to glance out into the garden. "You think your uncle is working in the greenhouse?"

"I doubt it. I saw him earlier today. He gave me back the key to the side gate. He'd have to crawl over the wall like you did to get inside."

"Assuming he didn't make himself a spare key," Reid said.

"Why would he do that? Why not just keep the original key? I never asked for it back."

"Maybe he thought you would eventually. I'm just thinking out loud." Reid went over and opened one of the doors, letting in the late-afternoon breeze. He moved out into the garden and Arden followed reluctantly. If the house unnerved her, the garden put her even more on edge, especially when the sun went down and the bats came out.

She folded her arms around her middle. "I saw him today. My uncle Calvin. He gave me a portrait he'd painted of my mother. He said he worked from a picture of her that was taken here in the garden on the night of the Mayor's Ball. I remember the dress she wore that night. Red chiffon. It floated like a dream around her when she walked. And she'd tucked a magnolia blossom in her hair." Arden paused, suddenly drowning in memories. "You can't imagine how beautiful she looked."

"I think I have some idea," Reid murmured. "Some people think you're the spitting image of Camille."

"A pale copy, maybe." His gaze on her was a little too intense so Arden made a production of plucking a sprig of jasmine and holding it to her nose. "Should we check the greenhouse while we're out here? I don't think my uncle came by, but I'd like to make sure the door is secure. The latch sometimes doesn't catch and I'd rather not have the wind bumping it at all hours…" She trailed off, letting the jasmine drop to her feet as she stared up into the trees. The light shimmering down through the leaves was already starting to wane. Twilight would soon fall and then darkness. She pictured the shadowy sidewalks outside the walls of Berdeaux Place and shivered. "Do you remember how it was that summer?" she asked.

"The summer your mother died?"

"Yes, I mean afterward, when we started hearing about the other victims. No one ever talked about the Twilight Killer in front of me, of course, but I overheard just enough to be terrified. I used to wake up in the middle of the night and think that I could hear his heartbeat in my room. I imagined him underneath my bed or hiding in my closet. Sometimes I would get up and go over to the window just to make sure he wasn't down in the garden staring up at my window."

"It was a very dark time in this city."

"Reid, what if we were right all those years ago?" Arden turned to him in the failing light. He stood in shadows, his features dark and mysterious and yet becoming once again as familiar to her as her own reflection. "What if the person who murdered all those women, including my mother, is still out there somewhere? The real Twilight Killer. Maybe he's taken more lives over the years, even before Haley Cooper. He could have broadened his hunting ground and spread out his kills so that the police never connected his victims. An animal with those kinds of cravings can't remain dormant forever. If he is still out there, then he framed an innocent man once. Maybe his impulses are growing stronger and he feels another spree coming on so he needs another scapegoat. He started seeding the ground with Haley."

"By scapegoat, you mean me?"

"That's what worries me," she said.

Reid didn't chide her for letting her imagination get the better of her as she thought he might. Instead, he let his gaze travel over the grounds, settling his focus on the summerhouse dome. "Assuming Orson Lee Finch really is innocent, he made the perfect patsy. Nearly invisible and moving at will in and out of the gardens South of Broad Street. Plenty of opportunities to observe and follow his victims. And once arrested, he had to rely on a public defender. No money, no friends, no family to speak of." He turned back to Arden. "I'm not Finch. I have access to the finest defense team in the city, not to mention a plethora of private detectives. I'm hardly powerless, so you have to ask yourself why a spree killer would want to try and frame someone with my resources. That doesn't make sense."

"Unless you're not even the real target. Maybe I am." Arden shivered. With the setting sun, a stronger breeze blew in from the harbor, carrying the faintest trace of pluff mud through the trees. Her grandmother used to call that particular aroma the perfume of rumors and old scandal. The fecund smell was there one moment, gone the next, replaced by the ubiquitous scent of jasmine.

"Maybe we're overthinking this," Reid said. "Trying to connect everything back to the Twilight Killer is making us overlook the revenge angle. Maybe this is nothing more than a simple frame job. A way to get to my father because Brody can't touch him."

"So Detective Graham being in the bar the night of the murder was just a coincidence?"

"I don't know what to think about Graham." The breeze ruffled Reid's hair, making Arden long to run her fingers through the mussed strands. "I need to tell you something else about my conversation with Boone today."

His tone made her breath catch. "What?"

"He suggested that we should take a look at your family photo albums."

"Why?" she asked in surprise.

"He thinks Clement Mayfair might not have been your mother's biological father."

Arden whirled. "What?"

"You've never considered the possibility?" Reid asked. "You never heard any talk to that effect?"

"Not a word. But..." She trailed off as her mind went back through those photo albums. So many portraits and candid shots of Arden and her mother and grandmother, fewer of Calvin, and none at all of her grandfather. Hardly surprising considering the lingering animosity. "If I'm honest, I can't say that would surprise me. It makes a sick kind of sense, doesn't it? Why Grandmother took my mother and left Calvin behind with my grandfather? He probably threatened to take both her children away from her."

"Has he made contact?"

"No. But I'm more certain than ever that his real interest is in acquiring this house. He doesn't care anything about me. He never did."

"His loss," Reid said.

Arden shrugged. "I'm sure he doesn't see it that way. I think I should go see him. I know you advised against it, but I want to make it clear that I'm not afraid of him and that he is never going to get his hands on Grandmother's house."

"Just hold off for a bit," Reid said. "Everything we've talked about is pure speculation. There's no point in antagonizing him until he makes a move. It's possible that he really does want to make amends."

"I'll wait. But not forever." Arden turned to make her way to the greenhouse. Reid had stopped on the path and was staring in the opposite direction. "What's wrong?"

"Let's check out the summerhouse first." He nodded toward the ornate dome. "We're right here and I'd like to see how it's held up over the years."

"I'd rather not. I don't like going inside," Arden admitted.

"Since when? You used to love the summerhouse. It was our place."

"It was his place first," she said.

He gave her a bemused look. "Are you talking about your mother's killer? There was never any evidence that he hid inside."

"The magnolia blossom on the steps would suggest otherwise."

"Okay, but that was a long time ago, and you and I made this place our headquarters for years. Why so reticent now?"

"I can't explain it," Arden said. "It just feels...wrong. Evil."

"It's just a place. A beautiful old summerhouse. You've been away too long. You've forgotten the good things that happened inside. Maybe a quick look around is all you need to put the ghosts to rest. You may find the good memories outweigh the bad."

Maybe that's what I'm really afraid of.

Nevertheless, she followed him up the steps and into the summerhouse. The latticework windows cast mysterious shadows on the floor while twilight edged toward the domed ceiling. Arden turned in a slow circle. The pillows that had cushioned their heads as they'd lain on their backs staring up at the stars were gone, along with all their treasures. The place smelled of dust and decay. But some things remained. Somewhere on the wall were their carved initials; Arden didn't want to look too closely. She didn't want to remember how much she'd given up when she left Charleston fourteen years ago.

"It's a little the worse for wear," Reid said as he moved around the space. "But it does bring back memories."

"Our first grown-up kiss was here," she murmured. "Do you remember?"

"Of course, I remember."

She turned at the tenderness in his voice. Tenderness… and something more. Something darker and headier. Desire. Throbbing just below the surface. Not so strange, she supposed, that they would both feel strong emotions in this place.

"I kissed you and then you ran away," he said. "It was quite a blow to my ego."

"I was afraid."

"Of me?"

"Of what it meant. I knew after that kiss that nothing would ever be the same. I was afraid of losing my best friend."

His voice lowered intimately. "You didn't lose me."

"Easy to say. Not so easy to believe after fourteen years."

"I've always been right here, Arden." He slid his fingers into her hair, tilting her head so that he could stare down at her. "See?" he said. "There's nothing to be afraid of in here."

Arden wasn't so sure. She parted her lips, waiting to see what he would do.

Into the quivering silence came a distant sound, a rhythmic thumping that she could have easily believed was her own heartbeat.

Reid glanced toward the door as his hand fell to his side. "Did you hear that?"

She turned to peer out into the garden. "It's coming from the greenhouse. The wind is rising. It must have caught the door."

Reid was all business now. "We'd better go have a look."

They hurried down the steps together and Arden was overly conscious of Reid beside her, of the memories that still swirled in the ether as they approached the greenhouse. Enough daylight remained so that they could see inside the glass walls. Arden was once again reminded of her uncle's paintings and the feeling his art had evoked of being on the outside looking in.

She gazed down the empty aisles toward the back of the greenhouse, where she could see the silhouette of her mother's cereus. "I should check the progress while we're here. I don't want to risk missing the blooms and that luscious scent." *Like moonlight and romance and deep, dark secrets*, her mother would say.

"Arden, wait," Reid said as she stepped through the door.

"It's fine. There's no one here. Come have a closer look."

She was well down the aisle when she heard a loud crack above her and glanced up a split second before Reid grabbed her from behind. They dropped to the ground and instinctively rolled beneath one of the worktables. Arden tucked her legs and wrapped her arms around her head as Reid covered her body with his. She heard a series of pops as one of the heavy panels gave way and crashed to the stone floor beside them. The tempered glass exploded into harmless chips, but the weight of the panel would have crushed anyone standing in the aisle.

Chapter Fourteen

A structural issue—that was the consensus of the inspectors Arden hired to check out the greenhouse. Over the years, some of the clips that held the glass panels in place had come loose or fallen off altogether and the elements had eroded the silicone sealant. Add in a rusted frame, and the roof panels had been one stray breeze away from disaster for years. Everything pointed to coincidence, and Arden told herself she should just be thankful no one had been hurt. Still, she couldn't stop the little voice in her head that whispered of sabotage.

Before the greenhouse was disassembled and carted away, she had workers move her mother's cereus to the terrace. She liked that location better anyway. Now she could watch the blooms open from the safety of a locked door if she so chose.

Her return to Charleston had been harrowing, to say the least. Luckily, she knew how to tuck and roll and keep her head down. She spent a lot of time at work, burying herself in research and planning. Reid had outside meetings almost every day so she spent hours alone in his house. The solitude never bothered her, which was strange since she could barely spend one night alone in Berdeaux Place without succumbing to her dark imagination. She hadn't experienced any more strange sounds or scents, but every now and then her gaze would stray to her mother's bedroom door and she would wonder again if someone had been inside burning that magnolia-scented candle.

By Friday, the website had gone live, the business cards were printed, and everything was in place to approach Ginger Vreeland's uncle—a retired welder named Tate Smith—about her whereabouts.

She and Reid made the trek down south into marsh country together. The drive was pleasant, the day crystal clear, but the results of their search proved frustrating. Although Arden had searched public records for the last known address, the house appeared abandoned, as if no one had lived there in months, if not years. No one answered the door and none of the neighbors claimed to know Tate Smith or his niece. Arden wondered if Mr. Smith had been that reclusive or if the neighbors were simply protecting his privacy. She clipped a business card to a hastily scribbled message and slipped it underneath his door. Then she and Reid headed back to the city.

The weekend passed without further incident, but Arden couldn't relax. She worked in the office for a little while on Saturday morning and then went home to finish the list of everything that needed to be done to Berdeaux Place. Obviously, with the greenhouse failure, things were direr than she'd anticipated. As she explored the premises and grounds, she kept an eye out for her uncle so that she could explain what had happened. He never turned up. Dave Brody had vanished, as well. The deadline he'd set for Reid had come and gone, but for the moment, he seemed intent on keeping a low profile. Or else he'd gotten a message from Boone Sutton. No Dave Brody, no Detective Graham. No word from her grandfather, either.

Still, Arden knew better than to let down her guard, and as the days wore on, a pall seemed to settle over the city.

An encroaching gloom that portended dark days ahead. She wanted to believe that Haley Cooper's murder had been random, a victim caught in the wrong place at the wrong time, but she had a feeling nothing about the woman's death or the killer's agenda was random. She now had an inkling of what Charleston had experienced during the Twilight Killer's reign of terror. The waiting. The imagined sounds. The impulse to hurry home before sundown and sequester oneself behind locked doors as shadows lengthened and dogs howled behind neighbors' fences.

She feared this quiet time might be the calm before the storm.

Another worry began to niggle. Reid had said nothing about extending her assignment, much less making the arrangement permanent. She hated to think of their time coming to an end. They'd settled into an amiable working relationship and Arden loved having a place to go to every morning. She admired his long-term plans for the firm, and, more than anything, she wanted to contribute to the success of those plans. But she refused to press him for an answer. His firm, his call.

Since the greenhouse incident, he'd kept things casual and that was a very good thing, Arden decided. The easy camaraderie had given them a chance to become friends again. Perhaps not the best buddies of their childhood—not yet—but the tension lessened with each passing day.

Or so she'd thought.

One afternoon she looked up from her work to find Reid standing in the doorway watching her with a puzzled expression, as if he couldn't quite figure her out. The intensity of his gaze caught her by surprise and her heart thudded, though she tried to keep her tone light.

"Everything okay?"

He folded his arms and leaned a shoulder against the

door frame. He didn't have outside meetings that day and was dressed casually in jeans and a dark gray shirt open at the neck. "Do you ever wonder what our lives would be like now if things had worked out differently fourteen years ago?"

The question took Arden by surprise. She pretended to write herself a note while she pondered an answer. "I think about it sometimes, but I try not to dwell. We can't change the past." She shrugged. "Why bring it up now? I thought we'd moved past all that. We're working well together, aren't we?"

"We are," he agreed. "But don't you ever get the feeling we have unfinished business between us?"

Her heart knocked even harder against her rib cage. "What do you mean?"

He shifted his gaze to the window, frowning into the sunlight that streamed through the glass. "I've always wondered why you left the way you did. Why you barely even took the time to say goodbye. We were so close and after everything we'd been through, ending things the way we did felt…wrong."

"I thought it was better to get it over with quickly. Rip the bandage off and all that." She paused thoughtfully. "You always make it sound as if my leaving came out of the blue, but you know that's not the way it happened. We agreed that time apart would be good for us. Separate colleges gave us a chance to be independent. We were so young, and we had so much growing up to do. Maybe things worked out for the best. What's the point in looking back?"

He came into the office and sat down in a chair facing her desk. "It's not healthy to leave issues to fester."

"What issues?"

"All those times you were in Charleston for holidays

and summer break. You *visited*, but you never really came back. You were here physically, but your mind and your heart were a million miles away. It was like you couldn't even stand the sight of me anymore. Like you hated me for what happened."

How would you know? Arden wanted to lash out. *You all but ignored me when I came home. You made me think there was nothing left for me here.*

Instead, she said, "That's what you thought? I didn't hate you. I never could. It was just hard for me to be here after everything that had happened. I felt so guilty. If only I'd taken better care of myself. If only I'd gone to the doctor sooner, if only I'd gotten more rest. And I felt even guiltier because a part of me was relieved when it happened. I know how awful that sounds, but it's the truth. That guilt is why I couldn't look at you."

"What happened wasn't your fault," he said.

"I know that. I probably knew it then, too, but my emotions were so fragile and everything between us seemed to be falling apart. We wanted different things, and that was never more apparent than in the way we each coped with our pain. You took comfort in the familiar. You wanted to cling to what we had. I wanted to run away. Maybe I should have tried harder to explain my feelings to you, but I probably didn't even understand them myself back then. I just knew I needed to get away from my grandmother's house."

"And from me."

"Yes, if I'm honest. We'd been inseparable since childhood. I needed a fresh start. I wanted to meet new people, have new adventures."

"I always thought we would have those adventures together," he said. "I didn't see why a baby had to stop us. I was young and stupid, and I had some crazy, romantic notion of how it could be, the three of us taking on the world. I never took into account what you would be giving up for my dream."

"As long as we're getting everything out in the open, I've always wondered why you never came to find me," she said. "In all those years, not a single phone call, email or text."

"You wanted your space."

"I thought I did." She shrugged. "Things don't always work out the way we want them to."

"And sometimes they work out in the way we least expect." He held her gaze for the longest moment before he rose to leave.

"Reid?"

He glanced over his shoulder.

"Thank you for what you said just now. That it wasn't my fault."

"It wasn't. I should have told you a long time ago."

"You did. You told me over and over. I just wasn't ready to listen. Anyway…it's good to clear the air."

"Yeah."

He went back to his office without further comment.

Arden sat quietly for a few minutes and then got up to follow him. She said from his doorway, "Can I ask you something else? It's not about the past. Actually, it's more of a favor than a question."

He set aside his phone. "Should I be worried?"

"No, it's not like that." She pulled a creamy envelope from her dress pocket and walked over to slide it across his desk.

He picked up the envelope and glanced at the address. "What's this?"

"An invitation to the Mayor's Ball. It was delivered to Berdeaux Place earlier this week."

He glanced up. "That's cutting it a little close. Isn't the ball tomorrow night?"

"I was obviously a late addition to the guest list," she said. "I assume you got your invitation weeks ago."

He didn't seem the least bit interested. "I remember seeing one in the mail. Probably still around here somewhere."

"You weren't planning on going?"

He leaned back in his chair with a broad smile, the seriousness of their earlier conversation forgotten. "That's one of the perks of having my own firm. I no longer have to climb into a monkey suit to please my old man."

Arden sat down in the chair across from his desk, reversing their roles. "Did you happen to notice that it's being held at Mayfair House this year?"

He gave her a curious look. "How do you feel about that?"

"It's very strange. I never remember my grandfather having so much as a dinner party. He hated anyone, including me, intruding on his privacy, and now, suddenly, he's throwing open his doors to half of Charleston."

"My father said he'd heard rumblings about the old man trying to rehabilitate his image. He thought it might be for your benefit."

Arden shrugged. "I don't see how it could be. This had to be in the planning for months. Still, if I didn't suspect he was up to something before, I certainly do now."

"You really don't trust him, do you? Are you sure you aren't letting your grandmother's animosity cloud your judgment?"

She gave him an incredulous look. "You're asking me that after the conversation you had with him last week? Aren't you the one who told me to stay away from him?"

He leaned forward, his expression suspicious. "Yes, I

did. Which is why I'm hoping you aren't planning to go to this thing tomorrow night."

She plucked at an invisible thread on her dress. "Of course, I'm going. It's the perfect place to interact with him for the first time. If I'm lucky, I may get some insight into what he's up to."

"Assuming he does have an agenda, he won't give himself away that easily," Reid warned. "Mayfair Place will be packed. Lots of press, lots of cameras. He'll be on his best behavior."

"Unless he's caught off guard."

"Arden." He drawled her name in that way he had. "What are you up to?"

"Nothing," she said innocently. "I just want to talk to him. And if you're really concerned about my safety, you'll go with me."

His eyes glinted, reminding her of the old Reid Sutton. "As your date?"

She hesitated. "As my friend or my boss. Whatever makes you feel most comfortable."

"Nothing about the Mayor's Ball makes me comfortable."

"Because you're looking at it all wrong," Arden insisted. "This is no longer about your father. This is about you and the future of your firm. Think about the guest list. Word will already have gotten around about Ambrose Foucault's imminent retirement. His clients will be there, ripe for the picking."

"I thought I wasn't allowed to go after his clients until his retirement is official," Reid said.

Arden tucked back her hair. "That was before he shared a private conversation with my uncle and possibly my grandfather. All bets are off now. As far as I'm concerned, anyone who comes to that ball is fair game. Think of it as a scouting expedition. I may be a little rusty, but I daresay I can still work a room. And we both know you can charm birds out of a tree when you set your mind to it."

"Listen to you being all cutthroat."

She met his gaze straight on. "No, I'm being practical. A few of those old-money clients could help subsidize the other cases we want to take on." *You. The other cases* you *want to take on.* She started to correct herself, then decided changing the pronoun would call too much attention to her slip. Instead, she rushed to add, "If I haven't convinced you yet, then imagine all those wagging tongues when we walk into Mayfair House together."

He tapped the corner of the envelope on his desk. "I'll think about it."

She pounced. "What's there to think about? You know I'm right. I assume you still have a tux?"

"Buried in the back of my closet, where I like it."

"Dig it out for just this one night. And I'll wear something appropriately provocative."

"I'm almost afraid to ask what that means."

She merely smiled. "The invitation says eight. We'll arrive no earlier than nine thirty. Parking will be a nightmare, so leave your car at my house and we'll walk over together. It'll be so much easier than dealing with the valet service."

"You've got this all planned out, I see."

"Yes. All you have to do is show up on time." She stood to leave.

"Arden?"

She paused at the door.

"This surprise you're planning for your grandfather… You're not going to catch me off guard, too, are you?"

"You worry too much. It'll be a fun night. You'll see."

"Famous last words," he muttered.

ARDEN SPENT SATURDAY morning running errands. She picked up her dress at the dry cleaners and then dropped off her favorite necklace at a jewelry shop to have the clasp replaced. While she waited for the repair, she window-shopped along King Street, browsing some of the high-end boutiques to kill time. A crystal-studded belt in a window caught her eye, and she wandered in to check the price. A candle flickered on the counter next to the photograph of a young blonde woman whom Arden recognized as Haley Cooper.

The smiling countenance of the murder victim shocked her. She couldn't seem to get away from the horror. Then she remembered reading somewhere that Haley Cooper had worked in a shop on King Street.

She found the belt and decided the accessory would go so well with her gown that the splurge would be worth it. Plus, the purchase gave her the opportunity to speak with the woman behind the counter. As she rang up the item, Arden nodded to the photograph. "That's Haley, isn't it?"

The woman glanced up in surprise. "Did you know her?"

"No. I just recognize her photo from the news."

The woman gave her a grim smile. "At least you called her by name. Most of the people who comment on the photo ask if she's the dead woman. It's so impersonal to them. Just a news item or a crime statistic. They forget that Haley was a human being with friends and family who still miss her terribly." She bit her lip. "I'm so sorry. I don't know why I dumped all that on you. The last two weeks have been difficult."

"No apology necessary. Sometimes it's easier to talk to a stranger," Arden said with genuine sympathy. "Were the two of you close?"

"We became good friends after she started working

here last year. She had a great personality. Funny. Smart. She was good with the customers, too." The woman hesitated, as if she wanted to resist but needed to get it all out. She busied her hands with tissue paper. "I know it must seem macabre that I have her photograph on display, but it's my shop. I can do what I want."

"Of course. And I don't think it's macabre at all," Arden said. "You're paying tribute to your friend."

"Yes, that. And I also promised myself I'd keep that candle burning until her killer is brought to justice. But, after two weeks, I'm starting to lose hope."

"I understand better than you think," Arden said. "My mother was murdered. Months went by before an arrest was made. I was young, but I remember the toll it took on my grandmother."

The woman's voice softened. "I'm so sorry. What a terrible thing to have happen to you."

Arden nodded. "It was a long time ago. But you don't forget." She paused. "Do you know if the police have any suspects?"

The woman carefully folded the tissue paper around the belt and secured it with a gold-embossed sticker. "They have *a* suspect. Who knows if anything will come of it?"

Arden tried to keep her tone soothingly neutral. "Do you know who it is?"

The woman took a quick perusal of the shop. A sales associate was busy with another customer at the clearance rack, too far away to overhear. The owner dropped her voice anyway. "You know what they say. It's always the spouse or boyfriend."

Arden lifted a brow. "Haley was seeing someone?"

"Yes. I never met him and she wouldn't say much about him. I had the impression he was an older man with money. That would have impressed Haley. She liked nice things."

"She never mentioned a name?"

"She was always careful not to let anything slip. She said he would be very upset if he knew she had mentioned him at all. He guarded his privacy. That didn't always sit well with Haley. She was young and she liked to go out. She wanted to be wined and dined."

"I heard on the news that she'd gone out to meet someone on the night of the murder. Do you think she met this man?"

The woman shrugged. "It's possible. But I know they had a falling-out a few days before it happened. Haley was seeing someone on the side, but I never got the impression it was romantic. If anything, I think she was trying to spite the older guy."

"Then that would make two suspects," Arden said.

The owner looked as if she wanted to comment further, but three young women came into the shop talking and laughing and drawing her attention. She placed the belt and receipt in a glossy black bag and handed Arden the purchase.

"Enjoy the belt. I'm sure it will look lovely on you."

"Thank you."

Arden walked out of the boutique and glanced around. Her uncle's studio was just up the block. She wondered if she should stop by and warn him about the greenhouse. No, he was probably busy and she'd be seeing him later that night anyway. She realized she was avoiding him and she wasn't sure why. He'd been nothing but cordial and welcoming, and yet she sensed that he, too, had an ulterior motive for his interest in her.

Her phone rang as she walked back toward the jewelry store. She fished it out of her bag and then realized the ringtone belonged to the burner phone she'd purchased for contacting Ginger Vreeland. She didn't recognize the incoming number. Lifting the phone to her ear, she said crisply, "Arden Mayfair."

Silence.

"Hello? Anyone there?"

A female voice said anxiously, "I hear you've been looking for me."

Arden's pulse jumped. "Is this Ginger?"

"Don't say that name."

"Sorry." Arden backed up against the building so that she didn't block pedestrian traffic. "You got my message?"

"What do you want?" The woman's Low Country drawl was deep and hardened by suspicion and hostility.

"As I tried to explain in my note, we need to see you in person so that—"

"You think I don't recognize a con when I hear one? There's no bank, there's no money and I seriously doubt you're an attorney. You have five seconds to tell me what you really want."

"I just want to talk."

"What about?"

"Did you know Dave Brody is out of prison?"

A brief pause. "So? What's that to do with you?"

"I work for an attorney named Reid Sutton. I'm sure you recognize his name. Brody is threatening to make life unpleasant for a lot of people if we don't get him what he wants."

"Which is?"

"He thinks someone paid you to leave town before you could testify on his behalf, and he wants to know who and why. Personally, I think you were threatened. I think you left town because you were afraid."

A longer pause. "You don't know anything about me. If you're smart, you'll keep it that way."

Arden's pulse quickened. She'd hit a nerve. "We can

help you. Just name a time and place and we'll come meet you."

"That's not going to happen."

"Why not?"

"Did you really think he'd stop at one?"

The hair prickled at the back of Arden's neck. Phone still to her ear, she turned to glance over her shoulder, scouring the street behind her. "What do you mean?"

"The body that was found in the alley," Ginger said. "She wasn't his first victim. If you're not careful, she won't be his last."

"If you know who he is—"

"Just leave me alone, okay? I can take care of myself. And whatever you do, don't contact my uncle again. If anything happens to him, his blood will be on your hands."

Arden could hear traffic noises over the phone before the connection dropped. She positioned her body so that she could watch the sidewalk in both directions. No one looked suspicious. No one stared at her for an unseemly amount of time. That made no difference. Her every instinct warned of danger.

Somewhere close by, a coiled snake lay in wait.

Chapter Fifteen

Reid found himself surprisingly nervous when he arrived at Berdeaux Place that night. He told himself he was being ridiculous. Arden had gone out of her way to clarify that she didn't consider this a date. He was escorting her to the Mayor's Ball as a friend or her boss. *Whatever makes you feel more comfortable.*

He tugged at his bow tie as she buzzed him in through the gate. He parked, locked his car and then headed across the side lawn to the garden doors. She whisked them open and stepped out onto the patio, backlit by the lamplight spilling out from the parlor.

Reid froze, his breath escaping in a long, slow whistle as he took her in.

She spun so that the airy fabric of her gown caught the breeze. The scent of jasmine deepened in the dark, and the moon rising over the treetops cast the garden in a misty glow. The night suddenly seemed surreal to Reid, as though he were remembering a dream.

He shook his head slightly as if to clear his senses. "That dress…"

She lifted the frothy fabric. "Do you like it?"

"You look… Well, I suspect you already know how you look." Her hair fell in gleaming waves about her bare shoulders, and when she moved, moonlight sparked off the diamond studs in her earlobes and the crystal belt she wore around her waist.

"It was my mother's," she said. "I found it in my grandmother's closet. I didn't have time to shop for a new one, and since I got rid of most of my wardrobe before leaving Atlanta, it was either this or nothing." She turned slowly this time so that he could appreciate the full effect of the flowing fabric. "The fit isn't perfect, but I don't think anyone will notice."

The dress fit her like a damn glove. Reid shook his head again, this time to try to get her out of his head. Not that it had ever worked for him before. "Is this the surprise you have planned for your grandfather? Turning up at the ball looking the spitting image of your murdered mother? You said you wanted to provoke a reaction. This should do it."

"Yes, but it's not just for his benefit. I want to see if anyone else is provoked."

Reid frowned. "You mean the killer? Is that what this is all about? You're trying to draw him out? I'm surprised you don't have a magnolia blossom in your hair."

"I have one inside."

"I hope you're kidding."

She picked a spray of jasmine and tucked it behind her ear. "Better?"

"Not really."

She removed the spray and lifted the tiny blossoms to her nose. "Okay, maybe I am trying to stir the pot. Listen, there's something you don't know. I talked to Ginger Vreeland today. She called on the burner phone."

Reid stared down at her in the moonlight. "Why didn't you tell me earlier?"

"Because I knew I'd be seeing you tonight. And because I didn't want you to try and talk me out of going to the ball. Reid, she knows who killed Haley Cooper."

"She said that? Who?"

"She wouldn't give me a name. She wouldn't agree to meet me, either. She's still afraid. She said Haley wasn't his first victim and if he's not caught, she won't be his last."

"So you decided to bait him?" Reid moved in closer. He wanted to take her by the arms and shake some sense into her. Not literally, of course, but what in the hell was she thinking?

"Someone has to do something. He's eluded the police for weeks, maybe even for years. If this dress or my appearance catches him by surprise, maybe he'll give himself away."

"Or maybe he'll come after you." Reid turned to scan the dark garden. The ornate dome stood silhouetted against the night sky, reminding him all too vividly of Arden's certainty that the killer had watched her from inside the summerhouse, still with her mother's blood on his hands. He turned back to Arden. "You know this is a terrible idea."

"What else are we going to do? Sit around and wait for him to kill again? If this is the same person who murdered my mother, you think he won't come after me anyway? Why do you think he left a white magnolia blossom on the summerhouse steps? He was warning me even then that he'd someday come back for me."

"You don't know that."

"Do you have a better explanation?" When he didn't reply, she shrugged. "Maybe I am off-base. Maybe Orson Lee Finch really did kill my mother. In which case, we have nothing to worry about. Let's just go tonight. Maybe we can even have a little fun. Nothing is going to happen with so many people around."

"You sound so sure of yourself," Reid said. "But it's afterwards that I'm worried about."

"I've taken precautions. Changed the locks, updated the

security system. I'm safe here. Try to relax, okay? Maybe we should have a drink before we go. Just a little something to calm the nerves."

"Calm my nerves, you mean. You're as cool as a cucumber."

She gave an excited little laugh. "Not really. I feel buzzed even without anything to drink."

"You're enjoying this," he accused.

"So are you. You just don't want to admit it."

She turned and moved back inside. Reid followed, closing and locking the French doors as he stepped into the parlor. Evidently, Arden had found the key to the liquor cabinet. A crystal decanter, an ice bucket and two glasses had been arranged on a drink cart. Arden went over and picked up the tongs.

Reid watched her move in that dress. The bodice was strapless, the skirt so gossamer that when the light struck her from a certain angle, he could glimpse the silhouette of her long legs beneath.

"Sure I can't tempt you?" she asked.

He swallowed. "Maybe just a small one."

She put ice and whiskey into the glasses and held one out to him. "To partners in crime," she said.

He clinked his glass to hers. "To surviving the night." He downed the contents in one swallow. "It's getting late. Should we go?"

"In a minute." She set her glass aside untouched. "Do you mind helping me with my dress first?"

His gaze dropped appreciatively. "What's wrong with it?"

She turned her back to him. "I managed the zipper, but I couldn't reach the hook. Do you mind?"

He felt clumsy all of a sudden, but it wasn't the alcohol

that made him fumble with the hook. It was the situation, the woman. All those memories.

"Do you see it?"

"Yeah." He dealt with the fastener, but his hand lingered. Her skin felt like warm satin. Reid had never touched anything so sexy.

His hands drifted to her shoulders as he bent to drop a kiss at her nape. He felt a shudder go through her, but she didn't turn, she didn't move away.

She said in a tremulous voice, "Reid?"

"Arden."

HER HEART WAS suddenly beating so hard she couldn't breathe. She took a moment to try to collect her poise before she turned to stare up at him. A mistake. How well she remembered that smoldering intensity. The tilt of his head. The knowing half smile.

She drew a shaky breath as she held his gaze. "Is this really a good idea?"

He caught her hand and pulled her to him. "Nothing about this night is a good idea. But you can't open the door looking like that and expect me not to react."

Her hands fluttered to his lapels. "We'll be late."

"When has that ever stopped us?"

Never. Not any event, not any curfew. Nothing had ever stopped them when they wanted to be together.

"We're not kids anymore," she said. "Our actions have consequences. If we do this, our working relationship will never be the same."

He slid his hands down her arms, drawing a shiver. "You said it yourself. Nothing has ever been the same since the first time we kissed in the summerhouse."

She closed her eyes briefly. "Fourteen years is a long time. What if the magic is gone?"

His arms were around her waist now, holding her close. "What if it isn't?"

She reached up to touch his cheek. He caught her hand and turned his lips into her palm. Such a soft kiss. Such an innocent touch. Arden whispered his name.

His kissed the inside of her wrist, a more sensuous seduction she could hardly imagine. She turned silently in his arms, allowing him to undo the hook he'd fastened mere seconds ago. Then he slid down the zipper and Arden took care of the rest, stepping out of the red chiffon dress and then her high heels.

She untied his bow tie, unbuttoned his collar and slid his jacket off his shoulders. He shrugged out of the sleeves and inhaled sharply when her fingers brushed across his zipper as she tugged loose his shirt. She took his hand, leading him out of the parlor, across the foyer and up the stairs. He paused on the landing, pressing her against the banister as they kissed.

"I didn't come here expecting this," he said.

She threaded her fingers through his hair. "Are you trying to tell me you're unprepared?"

"I'm always prepared. Isn't that the Scout Motto?"

"You were never a Scout, Reid Sutton. Not even close."

He shed his shirt as they kissed their way down the hallway to her room. Moonlight filtered in from the long windows, throwing long shadows across the ceiling.

"Nothing's changed," Reid said as he glanced around the room. "I wonder if you can still shimmy down the trellis."

"I wonder if you can still climb up." She lay down on the bed and propped herself on her elbows, spreading her legs slightly as she watched him undress.

He didn't seem to mind her stare. He'd never been the least bit shy about intimacy. Nor had she, for that matter.

But fourteen years was a long time. Thirty-two was not the same as eighteen.

He placed a knee on the bed and she lay back as he moved over her. Arden found herself thinking about those fourteen years, the loneliness and disappointments. The guilt and then the pride that had kept her away. She thought about their first kiss in the summerhouse, the first time they'd made love at the beach, the first time he'd told her he loved her. She could drown in those memories, good and bad, but she didn't want to lose herself to the past. Not with Reid's tongue in her mouth and his hand between her thighs. Not when that delicious pressure just kept building and building.

Slipping her hand between them, she guided him into her, then wrapped her arms and legs around him. He was leaner than she remembered. Older and more experienced. And yet he still knew her. Knew where to touch her, when to kiss her, how tightly to hold her when her body began to shudder.

And when it was over, he remembered to clasp her hand as they lay on their backs and stared up at the ceiling.

Chapter Sixteen

Reid couldn't take his eyes off Arden. He could barely keep his hands off her.

He tugged at his bow tie as he leaned a shoulder against the wall and watched her move about the room. He told himself he should be on the lookout for anyone suspicious or anything out of the ordinary. Arden's dress was bound to provoke strong reactions, but his gaze lingered as his mind drifted back to earlier in the evening.

If he'd had his way, he'd still be comfortably stretched out in her bed, but Arden had insisted they make an appearance at Mayfair House. So they'd climbed out of bed, hit the shower, and one thing had led to another. He closed his eyes briefly, imagining her hands flattened against the tile wall as she pressed her glistening body against his.

Afterward, she'd dried her damp hair, foregoing the magnolia blossom at his insistence, and touched up her makeup. Then they'd redressed like an old married couple. He'd zipped her gown and she'd straightened his bow tie. Now here they were, clothing looking the worse for wear, but totally worth it.

He brushed an invisible speck of dust from his sleeve as he forced himself to survey his surroundings.

He tried to remember the last time he'd been in Mayfair House. He and Arden had been kids, and she'd talked him into going with her because she hadn't wanted to spend the evening alone with her grandfather. Clement hadn't been pleased to see him. All through dinner, he'd stared at Reid in moody silence and as soon as the dishes had been cleared, he'd had his driver take them home.

"This place is something, isn't it? Flowers, champagne, live band. Must have set the old man back a pretty penny. And would you look at those chandeliers."

Reid turned to acknowledge his father, and lifted his gaze to the ornate ceiling. "Imported from Italy," he said.

"What?"

"The chandeliers."

"Is that so? I thought for a moment you were talking about Arden's dress. She's something, too. A real head-turner. Though I have to say, I'm a little surprised to see the two of you here together."

"Why's that?"

Boone gestured with his champagne flute. "You made a point of telling me she's not your girlfriend, remember?"

"She's not. We work together."

Boone smirked. "Do you look at all your employees that way?"

"I only have the one. And I don't think you're in any position to cast stones."

"Oh, I'm not casting stones. I'm just here to enjoy the show."

"Is Mother with you?" Reid asked pointedly.

Boone sipped his champagne. "She isn't feeling well tonight. I'm flying solo."

"Just the way you like it."

"Let's make a deal. You stay out of my private life and I'll stay out of yours."

Reid shrugged. "Whatever you say."

Boone set his glass on a passing waiter's tray. "Since

you and Arden have only a working relationship, you won't mind if I ask her to dance."

"Knock yourself out," Reid said. "But don't be surprised if she wants to lead."

"I think I can handle Arden Mayfair."

"Yeah. That's what I used to think, too."

ARDEN HAD FORGOTTEN how charming Boone Sutton could be. Handsome and debonair, and always just a little too smooth in her book. She was surprised when he had asked her to dance. She used the opportunity to glance around the room as they moved over the floor. Curious eyes met hers. She nodded to acquaintances and smiled at her uncle, who stood watching from one of the arched doorways.

"Strange guy," Boone muttered.

"My uncle? I would say he comes by it honestly, wouldn't you? My grandfather is nothing if not eccentric." Her gaze strayed again to the edge of the dance floor where she'd last seen Reid. He'd disappeared, but she couldn't imagine he'd gone far. She turned her attention back to Boone. "Reid told me about your theory. You think my mother wasn't Clement Mayfair's biological child. That would explain a lot, actually."

"Well, it is just a theory." He spun her unexpectedly. Arden had to concentrate to keep up.

"You knew my grandmother well," she said. "She never confided in you?"

"Evelyn kept things close to the vest. She wasn't the type to air dirty laundry even among friends. I don't pretend to know what went on in this house before she divorced Clement, but I can say with utter confidence that she would have done anything to protect her family. You and your mother were everything to her."

"What about her son?"

"As I said, Calvin is a strange fellow. Always has been."
A frown flickered as if he'd thought of something unpleasant. "I was surprised to hear that you'd moved back to Charleston. I thought you were done with this city for good. Maybe that would have been for the best."

"For Reid's sake?"

He hesitated. "For your own. These are troubling times. Reid has gotten himself into something of a bind, it seems. It would be a shame if you became entangled in that mess, too."

"You surely don't think he had anything to do with Haley Cooper's murder."

A shadow flitted across his expression. "Of course, I don't. But he put himself into a position of being blackmailed by the likes of Dave Brody. A man in Reid's position has to be more careful. Someone like Brody is always looking to take advantage."

"Maybe Brody isn't the real problem," Arden said. "He claims someone powerful is trying to frame Reid. Maybe that same person paid Haley to spike Reid's drink."

Boone froze for half a beat. "What are you talking about?"

"Reid didn't tell you? She slipped something into his drink that night at the bar. Why would she do that to a perfect stranger unless someone paid her? From what I understand, she liked the finer things in life."

"She wasn't—"

"She wasn't what?"

"Nothing."

No sooner had the conversation fizzled than something the shop owner had revealed came back to Arden. Haley had been seeing someone older, someone wealthy. Someone who guarded his privacy. Because he was married?

She told herself she was being ridiculous. Any number

of men in the city fit that description, many of them here at the ball. Boone Sutton was a lot of things, but he was no murderer.

How do you know?

Her gaze met her uncle's again, moved on and then came back. He couldn't seem to take his eyes off her, and no wonder—he'd painted her mother in this very dress.

Suddenly the walls started to close in and Arden wished she'd heeded Reid's warning. Coming here tonight had been a very bad idea.

The music ended, but Boone's arm seemed to tighten around her waist. "Something wrong?"

"No, of course, not." Arden backed away. "Thank you for the dance, but I think I'll go find Reid now."

She wandered through the house, avoiding anyone who looked familiar while she searched for Reid. The terrace doors in the library were open and she stepped through, scanning the silhouettes that lingered in the garden. A cool breeze blew in from the harbor, stirring her hair and fanning her dress. She turned to go back inside, but someone blocked her path.

Her heart beat a startled tattoo as she stared up at her grandfather. He had always intimidated and unsettled her; however, she was a grown woman now. No reason to fear him.

"Grandfather," she said on a breath. "I didn't hear you come up."

He said nothing for the longest moment, just stood there in the dark staring down at her.

"I'm looking for Reid," she said. "Have you seen him?"

"I have not."

His voice was like a cold wind down her back, devoid of warmth or affection. Hard to believe that he had actually warned Reid away from her. Why would he even care?

"This is quite an event." She waved a hand toward the terrace doors. "You've outdone yourself."

"As have you."

She suspected he was talking about the dress, and she pretended not to understand. "I was surprised to hear that you were hosting the Mayor's Ball this year. Somehow it doesn't seem your kind of thing."

Moonlight reflected off his glasses as he tilted his head slightly. "And just what is my kind of thing?"

"You never used to like company, much less a crowd. But then, I've been away for a long time. People change, I suppose."

"You haven't. This is exactly the kind of stunt you would have pulled as a child. You're an adult now. I had high hopes that you would outgrow your unseemly tendencies. But you're too much like your mother. Evelyn always had to be the center of the universe. You apparently have her morals, too."

A chill shot down Arden's backbone. "Evelyn was my grandmother. I'm Arden."

"Go home, girl. Don't come back until you've learned how to dress and behave like a lady."

"Grandfather—"

A commotion from inside the house drew their attention. Arden trailed her grandfather inside as he headed toward the raised voices. The music had stopped and everyone seemed suspended in shock. Arden followed their gazes. Detective Graham and two uniformed cops had surrounded Reid.

Arden rushed toward them. "What's going on?"

One of the officers put up his hand. "Stand back, miss."

"Reid?"

"There's nothing to worry about," he said in a calm

voice. "Detective Graham has a few questions that apparently can only be answered at police headquarters."

"This couldn't have waited until the morning?" Clement demanded.

The two men exchanged glances.

The detective said in a conciliatory tone, "My apologies for the disturbance. We felt this a matter of some urgency."

"Oh, I'm sure you did." Boone materialized at Arden's side. "I'm sure the urgency had nothing at all to do with the press being here tonight or the fact that your picture will likely be on the front page of the newspaper tomorrow."

The detective's expression had grown cold with contempt. "I'm just doing my job."

"Is he under arrest?"

"We just have a few questions."

Boone turned to Reid. "Don't say a word. Not one word. You hear me?"

"I know what I'm doing," Reid said. "Let's just get this over with. No need to ruin everyone else's evening."

They all traipsed outside to a waiting squad car. After another few minutes of discussion, Reid willingly climbed into the back and the car pulled away. Boone waited for the valet service to fetch his car while Arden called a cab.

"I hope you called that cab to take you home," Boone said.

"Of course not. I'm going to police headquarters."

"That's not a good idea. You heard the detective. Reid isn't under arrest. Let's make sure we keep it that way."

"Someone is trying to set him up," Arden said. "We can't let that happen."

"Which is why I need you to do something for me." He pulled her away from the crowd that had assembled on the steps and lowered his voice. "Go to Reid's place right now and make sure everything is clean."

Arden frowned up at him. "What are you talking about?"

"Use your head. You think a dirty cop like Graham is above planting evidence?"

"But—" Arden started to protest being sidelined. If nothing else, she wanted to offer Reid her moral support. Then she thought of the note that had been left in his closet by the intruder. What if Graham had somehow managed to plant the murder weapon inside Reid's house?

She swallowed back her panic and nodded. "Okay. But you take care of this. You get him out of there, you hear me?"

ARDEN HAD THE DRIVER drop her off at the end of the block, and she hurried along the shadowy street to Reid's house. Glancing over her shoulder, she let herself in and locked the door behind her. She moved quickly from room to room, drawing the blinds at all the front windows before she turned on the lights.

She started the task in his office and worked her way through the house, combing the obvious places and then looking for more obscure hiding places. When a third search turned up nothing, she had the unsettling notion that maybe evidence had been planted elsewhere. Some-place less likely yet still incriminating, like the summer-house at Berdeaux Place.

She called another cab and paced the front porch until the car arrived. Five minutes later she was home. She let herself in, locked the door behind her and turned off the security system. Then she headed through the parlor to the French doors.

Her hand froze on the latch. Her mother's cereus had bloomed during the evening. Someone had cut off every last flower and chopped the petals to bits with her grand-mother's antique katana.

Shredded them in a rage, Arden thought.

The katana had been tossed aside in the grass. The sword had been in its usual place when Arden and Reid had left for the ball. Someone had been inside the house. How was that possible? The alarm had been set, the front door locked tight...

She whirled, her focus moving across the room to the foyer. Someone was coming down the stairs, slowly, deliberately, taking his time as he anticipated the encounter...

Arden reacted on instinct. She went out the French doors and grabbed the katana. The lush, heady fragrance of the destroyed blooms filled her nostrils. The moon was up, flooding the terrace and garden with hazy light. She dove for the shadows, concealing herself as best she could as she rushed toward the side entrance. The wrought-iron gate had been padlocked from the other side and the low-hanging limb that she had once used to propel herself over the wall had long since been cut away.

She was trapped in the garden. No way out except to go back through the house.

Whirling, she moved down the path toward the summerhouse. She couldn't hide there, of course. He would surely look for her inside. She broke off a sprig of jasmine and tossed it to the ground and then another. Deliberate breadcrumbs. Then she plunged deep into the shadowy jungle of her grandmother's garden and hunkered down out of sight.

He came along the path, calling out to her. "Come out, come out wherever you are!"

Arden pressed herself back into the bushes, clapping a hand over her mouth to silence her breath. She knew who he was now. Knew why the Twilight Killer had come back for her.

"Did you really think you could keep me out of

Berdeaux Place by changing the locks?" he called. "Did you really think I wouldn't have my own way in without tripping the alarm? I know every square inch of that house. Every nook and cranny. Every single one of your little hiding places."

Her uncle was at the summerhouse steps now. He climbed the stairs slowly, a kitchen knife glinting in his hand. He turned at the top and surveyed the garden before ducking inside. Arden shifted her weight, positioning herself to make a dash for the house, but he came back out too quickly, pausing again on the steps as his gaze seemed to zero in on her hiding place.

"I used to come here all the time after Mother left me. I'd sneak inside and stand at Camille's bedside while she slept. Mother caught me once. She told Father, and the next day he sent me away to boarding school. Military school came next and then university. They did what they could to keep us separated. Did you know that's why Mother took Camille away from Mayfair House? She was afraid for her. Afraid of me. Her own son."

Arden was trembling now, picturing him creeping through the house. Watching her mother sleep. Watching *her.*

"That night when I saw her in the garden wearing the red dress, I knew it had to be her. She would be my first. The waiting became unbearable so I came back a few days later and did what I had to do. You saw me that night, here in the summerhouse. I left a magnolia blossom just for you. Do you remember?"

Arden clutched the handle of her grandmother's sword. She'd put her bag down with her phone when she first came in. She couldn't call Reid or the police for help. She was on her own. She had to somehow get inside the house. Lock the doors. Find her phone…

But what good would that do when he had a secret way in?

"I have something else for you tonight," he said. "I know you can see me. I know you're close. I can hear your heartbeat. Can you hear mine?"

Yes, yes, there it was, a throbbing that filled her senses until she wanted to press her hands to her ears and scream. She knew on some level that it was her own heartbeat thudding in her ears, and yet she could have sworn the cacophony filled the garden just as it had on the night of her mother's death.

"Look what I have for you, Arden."

She peered through the bushes, wanting to glance away but mesmerized by the red magnolia petals he scattered across the summerhouse steps. The breeze lifted one and carried it toward her. The crimson kiss of death.

"That night was magical," he said. "So thrilling I can hardly believe it actually happened. The others that came afterward were just pale imitations. I thought I'd never again experience such ecstasy until you walked into Mayfair House tonight wearing that red dress." He came down the steps and stood in the moonlight, staring through the bushes straight at her. "Come out, Arden. Come see what else I have for you."

She stood, hiding the katana in the folds of her gown. "You killed my mother. You killed all those other women, leaving their children motherless, and then you let an innocent man rot in prison for your crimes."

"I'm a Mayfair," he said, as if that were the only explanation needed.

He moved toward her slowly, a cat closing in on his prey. Arden stood her ground, gripping the handle of the hidden weapon until he was almost upon her. He pounced, more quickly than she had anticipated. She swung the katana, slicing him across the lower rib cage, wounding but not felling him. He staggered back, eyes wild, expression contorted as he gripped his side and took several deep breaths.

Arden sprinted away from him, nearly tripping as the bushes caught the gossamer layers of her dress. She kicked off her shoes and ran barefoot toward the house, spurred on by fear and pure adrenaline. She had almost made it to the terrace when he tackled her from behind and she landed face-first on the stone pathway.

Dazed and breathless, she tried to fight him off. The blood from his wound soaked her dress and dripped onto the grass as he pulled her deeper into the garden, to the exact spot where he had taken her mother's life.

She'd lost the katana, Arden realized. She dug her fingernails into the ground, trying to stop his momentum, while on and on he dragged her. She kicked and writhed, but he seemed to have supernatural strength. Bloodlust drove him. Years and years of pent up rage and resentment.

Pinning her arms with his knees, he rose over her, backlit by the moon. He gazed down at her as he must have stared down at her mother. He lifted the knife overhead, preparing for a thrust that would take her life just as he had taken her mother's.

She heard voices. Someone called out her name. A shadow appeared in the garden and then another.

One of the shadows tackled her uncle, knocking him back into the bushes. The two men fought viciously. The knife struck home, slashing Reid's arm. He grunted in pain and grabbed Calvin's wrist, holding the weapon at bay. Arden looked around desperately for the katana. She grabbed it, stumbled forward. Before she could strike, a shot rang out. Her uncle froze for a split second and then he toppled backward to the ground, his eyes open as he stared blindly at the moon.

Arden rushed to Reid's side, checking his wound and holding him close. They both gazed up at Boone Sutton, who still clutched his weapon. He said to no one in particular, "Sometimes the mad dog has to be put down."

Then he turned and walked away, giving them a moment of privacy before the police descended once again on Berdeaux Place.

Chapter Seventeen

"Orson Lee Finch will soon be a free man," Reid said the next day as he reclined back in his chair. His feet were propped on his desk, his arm in a sling. Everything considered, he looked cool and collected.

Arden was seated in the chair opposite his desk. She was still strung out from the night's events and from the hours she'd spent at police headquarters. It would take a long time before she felt normal again, but at least something good had come from tragedy. "I read that his daughter and grown grandchildren will be there to greet him when he walks through the gate. I can hardly imagine what they all must be feeling right now. If only I'd recognized my uncle that night. If only I'd been able to stop him."

"None of this is your fault," Reid said.

"I know. I was just a child when Mother died. Whatever I saw that night… I couldn't make sense of it."

"Boone knew. Or at least he suspected. That's why he helped Ginger Vreeland leave town. Calvin had roughed her up, and she was afraid he'd come back and kill her. He says he told the police, but Clement Mayfair is a powerful man. You don't go after his son unless you have irrefutable proof."

"Grandmother knew, too," Arden said. "That's why she

took my mother away from that house. Why she left her son behind. She knew even then what he was."

"What a terrible thing to have to live with," Reid said.

"She was never the same after my mother's death. None of us were." Arden fell silent. "Why do you think he killed Haley Cooper? She wasn't a single mother. She didn't fit his usual profile. Why her?"

Reid shrugged. "We can only speculate. She'd had a brief relationship with Boone. Calvin probably used her and Dave Brody to set me up. It was never about a conviction. He wanted to cast doubt on my father's character so that if he came forward with his suspicions, it would seem as though he was casting aspersions to clear his own son."

"My uncle must have started planning this as soon as he heard I was coming back."

"That's why your grandfather wanted Berdeaux Place so badly. He thought if he took that house away from you, you'd have no reason to stay in Charleston."

"And that's why he warned you away from me," Arden said.

"For all the good it did."

She got up and rounded the desk, leaning against the side as she gazed down at Reid. "In all the commotion, we haven't had time to discuss us."

"What's there to discuss?" He took her arm and pulled her down to his lap. "I let you go once without a fight. I'm not about to do that again."

"You don't see me running, do you?"

"Partners in crime?"

"Partners in crime." She settled in, taking care not to jostle his wounded arm as she reached up and touched his cheek. "But you still have to say it."

He smiled. "Why do I have to say it? You already know how I feel."

"Because a girl needs to hear it."

"All right then." He held her close. "I love you, Arden Mayfair. I've loved you from the moment I first laid eyes on you, and I'll love you until my last day on this earth. How's that?"

"That'll do just fine," she said with a sigh.

* * * * *

THE DARK WOODS

DEBRA WEBB

This book is dedicated to the outstanding police officers and deputies in Winchester and Franklin County, Tennessee. Thank you for all you do.

Chapter One

Sasha Lenoir struggled to keep her smile in place as her lifelong friend Audrey Anderson showed the last of the guests to the door. The gathering after her grandmother's funeral was a tradition as old as time, and Sasha had managed to muddle through the event without embarrassing herself by bursting into tears. As the social requirements of the day drew to an end, however, her nerves had grown ragged and her wherewithal dwindled.

She needed to close herself away in a quiet room for a few hours to recharge, to collect her emotions and tuck them neatly away once more. She had spent many years sharpening her skills at controlling her reactions and feelings. Despite the pressure or the insurmountable odds, any crisis manager worth her salt would never allow the slightest crack in her carefully constructed veneer for the rest of the world to see.

But today had been different. Today was personal. The only remaining family member, besides her daughter, she had left in this world was now gone. Dead and buried. There was no one left to ask about her history.

No one to remind her of all she had overcome, become and could do in the future despite that history.

Life would never be the same.

Viola Simmons had been more than a mere grandmother. She had been mother, father, sibling, best friend, confidante, cheerleader and, most important, the keeper of the faith. Not once had she ever lost faith in Sasha or let her down in any way. The sweet, brave lady had believed in Sasha when she barely believed in herself. She had picked up the shattered pieces of their lives and soldiered on when she had every right to want to give up.

There was a gaping hole in Sasha's life and in her heart now.

"I should stay tonight," Audrey offered as she entered the drawing room once more. "You shouldn't be alone."

Sasha dredged up a weary smile for her old friend. "I appreciate everything you've done, Rey. I'm not sure I would have been able to pull this off to my grandmother's standards without you, but right now alone is exactly what I need to be."

Everyone close to Audrey had always called her Rey. Nicknames were a mainstay of Southern culture. When Sasha was a small child, her parents—even her grandmother—had called her Sassy. By age twelve, no one dared to do so—not without the fear of a black eye or a bloody nose. Only once in her career as a top crisis manager in New York City had Sasha's childhood nickname surfaced. She had quashed that errant leak in a heartbeat.

"Are you sure?" Rey's face lined with worry. "I really hate to go and leave you in this big old house all by yourself."

Sasha hugged her arm around her old friend's and guided her to the door. "You've done more than enough." They faced each other in the entry hall. "You handled the outreach to her friends. You went over my grandmother's wishes and arranged the entire service at DuPont's with hardly a nod from me. You organized the lovely gathering here afterward. You've gone above and beyond already. Go home, kick your shoes off and have a glass of wine—or two…or three. Snuggle with Colt."

They laughed together. But instead of sounding happy, it seemed sad. It was the end of an era and Sasha suspected Rey was thinking of her own mother, who wasn't getting any younger and whose health had been plagued by dementia. Time stopped for no one and it felt as if it was slipping away far too fast.

Rey sighed. "The service was beautiful. I know your g'ma would have been proud." Rey shook her head. "It's such a shame about Mr. DuPont. I can't believe a close colleague of his daughter's murdered him. I'm certain she must be completely devastated."

The news of the DuPont murder had rocked the small town of Winchester, Tennessee. DuPont Funeral Home had served the community for more than a hundred and fifty years. Edward had been the fourth generation DuPont undertaker. His daughter Dr. Rowan DuPont was now the fifth. Strange, Sasha realized, the DuPont family's history was littered with as much tragedy as her own. Rowan's identical twin sister drowned when she was twelve and a few months later their mother committed suicide. Worse, her mother hanged herself in the funeral home and Rowan was the one to find her.

"I was surprised to hear she'd decided to return to Winchester and take over the funeral home." Like Sasha, Rowan DuPont had carved out a good life and a successful career elsewhere. With her father's murder she had apparently made the decision to give up everything to come home and take over the family business. There was likely more to Rowan's decision than what the media had covered. Whatever her reasons, Sasha applauded her courage. It took guts to come home after a tragedy and to start over.

Particularly with the guilt of her father's murder hanging over her like a dark cloud.

"Life has a way of sending us down a different path sometimes," Rey said almost to herself.

Sasha inwardly cringed. Her friend was right; no one understood that stark fact better than Rey. A hitch in her career had brought her home to some immensely dark history of her own that just last month had surfaced for the whole world to see.

"I guess we never know what the future holds." Sasha chafed her bare arms with her hands, chasing away the sudden chill that came from deep within her bones. "Don't you find it odd that the three of us have suffered such similar tragic pasts?" Sasha shook her head. "Winchester is a small town and that's a lot of skeletons rattling around."

Rey made an agreeable sound. "I suppose every small town has its secrets."

"My grandmother probably knew them all." Sasha laughed, the sound strained despite her effort to lighten the moment. "No one was privy to more rumors and gossip than Viola Simmons."

Rey smiled. "There was something about her—an aura maybe—that made you want to spill your guts." Rey grabbed her handbag from beneath the table next to the door. "Don't forget I want to do a reflection piece on her. Everyone loved Vi. It'll be a great way to pay tribute to such an admired lady."

"She would be so honored, Rey." Sasha's grandmother would love the notoriety. "We'll get together next week and talk."

Rey paused, her hand on the door. "Does that mean you're hanging around for a few days longer than you first anticipated?"

Sasha didn't hesitate. She took the plunge. "I told my partners I would be gone for at least two weeks. If there's an emergency they know how to reach me."

"I am so glad to hear that." Rey nodded. "You should take your time and do what you need to do before you jump back into work." A frown tugged at her lips. "Will Brianne be okay with you staying so long?"

"She's having a blast with her nanny. The woman spoils her rotten."

"And," Rey pointed out, "you get some *me* time. I have a feeling that doesn't happen often."

"No kidding. I can definitely use it." Though, in truth, it was work that stole most of Sasha's time, not her precious daughter.

The two hugged for a moment and then Rey hurried to the street and the car she'd left there that morning. She'd arrived early to help Sasha get ready for the funeral. She was a good friend and Sasha genuinely appreciated her help. Three times each year Sasha had visited her grandmother—on her birthday in September, Mother's Day and at Christmas. She and Rey, on the other hand, had lunch at least every other month since Rey lived in DC—or at least she had until she suddenly rushed back to Winchester to take over the family newspaper late last year. Sasha would never in a million years have considered that Rey would move back to Winchester. Not after the way Sheriff Colt Tanner, her first love, had broken her heart when they were in high school. Not only was Rey back in her hometown, she and Colt were giving their relationship a second go. Sasha definitely had not seen that one coming, though she was immensely happy for her dear friend.

Maybe happy endings weren't a total myth after all. Certainly there was a theme going on with the whole homecoming thing.

Sasha had made her own happy ending far away from Winchester and without any help from the man she had fallen head over heels for when she was too young to understand what heartbreak was. She and Brianne were a strong, complete family. They would both miss G'ma but they still had each other.

Sasha closed the door and, out of habit, locked it. She'd lived in Manhattan for the past thirteen years. One didn't leave the door unlocked in the city. No matter that almost two decades had passed since she'd lived in Winchester, folks in her small hometown hadn't changed very much. Doors were still left unlocked more often than not and neighbors still checked on each other on a regular basis, which was the reason her grandmother had been found so quickly after her unexpected death. She hadn't come out for her newspaper. Viola Louise Simmons would never have left her newspaper lying on the porch until noon. A neighbor had noticed and knocked on the door to check on Vi, as her friends had called her.

A heart attack had taken her as she sat down for her morning tea. At eighty-three, no one could complain that Viola hadn't lived a long and productive life. Yet Sasha still grieved the loss, felt shocked at the idea that her grandmother was no longer here. She leaned against the closed door and surveyed the familiar surroundings. She had lived in this big old house from age nine until she went off to college and after that she'd spent holidays and summers here.

Growing up, this house had been more her home than any other place. Even when her parents were still alive, she was with her grandmother far more often than with them. Sasha pushed away from the door and moved along the hall, studying the family portraits and photos that had captured a place in time, curating the moment for all eternity. She stopped and stared at one portrait in particular, the last one of her with her parents before they died. Memories of the photographer urging Sasha's mother, Alexandra, to smile whispered through her mind. Her parents had both looked uncomfortable that day. But Sasha had been a kid, so she hadn't really noticed at the time. Two weeks later they were dead.

The remembered sound of gunshots blasted in her brain, making her jerk.

Sasha banished the haunting memories and walked to the kitchen. Maybe a cup of tea would settle her nerves.

She put the kettle on, lit the flame beneath it then reached instinctively to the pocket of her suit jacket and found nothing. She sighed. *Upstairs.* Her cell phone was upstairs. The device was as much a part of her as her two hands. It was never beyond reach…except for today. Out of respect for her grandmother she had left it in her room. Viola had hated cell phones. Rather than money, she had been convinced the invention of the cell phone was the root of all evil.

Sasha smiled as she took the rear staircase up to the second floor. The house was an early nineteenth-century American Foursquare. Sasha loved this place, but she wasn't sure what she would do with it. Her life was in New York and she couldn't possibly move back here. Never in a million years.

She found her cell on the bedside table in her old room. A text flashed on the screen. Sasha smiled as she responded, typing the words I miss you, too, followed by three kiss emoji. Her heart swelled. She was really glad Brianne wasn't angry with her anymore. Her daughter had been furious when Sasha told her she couldn't come to G'ma's funeral. She had school and Sasha wasn't sure how long she would need to remain in order to settle her grandmother's affairs. At least Brianne was speaking to her now. Five minutes after Sasha was out the door, her daughter was planning all the things she and her beloved nanny could do together. Twelve was a tough age. Sasha remembered it well.

Love you.

Sasha sent the text and tucked the phone into her pocket. Downstairs the kettle screamed for her attention. She could taste the bitter tang of the tea already. Her grandmother was a die-hard Earl Grey fan. Sasha compensated with an abundance of sugar and milk.

With a quick twist of the knob she doused the fluttering flame under the kettle. She grabbed a cup and the ceramic box where her grandmother stored her tea. She dropped a bag into the cup and grabbed a mitt to pour the hot water. While the tea steeped she went to the refrigerator for the milk and rounded up the sugar.

The doorbell rang, echoing its Westminster chime through the house. Hoping it wasn't another plant since the front parlor was full already, Sasha made her way to the entry hall. Rey had suggested the plants be donated to one or more of the nursing or assisted living homes in the area. First thing tomorrow a local floral shop was sending a van to collect the plants and divide them up among the three homes in the Winchester area. It was a good solution, one her g'ma would approve of. Sasha peeked beyond the drapes, didn't see anyone on the porch or in the drive. Frowning, she unlocked the door and opened it. Definitely no one on the porch or in the driveway.

When she would have turned away, she spotted the corner of a pink envelope sticking up from the mail-box hanging on the wall next to the door. Had some-one dropped off a sympathy card? Maybe a neighbor who hadn't been able to make it to the service or to the gathering.

Sasha tugged the envelope from the mailbox, then went back inside and closed the door. Her name was scrawled across the front. She turned the envelope over, noted the bold *H* stamped on the flap. Her heart stum-bled as she opened it. The single page inside was folded twice. Frowning, Sasha unfurled the page and read the brief note that went straight to the point and then the name signed across the bottom of the page.

There are things your grandmother should have told you...about your parents. We should talk. Arlene Hol-loway.

For twenty-seven years the world had believed Sa-sha's father had killed her mother and then himself.

Deep down she'd had questions, had doubts. But each time Sasha had broached the subject, her grandmother hugged her and said that sometimes bad things hap-pened to good people. Her grandmother was like the policemen who came to her parents' house that night. They didn't want to listen to what a traumatized nine-year-old had to say. Two people were dead and nothing on earth was going to bring them back.

But Sasha remembered vividly what no one had wanted to believe.

She had heard at least one stranger's voice that night…maybe two. Voices that didn't belong to her mother or to her father or to anyone else she recognized.

Someone else had been in the house the night her parents died.

Chapter Two

Arlene Holloway was born and raised in Winchester. Sasha stood at the woman's front door as the sun dipped behind the trees and mountains that surrounded her hometown. Mrs. Holloway was—had been—Vi's best friend. Didn't matter that Vi was black and Arlene was white and that their childhood era had not been amenable to multicultural relationships of any sort. The two had weathered that storm and become stronger because of it. Through marriage and childbearing and widowhood Vi and Arlene had grown even closer over the years. Both had warned Sasha's mother nearly forty years ago how difficult life could potentially be if she chose to marry a white man. Alexandra had ignored the warning and married Sasha's father. Sasha had the dark curly hair of her mother and the pale skin and green eyes of her father.

More important, she had the determination and relentlessness of her grandmother. Both had served her well in the high-stakes world of celebrities and politicians where ruthless tactics and colliding egos were par for the course. Handling the high-profile issues of the rich and famous as well as the influential and powerful required a certain skill set, including fearlessness. The fearlessness as well she had inherited from her grandmother.

But for her parents, as predicted, life had been difficult and far too short.

Sasha knocked on the door a second time, and when the knob turned, her heart took another of those troubling tumbles. Was it possible that after all these years she might be on the verge of learning something new about what happened that night? If her grandmother had possessed some knowledge as to the events that unfolded that fateful night, why would she not have told Sasha years ago? The answer was easy—Viola Simmons would have done anything, gone to any lengths to protect her only grandchild. She firmly believed the past should stay in the past. Viola had wanted desperately for Sasha to move forward with no dwelling in a history that could not be changed.

But what if some aspects of it could change?

Why would Vi ignore that possibility?

The door swung inward and Sasha prepared to launch into her planned spiel about how she and Mrs. Holloway hadn't had the opportunity to properly catch up during the funeral or later at the graveside service or even at the gathering. She decided she wouldn't bring up the mysterious letter until the older woman did.

Except it wasn't eighty-five-year-old Arlene Holloway staring at Sasha when the door opened fully. It was Branch... Mrs. Holloway's grandson.

US Marshal Branch Holloway.

The boy Sasha had loved from afar since she was thirteen years old. The man she'd finally—after a decade of fostering a secret crush—made love with in his truck on the heels of having had far too much champagne at her five-year high school reunion.

The *man* who was the father of her twelve-year-old blond-haired, blue-eyed daughter.

A fact the man in question did not know.

That trademark grin spread across his handsome face—the same face she saw in her daughter every day. "Sasha Lenoir...aren't you a sight for sore eyes."

And just like that her heart melted and she wanted to lean into him the way she had that one night almost thirteen years ago. It would be so easy to cry on his wide shoulders after losing the only real parent she'd had. To lose herself in the warmth and promise of his arms and forget that she, like her grandmother had been, was on her own now, raising a child.

Except Sasha had far too much to lose to even think of going down that path. Her decision not to tell Branch about her pregnancy and the daughter she'd had nine months later had been based on fear and self-doubt during an intensely stressful time. She'd just graduated with her master's and had dozens of job interviews in front of her. Two months later she'd barely settled into her new career when she realized she was pregnant. Her life had already been far too complicated; she couldn't drag Branch into it. He was kicking butt and taking names in Chicago. There simply was no common ground for them to find for raising a child together. She'd made the decision not to tell him and her grandmother and Rey had kept her secret.

Now the decision seemed like the mistake it no doubt was. Brianne was missing out on the wonderful man who was her father and the still unmarried Branch had no idea what an amazing daughter he had helped create.

Remorse heaped onto Sasha's shoulders. What had she done?

She'd also caused her grandmother to keep that se-

cret from her lifelong best friend. Her poor grandmother
had taken that weight with her to her grave.

More guilt accumulated to the point Sasha almost
sagged. But didn't.

All at once regret claimed Branch's expression. "I'm
as sorry as I can be about your grandmother. I would
have been at the funeral today but there was an emergency with a prisoner transfer."

Arlene had explained Branch's absence. Not that
Sasha had really expected him to come to the funeral. They hadn't exactly been close friends back in
school. He was two years older and had been too popular to have time for a mere human like Sasha and her
friends. But he'd always been kind. Besides being incredibly handsome and spectacularly charming, one
thing Branch Holloway had always been was kind. Fear
abruptly clutched Sasha's heart. How kind would he be
if he ever learned her secret? She had stolen a dozen
years of his daughter's life from him.

She pushed the negative thoughts away. No one was
better at keeping shocking secrets or neutralizing the
rumors around those secrets than Sasha. They didn't
call her the queen of spin doctors for nothing. As for
her personal dilemma, she had made her bed; she would
lie in it.

Steadying herself, Sasha produced a smile. "Thank
you. I apologize for the unannounced visit. I was hoping
for a few minutes with Mrs. Holloway." Sasha leaned
to the left and peered past him into the cavernous foyer
beyond. "Is she home?"

"She sure is. Come on in." The long fingers of one
hand wrapped around her arm and ushered her across
the threshold. "Gran and I have dinner together every
Sunday. We were just about to sit down at the table.

We'd be thrilled to have you join us. There's always plenty to eat."

Sasha dug in her heels, stopping their forward momentum. "I couldn't possibly impose." Good grief, she had forgotten how early people had dinner around here. It wasn't even six o'clock.

"Nonsense. It's no imposition."

Before she could react to the statement, he'd taken her by the arm again and was guiding her through the house. Mrs. Holloway was beaming when they entered the dining room.

"Sassy, how sweet of you to come to dinner."

Branch pulled out a chair at the table and ushered Sasha into it. She managed a "Thank you." Then she propped a smile into place for the elderly woman across the table while Branch laid a setting for her. "It wasn't my intent to intrude. I came by to speak with you about—"

"Say grace, Branch," his grandmother ordered. "This girl needs to eat. She's as thin as a rail."

"Yes, ma'am." Branch shot Sasha a wink before sitting then bowing his head.

After the shortest dinner blessing she'd ever heard, he announced "Amen" and picked up the bowl of potatoes and passed it her way. "If you need anything at all while you're in town, you let me know. I'm sure you have your hands full."

"The hard part's over," Arlene insisted before Sasha could respond to Branch's offer. "The rest is as easy or as difficult as you choose to make it."

Funny, the older woman was far more right than she likely knew. "I appreciate the offer, Branch," Sasha said, her voice steadier than she'd hoped for. "My grandmother was very organized. She left specific instructions for everything."

Sasha nibbled at the food on her plate in an effort to appease her host and hostess. She listened avidly to their chatter about who had done what and the excitement of last month's organized crime case. Branch was still fielding offers for top assignments across the country but Arlene was hoping he would stay in Winchester.

Coffee had been poured and dessert served before Sasha had the opportunity to speak openly to Mrs. Holloway. Branch had excused himself to take a work call. Sasha wasn't sure how much time she had, so she went straight to the point.

"Mrs. Holloway, did my grandmother ever mention any second thoughts as to what happened to my parents? Did she feel satisfied with the police reports?"

Arlene stared at her for a long moment...long enough for Sasha to fear she'd shocked the poor woman.

"You received the note I had delivered."

Sasha nodded. "I did. I was quite surprised. You've never mentioned anything before."

"Your grandmother wanted the past left in the past. I felt her decision was a mistake but I held my tongue until today. Now it's time for the truth to come out, so long as you understand there will be consequences."

Sasha studied the older woman's face for some indication of exactly what she meant. "Certainly, I understand. I want the truth and I've always felt as if the truth was swept under a rug all those years ago."

There, she'd said it. It was past time she stopped pretending the truth didn't matter. It wouldn't bring her parents back but perhaps it would right a terrible wrong.

Arlene continued to stare at her, her blue eyes faded to a pale gray beneath the thick lenses of her glasses.

"Your grandmother never wanted you to pick at that ugliness. Are you sure you want to go against her wishes? She's scarcely cold in her grave."

Flustered and frustrated, Sasha held her ground. "Mrs. Holloway, with all due respect, you are the one who contacted me."

"I only made the offer—this is your journey to take."

Grappling for patience, Sasha asked, "Do you or don't you know what really happened?"

Arlene reached for her iced tea glass, took a long swallow. "I'm not sure anyone knows for certain but with the proper guidance I'm certain you could uncover the whole story."

"I'm thinking of hiring a private detective," Sasha confessed.

"A private detective?"

Branch's deep voice shook her. Sasha's attention swung to him. She hadn't realized he'd walked into the room. When she found her voice, she said, "Yes."

He pulled out his chair and dropped back into it, automatically reaching for his coffee. "Why do you need a PI?"

"She wants to know what really happened to her parents," Arlene explained. "She doesn't believe the police reports any more than I do."

Sasha cringed, as much at Branch's look of surprise as at Mrs. Holloway's words. "It's not that I don't believe the reports—I'm just not certain the investigation was as thorough as it could have been."

Branch nodded slowly. "I'm confident the investigators attempted to be thorough. Sometimes it's a matter of a failure on the part of the investigator and sometimes it's just a lack of communication. You were really young when your parents died—I can see how you would have questions now."

Sasha reminded herself to breathe. "I think you've nailed my feelings on the matter." She considered pointing out that she hadn't just shown up at his door with these questions. His grandmother had sent her a note. But she decided against that route for now. She had a feeling his grandmother had set them up for precisely this result. Sasha cleared her throat and pushed on. "With my grandmother's passing it feels like I need to settle my own affairs as well as hers. I would like to put the past to rest, I suppose."

"You can help with that, can't you, Branch?" Arlene suggested. "You're on vacation. What else have you got to do?"

He smiled patiently at his grandmother but the gesture didn't quite reach his eyes.

"No." Sasha shook her head. "I don't want to bother anyone. This is really something I need to do on my own. It's very personal."

His gaze rested on hers. "Gran's right. I'm on a long-overdue vacation and I don't have a lot planned. I can help you look into the case—if you feel comfortable with me digging around in your personal business."

If he'd said her hair was on fire she wouldn't have been more startled. Anticipation seared through her. Branch was a lawman. He would know how to conduct an investigation—that much was true. He would be able to spot the holes in the decades-old investigation. She could trust him. He would be thorough. His assistance would be invaluable.

What on earth was she saying?

She couldn't spend that kind of time with the man. There was too big a risk that he would discover her secret. Or that those old feelings that still stirred when she thought of him would be ignited all over again.

Either possibility was a chance she could not take.

"Perfect," Arlene announced. "I've always wanted to know what really happened. Out of respect for Vi, I kept my questions to myself. She never wanted to talk about it. I'm certain she was afraid of the consequences."

This was one aspect of the past Sasha had not considered. She knew in her heart that someone else was involved in the deaths of her parents. The fact that no one else seemed to feel that way and that her grandmother had been so opposed had prevented Sasha from pushing the theory over the years. But Arlene was right. If someone else was involved there would be consequences. That person or persons would want to keep the truth hidden as desperately as Sasha wanted to reveal it. Just another reason to be grateful she hadn't brought her daughter back to Winchester.

Finding the truth might be more dangerous than she had anticipated.

"When would you like to begin?"

Branch's deep voice drew her attention from the disturbing thoughts. *Breathe.* "I was hoping to start immediately." She blinked, realized it was Sunday evening only hours after her grandmother's funeral. "Tomorrow, I suppose."

He nodded. "I have a lunch meeting in Nashville tomorrow, but I can pick up the file and meet with you first."

"I would genuinely appreciate it." Anticipation lit inside her. This was really happening. "I can work with your schedule."

"I'll call Billy and let him know I'm picking up the file and we'll go from there."

Billy Brannigan was the Winchester chief of police. Sasha nodded. "Sounds good."

She thanked Mrs. Holloway for dinner and made her excuses for heading home without finishing her dessert. She wanted to spend some time going through papers and mementos at her grandmother's. Primarily, she wanted to put some distance between her and her teenage idol. Except just when she thought she was in the clear, Branch insisted on walking her out.

When they reached her car he opened the door for her and smiled; his expression looked a little sad. "I'm sure sorry about the circumstances," he offered, "but it's good to see you, Sasha. It's been a long time."

She wondered if he ever noticed that she carefully avoided him whenever she came home for a visit. Probably not. He was a busy man. She likely rarely crossed his mind, if at all. All these years, she had brought her daughter three times each year to see her g'ma and she had somehow avoided ever bumping into Branch. It was a miracle really in a town this small. And yet somehow she'd managed.

Doubt regarding the intelligence of this plan to investigate the past nudged her again. She at times second-guessed her decision about keeping Brianne a secret. But it was too late to undo that now.

All the more reason this was a really bad idea.

"It has been a while." She moved around the door, using it as a shield between them. "I'm usually only here for a couple of days when I visit. Between G'ma and Rey, I hardly see anyone else."

He nodded. "I hear you have a daughter."

Uncertainty whooshed through her like the flames from a roaring fire catching on dry kindling. She managed a laugh. "We really are behind. The daughter came into the picture ages ago."

He chuckled. "I didn't know you'd gotten married."

Her nerves jangled. "No wedding. The relationship was over before it began."

Before he could ask anything else, she threw out a few questions of her own. "What about you? Wife? Kids?"

The answer to both was no, of course. The idea that she knew this was intensely sad.

"No and no."

"Well, that's a shame, Branch. You don't know what you're missing. My daughter is amazing and brilliant. Being a parent is the best thing that ever happened to me."

Had she really just said that? Her heart swelled into her throat. Obviously she needed to go home. Today had been overwhelming and she was clearly not thinking straight.

"It's hard to be a parent without finding the right partner first." He winked at her. "I'm beginning to think I let the only one for me get away a long time ago."

The warmth that gushed through her was at once exhilarating and terrifying. "I'll see you tomorrow." Sasha dropped behind the wheel and closed the door before Branch could say anything else.

He watched as she backed from the drive and drove away.

Branch Holloway had always been incredibly charming. He hadn't meant what he said the way it sounded— the way her mind and body took it. Sasha was certain on that one. Being kind was one of his most well-known traits. It was as natural as breathing for him.

He hadn't actually meant that she had stolen his heart

and ruined him for anyone else. They'd had a one-night stand after years of her pining after him.

End of story.

At least, for Branch, it had ended there.

For Sasha, that night had only been the beginning.

Chapter Three

Monday, March 25

Chief of Police Billy Brannigan was waiting in his office for Branch's arrival. Billy had personally dropped
by the archives and picked up the Lenoir file. He stood
and extended his hand across his desk when Branch
walked in.

"Morning, Branch. I thought you were on vacation."

Branch clasped his hand and gave it a shake. "I am.
Just helping a friend."

Billy settled into his chair and tapped the file box on
his desk. "This is everything we have. You looking for
something in particular with this old case?"

Though Billy had been a senior when Branch made
the team, they'd spent one year on the high school football team together. They'd been friends and colleagues
most of the time since. Billy was a good man. He'd spent
his life giving back to the community. Branch respected
him, trusted him. He saw no reason to beat around the
bush on the subject.

"You're aware Mrs. Simmons just passed away."
Branch had spotted him at the funeral.

Billy nodded. "Viola was one of the people who insisted I step into the position of chief of police. She and

about a half a dozen descendants from the town founders showed up at my door and practically demanded that I take the mayor up on his offer. Until the end of her life she still attended every single city council meeting."

"She'll be missed," Branch agreed. "You remember her granddaughter Sasha."

It wasn't really a question. Even those too young or old to remember Sasha Lenoir from when her parents died, most everyone had heard about how she worked with some of the biggest celebrities in the country. Sasha had set the gold standard for turning around a media crisis.

"I spoke to her for a moment at visitation on Saturday afternoon."

"She wants to go over the case, mostly to put that part of her past to bed once and for all. There are a lot of questions in her mind about those days. I'm hoping I can help her clear those up. She mentioned hiring a PI, but since I have some time on my hands I thought I'd save her the trouble, see if we can't find the answers."

Billy nodded. "Understandable. She was just a kid when it happened. I'm sure she has questions she wasn't mature enough to ask at the time."

"From what I gather, her grandmother didn't want her looking back, so they never talked about what happened. Now that she's gone, Sasha feels it's time to open that door."

"I'm entrusting the case file to you," the chief reminded him. "All I ask is that you keep me advised of anything you find contrary to the investigation's final conclusions and return these files intact to me when you're finished."

As chief, of course he wanted to be kept advised and aware of any red flags. Any contrary conclusions reflected on his department. "Understood." Branch got to his feet and reached for the box.

"Look forward to your insights."

Branch exited city hall and loaded the box into the back seat of his truck. It was still fairly early, only eight thirty. He imagined Sasha was still operating on Eastern time. Since he didn't have her number he couldn't shoot her a text before showing up. He'd just have to take his chances.

When he reached the Simmons house, Sasha was sitting on the front porch. Like a number of other homes in Winchester's historic downtown, the Simmons home wasn't far from anything. On the other hand, the house where Sasha had grown up—where her parents died—was outside Winchester proper, deep in the woods on the family farm. His grandmother had often commented that she didn't know why they hadn't sold that place rather than allow it to sit empty and falling into disrepair. Maybe it had been too painful to make a decision.

He grabbed the case file box and headed for the porch.

"Good morning. Would you like coffee?" She gestured to a porcelain pot waiting on a tray. "I have blueberry scones. I made them this morning."

"You've been busy." He placed the box onto a chair and settled into the one next to it.

"I'm not the only one." She poured his coffee and passed the delicate cup to him. She placed a scone on a dessert plate and handed it along next. The china was covered in pink roses and looked far too fragile for a guy like him to handle.

"Thank you, ma'am." He felt kind of foolish drinking from the fancy little cup but the scone was far tastier than he'd expected. "This is not bad, Sassy."

She lifted her eyebrows at him and he winced. "My apologies. I guess I had an awkward flashback."

Sasha laughed. "Forgiven. But just this once."

"Whew. I was worried," he teased. "I remember you socking Randy Gaines in the nose. Bled like a stuck hog."

Her hand went to her mouth to cover a smile. "I always felt bad about punching him—not at that precise moment. After I'd had time to cool off. Eventually I apologized to him. I think it was like ten years later at our first class reunion."

She looked away and silence expanded between them for the next minute or so. It didn't take a crystal ball to comprehend that she was thinking the same thing he was. They'd had sex in his truck the night of her five-year reunion. Heat boiled up around his collar. He hadn't exactly shown a lot of finesse. Since that night he had wished a hundred times for a do-over. His gut clenched at the thought. Memories of how she'd felt in his arms, the soft sounds she'd made, the way her skin had smelled, echoed through him and his body tightened with lust.

"So, have you had a look yet?" She nodded toward the box, careful to avoid eye contact.

He polished off the last bite of his scone. "No, ma'am. I waited so we could do it together."

Their gazes locked and that same lust he'd experienced a moment ago flared again. She looked away. He reached for the box. He should get his act together. She'd just lost her grandmother and she was vulnerable. The last thing he wanted was her picking up on his crazy needs.

"Let's see what we've got."

While he removed the stacks from the box, she gathered their dishes and set them on the tray. Then she disappeared into the house. By the time she returned with glasses of ice water, he'd arranged the files in chronological and workable stacks.

"So what we have here—" he opened the first folder "—are the investigator's reports, the coroner's report, crime scene photos and the medical examiner's report." He studied Sasha for a moment. He wondered if she realized how difficult this was going to be. She had the prettiest green eyes and he loved all those soft curls that fell over her face and shoulders. She was a beautiful woman. He blinked, reminded himself to stay focused. "Are you sure you want to see all the grisly details?"

She stared at him, her eyes hot with determination. "I was there, Branch. I saw everything that night. Heard my mother's screams and my father's pleas."

He nodded. "All right, then." He opened the folder and spread the photos across the table. "Your mother was lying on the living room floor. She'd been shot twice in the chest." He read the description of her father's injuries. "Your father took—"

"One shot to the head. He was dead before he fell onto the sofa. Blood was everywhere." Her voice was hollow, distant. "I had to stand on the fireplace hearth to avoid the blood."

His chest ached at the image of her as a little girl, the pigtails he recalled so vividly and those big green eyes, standing alone and surrounded by a sea of red pouring from her mother's lifeless body. "There was no indication of forced entry. The responding officers had to break down the door to get inside."

Sasha stared at the photos. "I tried to wake them up, but I couldn't. Then I called 911. But I was afraid to unlock the door when they pounded and called out to me. I'm sure I was in shock."

Her voice had gone small, like the child she had been when the tragedy happened. The urge to take her hand and remind her that she was safe now tugged at his gut.

"How about we go over the reports and you tell me if you recall anything differently than the way it was documented."

She nodded and took the pages he offered. While she read over the reports, he studied the ME's report to see if either victim showed any indication whatsoever of a struggle. The ME noted wisps of Alexandra's hair having been torn out. So he—presumably her husband—held her by the hair rather than by the wrist or arm. No scratches or bruises on either victim. No alcohol or drugs found in her mother; her father had been drinking fairly heavily. The evidence reports showed a number of unidentified fingerprints found in the house. Not unusual. People had visitors. Visitors left prints. That alone didn't mean anyone besides the family or close friends had been in the house that night or any other.

Sasha laid the investigator's final report aside and took a breath.

"Thoughts?" He waited, gave her time to collect herself. This was hard. This was exactly, he imagined, why or at least part of the reason her grandmother had never wanted to take this journey.

"That night and then again about a week after...*that night*, I told my grandmother I'd heard another voice, maybe two in the house besides my parents'. She took me to see Chief Holcomb but there's nothing in the report about my statement."

"It's possible—" Branch hoped to convey this without being too blunt "—the chief didn't feel your statement was reliable enough to enter into evidence, particularly if it was days later."

She made a face that spoke of her frustration and no small amount of anger. "I suspected that was the case. I remember Chief Holcomb suggesting that I'd dreamed about that night and my imagination had added the voices in an attempt to divert guilt from my father. He urged my grandmother to take me for counseling and she did, but those sessions didn't change what I remembered."

Branch could see how Holcomb might have come to that conclusion. For an officer of the law, logic had to be first and foremost when looking at an emotional situation. Anyone could imagine the horror and pain involved with an event like murder, but that empathy could not dictate how an investigator tackled a case.

"Denial is a powerful emotion. It's possible what Chief Holcomb suggested was exactly what happened."

She stared at him for a long moment before shaking her head. "That's not what happened. I know what I heard. I was simply too traumatized at first to explain my impressions. I've lived with this for a long time, Branch. I know what I heard. Those voices have played in my thoughts and in my dreams for twenty-seven years."

"All right, then. Let's talk about the voices." Was it possible someone else was involved? Absolutely, and if he found even a speck of evidence to support that theory, he was going the distance with it. He shuffled the crime scene photos together and placed them back into the folder. There was no need to leave those gruesome images lying in front of her. "Let's talk about the voice or voices. What exactly did you hear?"

"I heard a voice and it wasn't my father's."

"And it wasn't your mother?"

"No. It was a male voice. Deep, really deep—and mean. I remember shaking when I heard it even though I didn't understand the words. Then I heard my mother crying and my dad pleading with someone to let her go. He kept saying *Please don't do this. Just let her go.*"

Her voice trembled with the last. "At what point did you hear the second unidentified voice?"

"When my mother started to scream, I heard another male voice. This one wasn't as deep. It sounded like he said *There's another way we can do this.* It's possible, I guess, that it was the same man, but I believe it was someone different from the first voice I heard."

Branch braced his arms on the table and considered her recounting. "Where exactly were you in the house?"

This was the point in the conversation when she shrank down in her chair, her shoulders visibly slumped, her eyes reflecting the remembered horror. "I was hiding under the stairs. When Mom and Dad argued I always hid in the closet under the stairs."

This would explain why she hadn't actually witnessed what happened. "After the gunshots, how long did you stay under the stairs?"

She shook her head. "I don't know. Minutes. An hour. Until it had been quiet for a really long time. I was too afraid to move."

Branch hesitated but then asked, "So there were sounds after the gunshots?"

She blinked. "Yes." She paused as if she'd only just considered that idea. "There were sounds. Footsteps." Her brow furrowed in concentration. "A door opened and then closed."

Branch found himself leaning forward. Every instinct he possessed told him she was telling the truth or at least what she believed to be the truth. "Were the footsteps heavy or light, a shuffle or more like a march or big steps?"

"Heavy, like the person walking was big."

"What about the door? Did he use the front door or did he exit through the back of the house?" If he remembered correctly, the staircase in the old Lenoir house was very near the front door.

"Not the front door. Farther away." She cocked her head as if trying to remember. "It must have been the back door." She suddenly nodded, the movement adamant. "Definitely the back door because I heard the squeak of the screen door, too. There was no screen door on the front."

"What happened after that?" It was important that he didn't lead her in a particular direction. Just a nudge from time to time to keep her going.

"I opened the closet door a little to try to see." She moistened her lips.

He watched, wished he hadn't. More of that foolish lust had his fingers tightening into fists.

"I didn't hear any more sounds and I couldn't see anyone, so I crawled out of the closet. I called for my mom and dad." She shook her head. "They didn't answer. So I got up and started to look for them. That's when I saw the blood." Her eyes grew bright with emotion. "I tried to wake her up. Got blood on my dress and shoes." She shuddered. "I ran to the sofa—to my dad—but there was a sizable chunk of his skull missing. I don't know how I remembered to grab the phone from the end table, but I did. I ran to the hearth and that's where I stayed until help came."

"Let's talk about what was happening in the days prior to that night." He needed to pull her away from that ugly scene. He would be talking to Holcomb about her statement. Her recounting certainly seemed credible to him. But she was an adult now. She'd had years to refine her memory. "Your parents were arguing, you said. Was the argument any more serious than usual?"

"My father had lost his job. Mother accused him of drinking too much. I think that's why he was fired. She was tired and angry. And under a lot of pressure at her job."

"Your mother worked at the municipal office."

"She was a supervisor at building inspections. The job came with a lot of stress."

He knew most of this because he'd grown up right here in Winchester with Sasha. The more they talked, the more he remembered. Looking at those photos of Sasha as a kid, a terrified, emotionally traumatized kid, tore him apart.

"I'll speak to Luther Holcomb. See if they had any leads relating to any other scenarios. Anyone who had it in for your dad or your mom."

She sat up straighter then. "Does that mean you believe me? You don't think I imagined the voices and the…?" She waved her hand in the air. "The other stuff?"

"I believe—" he chose his words carefully "—there was more to what happened than what we're finding in the reports."

"So what do we do now?"

"Now we start at the beginning of when any trouble began and we work our way up to that night. We put together the pieces we find until we discover the parts no one else has found before. We turn over every rock, we shake every tree and then we do it again until we unearth anything we didn't know before."

"But it's been so long." She pressed her fingers to her lips. "Do you think we can find the truth? Will anyone else remember?"

If Sasha's father did not murder his wife and then shoot himself, that meant someone else did. Branch could guarantee that person remembered what happened, and if Sasha's recall of the voices was accurate, at least one other person would remember, too.

"I don't know how successful we'll be but we can try."

She nodded, stood abruptly. "Thank you for agreeing to help me. You said you have a meeting in Nashville. I don't want to keep you."

Branch pushed to his feet, picked up his hat. "I'll call you as soon as I get back."

"I'll keep digging through all those reports and see what I can find."

He gave her a nod and she walked him down the steps, then waved as he crossed the yard to his truck. Whatever truth there was to find, he would help her find it.

He just hoped the truth turned out to be what she wanted to find.

Chapter Four

Sasha stood on the sidewalk surrounded by overgrown
shrubs and knee-deep grass. It all seemed so small now
or maybe it was only that the woods were swallowing
up the yard and the house, ruthlessly invading all within
its path. White paint once gleamed from the wood siding; now it was chipped and curled away like the skin
slithering from a snake. Green moss had taken up residence on the gray roof. The house looked old and tired,
broken-down.

This was the first time Sasha had set foot on the
property since she was nine years old. Her fingers tightened on the key she had dug from a drawer in the mudroom. After Branch had left she'd gone up to her old
room and dug out a pair of boots to go with her jeans.
She'd added a sweater over her blouse and buttoned it
to the throat. She'd started to bring a flashlight but then
she'd remembered that the electricity and the water remained on for insurance purposes. Her grandmother
had arranged for any necessary expenses related to
the property to be drafted directly from her bank account. Beyond that step, she had washed her hands of
the property.

Weeds poked through the cracks of the sidewalk
and steps. Memories of drawing with chalk and play-

·ing hopscotch sifted through her mind. She climbed the steps and crossed the porch, boards gray with age creaking beneath her weight. Unlocking the door took some doing. The lock probably needed oiling. After a couple of minutes of frustrated twisting and turning, the tumblers gave way and the lock turned.

Darkness and dust motes greeted her beyond the threshold. A memory of swiping the switch next to the door prodded her to slide her hand across the wall. An overhead light came on.

For a long time Sasha stood staring at the narrow entry hall. It wasn't very large, perhaps seven by nine. Dust was thick on the wood floor and the wool rug that might be blue or gray. Some sort of pattern attempted to emerge beyond the layer of dust but failed miserably. Cobwebs draped across the ceiling, making a path over the chandelier with its two bulbs out of six struggling to light the space. A table sat against the wall, a set of keys amid the layer of dust there. Above it a mirror hung on the wall, the glass like the windows, heavy with years of buildup.

Deep in her chest, her heart hammered as if she'd run miles and miles.

The worst was the smell. Decades of mustiness with an underlying hint of copper. The stillness gave the sense of a lack of air. It was hard to breathe. Sasha drew in a deep breath that seemed to dissipate before it reached her lungs. To the right was a small parlor that her mother had used as a home office and straight ahead was the living room, a hall, dining room and the kitchen and a bathroom. The bedrooms and another bathroom were upstairs.

If she kept going, only a few more steps, she would enter the living room. Someone had cleaned up the bloody mess. She'd heard her grandmother discussing it a few weeks after that night. Friends or neighbors had rid the place of all indications of the bad thing that had happened.

Bad thing.

A very bad thing had happened in this house. Sasha forced one foot in front of the other. As she entered the parlor, voices vibrated in her mind. Her mother crying…her father pleading…the other voices growling with such menace. Sasha stood very still; she stared at the staircase and the door that was hidden until you walked beyond the newel post. She'd hidden there so many times.

Her heart pounding harder and harder, she continued on, along the hall and into the kitchen, turning on lights as she went. It looked exactly the same save for the cobwebs and dust. The teakettle still sat on the stove, the red-and-white-checked mitt hung from a drawer pull nearby.

You'll be late for school.

Her mother always worried that Sasha would be late for school. Or that she wouldn't finish her homework or her breakfast.

The newspaper from their final morning in the house lay on the kitchen table where her father had left it.

She stared at the headlines from that date. Man Is Killed by Lightning Strike while Working on Barn Roof. New Hospital Construction Is Moving Forward.

Sasha walked through the dining room on her way back to the living room. This time she forced herself to take a closer look. The spot on the floor in the center of the room where her mother had fallen. The rug that had once been there had been taken away. The sofa was gone, as well. Her father's blood and brain matter had been sprayed over the upholstery. All that remained were two chairs with a table between them. The princess-style phone still sat on the table. Sasha had dragged its long cord over to the hearth that night to escape the reach of her mother's blood flowing across the floor.

Please don't do this. Just let her go!

Sasha blinked away the voices and moved toward the stairs. The runner was coated in dust. The steps creaked as she climbed upward. Her fingers trailed along the wooden banister the same way she'd done as a child. Her father had grown up in this house. His grandfather had built it. Her father had been a good man. Never raised his voice. Was always a gentleman with her or her mother. No one could understand what happened to his temperament. Surely losing his job had not turned him into a killer.

No. Sasha shook off the notion. Someone else had been in the house. Her father had not done this and it was time she proved it and cleared his name. Both he and her mother deserved justice.

Someone had murdered them. Sasha was certain of it.

Two doors on the right were the guest room and a bathroom; on the left was her room and then that of her parents. She walked through her parents' room first. The bed was made. Sasha crouched down and checked underneath the bed skirt on her father's side. His old high school baseball bat was still there. He had called it his security system. Anyone broke into their house, the security system was going off.

Sasha stood and moved to the other side of the bed. Her mother's heels lay next to the closet door where she'd come home that evening and shed her work attire. She always stripped off the suit and pulled on jeans and a tee or a sweater. Her father wore jeans and work boots all the time. His work as a construction superintendent rarely required a shirt and tie. They had been so different and yet so suited for each other.

At least until the last few weeks of their lives. Things had been tense. Very tense.

Even as a child Sasha had sensed the extreme tension.

Her mother's pearls lay across a small mirror on the dresser. Sasha fingered the necklace. Alexandra Lenoir had worn those pearls every Monday and Friday. She had laughed and said she wanted to feel special on Mondays and she wanted to be ready to celebrate on Fridays. The pearls were a gift to her mother from her father, Sasha's grandfather, when her mother was sixteen, the year before he died. They were the only piece of jewelry her grandmother hadn't had the heart to remove from the house. She'd wanted the pearls to stay exactly where her daughter left them.

Sasha stared at her reflection in the mirror standing above the dresser. Other than the lightness of her skin and the green eyes, she looked exactly like her mother. Same features and profile. Her mother had been a very beautiful woman.

She turned away from her reflection and walked out of the room and into the one that had belonged to her as a child. Her white canopy bed with its pink lace and mound of stuffed animals was heavy with dust. Posters of cartoon characters and butterflies dotted the walls. Her favorite doll was at her grandmother's. It was the only item Sasha had wanted to take with her.

Her grandmother had bought her an entire new wardrobe so she wouldn't have to be reminded of her former life if she didn't want to be. Looking back, she and her grandmother had both been in denial. They had looked forward, never once looking back, and pretended the bad thing had not happened. It was easier that way. They became a family unit.

No looking back. No looking back.

Sasha sat down on her bed and allowed her surroundings to soak in. The lavender walls and the hair bows on the dresser. Her mother had loved brushing and braiding Sasha's hair. Giggles and the sound of the brush stroking through her hair whispered through her mind.

Life had been good here all the way up until it wasn't. She should have looked back, should have cherished the memories rather than trying to forget them.

But her grandmother had wanted to protect her. How do you protect a child? You insulate her from danger, from harm.

The denial, the memories that refused to stay buried had haunted her. It was time to unearth them and learn the truth.

Sasha descended the stairs and rounded the newel post. She grasped the knob of the closet door and gave it a twist, opening the door. The closet looked even smaller now. Maybe two feet by three. The only thing inside the closet was dust. There had been raincoats as she recalled. She could only assume they had been moved during the processing of the house for evidence. After all, she'd been hiding in the closet.

Sasha stepped into the closet and pulled the door closed, pitching the tiny space into darkness. She squatted down, hugged her knees and allowed her bottom to slide down to the floor. Then she closed her eyes.

You had a chance to save yourself...

Her eyes shot open as the voice echoed through her. It was the man's voice—the one with the deep, menacing voice.

Please don't do this. Just let her go.

Gunshots erupted in the darkness.

Sasha bolted upward and pushed out of the cramped space.

She couldn't breathe.

She ran out of the house and across the porch, down the steps. *Deep breaths. Slow it down.*

Perspiration covered her skin.

She focused on her breathing, told herself over and over to calm down.

A panic attack had not managed to get the drop on her in ages. Not since she was a teenager.

She braced her hands on her hips and breathed. Her heart rate began to slow. Still the dense woods seemed to close in on her.

If you go down to the woods today...you'd better not go alone.

The old nursery rhyme murmured through her. She'd loved exploring the woods around their home when she was a kid, but after that night she had been terrified of the woods. She'd gone camping once with a friend and her family and suffered her first panic attack that night in the woods.

Pulling herself together, Sasha walked back into the house and turned out the lights and locked the door. She climbed into her car and backed away, the trees closing in on the place sticking in her mind as she drove back into town.

She had a feeling if she didn't find the truth soon it would vanish forever.

TAREK MARTIN STILL lived in the same house he'd bought when he and his wife married, the same summer Sasha's mother and father had married. The two couples had their daughters within two years of each other and both men worked at Kimble & Douglas, K&D, the largest construction firm in a tri-county area. Sasha's father, Brandon, had often joked that imitation was the purest form of flattery and that Tarek had been flattering him for years.

Mr. Martin was one of the few people who had stood by her father during the investigation. He had insisted that Brandon Lenoir would never hurt his wife. His insistence hadn't changed the coroner's report.

Burt Johnston, the same man who was county coroner now, had concluded murder-suicide, and the medical examiner's autopsy, though inconclusive, had not disagreed.

Sasha had almost called Mr. Martin before driving to his home, but she'd decided that surprise would be a handy element under the circumstances. Never allow one's adversary an advantage. An announcement that the daughter of your former best friend was going to pay you a visit after more than two decades was turning over a fairly large advantage.

She opened the screen door, it squeaked and she knocked on the door. A television blasted the laughter and cheers of a game show. When she knocked a second time a dog barked. Sounded like a small breed. Sasha allowed the screen door to close between her and the wood door just in case the dog made a dive for the stranger doing all the knocking.

The knob twisted and the door opened. The voice of the talk show host blared out around the big man filling the door frame. Tarek Martin was considerably heavier than he'd been the last time Sasha saw him and his hair was gray through and through; his face looked significantly craggier but she easily recognized him.

His breath caught and he hissed it out between his teeth. "Sassy Lenoir, as I live and breathe."

She opted not to call him on the use of her nickname. "Mr. Martin, how are you, sir?"

"Well, I'm fine." He reached to push the screen door open. "Come on in here, little girl." He hollered over his shoulder, "Edie, come see who's here."

The little white dog hopped around his feet, yapping madly.

Sasha dared to step inside, expecting a snip at her heels. But the little dog just continued to bounce and bark.

A woman, obviously his wife, wandered into the living room, drying her hands on her apron. "I swear, you look just like your mama, honey."

Sasha didn't remember Edie Martin. Her voice was vaguely familiar but her face drew a blank. "Thank you."

The older woman's mouth formed an O. "I am so sorry about your grandmother. We came to the funeral but we didn't get a chance to talk to you. It was so crowded."

Sasha nodded. "G'ma had a lot of friends."

"She sure did," Mr. Martin said. "Come on in here and sit down. Can we get you something to drink? Coffee or tea?"

Sasha shook her head. "No, thank you. I just wanted to ask you a few questions if you have a moment."

"Course." He gestured to the sofa as he and his wife claimed the chairs they obviously preferred.

"I suppose you're busy taking care of your grandmother's affairs?" Mrs. Martin commented.

"Yes, ma'am. There's lots to do."

Mr. Martin grinned. "You sure enough pulled that pop star out of the fire last month."

Sasha smiled, her first real one of the day. "Yes, I did." The pop star in question had really blown his image on social media recently. Sasha had turned the situation around for him and set him on a better track. It was up to him now to stay the course.

"Your grandmother was so proud of you. She was always talking about you everywhere she went."

"I appreciate you sharing that with me."

Mr. Martin's craggy face scrunched up. "You said you had some questions. You know we're happy to help any way we can."

Sasha squared her shoulders. "When my parents died, Mr. Martin, you were the one person who stood up for my father. You insisted he would never have done such a thing."

Mr. Martin shook his head firmly from side to side. "I stand by those words still. There is no way Brandon would have hurt Alexandra. No way in the world."

"No way," his wife echoed. "They were having some problems with him getting fired and all, but they loved each other. He wouldn't have hurt a fly, much less his sweet wife."

Sasha blinked back the tears that threatened. "I tried to tell everyone that myself, but no one listened." She swallowed the lump in her throat and pushed on. "Can you think of any reason anyone would have wanted to hurt either of my parents?"

"You see," Mr. Martin said, "that's the thing. Everybody loved those two. I mean you had your jerk who made some remark about the fact that your mama was black and your daddy was white, but that was rare. I honestly can't remember more than one occasion that it happened and that was years before...that night."

"Why was my father fired? The reports say he was drinking on the job."

He scoffed. "That's another thing that was stretched out of proportion. Yes, he'd had a couple of drinks, but he was not falling-down drunk. Your daddy wasn't much of a drinker in the first place. The real problem is he crossed the wrong person and that person was looking for a way to be rid of him."

"Who did he cross?"

"Dennis Polk, the crew chief at our site. Dennis didn't like your daddy. To tell you the truth, I think he had a thing for your mama and didn't like the man she chose. I think I heard something about her dating Dennis back in high school but that's pure hearsay."

"Whether she did or not—" Mrs. Martin took over from there "—your mama had no use for the man. He had it in for your daddy, and as soon as he got that promotion to crew chief, he found a way to get him in trouble." She shook her head. "But they were working that situation out. Your mama had a good job that included a health insurance plan. They had the house they'd inherited. There were no real money issues. I think your daddy just felt like he wasn't pulling his weight those last few weeks and that caused tension."

Words echoed through Sasha. Her parents arguing over his need to find work and to stop moping around. She pushed the memories away. "Is it possible Mr. Polk may have wanted to hurt my parents?"

Mr. Martin moved his hands back and forth as if to erase the idea. "Oh, no, not in a million years. Polk was a weasel, rightly enough, but he didn't have the guts to do anything like that. He was all talk." Martin laughed. "Still is, as a matter of fact."

"There was that drug operation," Mrs. Martin said. "Brandon came across it deep in the woods behind your house in that old shack. Remember?" She directed the question to her husband.

"I sure do. We told the chief about it and he looked into it, but those knuckleheads were long gone. Drifters, I think."

"I didn't read anything about that in the reports from the investigation."

"I know it was looked into," Mr. Martin countered. "I took Chief Holcomb through those woods personally. Showed him the shack and told him the whole story same as Brandon told me."

"What about my mother?" Sasha looked from one to the other. "Did she have any enemies who might have wanted to hurt her?"

Both shook their heads. "Folks loved her. She was always so helpful with the permits and zoning issues. Anytime anyone wanted a permit to build or change something on their home, they went to Alexandra first even though she was in planning and development. She did it right and she did it fair. None of that playing favorites or making things more difficult than necessary."

"Your mama was under a lot of pressure that year," Mr. Martin said. "Her boss had a heart attack and that left only her to oversee everything going on in the county and to keep up with all the inspectors. It was a difficult time. Especially with the hospital and the big-box store going up that year. It was a real mess."

Frustration inched up Sasha's spine. These were the people closest to her parents. If they didn't know of anyone who wanted to hurt one or both, who would?

"But there was no one related to her work who might have wanted to hurt her or have revenge for some action she'd taken or failed to take?"

More shaking of heads. Sasha felt her hopes deflate.

"Can you tell me where Mr. Polk lives?" She might as well talk with him, too. She had nothing to lose but time.

"Over at the Shady Pines nursing home," Mr. Martin said. "He had a stroke some years back and he can't get around too well, but he can talk. He's a little difficult to understand at times."

"I appreciate your help." Sasha reached into her handbag for a business card. She passed it to Mrs. Martin. "If you think of anything at all that you feel might be useful in my search for answers, please call me. I would really like to find the truth."

Mrs. Martin saw her to the door. Both she and her husband assured Sasha they would contact her if they recalled anything useful.

If she had to interview every single person who had known one or both of her parents, she intended to do so. Someone had to have seen or heard something.

Murder didn't happen without leaving ripples.

Chapter Five

The Shady Pines assisted living facility had been around as long as Sasha could remember. As a child her grandmother had brought her here to visit one of her teachers, Ms. Clements, who had been in a terrible accident. She had no husband or family, so she'd had to stay in this facility through her rehab. Three months later she was able to return home but she was never able to teach again. Ms. Clements had been Sasha's favorite teacher. She was the one to sit in the bathroom with her whenever she felt the need to cry that first year back at school after her parents died.

Sasha should visit her while she was in Winchester. Ms. Clements would love seeing photos of Sasha's daughter. She smiled to herself as she thought of all the things about her childhood that she needed to show her daughter...including the father her daughter didn't know.

The realization startled Sasha but there was no denying the truth.

She put her car in Park and shut off the engine. For years now she had been telling herself that she should talk to Brianne about her father. Her daughter had gone through that phase where she'd asked every other day about her father. Sasha had told her that he was a good man but that he didn't know he had a daughter. So far Brianne hadn't questioned her mother further but Sasha understood the time was coming. Her daughter was quickly going from a child to a teenager.

The truth was, how could Sasha be so intent on having the truth about her own childhood when she concealed her daughter's? She had been afraid to tell Branch. Not at first. At first she'd been certain he wouldn't be interested, so she had chosen not to tell him. Their one night together hadn't been about love or the promise of a future; it had been about need and happenstance. Neither was a good foundation for a relationship. She had told herself that Branch wouldn't want to be weighed down with fatherhood and at the time that was most likely the case.

Years later, on a visit to her grandmother, she had run into him again. He, too, was home for a visit and he had talked and talked about how exciting his work was in Chicago. He had been happy, focused singularly on his career. Again, Sasha had told herself that she had made the right decision. But then, two years ago her grandmother had shared Arlene's concerns about how lonely Branch was. He'd mentioned to Arlene that he worried that he'd waited too long to pursue a real relationship… that maybe a family wasn't in the cards for him.

Sasha had always intended to find a way to tell him, but time had slipped away. Her grandmother had never advised her either way. She'd said Sasha would know what to do when the time came.

"I'm still waiting for that time to come, G'ma."

She climbed out of her car, draped her bag over her shoulder and headed for the assisted living center entrance. After a stop at the registration desk, she wove her way along the corridors until she found the room belonging to resident Dennis Polk. Though the facility wasn't a five-star resort, it was certainly well maintained.

Sasha knocked on the door and a surprisingly strong male voice shouted for her to come in. She opened the door and stepped inside. The room was neat and spacious. Mr. Polk sat in a chair by a large window that washed the room in sunlight. His bed was made, a patchwork quilt folded across the foot, and a small arrangement of flowers sat on the bedside table. The television was tuned to a news channel.

Mr. Polk eyed her over the top of his reading glasses for a moment. His curly dark hair had gone mostly gray now. She vaguely recalled meeting him at a company picnic once. His tall frame was far thinner and his ebony skin sagged from his chin. But his eyes were bright and alert.

"Mr. Polk, I'm—"

"I know who you are." His words were a little rough and clipped but easy enough to understand. He closed his book and laid it on the window ledge. "You're Alexandra and Brandon's girl."

She smiled and moved a little closer. "Yes, sir. I am. I'd like to ask you a few questions if you have the time."

"I have all the time in the world, young lady." He gestured to the small sofa. "Please, join me."

Sasha took the offered seat. "I don't know if you heard, but my grandmother passed away."

"I heard." He nodded to the small radio perched on the table next to his chair. "I listen to the local talk show every morning. They always announce who's married and who's passed and so forth. She was a good woman and a lucky one. Her granddaddy made a fortune on a land deal when the dam came in and he bought his wife one of those stately historic homes. They were the first folks of color to own one. Did you know that?"

Sasha nodded. "I did." Her grandmother had told her the story when Sasha was just a child but she never spoke of it again. Viola Simmons did not believe in rehashing the past. She was a firm believer in moving forward without looking back and dwelling on the things that had already occurred. All the more reason Sasha needed to find the truth—whatever it was—and move on with her life. There was no future in dwelling in the past.

"I was in love with your mama. Did you know that?" His expression was a little sheepish now.

Sasha met his gaze and asked the question burning inside her. "Is that why you got my father fired from his job?"

His eyebrows shot up. "There were folks who believed that was the reason and I have to tell you that I certainly was looking for a reason to give him his comeuppance. But no, I didn't turn him in on account of how I felt about your mother. I turned him in because he came to the job site drunk. Drunker than a skunk, I'm telling you."

Hurt speared through her. She had wanted to believe otherwise. "My father wasn't much of a drinker." This she remembered quite well, which was why she'd held out hope that the story was wrong.

"That's true and that's also why I was so surprised that he came into work at six in the morning with alcohol on his breath and staggering. I took him off to the side and asked him what was going on. He got defensive and told me it was none of my business." Polk shook his head. "I surprised myself when after all that time of looking for a reason to get him into trouble, I felt sorry for him instead. I knew something wasn't right. Brandon Lenoir wasn't a drinker."

The ache inside Sasha eased. "Did he tell you what happened?"

"He and your mother argued over something. He wouldn't say what. He just kept repeating that there was nothing he could do. He couldn't fix it and that seemed to have him awfully upset."

"Do you have any idea what he meant?"

Polk shook his head again. "I don't. I tried to talk to him, to reason with him, but he was having none of it. I told one of the other guys to take him home and I warned your daddy to sleep it off and come back the next day. I'll be damned if he didn't take a swing at me. Knocked me flat on my back but good, I'm telling you. I thought he'd broken my jaw, but lucky for me the worst damage was to my pride." He shrugged. "I didn't have a choice then. I had to fire him but I told him when he got his act together to come back and we'd work something out. The next thing I knew, he and your mama were dead."

His tone and his downcast gaze told her he felt partially responsible. "Did you ever hear any rumors about what happened? Maybe an opinion that differed from the official conclusion?"

His faded brown gaze lifted to meet hers. "I heard lots of opinions but none of them were any truer than the one the police came up with."

Her pulse rate accelerated. "So you don't believe my father killed my mother and then himself."

Polk shook his head firmly from side to side. "There is no way on God's green earth that Brandon Lenoir hurt his wife. He loved her too much. He would've done anything for her."

Sasha took a much-needed breath, hadn't realized she'd been holding it as he spoke. "Then who killed them?"

"That's the question, isn't it?" He stared out the window for a time as he spoke. "I'm pretty sure they didn't have any enemies. In a small town you hear those sorts of things. Never heard any talk like that about your folks."

Sasha hesitated. Should she tell him what she remembered hearing? Why not? Maybe it would spur some lost memory of his. "I heard at least one other person in the house that night. It was a man, perhaps two. My father pleaded with him or them to let my mother go."

Polk's gaze locked onto hers again. "Did you tell Holcomb about that?"

She nodded. "Apparently he felt my statement was too little too late. By the time I could tell someone they'd already concluded the murder-suicide scenario based on the lack of evidence for any other theory. I can't really blame the police. You said yourself my parents had no enemies. There was no evidence to support what I heard."

"It's been twenty-seven years. Digging at it won't change nothing at all. Sometimes it's just best to let sleeping dogs lie." He reached for his book and opened it, started to read once more—or pretended to.

Sasha recognized the cue. He was through talking. She retrieved a card from her bag and placed it on the table next to him. "If you think of anything else that might help, please call me."

He gave a single nod but didn't look up from his book. Sasha left his room. How could everyone be so convinced her father would never do this and yet sit back and let the whole thing go as if it made no difference?

Outside she unlocked her car and slid behind the steering wheel. The question that haunted her now echoed in her brain.

What difference will it make? Dead is dead. Her grandmother had said those words to her once when Sasha was fifteen and demanding answers.

She started the engine, braced her hands on the steering wheel. What now? Who else should she interview? Years ago she should have demanded that her grandmother help her do this. Now the one person who had known her parents better than anyone was dead. How was she supposed to piece together this mystery without her grandmother?

Tears spilled down her cheeks. Despite her best efforts to contain the flood, Sasha surrendered. She laid her forehead against the steering wheel and let them flow. She hadn't allowed herself to cry—to really cry—since she got the call about her grandmother. She'd been too busy, too shrouded in disbelief to totally break down.

Apparently there was no holding it back any longer. She pawed through the console of the rental car looking for a tissue or a napkin, anything with which to wipe her eyes and nose. The more she searched for something to dry her tears, the harder she cried. By the time the stream had slowed, she was exhausted and weak with an odd sort of relief.

She finally found a pack of tissues in her bag. She cleaned up her face as best she could and took a long, deep breath. She would get through this. As much as she had wanted to have her grandmother around forever, that wasn't possible. But what she could keep for the rest of her life were the memories. Memories that she would pass down to her daughter.

Sasha put the car in Drive and rolled out of the parking lot. The most important thing she could do for the memory of her family was to prove her father's innocence and to see that the person who murdered her parents was brought to justice.

If that person was still alive. Twenty-seven years was a long time. He could be dead or in prison or in a nursing home.

But, if he was alive, he had gotten away with murder for more than a quarter of a century. It was well beyond time to rectify that wrong.

THOUGH IT WAS still hours until dark, the sun had dropped behind the trees, leaving the old Lenoir home place cast in shadow. Sasha parked in front of the house and climbed out. She had her cell for all the good it would do. Cell service in the area was sketchy at best.

She unlocked the house and tucked the key into the hip pocket of her jeans. First, she walked through the downstairs and turned on lights, chasing away a portion of the creep factor. It was impossible to shake the idea that the deep, dark woods that surrounded the house appeared to be closing in a little more each year. She should probably have a service come out and clear the yards back to the original boundaries.

Upstairs she noted a few dark spots on the ceilings. The roof was deteriorating. She had to make a decision about this place soon or it was going to collapse into a heap. Her grandmother hadn't cared. She never wanted to come back here. But Sasha had cried each time she spoke of selling it. Some part of her had hoped one day she would wake up in her bed in the room she'd slept in as a child. That her parents would be gathered around the breakfast table, smiling and wishing her a good morning.

But she was not a child anymore. All the hope and wishing in the world wouldn't bring her parents back. It was time she did what needed to be done.

That would mean clearing out her parents' things as well as her childhood possessions. She felt confident there was someone she could call to donate whatever remained usable.

But first she had to determine what, if anything, she wanted to keep. Her grandmother had left most all their worldly possessions right here in this house. There were photo albums and keepsakes. The family Bible and a million other things that Sasha needed to consider before walking away.

She started with her parents' bedroom. The bedside tables were first. She went through each drawer, her mind instantly conjuring a memory connected to each object she touched. From her mother's favorite lotion to her father's wallet. She thumbed through the contents of the wallet. On the very top inside was a photo of Sasha and her mother. It was worn from being stored in his wallet but the images of their smiling faces said it all.

Happiness.

What had happened to change that?

Another thought occurred to Sasha. She glanced around the room. Where was her mother's purse? She summoned the image. White leather trimmed, a sort of tan-colored bag, some straw-like material since it was summer. The end of June.

Sasha searched the closet, looked under the bed, and then she went to the single shared bath on the second floor. No purse. Downstairs, she started with the small mudroom off the kitchen. Her mother's sweater hung on one of the hooks near the door. A windbreaker that had belonged to her father was there, too. She checked the pockets. A piece of peppermint candy was in her mother's right pocket. Beneath the sweater was her purse. Her wallet was there. Staring at the driver's license photo made her stomach hurt. The pressed powder compact, a brush and lipstick cluttered the bottom of the bag. A receipt from the local grocery store dated two days before her death.

Sasha walked through the kitchen, checked under the table and in all the cabinets, though she couldn't see her mother storing any big secrets in the cabinets. Then she moved on to the dining room and living room. She checked under tables, behind chairs and in bookcases. No surprises.

The same in the entry hall. An umbrella stood in the corner.

Her mother's office was cluttered and as dusty as the rest of the house. Framed accolade after framed accolade filled one wall. Her mother had graduated from architecture school at the top of her class. She'd spent two years in Nashville working but then she'd fallen in love with Sasha's father and she'd come home to marry him and to start a family. It wasn't until Sasha was in kindergarten that her mother took the position with the city in planning and development.

Sasha surveyed the rolls and rolls of plans on her mother's desk. There were dozens of notes in a stack next to the phone and more on the bulletin board; all appeared to be about work.

One by one she scanned the notes on the bulletin board. All were related to upcoming deadlines at work. A stack of file folders waited on one corner of the desk.

Her mother had made notes on call sheets and forms attached to the folders. Most looked like copies, not originals. Sasha assumed she had a working copy at home and the originals at work. Her fingers stalled on the photos tucked under the glass on the desk. Sasha's green eyes and big smile beamed out from the one in the middle. There was another of her parents in a hug, their lips just touching. Her heart squeezed. How had two people who seemed to love each other so much and who had everything necessary for happiness ended up dead in such a violent, heinous manner?

Sasha banished the question and moved on to the drawers. She found her mother's peppermint stash. She unwrapped a piece of the red-and-white candy and popped it into her mouth. Still tasted okay. More work files and office supplies but nothing else.

A memory of her mother working late in this office flashed through Sasha's mind. Her position had been very stressful and demanding. But could it have had anything to do with her death? Sasha couldn't see how. She'd only been in the position for four years. Perhaps an outsider coming in and taking a top spot had caused some resentment. But was that enough motive for murder?

There was that woman with whom her mother had lunch occasionally. What was her name? Penny something. Sasha remembered her, mostly because she always seemed to be intense, so needy. She should find the woman and ask her about her mother's work. First, though, she had to figure out what the woman's name was. Her attention settled on the old Rolodex and she reached for it. Seemed like a good place to start looking for names.

She moved from *A* to *B* and so on, turning the wheel to the next letter. Still no Penny. Maybe she had the name wrong. Could be some other *P* name. Patty? Pricilla? Penelope?

The digital number on the phone snagged her attention. It was one of those old-fashioned phones with the built-in answering machine.

"Old as dirt." Sasha studied the device. The handset was cordless, so not entirely ancient.

A number 2 stared at her from the small window that displayed the total of stored messages on the answering machine. Sasha had no idea if the machine still worked, but the small button glowed red for answering machine on.

With nothing to lose, she pressed the play button. The first message was from the dentist's office, reminding Mrs. Lenoir that her daughter Sasha had an appointment the next day.

That appointment hadn't taken place for another month.

Another voice echoed in the room. The sound quality was a little scratchy but it was certainly clear enough to understand.

We need to talk, Alex. Call me as soon as you can. It's important.

The date-and-time stamp indicated the message had been left the afternoon of the day before her parents died.

Was this the woman who had been her mother's friend? Penny or Patty or whatever?

It's important.

Maybe this woman had the answers Sasha needed. All she had to do was figure out who her mom's friend was and then find her...assuming she was still alive. And that she was the woman who had left that message.

With nearly three decades having elapsed, anything could have happened.

Chapter Six

It was almost dark by the time Branch reached the Winchester city limits. He had tried to call Sasha since he passed the Tullahoma exit but she hadn't been answering. He just kept getting her voice mail. Since he had promised to catch up with her as soon as he was back in town, he headed to her grandmother's house.

He'd done a lot of thinking on the drive back from Nashville and none of it was about the offer he'd been made in the meeting. The promotion and the opportunities available in Nashville were a far cry from the future he could expect in Winchester and still he hesitated.

As crazy as it sounded, he had sort of grown accustomed to the slower pace in Winchester and being around family and old friends. But the Nashville offer was one he'd been hoping would come his way for a long while now. He'd been certain the trouble in Chicago early last year had set his career back at least a decade. Last month's high-profile takedown had launched his career back up to where it belonged.

As gratifying as the offer was, at the moment he couldn't keep the Lenoir case off his mind. There was more to what happened twenty-seven years ago than was in the pages of those investigation reports. Maybe it was all the years of his grandmother shaking her head and commenting about what a travesty the investigation into the case had been.

She had insisted that Brandon Lenoir would never have murdered his wife. The question was, why hadn't Viola Simmons demanded the case be reopened? She had kept quiet and allowed the police to do their job, whatever the outcome. Not once had Branch ever heard his grandmother mention Mrs. Simmons's thoughts on the matter. Maybe Mrs. Simmons believed his grandmother spoke loudly enough for both of them. But he had watched the elderly lady go after councilmen in city council meetings. He'd witnessed her speaking on behalf of the lack of opportunities for young black women in the area. When Viola Simmons believed in something, she went the distance.

Why hold back when it came to the murder of her own daughter?

It just didn't fit.

He parked in front of the Simmons home and made his way to the door. He knocked twice. No answer. No sound inside. Sasha's rental car wasn't in the driveway or on the street. She had said she would be reviewing the reports. Maybe she'd found something she wanted to follow up on. He sure wished she had kept him informed. He would have to talk to her about the need to stay in touch. Going off on her own wasn't a good idea. She could run into trouble and he'd have no idea what happened.

He called her cell again and this time it went straight to voice mail.

For the next half minute he considered what he would do if it was his history he was attempting to dissect and correct.

First, he wouldn't have screwed things up with her

all those years ago. He'd been attracted to her since high school but she had completely ignored him. She'd always been busy with her friends. Always had a boyfriend hanging around. No surprise there. Sasha was the prettiest girl in school. The biggest stumbling block had been his grandmother. She had warned Branch about doing anything that might in any way take advantage of or hurt Sasha. She had been through enough, his grandmother cautioned.

And he had. He'd done exactly what his grandmother told him...until that fall Sasha showed up for a high school reunion. If she had been pretty growing up, she had become a stunningly beautiful woman. Just looking at her had taken his breath. That one night, thirteen years ago, had turned him inside out. He hadn't managed a serious relationship since. Oh, he'd had plenty of dates, but none that had gone beyond the physical. He hadn't met anyone who made him want more.

Work had consumed his life. And he had been exceedingly good at his job. Then he'd made the mistake of his life by getting involved with a witness and she'd lost her life because of his error. That wasn't entirely true. He had been cleared of wrongdoing related to her death, but deep down he would always feel that if he'd done things differently maybe he could have seen what was coming.

He would second-guess himself on that one for the rest of his life.

Clearing his head of the troubling memories, he decided to check the old Lenoir place. It was possible Sasha had decided to have a look around in the house without him. Not that he could blame her. There was no better way to put herself in the middle of the past than by going back to the scene of the crime.

The Lenoir house wasn't that far outside Winchester proper, still in the city limits but nestled deep in the woods off South Shephard and Gem. The area was densely wooded and the old place had been abandoned since Sasha's parents died. Mrs. Simmons refused to allow the property to be sold or rented, or even maintained.

Weeds had encroached on the long driveway, making it narrower. Cracked and broken asphalt aided the weed coup. He breathed a little easier when he spotted Sasha's rental car parked near the house. He had no more appointments for the next few days, which left him free to focus on this investigation. And her.

He shook his head, reminded himself that he had to look at this as a case—not as a personal venture. This was not about spending time with Sasha—well, maybe it was in part—it was about finding the truth. There was an aspect of the case he needed to find an opportunity to present to her. As much as she wanted to clear her father completely of any fault in what had happened, Branch worried that wouldn't be possible. One of the two victims, either her father or her mother, was involved on some level. People rarely got murdered in this manner—planned and executed—without some degree of involvement.

First thing, they needed to set some ground rules. Although he had no reason to believe either of them was in danger related to this exploration of the past, it was best not to take any chances. If they learned someone else was responsible for her parents' murders, that person in all probability would not want his secret revealed.

If that person was still alive.

Branch wanted to remain objective on this case but he was having a difficult time doing so. Maybe because of his grandmother's certainty, maybe simply because he wanted a different ending for Sasha.

He thought of her daughter. Was there still a connection between her and the girl's father? She hadn't mentioned a relationship with the man but it was more likely than not. After what Sasha had been through losing her parents, he felt confident she would want her daughter to have a relationship with both her parents if possible.

He walked to the door and knocked. It was quiet inside. He glanced around the overgrown yard. He would call the lawn service his mother used and have them come over and work on the property. Sasha would potentially want to put it up for sale now. He wasn't sure it would pass any sort of inspection considering the condition of the roof and the siding, but all those things could be repaired. It could be a nice place again. A little TLC would go a long way.

He reached up to knock again and the door opened. She started, stared up at him in surprise.

"You didn't answer your phone." He removed his hat, held it with both hands, mostly to keep them busy since his first instinct was to reach out and touch her.

She frowned. "The service is really bad out here. Sorry. I guess I should have sent you a text to let you know where I'd be."

"How's it going?"

"I haven't found anything earth-shattering." She shrugged. "Anyway, come in. I can't offer you any refreshments because there's nothing here."

He followed her through the entry hall and then into a room to the right. Her mother's office. Sasha went around behind the desk and sat down. She pushed a button on the phone. "Listen to this."

He listened through two messages. The first was an

appointment confirmation; the second was from a female who urged Alexandra to call her. "Do you know the caller?"

She shook her head. "I tried to review the numbers on the caller ID but they're no longer available. The only reason the messages are still there is because it's one of those old answering machines with the cassette tape."

"The voice doesn't sound familiar to you?"

"It's too scratchy or low, maybe both. I know Mother had a friend, Penny or Patty. Something like that. I've been looking through her Rolodex and her notes. I haven't found a reference to a female with a name that starts with *P*."

"Rolodex? Really?"

The hint of a smile peeked beyond her obvious weariness. "Believe it or not, there are people in this world who would die protecting their Rolodex. For a businessman or woman who's been around since before contact lists and smartphones, a Rolodex is sacred."

She gave the Rolodex wheel a spin; the alphabetized cards tumbled around the wheel. "I can ask my grandmother if she remembers anyone in particular who was friends with your mom."

Sasha's gaze lit up. "That would be great. I considered calling her but I thought I'd exhaust my other options first."

"Frankly, I'm surprised the phone and the answering machine weren't taken into evidence."

"That was my first thought," she agreed. "It feels like the investigators had made up their minds and simply didn't bother looking for evidence."

He wasn't prepared to go that far just yet, but he had to admit that there was a lot that had been missed. Then again, hindsight was twenty-twenty.

"Why don't you give me a tour—if you're up to it." Branch had been here a few times growing up, but he never paid much attention to the layout of the house. He'd always been focused on the green-eyed princess who lived here.

"Sure." She pushed away from the desk and stood. "Obviously you can see this was her home office. She worked a lot of long hours and she didn't like spending so many away from Dad and me. So, she brought homework from the job nearly every day."

They moved into the living room and she walked him through the scene though he already had a good grasp from the crime scene photos. The closet where Sasha had been hiding was literally less than a dozen yards from where her parents had died. God Almighty. No child should have to go through that kind of trauma.

The kitchen and dining room were next. Branch stared out the rear windows at the gathering gloom. "Do you remember exploring those woods as a kid?"

"I do. There was an old shack. Rey and I used to use it for a playhouse. We spent hours pretending to clean and cook."

He wondered if that was the same one where the drug cookers had taken up residence during the time frame when the Lenoirs died. He would look into the exact location. "You never ran into anyone out there?"

She shook her head. "Never."

As they walked back into the living room, Branch studied the scene once more. The living room was located about midway between the front door and the back. If there was someone else in the house and they went out the back, as Sasha recalled, then they must have cut through the woods to get to where they had parked.

Otherwise they would have had to go around front and to the main road and risk being seen by neighbors.

"How far through the woods until you reach another road?" he asked.

"Not that far. The woods are dense and there's probably a lot more undergrowth now since no one's been keeping it tramped down. For an adult running, maybe fifteen minutes. As a child it took a little longer."

Branch would follow up on where the shooters might have parked and, if they were lucky, someone who still lived nearby had seen someone. It wouldn't have mattered twenty-seven years ago because apparently no one was looking for a killer beyond the husband.

"Have you gone through the bedrooms?"

"I poked around a little. No serious digging."

Her arms went around herself as if she were cold and needed to protect herself from potential harm. She was tired and not entirely comfortable here, no matter that she wanted to appear strong and capable.

"Did coming here prompt any new memories?"

That was the real question. She hadn't been in this house since the night of the murders. It was possible seeing everything with new eyes had nudged one or more hidden memories.

"Nothing important that I didn't already know. There were two men in the house that night besides my father. I heard their voices. I'm almost certain there were two distinct voices." She shook her head. "My father didn't do this, Branch. No matter what the reports say and no matter how bizarre it sounds after all these years. My father did not kill anyone."

The thing was, he believed her.

Chapter Seven

Sasha chafed her arms to chase away the chill. Branch watched her so closely, his blue eyes seeming to see right through her. She wanted him to see her strength and determination but at the moment it felt as if all he saw was her fear that she wouldn't be able to prove what she believed in her heart.

And what if she was wrong?

No. She refused to believe her father had done this. Her entire life she had known, without doubt, that he was innocent. Now she had the opportunity to prove it and she was extremely fortunate to have Branch offering to help. Local law enforcement would lend far more credence to his investigation of an old case than to that of a member of the family—particularly the daughter determined to prove her father's innocence.

"Why don't we call it a day?" Branch glanced around. "You've taken in a lot today. Maybe let it filter tonight and start fresh tomorrow."

Not until that moment did Sasha realize how incredibly tired she was. It was as if his words somehow prompted her to relax, to stand down from the fight. "Good idea. I am unreasonably exhausted."

"I'll take you to dinner," he announced. "You can

give me your thoughts on today's effort and I'll give you mine."

If she was smart she would pass. If she was smart she would go directly home, take a shower and hit the sack.

If she was smart she would recognize how very precarious this cliff upon which she had perched herself really was.

But she wasn't smart when it came to Branch Holloway and the past they shared.

"I'm not really dressed for going out." *Good job, Sash.* At least she tried, despite the idea that she felt herself leaning toward him, waiting for him to give her one good reason why her manner of dress didn't matter one little bit.

"The Back Porch is a great pub just off the town square." He looked her up and down, her skin heating with the move that even in an innocent moment like this one exuded sex appeal. "Nothing fancy, but great food."

There it was, the excuse she needed. "Well then, let me lock up here."

He followed her to the kitchen, where she locked the back door. "We can drop your rental off at your grandmother's and you can ride with me, if that's okay. No need to take both vehicles. Parking is sometimes at a premium."

She glanced at him. "Sure."

He trailed her back to the front door; she turned off the lights as she went. They stood on the porch while she locked the front door. No matter that it wasn't completely dark yet, it was utterly dark on the porch. The dense woods blocked the fading sunlight from reaching this far. She thought of all the times she had chased the looming shadows across the yard. She had never once been afraid here…not until that night.

When she was loaded in her car, he settled his hat into place and gave her a nod. "See you at your grand-mother's."

Sasha gave him an answering nod. She told herself to smile but somehow being in the dark with Branch left her unable to do so. She rolled away from the gloomy house and the woods that held it hostage, and breathed a sigh of relief when she reached the main road. She felt as if she hadn't managed a deep breath since she set foot in that old house. All the dust, she told herself.

Layers and layers on top of the memories…the pieces of her life.

The drive to her grandmother's home was wrought with building tension. Hard as she tried not to, she had worked herself into an emotional frenzy by the time she parked in front of the house. She should have bet-ter control than this.

He hopped from his truck, skirted the hood and opened the passenger-side door for her.

Control? Ha! This was Branch Holloway. She'd never had any control when it came to him.

She climbed into the truck and he closed her door. All through her teenage years she had been besotted with him and he had barely acknowledged her exis-tence beyond the Sunday lunches their grandmothers had shared. He slid behind the wheel of his truck, that big black cowboy hat of his lying on the seat between them. Of course, they'd run into each other outside school. Their grandmothers had been best friends. But he'd been two years older and always busy with football or being the most popular guy in school.

Sasha had been reasonably popular as a teenager. There were several difficult years right after her par-ents died but those may have been more about her inability to interact than about anyone else. She'd crept into a shell for a while. What child wouldn't under the circumstances?

A furtive glance in his direction had her gaze lingering there. He'd always had that perfect square jaw. The kind of face—particularly his lips—romance novel heroes were written about. Her daughter had those same lips as well as his blond hair and blue eyes. Brianne was the female version of Branch Holloway. So many times Sasha had wanted to tell her...had wanted to get out her old high school yearbooks and show off the child's handsome father.

But fear had kept her from doing so. Sasha, the woman who was fearless in every other aspect of her life, was terrified of what she had done and it was too late to fix that huge misstep.

Funny how she was here now, spending time with Branch to try to rectify a part of her past, and she was keeping this life-altering part of his from him.

He would hate her when he learned that truth.

Her stomach roiled. Any appetite she had possessed vanished. What was she thinking? Allowing him to help her with this investigation would only make him feel used in the end. This had been a very bad idea.

Branch parked at the curb across the street from The Back Porch. Sasha recognized the corner shop. It had been an old antiques store the last time she was here. Now it was a happening place from all appearances. Lights were strung over the sidewalk on both street-facing sides of the establishment. Beyond the big windows tables were filled with patrons. Waitresses were running around with laden trays.

The passenger door opened before she realized Branch had gotten out of the truck and walked around to her side. He held out his hand and helped her down. She tugged at the hem of her tee and wished she had taken the time to change. He was right in that the place looked very casual, but she felt dusty and rumpled after plundering through her mother's office for so long.

"I can't say for sure what'll be on the menu tonight, but I can tell you that anything you order will be excellent."

She glanced at him, produced a smile. "Smells great." The aromas emanating from the screened entry doors had resurrected her appetite.

He smiled and her heart reacted. She looked away. She spent her days and weeks managing other people's personal and professional crises and she couldn't keep her own ancient history under control? How sad was that?

Pull it together, Sash.

Branch opened the door and the music washed over them. A recent country hit, strumming through the sound system and through her. Inside, the floor was rustic, reclaimed wood as were the walls. A bar ran the length of the far wall. Every stool was occupied. Branch spoke to the waitress who looked up at him as if she was a mesmerized fan and he was her favorite rock star. Then she directed them to a table. It was tucked into a dark corner and Sasha was thankful for the out-of-the-way location.

The waitress took their drink orders; Branch suggested the house specialty—their craft beers. Sasha could use a beer to settle her nerves. Maybe she would sleep better, as well. Last night had been a battle with the covers all night. She'd awakened more tired than when she went to bed.

When the waitress returned with their beers, they

ordered burgers and fries. Brianne would be appalled. She would strictly eat only healthy food. Sasha sipped her beer and relaxed. She loved that her daughter was so independent and strong-minded.

"How did your meeting go?" They had spent most of their time together talking about her and her parents; she felt bad that she had asked so few questions about him and his life.

He stared at the beer in his glass. "Great. It went great. They made me a terrific offer for a position in Nashville—a promotion." He shrugged. "The whole thing went better than I expected."

Sasha laughed. "Wow. I have never heard a guy sound so down-and-out over such good news. Is this your excited face?"

He stared at her for a long moment, that mask of uncertainty not shifting the slightest. "I'm undecided. To tell you the truth, I like being close to my family. It's an unexpected development, that's for sure."

He sipped his beer and Sasha bit back the words she wanted to say. Branch was a good guy. He recognized that his parents and his grandmother were getting older and he felt compelled to stay close. This was just another perfect example of what made him so sweet. She, on the other hand, felt like scum. She hadn't once considered that it might be better if she moved closer to her grandmother. She was completely focused on her career and on her own life and that of her daughter.

"You should do what makes you happy, Branch." She turned the frosty beer glass round and round, kept her gaze focused on the rivulets of condensation sliding down the sides. "Too many people rush after the brass ring and lose out on happiness."

"Are you speaking from experience?"

Oh, damn. She'd said too much. She might as well confess now. "I have to say that I've considered the idea that I should have been here for my grandmother. I was the only family she had left and I was not around." If she'd hoped that confessing would make her feel better, she had been wrong.

Even after she'd found out she was pregnant, Sasha had been determined to forge her own life. She'd wanted to go far away from here and become someone else. Not the daughter of a man who had killed her mother and then himself.

"My grandmother always said your grandmother was very proud of you. She was very happy about your success. So don't go beating yourself up for something that wasn't real when she was alive and damned sure isn't real now. You're feeling guilty for a nonexistent issue."

She laughed. *God, if he only knew.* "So what are you, a shrink?"

He shook his head. "No. Just a guy with experience in the blame department."

No matter that she told herself she didn't want to know, she found herself asking, "What happened?"

"I broke protocol. Got involved with a witness and she died. My superiors cleared me of any blame in her death but that didn't seem to matter up here." He tapped his temple. "I still felt responsible. The two-week suspension for breaking protocol didn't seem like punishment enough."

"So you punish yourself by second-guessing whether or not you deserve this promotion."

The waitress arrived with their food before he could respond. Sasha poured a pool of ketchup on the edge of her plate and dragged a French fry through it. She nibbled the salty goodness. If she were completely honest she would admit that she devoted herself entirely to work and to her daughter because she didn't feel as if she deserved a personal life outside the relationship with her child. She lost that right when she gave up everyone who had been there for her during her life before college.

Her gaze drifted to the man across the table. Mostly because of him and how she'd left him out all these years.

They ate. Laughed at silly moments from high school. Shared the ways they had struggled to build their careers. When she'd devoured all she could hold of the best—bar none—hamburger she'd ever eaten and half a plate of fries, as well as a second beer, she asked the question that had been burning in the back of her mind for years.

"Why no wife or kids? And don't give me that ridiculous answer you gave before about letting the only one for you get away."

He shrugged. "Hey, it's true." He sipped his ice water. No second beer for him since he was driving. "How was I supposed to fall in love with someone else when you stole my heart when I was fifteen."

She rolled her eyes. "That is completely not true and certainly no answer."

He pushed his plate away. "I guess I just never ran upon anyone who made me want that kind of relationship. What about you? What went wrong with your daughter's father? The two of you aren't still together. Maybe you let the only one for you get away, too."

Fear pounded in her veins. "We were never together." She stared at her plate, tried to think what to say next. "I... I screwed that one up. He was a good guy but he's...he's out of the picture." She met his gaze then.

"I made a mess of everything and my daughter is paying the price."

A frown of concern lined his handsome face. "There's nothing you can do to work things out? He doesn't sound like such a good guy to me if he's not interested in having a relationship with his daughter."

Sasha felt as if she couldn't breathe. She had to change the subject. Now. "I visited the guy who fired my dad. Polk, Dennis Polk."

Branch angled his head, studied her face for a long moment. Then picked up on her cue, her change of subject. "What did he have to say?"

"He didn't fire my dad permanently." She explained how Polk had tried to handle the situation. Her tension eased a little as they drifted back onto safer ground. "The interesting thing was, he doesn't believe my father killed my mother either."

She also told him about her conversation with the Martins. A brief pause was required while the waitress cleared their table and asked about dessert, which they both declined. Branch insisted on paying. Another point of contention. She could not have him paying for her meals as if they were on a date. *This was not a date.*

"You were busy today." He leaned forward, braced his forearms on the table. "I'd like you to keep me informed of where you are and what you're doing from now on. Just to be safe."

She stared at him for a long moment, hoping to ascertain the motive for the statement. "Are you or Chief Brannigan concerned with my activities?"

Branch held up his hands. "No way. I just want to know you're okay." His arms dropped back to the table. "We have to face the fact that if your father didn't do this, someone else did. Whoever that someone else is, chances are they don't want us learning their secret."

It was a valid point. Certainly the idea had crossed her mind but she had chosen not to be put off by it. "What if that person or persons is dead?"

"Then we probably have nothing to worry about but we're talking about cold-blooded murder. A well-thought-out-and-executed set of murders. This was no impulse kill or robbery. It was planned carefully and carried out mercilessly. That tells us a number of things. First, someone powerful may have been involved—as in someone who paid hired professional thugs to do the dirty work. Or someone close to your family who knew the details of their daily lives and who could get in and out without being caught."

Planned and executed. She reminded herself to breathe. He was right. The images conjured by his words made her stomach clench and the taste of the burger she'd eaten turned bitter. Their deaths had not been about a robbery. Nothing had been missing—at least nothing of which anyone was aware. Certainly not money or jewelry or the usual valuables.

"Let's exchange contact information."

Once their cell numbers were added to each other's contact list, she asked, "So what do we do now?"

"We create a list of potential suspects. Anyone who was involved in the lives of your parents, either professionally or personally. Someone who had something to lose if a particular event occurred." His broad shoulders lifted and fell in a slight shrug. "We can probably rule out Polk. If he was in love with your mother, it's unlikely he would have killed her. The more reasonable path would have been to try to get your father out of the way."

"We might as well list everyone living in Winchester at the time." She rubbed at her forehead. The idea was overwhelming. "This is a small town, Branch. Everyone knows everyone else."

He nodded. "True. But not everyone has something to gain at the expense of someone else. This is what we need to find. What did your parents know or have that was worth killing for?"

She shook her head. "I should have made my grandmother talk about this. She refused when I was growing up. She said it was too painful. But I should have pushed the issue in recent years. Now she's gone."

Sasha rested her face in her hands. This was too much. Too, too much.

"Hey." Long fingers wrapped around one of her hands and tugged it away from her face. Blue eyes zoomed in on hers. "We'll figure this out. One step at a time. If you look at the big picture it can be overwhelming."

She dropped her free hand to her lap and told herself to pull her hand away from his but her body refused to obey. The sensation of his long fingers encircling hers made her feel safe and warm and not so lost and alone in this misery.

"We're going to look at this one piece at a time. We'll start with their personal lives. We dissect each piece. Were there financial issues? Had your grandmother been helping financially? I'll talk to my grandmother and see what she knows—if anything—that might help."

"Why are we starting with their personal lives first?" As a crisis manager, Sasha knew the value of a marketable commodity. For most people that was their professional lives. Certainly with celebrities the two often intertwined but the concept was the same. No matter that her grandmother liked to laughingly disagree, money—or the lack thereof—was usually the root of real trouble.

"This was up close and personal. Not a drive-by or a long-distance kill. Up close. Personal. There was intense passion behind these murders."

Sasha stared at him for a long moment; her hand felt cold despite the feel of his skin against hers. "Is that why the police were so convinced the killer was my father?"

Branch nodded. "In situations like this, it's almost always the husband."

"But not this time."

"I firmly do not believe your father killed your mother," he agreed.

There was a *but* coming. She could see it in his face, hear it in his voice.

"*But* there's a strong possibility the reason they both ended up dead is because of something your father knew or had done. This would be why he pleaded so for her life. He didn't want her to die for something he had done."

She drew her hand away from his, his skin suddenly burning hers. "I see your point, but I'll reserve judgment until we have more facts."

Sasha had spent her entire life believing her father was innocent. She wasn't about to throw him under the bus from a different perspective at this point without substantial evidence.

"Reserving judgment is warranted," he acquiesced. "We should both keep an open mind until we have all the facts—or as many as we can dig up."

"All right." She clasped her hands together in her

lap. "Are you certain you have the time to devote to this case? I know you're on vacation and obviously you have a decision to make."

Sasha stopped herself. What was she doing? Could she really spend the next several days working so closely with Branch without resurrecting those old feelings? Of course not. She was already struggling. Instead, she should be trying to figure out how she was going to tell him about Brianne. She had waited a very long time to find the truth. She didn't want to screw it up now.

What a mess she had made.

He started to answer her question but she held up her hands to stop him. "I'm sorry. I shouldn't be asking you to do this. You've been far too kind and giving already. This isn't your issue. It's mine. You have a life and I shouldn't be dragging you into my problems."

He chuckled but there was no humor in the sound, more a sad weariness. "First, I offered to help because I would very much like to be a part of resolving this case. Second, I have nothing else I need to do except make that career decision in the next few days about where I go from here. Seriously, I am totally available."

"Still," she argued, "this is too complicated, too personal…"

"I want to do this, Sasha. It means a lot to me. Your family means a lot to me."

She wished he hadn't said those words. Tears brimmed on her lashes before she could stop them. "I don't have any extended family left, Branch."

He grinned. "You have your daughter and you have me and my family."

"You're right. I'm feeling sorry for myself and I should get over it and get the job done."

He winked. "That's what I want to hear."

He stood. "Come on. I'll take you home. We have a lot to do tomorrow."

The drive to her grandmother's house was quiet but it was a comfortable silence. Sasha felt content with the decisions they had made. When he'd parked in front of the house and reached for his door, she stopped him with a hand on his arm.

"Now *I* have some ground rules."

He nodded. "All right."

"I don't need you to walk me to the door and I can open my own door." When he would have argued, she held up a hand and went on. "It's not that I don't appreciate it, but it's not necessary. Also, I pay for my own meals."

He made a face. "You're being unreason—"

"No exceptions. Tomorrow I pay since you paid tonight."

He held up his hands in surrender. "Fine."

"I don't mind keeping you informed of where I am—it makes sense. But I am a strong woman, Branch. I am completely capable of taking care of myself."

He nodded. "Got it."

"Thank you." She reached for her door. "Good night. I'll see you in the morning."

"Good night."

She climbed out of his truck, closed the door and walked straight to the front door without looking back. He didn't leave until she had unlocked the door and gone inside. She supposed she couldn't complain about that part.

Inside, she leaned against the door and closed her eyes to slow the spinning in her head. She really was in trouble here. She wanted Branch Holloway in a completely selfish way.

Sasha had developed a reputation for never giving in or giving up. She was relentless. Other than her time with her daughter, she had no personal life. Honestly, she could not remember the last time she'd been intimate. She wasn't an idiot. She understood the core issue at play here. Years of depriving herself had made her weak, had caused her to be vulnerable.

This was not a good time to be vulnerable.

But Branch made her want things she shouldn't want. All he had to do was walk into the room. He didn't even have to look at her. The very act of breathing was somehow sexy on him.

"Idiot."

Sasha pushed away from the door, locked it and headed upstairs. She needed to hear Brianne's voice, and then she intended to have a long hot bath and to get some sleep.

Whatever else tomorrow brought, she had to be prepared for spending time with the man without making a mistake that would impact her daughter.

She'd already made one too many of those.

Chapter Eight

Tuesday, March 26

Sasha's eyes opened.

It was still dark. She reached for her cell on the bed-side table.

2:06 glowed from the screen.

She closed her eyes and told her brain to go back to sleep. It was too early.

The whisper of a sound, the slide of a rubber sole across a wood floor, fabric swiped against a painted wall. Just a little swoosh.

Her eyes flew open again.

This time the darkness closed in on her, squashing the air from her lungs.

Heart pounding, she sat up, grabbed her cell. Her fingers instantly poised to enter 911.

Wait. She needed to take a breath and listen. Ensure she hadn't dreamed the sounds. She struggled to calm her racing heart and to quiet the sound of blood roaring through her veins.

The squeak of a floorboard…another soft whisper of a footfall.

Someone was definitely in the house.

She tapped Branch's name in her contact list as

she hurried soundlessly across the room. Holding her breath, she opened the closet door. Thank God it didn't squeak. She burrowed as deeply inside as possible, pulling the door soundlessly shut behind her.

"Hey—" Branch's voice echoed sleepily in her ear "—what's up?"

She turned her back to the door and whispered, "Someone is in the house."

"Hang up and call 911. I'll be right there."

She did as he asked and tried to flatten herself against the back wall behind the clothes from high school that still hung in her closet.

The dispatcher came on the line with her practiced spiel. Sasha gave her address and situation.

"Officers are on the way to your home, Ms. Lenoir. Where in the house are you?"

"Second floor, third door on the left. I'm in the closet."

"Good. Are you armed?"

Another brush of sound. This one on the stairs.

"What?" she murmured.

The dispatcher repeated the question.

"No." What she would give for a weapon. "Wait." Sasha used her free hand to feel through the darkness until her fingers tightened on the item she hoped to find. "I have my baton."

It was the baton she'd used in junior high. Just over two feet long and with a classic star ball on each end. A whack to the face or chest or private area could disable a man.

As long as he didn't have a gun.

Her fingers tightened around the baton.

Pounding echoed through the house.

Sasha's heart nearly stalled.

"Sasha! It's Branch. I'm coming in."

The door was locked. How would he get in?

"The police are turning into your driveway now, Ms. Lenoir."

Sasha tried to think. "US Marshal Branch Holloway is at the front door. I called him first. Should I go down and let him in?"

"Stay where you are, ma'am."

"Sasha!"

She couldn't just stay hidden like this. She opened the door and eased out of the closet. The moonlight coming in through the window had her blinking after being in total darkness for several minutes.

Standing very still, she listened for sound. Besides Branch's pounding she heard nothing else.

She burst out of her room and rushed down the stairs. "I'm coming."

A crash in the kitchen froze her feet to the floor.

For a single second she wanted to run after the sound. Good sense took over and she rushed to the front door instead and unlocked it for Branch.

"Are you all right?"

"Yes. I heard something in the kitchen just now."

"Stay close behind me."

Sasha fell into step right behind him. He flipped lights on as they went. Once in the kitchen he stopped. She bumped into his back.

"The back door is standing open," Branch said.

Sasha leaned past his shoulder, saw a uniformed police officer coming through the wide-open door. She had locked that door. She was certain of it.

"My partner's going over the yard," the officer said. "Are you clear in here?"

"I'll make sure. You take the exterior."

The officer disappeared into the darkness. That was when Sasha saw Branch's weapon.

Her breath caught.

Branch reached back with his free hand and gave her arm a squeeze. "I want you to stay close behind me while we look around inside. I'm confident the intruder is gone but let's not take any chances."

It wasn't until they had cleared the dining room and family room as well as the powder room that she realized she had dropped her cell phone. It lay on the floor at the bottom of the stairs.

She grabbed it. "I don't think he came upstairs. I think that was his intention but your pounding on the front door stopped him."

As they climbed, Branch asked, "Do you have reason to believe the intruder was a he?"

"Well, no. I'm just assuming."

"He didn't speak or make any sounds?"

"I heard the sound of his clothing brushing the wall or a piece of furniture and the whisper of his shoe soles on the floor."

"What woke you up?" He entered the first bedroom, the one her grandmother had always used for a guest room.

"I guess the sound of him moving about downstairs. I thought I imagined it, so I tried to go back to sleep. Then I heard it again. Really soft sounds."

They checked each room and found nothing.

"Now let's have a look downstairs and see if anything is missing?"

"Okay."

One side of his mouth hitched up into a grin. "Nice weapon."

Her fingers loosened slightly on the baton. "One of the girls on my team knocked a guy out with her baton."

He laughed. "I think I remember hearing about that. Gave him a concussion, didn't she?"

"That part was a rumor, I think."

"Marshal Holloway, I'm coming in."

Sasha turned toward the front door as it opened and one of the officers stepped inside. Since Branch was armed, the officer announcing his intentions was a smart move.

"We have a secondary scene outside."

Sasha wasn't certain what the term *secondary scene* meant but she was confident it wasn't a good thing.

"Stay inside with Ms. Lenoir and I'll have a look."

"Excuse me," she protested. "I would like to see this secondary scene, as well."

Branch looked to the officer, who said, "The yard is clear, Marshal."

"Take a second look around inside," Branch suggested. "Ms. Lenoir and I will talk to your partner outside."

"Yes, sir."

"Stay close," Branch cautioned again.

She followed him outside, down the steps and around the corner of the house. Obviously this secondary scene was in the backyard. The other uniformed officer was waiting near the porch.

"The perpetrator entered through the rear door," the young man, who couldn't be more than twenty-five, said. "There's evidence the lock was disabled."

"Good work, Officer Gabrielle. What else did you find?"

Gabrielle shone his flashlight onto the wall near the far end of the porch. Words had been spray-painted on the siding.

You were supposed to die that night...

For several seconds Sasha could only stare at the words; they wouldn't assimilate in her brain... Then suddenly they did. Her heart bumped against her sternum.

"I think you can safely say that you've kicked a hornet's nest," Branch announced.

Where's the kid? the man with the deep voice demanded.

At a friend's. She's not here. Her mother's voice. Terror pulsed in every syllable. *She's a child. She doesn't know anything!*

Sasha turned to Branch. "Whoever left that message was in the house that night. He knows I was supposed to die, too, but my mother told them I was at a friend's."

A sinking feeling had her knees going weak. Sasha steadied herself. At least now there was no question about what happened that night and it was no longer only dependent upon her unreliable memories. This was evidence.

Someone had murdered her parents.

DAYLIGHT HAD ARRIVED by the time the evidence collectors had come and gone. Sasha had made two pots of coffee and dragged out the leftover pastries from the gathering on Sunday evening.

She stood in the backyard staring at the words that had been sprayed with red spray paint. *You were supposed to die that night...*

Why did it matter to her parents' killer if she lived or died?

What could she have possibly known that counted for anything?

Had she seen the killer before? Was it someone she knew when she was a child?

She needed more coffee. In the dining room the pastries were mostly gone but there was still coffee. She'd had to set up in the dining room since the kitchen was a crime scene.

Crime scene.

She shuddered. No one should have to go through something like that twice in a lifetime. In New York she had a security system. Maybe she should have one installed here.

Should she sell the house at the same time she sold the Lenoir home place?

She hadn't really thought that far into the future. She had to talk to Brianne. This was her legacy, too.

Sasha poured the coffee and went back outside via the front door. Halfway around the house she ran into Branch and another man wearing a cowboy hat. Wait—she knew him. She just couldn't place his face.

"Sasha, this is Chief of Police Billy Brannigan."

She extended her hand. "I remember you. You played football for Tennessee."

"I did." He gave her hand a quick shake.

All of Winchester had celebrated when he made the cut. "Did your forensic people find anything useful?"

"Well—" he pushed his hat up a little and settled his hands on his hips "—it's too early to tell just yet, but I did want to speak with you about the case you and Branch are investigating."

Sasha glanced at Branch.

"We should talk inside," he offered.

Sasha led the way to the family room. She closed the French doors to the dining room as well as the door to the kitchen. She turned back to the two men waiting for her attention.

"Why don't we sit," Brannigan offered.

"Of course." Sasha hadn't had nearly enough sleep. Her brain was hardly working.

They settled around the coffee table, Branch on the sofa with her, Brannigan in the chair directly across from them.

"Ms. Lenoir—"

"Sasha," she protested.

"Sasha," he amended, "it's clear you've awakened a sleeping bear."

That was one way to put it. "It's also clear that my father didn't kill my mother or himself."

"I certainly believe we have justifiable cause to officially reopen the case."

Sasha barely restrained a cheer.

"We've established more than justifiable cause, Chief," Branch argued. "We've proven reasonable doubt in the initial findings. If there were any questions, the message outside should have alleviated those."

Brannigan nodded. "I agree, but I also understand that there are plenty of folks who like to stir trouble. It's possible someone you've spoken to—" this he said to Sasha "—has decided to give legs to your case. Folks were divided twenty-seven years ago. There were those who believed your daddy was guilty and those who were certain he was innocent. Your digging around in the past is the perfect opportunity to turn the tide of things in the direction they believed was the right one to begin with."

As much as Sasha wanted to dispute his assertion, his conclusion was reasonable and logical. Even in a small town people took sides in controversies, especially those that involved lifelong members of the community and murder.

"What're you suggesting we do moving forward?"

Branch asked, his tone as pointed as his expression. He obviously wasn't happy with where this was going.

Sasha spoke first. "Chief, I respect your thoughts on the matter but I have every intention of continuing my search for the truth. I'm well aware that as long as I don't break any laws or cause any obstruction of any sort that I can do as I please."

Branch turned his hands up. "I'm on vacation and I intend to help her do exactly that—in a completely unofficial capacity, of course."

Brannigan looked from one to the other. "Well, I won't waste my time trying to talk you out of it. I will, however, need the case file back so I can reopen the investigation."

"Do we have time to make a copy?"

Brannigan's lips formed a grim line. "It was one thing when this was a cold case, Branch. This is now an official police investigation. I can't have copies all over the place. We should step back and do this right. You know the drill as well as I do. Whatever we find, we don't want a simple technicality to cause trouble in the courtroom."

"I understand," Branch conceded. "The case file is at my house. I'll have it at your office before noon."

Sasha wanted to argue with him but decided to save her frustration for when it was just the two of them. A united front was what she needed right now. She was an outsider, no matter how many years her family had resided here. Branch was one of them and he was a member of law enforcement. Besides, the case file wasn't at his house; it was here. She trusted that he had good reason for not sharing that information with the chief.

In the end, they would figure this out, with or without the file.

"Thanks, Branch. I'll make sure Cindy is on the lookout for it. I'll have a meeting with my detectives and get the ball rolling and I'll keep you informed as well as I can."

"I appreciate it, Billy."

Brannigan stood and settled his hat back into place. "Thank you for your cooperation, Ms. Lenoir." He nodded to her and then to the other man. "Branch."

Branch followed him to the front door. Sasha strained to hear anything one or both might say.

"Keep an eye on her, Branch," Brannigan warned. "Obviously there is some danger here. I'm not sure she understands how complicated this could get."

"I'll keep her safe," Branch guaranteed. "A situation like this morning won't happen again."

When Branch returned to the family room, Sasha opened her mouth to protest having to turn over the file without a copy but Branch held up his hand for her to wait. He went back to the entry hall and checked out the window. When he returned to where she waited, he kept his voice low.

"We have a few minutes before Billy will become suspicious. Where's the case file?"

"In my bedroom. I put it in the closet." She shrugged. "Just in case."

"Good idea."

As they climbed the stairs, she whispered to him, "If he won't allow us to make a copy—"

"We can't make a copy but he didn't say anything about taking photos."

Sasha smiled for the first time today. "Smart thinking."

At the top of the stairs he paused, held her gaze. "I've been doing this a while. Never count me out."

She would know never to do that again. "Thanks."

During the next few minutes they snapped pics with their cells. Every page, every photo. Sasha's stomach churned as she took care of the crime scene photos. When the last one was complete, Branch repacked the files into the box.

"I'll tuck this back in your closet and pick it up on my way to Billy's office later today."

She nodded her understanding. Before she could ask what was next, he said, "Pack a bag. You're not staying here alone anymore."

"Where are you suggesting I stay?"

"You're staying with me." He carried the file box to her closet, deposited it on the floor and covered it with the same throw she'd had over it.

For a moment she only stared at him. He couldn't possibly think she would stay with him at his house... *alone.*

"I know what you're thinking." He tapped her on the temple. "Don't fight me on this, Sasha. Besides my grandmother, I'm the only one who's completely on your side in this."

"I can stay at a motel or at the inn." She wasn't actually sure of what establishments still operated in Winchester. Good grief. She could not spend time under the same roof with him. Not the way he was suggesting.

"Look. This is not some plot to take advantage of you. You can stay at my grandmother's if you prefer. I just don't want you alone at night—anywhere. We can use the evenings to go over what we find and compare notes and thoughts. We'll spend most evenings together anyway."

So maybe he had a point. "You have a guest room?"

"I do. You can take my room since it's upstairs. I'll

take the guest room downstairs. There will be an entire floor between us."

Now she just felt foolish. "Well, all right. I'll pack a few things."

"Good." He nodded. "I'll get out of your way."

Somewhere downstairs the sound of her cell phone ringing pierced the air.

Sasha headed for the door. "That's my phone."

"You pack. I'll get your phone."

She nodded. "Thanks."

With her smallest suitcase opened on the bed, she started layering in sleepwear and clothes. She groaned when she realized she'd been running around all morning in a nightshirt. At least she'd had the good sense to pull on one of her grandmother's sweaters once Branch had arrived.

"What a night," she grumbled.

"Mom?"

The sound of her daughter's voice reverberated up the stairs. Sasha's heart nearly stopped.

"I'm not your mom, but I'm taking the phone to her. Hold on a minute."

"Who are you?"

Sasha winced. That was her daughter's interested tone. She probably thought— Sasha shook her head. She didn't want to go there.

"I'm US Marshal Branch Holloway, an old friend of your mom's."

He walked into the room, grinning from ear to ear.

Sasha reached out; her hand trembled in spite of her struggle to keep it steady. "Thanks."

He placed the phone in her hand, her daughter's pic filling the screen. Her blond hair and blue eyes exact duplicates of his.

"I'll be waiting downstairs."

Sasha nodded. Not trusting her voice. When he'd left the room she took the phone off Speaker and said, "Hey, baby."

"Who was that?"

Sasha collapsed onto the bed. "An old friend, sweetie. He's helping with all this stuff that needs to be done." She had not told her daughter about her search into the past. Until she had some evidence one way or another, there was no point sharing any of this with anyone beyond official personnel. Though, technically, she did have some evidence now.

"Mom, he sounds hot. You should live a little. I'm doing a Google search on him right now."

Sasha's mouth went dry. "You know how photos on the internet are never like the real person."

"So when are you coming home?"

Sasha managed her first deep breath since her phone rang. "Next week, I hope."

"I don't understand why I can't come there. There was a death in the family. I can make up the homework and tests."

"We'll talk about that later in the week."

"OMG, he is straight fire."

"Why aren't you on your way to school?" Her heart was hammering again.

"Okay, okay. Chill. I won't be late."

In the background Sasha heard Avery's voice urging Brianne to hurry before she was late. Saved by the nanny!

Thank God.

"I'll talk to you after school, sweetie."

"Okay. Love you!"

"Love you, too."

The call ended but Sasha's heart didn't stop pounding. Her daughter had seen a photo of her father.

Branch had seen a photo of his daughter.

Sasha was running out of time and someone had threatened her life.

She stood. She couldn't control precisely how the investigation of this case went, but she could still navigate the other. She would not leave her daughter in the dark the way her grandmother had left her.

All she had to do was find the right moment to tell her the truth. First, she needed to tell Branch.

Chapter Nine

Arlene Holloway had come to her grandson's house as
soon as she heard the news. She also insisted on throwing together a late breakfast. Sasha tried to help but the
eighty-five-year-old woman shooed her away. So while
Arlene prepared eggs and toast and bacon, Sasha and
Branch discussed where to go next with their investigation.

"Come and get it!"

By the time they wandered into Branch's kitchen,
Arlene had already arranged her own plate and was
stationed at the head of the kitchen table.

Sasha had been certain she couldn't eat. Not after all
that had happened this morning. Apparently her emotional reaction had been a little delayed. By the time
they had driven from her house to Branch's, she was
trembling and feeling weak-kneed. She hated feeling
frail, hated even more for anyone to witness the episode.

"That's the way it always worked for me," the older
woman had said. "I was always the one who could keep
it together during a crisis, but then when it was over I
fell apart."

Weathering crises was Sasha's brand. No one was
better, but she had definitely had trouble holding herself
together after they left her grandmother's home. Sasha

understood the reason this situation was different was because it was personal. At work she was dealing with other people's crises. This was profoundly private and it went all the way back to her childhood.

"I've been thinking about what you asked me," Arlene announced, her attention moving from her freshly emptied plate to the man at the other end of the table.

"Did you think of anyone?" Branch asked.

Sasha looked from him to his grandmother.

"Your mother," she said to Sasha, "had lots of friends. She was a very busy lady, all about work, so she didn't do a lot of socializing. But there was one friend she lunched with fairly regularly. Vi and I sometimes ran into them at the diner."

"Is her name Penny or Patty?" For the life of her, Sasha could not recall the name. She was glad Branch had remembered to ask his grandmother.

"Not a Penny or a Patty. That's why I had to do some thinking. The name was wrong. It's Leandra Brennan. Her friends called her Lenny."

"Lenny." The name clicked. Sasha nodded. "That's it. Is this woman still alive?"

"She is. Still lives in the same house and works at the same job. Her house is over on North High Street. Six-oh-six. You probably won't find her at home on a workday though. She's Jarvis Packard's personal assistant."

"Jarvis Packard?" The name wasn't familiar to Sasha. She'd been gone a very long time.

"The biggest land developer in the Southeast," Branch said. He pushed his cleaned plate away. "His company is involved in any major project that happens in the area."

"Where're the Packard offices?"

"Over on South College," Arlene said. "You can't miss it. There's a huge sign."

Arlene scooted back her chair and stood. "Now you two get on about your business and I'll clean up here."

"Gran," Branch argued, "you've already done too much."

"Your mama told me to take care of you while she and your daddy are on vacation."

"I don't think she intended for you to cook for me," he protested as he took his plate to the sink.

Sasha followed with her own plate and fork. She loved hearing the two bicker. It was so cute to see the big fearless marshal concede to his little old grandmother. Sasha rinsed the dishes and tucked them into the dishwasher. Arlene wiped the table.

"You planning to visit Lenny?" Arlene asked.

"I am," Sasha confirmed. "If she was my mother's closest friend, perhaps she'll know if there was something unusual happening around the time of the murders."

It felt suddenly odd to speak about the murders in such an investigative manner. Twenty-seven years had elapsed since that night. Sasha had long ago come to terms with the pain of shock and loss. The events of that night had left lifelong wounds with deep scars. But she had chosen to move forward despite the trauma.

Now those emotions resurfaced with the same raw ache she'd felt as a child.

"I can go with you," Branch offered.

Arlene sent him a frown. "I doubt she will want to talk in front of you. Heavens, Branch, you know better than that. If the woman knows anything, she's far more likely to tell her friend's daughter than some lawman."

"She has a point," Sasha agreed.

"I'll follow you there on my way to see Luther Holcomb."

"Luther?" Arlene pushed the last chair into the table. "He was convinced your daddy did the killing, Sasha. He refused to see that night any other way. I remember arguing with him but it did no good whatsoever."

This was the part that nagged at Sasha. All her adult life she had ignored this aspect of the past but now it was simply impossible to ignore. "Why didn't my grandmother argue with him? Why didn't she fight for the truth?"

Arlene seemed to shrink into herself—as if the question had shaken her. Sasha immediately felt contrite for her poor choice in words.

"I think she wanted to protect you? The longer the investigation dragged out, the harder it was for you to move on. Like she said, *dead is dead*. No amount of hollering and screaming and making a fuss was going to bring her daughter back."

Sasha considered for the first time how painful her mother's death must have been for her grandmother. Alexandra had been Sasha's mother, but she had been Viola's only child. Sasha couldn't fathom even the concept of losing her own daughter.

"I can understand how she wanted to put the hurt behind her—behind the both of us." She pushed the painful thought away and turned to Branch. "I guess we should get started."

He nodded. "I need to talk to Luther," he explained, "before the official investigation shuts him down to those not part of that investigation."

"We'll connect after our meetings," Sasha said. She

could do this part on her own. Besides, they could get a lot more done going their separate ways.

He pointed a finger at her. "I want to know where you are at all times. When you leave one location headed to another, I want to know."

"I expect the same," she tossed back at him.

He grabbed his hat and settled it into place. "You got it."

"Thanks for breakfast, Mrs. Holloway." Sasha gave the lady a hug.

She patted Sasha on the back. "Your mama would be very proud of you."

The words haunted Sasha all the way across town. Her grandmother had told her often enough as a child that her mother would be proud of her, but Sasha hadn't considered how her mother would feel about her reopening this investigation.

"The truth is what matters," Sasha said aloud as she turned into the parking lot of the Packard building.

She watched Branch continue on South College. Sasha wasn't sure where former chief of police Luther Holcomb lived now. Her attention settled on the six-story building with the huge *P* on top that had not been here when she was a kid.

Sasha climbed out of the rental, tucked the strap of her bag on her shoulder and headed for the main entrance. She couldn't be sure if this Lenny person was at work today, if she was out of town on vacation or tied up in back-to-back meetings, but Sasha had to try.

Inside, the elegant lobby was massive with towering ceilings and a wall of plants behind the elegant reception desk. The other three walls were tinted glass. Sleek tile floors, combined with all the glass, gave the lobby a cold feel. The neatly arranged pit of leather seating didn't help.

Cold and austere.

Sasha was glad she'd chosen a gray sweater to wear with her jeans today. She didn't exactly look professional but she did look casually comfortable. She'd tucked her long, curly hair into a clip.

When the receptionist ended her call and looked up, Sasha smiled. "I'm here to see Leandra Brennan."

A practiced smile that didn't quite reach her eyes slid into place. "Do you have an appointment?"

"No," Sasha confessed. "I'm only in town for a few days and I thought I'd drop in. I'm Alexandra Lenoir's daughter. If you would just tell her I'm here."

"I can call her office and see if she's available," the receptionist offered.

"Thank you."

Rather than sit, Sasha wandered to the far side of the lobby where a freestanding glass wall featured ongoing and upcoming projects. A new mall in Tullahoma. A hotel near the interstate. A medical complex by the Winchester hospital. Packard was apparently involved in anything big in the tri-county area.

"Ms. Lenoir—" the receptionist's carefully modulated tone reached out "—Mrs. Brennan can see you now."

Surprised but thankful, Sasha went through the steps. She provided her driver's license and stood still for a photo. Then she was given the code for the ride upstairs. On the elevator she entered the code and the doors automatically closed and the car bumped into motion, stopping on the top floor.

As cold and austere as the lobby was, the top floor was anything but. Thick carpeting, rich wall colors and lavish furnishings. Another receptionist looked up from her desk and smiled.

"Please have a seat. Mrs. Brennan will be with you shortly."

"Thank you."

Sasha settled into a plush upholstered chair and worked on relaxing. She wanted to appear calm and intelligent, not emotional and desperate. This could be the step that made all the difference in discovering the truth she so badly wanted to find. If she had harbored any reservations about this endeavor, she certainly did not after last night's intruder. Someone knew what she was doing and that someone was worried. That had to mean something.

You were supposed to die that night...

Had her grandmother feared for her own and Sasha's lives? Was that why she hadn't pursued a different conclusion from the official one reached by the police department? Her grandmother had been a very intelligent woman. She would have realized that nothing added up. The concept that Viola Simmons might have been afraid shook Sasha. Her grandmother had always appeared so brave and strong.

But everyone had his or her breaking point. Sasha could not imagine surviving the loss of a child. Arlene was right. Viola's entire focus would have been on protecting Sasha.

Whatever it took, she would find the truth—for her parents and for her grandmother. Sasha's grandfather on her mother's side had died before Sasha was born, so she had never known him. She had heard stories that he was a shrewd businessman, which was why her grandmother had never had to worry financially. Her father's parents and sister had moved away after the murders.

Sasha had never once heard from them. She supposed they had been too devastated. But she had been a child and they shouldn't have abandoned her.

She had considered contacting them but she'd never pursued any search. If they hadn't cared about what happened to her, then she'd just as soon leave well enough alone. Unless they had information about what had happened?

Why would they not have stayed and fought for justice if they believed her father was innocent? Or had some proof?

Why hadn't someone done the right thing?

"Sasha."

Sasha looked up at the sound of the woman's voice. The red hair and blue eyes instantly triggered memories of her mother and this woman—a younger version of this woman—huddled over magazines and talking about decorating.

She stood and extended her hand. "Thank you for taking the time to see me, Ms. Brennan."

The woman nodded. "Let's go to my office."

Sasha followed her down the hall and into an office with a massive window; though the view of South College and the parking lot wasn't that spectacular, it did allow lots of light. The furnishings were elegant and numerous accolades lined the walls.

Brennan loosened a button on her suit jacket and settled into the chair behind her desk. She wore her hair down over her shoulders as she had decades ago. The gray streaks reminded Sasha just how much time had passed.

"Please—" the older woman gestured to the chairs opposite her desk "—have a seat."

Sasha perched on the edge of a wingback. Suddenly

she felt nervous. Perhaps it was foolish but she felt as if what this woman had to say could be a turning point in her search for the truth.

"You look well," Brennan said. "I was sorry to hear about your grandmother. She was a kind and gracious woman."

"Thank you. It was a blow." There was no other way to put it. Losing her grandmother had shaken Sasha's world. Perhaps that was why she was here as much as for any other reason.

"I hear you've made quite the name for yourself in New York." Brennan smiled. "Your mother would be proud."

Sasha nodded, the burn of emotion suddenly attacking her eyes. She really needed to get a hold on herself. "I'm good at what I do."

"And you have a daughter. I understand she's quite the dancer. I'm sure you have your sights set on Juilliard."

Sasha wanted to ask if Brennan had remained close with her grandmother but it didn't feel right. Why wouldn't her grandmother have mentioned talking to Brennan?

"She does," Sasha allowed. "Personally I have my hopes set on Columbia or Princeton."

Brennan nodded. "Sometimes things don't turn out the way we expect."

There was a sadness in her eyes and her voice as she said the words.

"No one knows that better than me," Sasha agreed. "One day my life was the perfect nine-year-old's world and the next my parents were dead. Murdered."

Brennan blinked. "It was a tragedy."

"My mother was worried about something those last

few days of her life," Sasha lied. She actually had no recall of her mother being upset about anything except her father's job issue. "You were helping her. I remember you calling and leaving her a message."

Fear or something on that order flashed in the other woman's eyes before she schooled the reaction. "Perhaps you didn't know that your parents were having a difficult time. Your father had lost his job and they were arguing a lot. I tried to be there for her but I'm afraid I failed her miserably. If I'd had any idea Brandon would go that far I would have done something. The fact is, I was out of town on business for days before and after... that night."

"Is that why the police didn't interview you?" It seemed strange to Sasha that the police would not have interviewed the victim's best friend.

"I suppose so. Why do you ask?"

One aspect of Sasha's work that she was particularly good at was reading her clients. It was extremely important that she recognize when one was lying. It wasn't that she took only clients who were honest and aboveboard—that wasn't the case at all. But she didn't take clients who lied to *her*.

Leandra Brennan was lying.

"Oh." Sasha frowned. "I guess you haven't heard."

Brennan frowned as if she had no idea what Sasha meant.

"Chief Brannigan is reopening the case. New evidence has come to light that suggests my father was innocent. In fact, the same person who murdered my mother murdered him, as well."

Blink. Blink. Shock. "What new evidence?"

Sasha sighed. "I'm afraid I'm not at liberty to discuss it. I can tell you that someone broke into my grandmother's house last night and left me a threatening message. It wasn't pleasant. The chief feels that's all the more indication that the new investigation is on the right track."

Sasha hoped the other woman wasn't so good at ferreting out untruths because she had just woven an elaborate tale that was only partly true.

Brennan put her hand to her chest. "That's terrible—about the break-in, I mean. I'm glad you're all right. What kind of message did the intruder leave?"

Sasha held her gaze for a long moment, mostly to drag out the tension. "He said I should have died that night. I guess the killers didn't realize I was hiding under the stairs and heard everything." She shook her head. "There were two of them in the house. It's a shame Chief Holcomb didn't listen to me all those years ago or my parents' killers wouldn't have gotten away with murder."

"I had no idea." Brennan's words were cold and stilted.

"No one did. But now they're going to know. Because I won't stop until I find the truth. Actually, I'm hoping you can help me."

Brennan looked startled. "How would I be able to help you?" As if she'd only just realized how her words sounded, she added, "Of course I will be happy to help any way I can, but I'm not sure how that's possible. It's always been my belief that Brandon was the one...and as I said, I was out of town."

Sasha stood. She reached into her bag and pulled out one of her cards. "I'm certain if you think about it, something will come to you. I still have your message to my mother the day before she was murdered. You were worried—you wanted to warn her about something. When you remember what that something was, call me. Please."

She placed her card on the desk and turned away from the woman's stunned gaze.

Sasha had a feeling she'd just shaken the lion's cage. A roar of a reaction would be coming.

Good. That was the point.

She rode the elevator down to the lobby and walked out of the building. She could almost feel Brennan's eyes on her as she climbed into her rental car.

All she had to do now was wait for the domino effect.

Chapter Ten

Luther Holcomb no longer lived in Winchester proper. After he retired four years ago, he divorced his wife and moved out into the woods in the middle of nowhere. He spent most of his time fishing or hunting.

Branch supposed a man who'd spent his life being a cop had the right to do whatever he wanted when he reached sixty-five without getting himself dead. Now, as Luther approached seventy, it seemed he rarely even came into town anymore.

Branch parked his truck and stared at the cabin directly in front of him. Was this what happened to a man who spent his life focused on catching criminals? Luther and his wife never had children and then after all those years they just walked away from so many decades invested in a marriage. Had they been living separate lives all along anyway? Branch knew lots of lawmen who did exactly that. The lives they led with the badge were the ones that consumed their existences. Their wives and kids had their own lives. Once in a while—like birthdays and holidays or graduations—those two lives intersected.

Branch didn't want that kind of life. Maybe it was the idea that he was barreling toward forty but he didn't want the family life he hoped to one day have to end up a casualty of his career. He wanted what his parents had. He wanted what his grandparents had shared.

He thought of Sasha and her daughter. What kind of life did they have together? Without the girl's dad in the picture? Her daughter—Brianne—had looked nothing like Branch had expected. He'd expected her to have her mother's dark hair and green eyes but she'd been blonde with blue eyes. Before he could stop his mind from going there, he imagined Sasha with some New York City hotshot. His gut tightened with envy.

A rap on the glass made him jump. His attention whipped in that direction to find Luther staring at him.

"You gonna sit in there all day?"

Branch couldn't believe he had allowed the old guy to sneak up on him. He opened the door and climbed out. "Hey, Luther, how are you doing?"

"Well, I'm still above ground, so that's always a good thing."

"Can't argue with that."

"Is this an official visit?" Luther eyed him speculatively.

"Kinda sorta." Branch closed the truck door and leaned against it. "Is that okay?"

Luther shrugged. "Sure. Why not? I just made a batch of shine if you're interested."

Branch shot him a grin. "I've had your shine before, Luther." He pressed a hand to his stomach. "I don't think I should go down that path today."

"When did they start making you guys so soft?" The older man laughed as he led the way into his house.

Branch followed, removing his hat at the door. "They like us to keep a clear head these days."

Luther grunted. "Is that supposed to make you better lawmen?"

"Presumably." Branch glanced around at the sparse furnishings and then at the bulletin board with its big calendar and all those crossed-out blocks. "You lining up your fishing calendar?"

"Oh, yeah." Luther poured himself a little shine in a mason jar and gestured to the seating area. "Sit. Tell me what you're up to, Mr. US Marshal."

Branch settled in the nearest chair. "Technically, I'm on vacation, but I'm helping a friend. You remember the Lenoir case?"

Luther collapsed into an ancient recliner. He knocked back a slug of his drink and then nodded. "How could I forget? It was an ugly mess. That poor little girl was shattered."

"That poor little girl is all grown up now," Branch commented, "and she wants to know what really happened that night."

Luther's gaze narrowed. "You think there was something wrong with the way I conducted the investigation?"

Branch had expected a bit of defensiveness. It was human nature. "No, sir. I reviewed the reports and I think you did everything you could with what you had to work with at the time."

The tension in Luther's expression relaxed marginally and he indulged in another shot of homemade liquor, winced at the burn.

"I actually just have one question."

"What's that?" Luther set the mason jar down. "The scene was cut-and-dry. Easy to read. A blind man couldn't have missed the clues to what happened that night."

"Almost too easy," Branch noted. Then he asked his

question. "Why didn't you put the little girl's statement in the file?"

Luther's eyebrows reared up. "You mean the one she came up with a week later?"

Branch didn't miss the guy's skepticism. "She insists she mentioned it the night her parents died but no one was listening."

"Let's take a minute and go over what I had," Luther suggested, "if you have the time."

"I have the time." Obviously Branch had struck a nerve. Not surprising. No lawman ever liked having one of his cases called into question.

"Brandon Lenoir got fired for drinking on the job. His blood alcohol level that night, by the way, was point one, well over the legal limit of impairment." Luther flared his hands. "Do the math. Taking into consideration his size, that means he had at least six beers or drinks in the couple of hours before he died. He didn't have a reputation for drinking, so I'm thinking that level of alcohol was unusual for him. People do crazy stuff when they're inebriated—especially someone not accustomed to being in that condition."

There was no denying that assessment. "So you're convinced Brandon Lenoir did this? No matter that he had no violent tendencies and from all reports loved his wife."

Luther shrugged. "Every killer starts somewhere. Many of them were never violent before their first kill. Sometimes people just snap. When he realized what he'd done, he killed himself."

"Why didn't he kill his daughter?" Branch countered. "He had to know where she was. If he wanted to kill his family, why leave her alive?"

Luther picked up the mason jar and had another

swallow. "We explored the possibility that his wife was having an affair, but we found no evidence of infidelity—on either side."

"So basically they were a happy family with no serious problems. In fact, losing his job wasn't a major blow to their financial stability."

"Maybe it was a pride thing," Luther offered.

Branch wasn't buying it, particularly after last night. "You didn't answer my first question."

"The victim's advocate urged Mrs. Simmons to take the child to a psychiatrist. I did the same. She made an appointment immediately and the psychiatrist's report indicated the girl's story was something her mind conjured to make her feel better—a defense mechanism. What else was I supposed to do? Pursue a lead on a voice or voices that didn't exist?"

Branch couldn't deny the conundrum the man had faced. "You know my grandmother is still convinced Mr. Lenoir didn't kill his wife."

"She made her feelings known well enough." He laughed. "She complained louder than Mrs. Simmons."

"Did you consider why Mrs. Simmons kept so quiet? Is it possible she was afraid for her granddaughter's safety?"

This suggestion got the man's attention. "Did she tell her granddaughter that?"

Branch shook his head. "Nope, but someone broke into Mrs. Simmons's house last night and left a message for Sasha. *You were supposed to die that night.*"

"I guess word has gotten around that she's looking into the case. Some folks don't like the past being dug up."

"Unless they have something to hide, why all the fuss?"

"You got a point there, Marshal." He tossed back the last of his shine. "Let's talk off-the-record."

"This entire conversation is off-the-record," Branch reminded him. "I'm on vacation and anything I do or say is strictly coming from just me."

"No one really believed Brandon Lenoir would kill his wife, but stranger things have happened. The evidence was clear. There were powder burns on his hand. No indication of forced entry. No evidence of foul play anywhere on the property."

"But," Branch argued, "I'm guessing it was the psychiatrist's conclusion that Sasha had made up the voices that convinced you to close the case?"

"If I have to pinpoint one thing, yeah. It was his report."

"Why isn't that report in the case file?" Seemed strange to Branch to leave out the primary reason for his conclusion.

"Mrs. Simmons didn't want any record of her granddaughter having emotional issues. I guess she was afraid the conclusion would haunt her in the future. I figure that honoring her wishes was the least I could do under the circumstances."

"Can I pass the psychiatrist's name on to Sasha? If he's still practicing she may want to meet with him."

"Sure. It was Dr. Bruce Farr. His office is across from the hospital. He doesn't see many patients anymore. He's some big-deal board member at the hospital these days."

Branch stood. "Thanks, Luther. I appreciate your help."

Luther pushed to his feet, gave Branch's hand a shake. "I'm not so sure I helped."

"If you think of anything else that might be useful, I would appreciate a call." Branch reached into his pocket and pulled out one of his cards.

"Sure thing." Luther took the card. "Bill called me. He wants to meet later to do this same thing."

Branch wasn't surprised. "It might be better if you don't mention I was here."

Luther grinned. "I never kiss and tell."

Branch was back on the main highway before his cell service kicked in again. He pulled over to review a couple of text messages from Sasha. She had met with Leandra Brennan and learned very little. Chief Brannigan wanted to meet with her, so she was headed to city hall. Branch sent her a message explaining he'd met with Luther and intended to follow up with the shrink who had examined her, and then the coroner.

She promised to call him as soon as her meeting with Brannigan ended.

Branch drove back to town and took the turn that wound around by the hospital. Dr. Farr's office was a brick building directly across the street. Branch pulled into the small lot and climbed out. He settled his hat into place and walked to the entrance.

The door was locked. The office hours posted on the door showed Wednesday through Friday from one to four. There was an emergency contact number but Branch preferred catching the man in person to question him. He didn't want to give him a chance to prepare answers or to blow Branch off.

He moved on, heading to the veterinarian's office on Decherd Boulevard. The drive took only a few minutes. Burt Johnston had been the county coroner for about forty years. He also operated two large veterinarian offices. By trade the man was a veterinarian. Though he mostly oversaw the operations from a distance these days, folks still considered him the top vet in the area.

Didn't seem to matter to anyone that he also pronounced their deceased loved ones.

A technician waved Branch through. He found Burt in his office. Branch knocked and was summoned inside.

"Well, if it's not our celebrity US marshal. You chasing down another big mob element here in Winchester?"

Branch laughed. "No, I think we've cleared all that up."

Burt gestured to a chair. "What can I do for you today, Branch?"

"Tell me what you remember about the Lenoir case. Anything that stood out as a question for you?"

Burt shook his head. "It was a pretty straightforward situation." He shook his head again. "That poor child was the worst part. She was crying at the top of her lungs. Until we got her grandma there, it was a nightmare."

"Did you see anyone near the house that night who shouldn't have been there? Maybe someone who was there to see the show?"

Crime scenes were like car accidents—people often went out of their way to see.

"Not that I can recall. Two of Luther's boys got there first. Officers Kenyon and Lacon. When I arrived, Kenyon was in the front yard puking his guts out and Lacon was trying to calm the kid down."

"No neighbors or code scanners showed up?" Some folks listened to the police scanners and rushed to the scenes of crimes. The internet had made the uploading of photos and videos for titillation a way of life.

"The officers were there. I came next. I was already in the area when I received the call. The ambulance was right behind me and then Luther brought up the rear."

"As you know," Branch ventured, "Viola Simmons passed away and her granddaughter is in town settling her affairs. She has a lot of questions about what happened and she'd like to have answers to those questions while she's here. She's waited a long time to put this behind her. I've offered to help her find those answers."

"A lot of people weren't satisfied with the conclusions from that one, and frankly, I was one of them."

In Branch's opinion, having the coroner a bit skeptical was saying something. "Looking back, is there anything you would do differently today?"

He appeared to contemplate the question for a bit. "I would have sent a team through the woods a second time. They did a search that night but I would have done another at daylight. Luther didn't think it was necessary. He had the case nailed shut already. Personally I think the decision not to do a second search might have been a mistake. I'm convinced ignoring the little girl was one. I don't know that either issue would have changed anything, but better to be safe than sorry. Especially since the child said she heard voices besides her parents' in the house that night."

Branch frowned. "You certain about that? There are some who believe she never mentioned the voices until about a week later."

"You'd have to ask Luther to be certain, but I recall her saying something along those lines that night. Course, I was pretty focused on the bodies, but I'm reasonably sure I didn't hear wrong. In fact, I told Chief Brannigan the same thing this morning."

It appeared Brannigan was on the same track. No real surprise. "Thanks, Burt. I'll talk to Luther," Branch assured him.

The problem was, he already had.

Chapter Eleven

City hall looked basically the same as it had when Sasha was a child except for the metal detectors and the bag search. She'd come here with her grandmother once or twice after her parents died. Her grandmother had always gone into the chief's office while Sasha sat in a chair in the small lobby with the secretary or assistant to the chief.

She sat in a similar chair now. The upholstered chairs were different from the ones that had been here when she was a child but the polished tile floor was the same. The nondescript tan walls were the same. A couple more framed photos of officers who had lost their lives in the line of duty had been added to the one blue wall.

Sasha wasn't anticipating anything new in the chief's investigation of her parents' deaths. He'd only decided to reopen the case a few hours ago. Of course, there was the chance they had discovered some piece of evidence at her grandmother's house related to the break-in. Frankly, she was grateful for any support on the case. She hadn't expected to garner this much attention.

"Ms. Lenoir," the older woman behind the desk said, "the chief is ready to see you now."

Sasha stood and the door across the small room

opened. The chief stepped out to greet her. "Thank you for coming, Ms. Lenoir."

Sasha thanked the secretary and entered the chief's office.

"Do you have some news for me, Chief?" She watched as he closed the door behind them.

"Actually, I have a few questions for you." He gestured to the pair of chairs in front of his desk. "Please, have a seat."

Sasha settled into one of the chairs and waited for the chief to do the same on the other side of the desk.

He leaned forward, scanned his notes. "I met with former chief of police Luther Holcomb and the county coroner, Burt Johnston. Both remembered the Lenoir case quite vividly. The trouble is I got conflicting stories about you from the two of them." Billy's gaze fixed on hers. "I know it's been a long time and that memories cloud with time, but this is one of those things that shouldn't be difficult to recall."

"How can I help, Chief?" Strange, Branch had the same two men on his list this morning. She wondered if he and Brannigan had run into each other.

"There seems to be some question as to when you actually mentioned hearing other voices—besides your parents'—in the house that night."

A frown tugged at her brow. She was surprised by this particular question. "Chief Holcomb didn't include a statement from me in the official case file. He didn't feel my statement was credible. Are you saying you think that was a mistake?"

"Before we talk about my thoughts, did Chief Holcomb explain his reasoning for that decision?" Brannigan asked.

"There was some question as to why I didn't speak

up earlier and the psychiatrist who evaluated me seemed to feel I was making up the whole story." Hurt and anger twisted inside her. She had been telling the truth. If everyone had listened to her then, maybe the investigation would have been conducted differently. Her grandmother had been so upset by Sasha's reactions to the sessions that she had refused to take Sasha back to see the man. At the time, Sasha had been glad. The doctor had made her feel strange, as if she were lying, and she had been telling the truth.

"I've tried to contact Dr. Farr, the psychiatrist who evaluated you, but he seems to be unavailable. The dilemma I have is that according to Burt Johnston, the coroner, you were talking about the other voices that very night, which directly conflicts with what Chief Holcomb says. Obviously, someone made a mistake. I just need to figure out which one is correct."

Sasha searched her memory of that night, tried to find a moment where she remembered speaking about the voices to someone amid the macabre activities happening around her. She remembered her parents' motionless bodies…the blood everywhere…the anguished screams of her grandmother…the uniforms of the officers and the men from the ambulance. Sasha had felt as if she was in an odd bubble lingering all around the insanity but not quite inside it.

"Chief, parts of that night are a complete blur. I was in shock. Traumatized. If I was talking, I'm sure I said something about what I heard. The problem is, I can't actually remember speaking. If my grandmother was here…"

But she wasn't. Viola Simmons was gone. And with her, any information she had possessed about that horrendous night.

After so many years, how could Sasha hope to ever really know the truth? So many who might have known more were either dead or in bad health or simply no longer remembered.

Brannigan nodded, his expression filled with concern. "I've known Luther and Burt my whole life. They're both good men and neither would purposely misdirect a case. I would trust either one with my life. That said, one of them is wrong. Is there anyone else who would have been close enough to you and your family to know the details of that night?"

There was only one person. "Arlene Holloway. My grandmother and she were best friends. She might be able to help."

"I'll drop in on Mrs. Holloway. Thank you for coming by, Ms. Lenoir. Whatever you believe, I want to get to the bottom of this the same as you do."

"Thank you, Chief. That means a great deal to me."

As Sasha left the building, she noticed Leandra Brennan at the security desk in the lobby. The older woman spotted Sasha at about the same time and their gazes locked. Sasha held her gaze until her mother's old friend Lenny looked away. What kind of friend withheld potential information that might be able to cast new light on an old tragedy?

"The chief's office is directly that way, ma'am."

Sasha turned, walking backward and watching the Brennan woman as she strode toward the chief's office. Funny, there was no statement in the case file from her mother's best friend. Sasha wasn't a cop or a private investigator, but she could not see how that was right under any circumstances. Anyone close to her parents should have been interviewed. It simply didn't make sense. Brennan had insisted that she was out of town and nothing she knew was relevant, and apparently Chief Holcomb had taken her at her word.

A huge mistake, in Sasha's opinion. The woman was definitely hiding something.

Outside, she stood on the sidewalk and stared at the fading afternoon sun. She had been back in Winchester since Thursday evening—mere hours after she received the call about her grandmother. Friday Rey had taken care of all the funeral arrangements and Sasha had gone through photo albums and boxes of her grandmother's stored treasures. It wasn't until sometime Saturday that the reality sunk in. Her grandmother was dead.

Sasha climbed into her rental and drove the short distance to the cemetery. She hadn't been back there since the burial on Sunday. Right now she just needed to go back. To be near her grandmother.

She drove to the section of the cemetery where the family plot was and parked. The breeze kicked up and she shivered. Growing up, she'd never liked cemeteries. She would never forget watching her parents' caskets lowered into the cold ground.

A part of her had vanished that day. She hadn't seen that little girl since.

She walked over to the family plot, which was quite large. Simmonses had been buried here for several generations. Sasha sat down on the bench her grandmother had had installed near her parents' graves. The double headstone sat right next to the double one for her grandparents.

There was still enough space in the plot right next to her parents' for another double headstone. Would she need a double? She hadn't even come close to the altar or even moving in with a significant other.

It was just she and Brianne.

Sasha studied the date on the headstone that belonged to her parents. She suspected that her grandmother had only buried them next to each other for Sasha's benefit. Looking back, what mother who actually believed a man had killed her daughter would want him buried in the family plot for any reason—even to appease her nine-year-old granddaughter?

Had Viola really believed the official conclusions?

So many aspects of the tragedy were contradictory. So many pieces didn't properly fit into place.

But was she looking for a reason to believe her father was innocent? Had someone else been doing the same thing when they broke into her house and left that note?

Now she was really grasping at straws. She reminded herself that Branch Holloway and Billy Brannigan would not be poking around in the case unless they suspected something was amiss.

Several headstones away, she noted a blonde woman wearing a dark sweater. Arms hugged tightly around her slim body, she stood staring down at a wide granite marker. Sasha watched her for a moment, sensing she should recognize her. The breeze pushed the hair back from her cheek and Sasha realized who she was. Rowan DuPont, the undertaker's daughter. She'd buried her father in this cemetery barely a week ago. Like Sasha, she was alone now—except Sasha had her daughter. But the last of her ancestors were gone. Somehow the realization made the loss all the more difficult.

She checked her cell. Nothing from Branch yet. She should go back to the house and look around some more. The memories had really been coming inside that old house, and as difficult as it was to be there, this—*venture*—was about revisiting the past. More often than not the truth was not comfortable.

Discomfort she was prepared for.

Sasha called her daughter as she walked back to her car. There were more questions about Branch and more teasing. Deep down it pleased Sasha that her daughter thought he was good-looking. She'd had a great day at school and only had one more test this week. She could leave for Winchester tomorrow afternoon and spend the rest of the week. Sasha managed to talk her out of that one. She promised to text good-night.

When the call ended Sasha was halfway across town before she remembered to text Branch with her change of plans. She had promised to keep him informed of her whereabouts. Not that she was opposed to doing so; she'd simply forgotten. After her late-night visitor, he was right about keeping in touch. When she made the turn onto the long narrow driveway, she braked long enough to send the text. Then she rolled the quarter of a mile to her childhood home.

This late in the afternoon it was almost dark on the porch. Sasha unlocked the front door and flipped on a light. She'd spent a lot of time in her mother's office when she was here before. No need to pilfer around in there today.

She climbed the stairs, turning on lights, watching the dust motes float through the air. Bypassing her own room, she walked into her parents' room. This time, rather than look through drawers, she went to the closet and started digging through pockets and bags. Her mother had owned a dozen or more handbags. Sasha fished through each one and found nothing. She ran her hands into each pocket on each pair of pants and blouse or dress. Not one thing. Not a scrap of paper, a business card or even a piece of lint.

Viola had taken most all her daughter's jewelry, except the pearls, to her house and put it away for Sasha, so there was nothing in the jewelry box. That left only one unexplored space—the bathroom. Of course, the original investigation had checked for drugs and anything that might be considered contraband.

Sasha checked each item in the bathroom. Every bottle of makeup, stick of deodorant and jar of liquid soap. There was nothing that should not be there. Nothing unexpected. She turned toward the door, her gaze landing on the tissue box on the back of the toilet. No point leaving a single stone unturned.

She picked up the box and pulled out tissue after tissue, allowing them to fall onto the closed toilet seat. Obviously she was losing it. Rolling her eyes, she started to put the box back and then she noticed the blue on the white tissues. Sasha picked up the one on top.

Major structural flaws.

She dragged another from the box. It, too, was marred with blue ink.

Material will be stressed beyond its strength.

Then another. *Monumental failure at some point in the future.*

And the next. *Don't know what to do.*

Sasha's heart was thundering by the time she reached the last tissue in the box.

Can't tell Brandon.

She wasn't sure what this meant but it had to be important. Why else would her mother hide the notes in the bathroom tissue box?

Sasha could imagine her mother sitting alone in this bathroom, worried and afraid, and making notes to herself...or to anyone who might find them.

Cold seeped into Sasha's bones. The idea of her mother being afraid twisted her heart.

She pulled her cell from her pocket and checked her screen. Why hadn't Branch responded to her text?

A red exclamation answered the question. Message failed to send.

A scan of the top of the screen explained why. No service.

She hit Try Again with the same result.

"Well, damn." Maybe the service would be better outside. She shoved the tissues back into the box and stowed it under her arm.

The house was utterly silent. No humming refrigerator sound. No soft purr of the heating or cooling systems. No ticking clock. So when a creak splintered the air Sasha froze in her tracks.

There was no gun in the house. No weapons that she was aware of... Maybe a knife in the kitchen.

But she wasn't in the kitchen.

Then she remembered the security system. She rushed to her father's side of the bed and dragged the baseball bat from under the skirt.

Her heart pounding, Sasha placed the box of tissues on the nightstand and gripped the bat with both hands. Moving slowly in hopes of not hitting a squeaky spot in the floor, she eased out of her parents' room. She made it to the hall without a sound. Downstairs the intruder wasn't so careful. He had just entered the kitchen.

Could it be the same guy from last night?

She was halfway down the staircase when the tread beneath her right foot creaked.

Sasha froze.

Silence seemed to explode all around her and yet there was utter stillness, utter quiet. It was the blood roaring through her veins that sounded like an explosion.

The crash of the back door banking off the siding

jolted her into motion once more. Sasha ran for the kitchen. As she reached the door that stood wide open, she spotted a male in dark clothes and a dark cap disappearing into the woods.

She hesitated for only a moment. Long enough to hit Try Again and then to send Branch another text.

Intruder!

Sasha shoved her phone into her pocket and ran for the woods, the bat held at the ready. "Stop!" she shouted.

When she reached the woods she scanned the trees, caught a glimpse of a dark shape fading into the shadows.

She hurried in that direction. "Hey! What do you want?"

Her voice reverberated around her, bouncing off the trees.

She ran until she stopped seeing glimpses of the fleeing man. Then she skidded to a stop.

Her breath heaving in and out of her lungs, she surveyed the gloom. Nothing. And it was so damned quiet. Frustrated and feeling completely ridiculous, she started to turn around. Branch would be furious when he found out what she'd done. She'd run toward the trouble rather than away.

Not smart, Sasha. Even if she did have her father's baseball bat.

The corner of something rustic and out of place captured her attention.

Wood and metal.

The shack. Sasha cut through the dense underbrush, following a now hidden path that she knew by heart.

Her jaw dropped as she stared at the dilapidated

structure. The shack was maybe eight feet by ten and perhaps seven feet tall. Her father had told her it was at least a hundred years old when she was a little girl.

This had been her playhouse by the time she was seven years old and knew how to sneak through the woods without her mother or her grandmother knowing she'd disappeared. She had come here nearly every day.

She reached for the old door. It wasn't a real door. Just a bunch of boards nailed together and hung on hinges. The wood was rotting around the edges of the door and the hinges squeaked when she pulled it open. Wood banged against wood as the door plopped against the exterior of the shack.

Inside she blinked to hasten the adjustment of her eyes. There were cobwebs and dust. Lots of dust like in the house.

Against the far wall was a blanket. A discarded soft-drink can and a bit of other food trash. Had someone been staying here?

No, wait. The layer of dust on everything suggested no one had been here in a very long time.

Sasha stepped into the small space and picked up a potato chip bag. She searched until she found the expiration date: one year after her parents died.

Whoever had been staying in here could very well have been here when her parents were murdered.

Why had no one checked this shack?

The more she learned about the investigation the more convinced she became that the chief of police at the time had not wanted to unravel the facts. Suddenly aware that she was contaminating a potential crime scene, she eased out of the shack. Bat gripped firmly in her hands, she surveyed the woods around her. Clear.

She headed back toward the house. She'd just passed the tree line when a hand snagged her arm.

Sasha tried to swing the bat, but he held her tight. Her scream rent the air.

Chapter Twelve

Branch.

It was only Branch.

Sasha dragged in a breath, tried to calm her racing heart.

"What the hell happened?" He glanced around the overgrown yard. "There was an intruder? *Here?*"

She had made it back to the yard. Branch had obviously just arrived and spotted her barreling out of the woods. The other man—person—was gone. "There was someone in the house with me. When he heard me he ran. I…" She moistened her lips, braced for his disapproval. "I followed him into the woods, but I lost him near the shack."

Branch visibly restrained his frustration. She watched the struggle play out on his face. "Did you get a look at his face?"

She shook her head. "He wore dark clothes and a skullcap."

"How tall was he?"

"Average." She shrugged. "Medium build, maybe a little on the thin side."

Her knees were slightly weak now with the receding adrenaline. She steadied herself and braced for whatever he had to say next. No doubt a lecture on common sense or something along those lines.

He looked away for a moment, his hands planted on his hips. She had a feeling he had planted them there to prevent shaking her. Now that she thought about it, maybe she needed to be shaken. She had come here—to this desolate place—alone. After last night she should have known better.

She hadn't been thinking. Sasha was accustomed to being strong and fearless. This sort of uncertainty was not the norm for her.

"What's this about a shack?"

So maybe she was going to skate through this without a raking over the coals from Branch. "When I was a kid I played there. My father said the shack was really old, like a century old or more. It looks as if someone was staying in there."

He frowned. "In the shack?"

She shook her head, then nodded. She wasn't making sense. "Not today, but back when the murders happened. Come this way—I'll show you."

He hesitated at first but then he relented and started forward with her.

"Point the way," he said, "and stay behind me."

"Yes, sir." She gave him a little salute. He shot her a look that said he was not playing.

Sasha guided him back to the shack with only one wrong turn. When she'd stumbled upon it a little while ago she'd been chasing the intruder and she hadn't been thinking. It had been twenty-seven years since she'd visited this shack.

She spotted a flash of rusty metal roof to their left. "There it is."

They moved through the overgrowth of saplings and

brush until they were standing beside it. The squatty primitive structure looked smaller with Branch looming nearby.

"Did you go inside?" he asked.

"Yes. For a moment."

He pulled the door open and used his cell as a flashlight to illuminate the interior. It was darker now, the setting sun withdrawing its feeble reach through the dense trees.

There was the blanket she'd seen and the food refuse.

"The chip bag shows an expiration date the year of my parents' deaths." She pointed to the bag, now wishing she hadn't walked inside. "It's possible someone was staying here when my parents were murdered. There could be prints or other evidence."

Branch leaned inside, surveyed the space more closely with the aid of the flashlight app. "The dust on the floor looks undisturbed before today."

Yes, she had made a mistake. "Whatever's in here could still be useful, though, right?"

Her desperation was showing. No one hated that kind of slip more than her.

"It could. Absolutely." He withdrew his upper body from the shack and put through a call on his cell. "Hey, Billy, we have a new development over at the Lenoir property."

While Branch explained recent events to the chief of police, Sasha surveyed the woods, hoping she might spot the man who had sneaked into the house. He had to have seen her car parked in front of it. If he knew she was there, why try sneaking in? Had he hoped to get a drop on her? He hadn't appeared to be armed—or even after her, for that matter. He'd run away. Was he only watching her? Or was he like her, searching for something that would lead to the truth?

"I wasn't able to talk to that shrink," Branch said, drawing her attention back to him. He propped one shoulder against the side of the shack to wait. "He apparently doesn't operate by his posted business hours."

"Brannigan couldn't reach him either."

There was something else she'd forgotten: to brief him on her meeting with Brannigan. They would have gotten around to it eventually, she felt confident. At his prompting, she explained the differing statements from Holcomb and Johnston as well as the idea that Brannigan seemed intent on getting to the bottom of the discrepancy.

"Unfortunately my memory of events after I came out of the closet that night is not reliable." She chewed at her lip and considered whether there was more she should be telling him. "And I saw Leandra Brennan going to the chief's office as I was leaving."

"Burt told me the same thing about that night," Branch said. "He feels Luther closed the case too quickly. Burt wasn't happy with the limited search around the property or the fact that Luther blew off your assertions. But then, Burt is the coroner. He's not a detective. Still, I agree with him. This—" he hitched his head toward the shack "—is a perfect example of why a more thorough and expansive search should have taken place that night. Nothing may come of this, but it should have been done back then."

Sasha didn't remember Luther Holcomb well enough to reach any sort of conclusion on this news, so she asked, "Is there any chance Holcomb was part of the cover-up?"

Branch's lips formed a grim line for a long moment

before he spoke. "I don't think so. There have never been any rumors about his work or about him. He had a stellar reputation when he was chief and no one has suggested otherwise. Course, I was gone for a lot of years. I'll talk to Billy and see what he thinks. Billy worked with him until he retired four years ago. If we have reason to be concerned about his actions in the investigation, Billy will know."

Sasha felt suddenly immensely tired.

For twenty-seven years she had been waiting for the truth about what happened to her parents. She had put off pushing for that truth as long as her grandmother was alive because it was too painful for her. She had told Sasha this only once when, at sixteen, Sasha had demanded she hire a private investigator. When Viola had tearfully begged for Sasha to put that part of the past behind her once and for all, she'd had no choice. She could not bear to hurt her grandmother.

Now she understood a little of what her grandmother did not want to face. It was overwhelming and frustrating and painful all at the same time. Those in law enforcement—like Branch—trying to help were so incredibly important to the probability of success. Now the chief of police and the coroner were involved. It was finally, really happening, and Sasha was drowning in all those overpowering emotions.

"We should walk back to the house," Branch offered. "Or Billy's officers will be swarming the woods after us."

Over the next hour Brannigan arrived and was escorted to the shack by Branch, and then the forensics unit was called. The part that made the chief of police so happy was the fact that the intruder hadn't appeared to be wearing any gloves. Until he asked, Sasha hadn't considered whether the man had or not, but when her mind replayed him running away, his hands were bare.

Maybe this was the break they needed.

EVENING HAD GIVEN way to night and it was well after dark when Branch insisted on driving her home.

"There's nothing else we can do here," he told her.

He was right, except a part of her wanted to stay as long as there was still activity going on, but she relented. "There's something in the house I need to grab first."

Branch followed her to the back door. She retrieved the box of tissues and declared she was ready to go. Branch didn't question the move. During the drive she thought of the things her mother had written on the tissues. Had she been brainstorming? Trying to work out a path to take some sort of action? Had she hoped that someone would find her notes?

How could they possibly?

By the time they reached Branch's house, Sasha felt agitated. Had her mother been in some sort of trouble? Who had known? Why hadn't someone helped her? Was this why the woman who had been her best friend pretended she knew nothing? Had she abandoned Sasha's mother when she needed her most? What had her father known? Was this situation related to his work at a major construction company?

Sasha closed her eyes for a moment. How in the world could she possibly find the answers after all these years?

"You okay?"

She opened her eyes and turned to Branch. They were parked in his driveway and he sat behind the wheel watching her.

"I'm not sure." She stared forward. "I'm really not sure at all."

"Let's go inside, have a bite to eat and tackle this one piece at a time. I think you're feeling inundated because of all the questions and all the possibilities."

He was right. She nodded. "Okay."

On the porch, she held tight to her box of tissues while Branch unlocked his front door. He flipped on the lights and inhaled deeply. "You smell that?"

Sasha stepped inside and took a deep breath. "I do. Smells like roast and fresh-baked bread."

He shoved the door closed, gave the lock a twist. "My grandmother has been here. She was afraid I wouldn't feed you right."

Sasha had to smile. "Well, it smells heavenly."

They followed the aroma into the kitchen. Arlene had left a note on the island.

Dinner is in the oven. Make sure she eats.

Sasha laughed out loud then. "I think we can make that happen."

"I'll get a couple of beers," Branch offered.

"I'll check the oven." Sasha left her bag and her box of tissues on a chair.

Branch had a nice house. It wasn't a new build but it was recently renovated. His kitchen was particularly stylish with modern appliances. The casserole dish in the oven was covered in aluminum foil. Sasha settled it on the stovetop and removed the foil. Potatoes and carrots and a roast. Looked as good as it smelled. On the counter was a basket filled with freshly made rolls.

Two bottles of beer landed on the counter then and Branch grabbed bowls and spoons. They filled their bowls and settled around the island. The roast tasted just as amazing as it smelled. The rolls melted on the tongue and the beer was the perfect contrast to all the smooth, rich tastes and textures.

When Sasha couldn't eat another bite, she pushed her bowl away. "Your grandmother is an amazing cook."

"She is." Branch pushed his bowl away, too. "She spoils me."

"I suspect this is something else you'll miss if you move to Nashville."

He nodded. "No doubt. Course, there's always Sundays. My grandmother feeds everyone on Sundays. The whole Holloway crew."

Sasha needed to start traditions like that. She and her daughter only had a couple. Traditions, even small ones, were important to future bonding. One day her daughter would be all grown up and have a family of her own. The thought terrified Sasha. She glanced at Branch, who was putting their bowls into the dishwasher.

This was another past wrong that Sasha had to make right. Soon. Very soon.

"I asked Billy if he could share any information about his interview with Leandra Brennan. He couldn't."

Sasha paused in her work covering the leftover roast. "But he did call her into his office about the investigation."

Branch nodded. "He also called her a hostile witness, so she didn't come in voluntarily."

Sasha shook her head. "I just want to know the story there. Arlene has no idea?"

"I asked her if she remembered any issues and she didn't. She says your mom and Brennan weren't really that close."

Surprised, Sasha started to question him further but she suddenly remembered the box of tissues. "There's something I need to show you."

She retrieved the box of tissues and went back to the island. Claiming a stool, she placed the box on the counter.

"I think we might need another beer," he said with a curious glance at the box.

"Good idea."

He grabbed two bottles from the fridge and joined her at the island.

"I searched everything in my parents' bedroom. As I was finishing up, I realized this was the one place I hadn't looked." She tapped the box. "So I pulled the tissues out, thinking something might be hidden inside—I guess I've watched too many movies. At any rate, this is what I found."

She spread the tissues with blue ink across the counter.

Major structural flaws.

Material will be stressed beyond its strength.

Monumental failure at some point in the future.

Don't know what to do.

Sasha's heart started that painful squeezing again when she read the last one.

Can't tell Brandon.

"You're certain this is your mother's handwriting?"

Sasha nodded. "Positive."

"Then it looks like we have ourselves a starting place."

Sasha met his gaze. "You think the murders were related to one or the other's work?"

"I was leaning in that direction already, but this makes it pretty clear." He searched her gaze. "Your mother was responsible for approving plans and architectural drawings for every building that was constructed in this county for as long as she held the position. Any issues with the plans would have been flagged by her office. These—" he tapped the counter near the tissues "—are the sorts of issues developers don't want to hear about."

"Are you saying someone could have wanted to stop her from doing her job?"

He nodded. "That's exactly what I'm saying."

Sasha put a hand over her mouth so he wouldn't see her lips trembling.

"I'm sorry. I didn't mean that to sound so callous."

"No." She put her hand over his, almost jumped at the soft zing that sparked between them. "You've been nothing but helpful and a great friend. I couldn't have done this without you, Branch."

With his free hand he reached up and stroked her cheek with the tips of his fingers. Warmth spread through her. "I'm grateful for the opportunity to do the right thing." He let his hand fall away but didn't draw from her touch. "I shouldn't have left the way I did."

She frowned, not understanding what he meant. Then she realized he was talking about the morning after their one-night stand. She held her hands up, withdrawing contact. "We were young. It was…"

"Thoughtless," he argued. "I had to be back in Chicago but I should have delayed my flight and at least spent some time with you."

If either of them had anything to be sorry for, it was her, but she couldn't bring herself to confess. She just couldn't go there right now. She needed his help. How selfish was that?

"You didn't do anything wrong, Branch."

He gave her a nod. "We can agree to disagree. For now, let's start a list of possible suspects."

She blinked. Okay, so they were back on the case now. Good. "You go first."

"Leandra Brennan."

Sasha was surprised. "Really?"

He gave an affirming nod. "She still works for the same developer. One of the largest, most powerful ones in the Southeast."

"Okay."

He came up with paper and a pen and they started their list.

She liked being shoulder to shoulder with him as they jotted down the names. She liked his smile and the sound of his voice.

She liked everything about him, actually.

Her daughter was right. He was hot.

Slow it down, Sash.

Right now she could without question say that Branch was a really good friend. Whatever happened after this, it had to be a slow build toward total honesty…and hopefully forgiveness.

She would need his when he had the whole truth.

Chapter Thirteen

Wednesday, March 27

Branch had just poured the coffee when Sasha appeared in the kitchen. He'd had a hard time sleeping last night, as much because she was sleeping in his bed as because of the case.

"Morning." He set a mug of steaming brew on the counter in front of her. "I hope you slept well." Toast popped up in the toaster.

"I did." She picked up the mug, cradled it in both hands. "Actually, I slept better than I have since I arrived." She sipped her coffee.

"I'm glad." He turned his own cup up to prevent saying more. He hoped she felt safe in his home...in his *bed*. He wanted her to feel safe with him. "I thought we could talk about the list over some toast."

They hadn't gotten very far on their list last night. *Brennan* was the only name scribbled there so far. He'd been toying with a few others. He'd already put in a call to Billy about pulling records to find out what planned developments Sasha's mother had been working on the final year of her life. There would hopefully be notes in the records if any of the developers or builders had given her any trouble or if any issues had cropped up with the properties during construction or later on.

"Toast would be perfect."

He slathered butter on both pieces, placed each on a small plate and offered one to her. "Jelly?"

"No, thanks." She nibbled a bite. "Perfect."

He devoured his in a few bites, washed it down with coffee.

"I've been thinking about Leandra Brennan." Sasha dabbed her lips with a napkin. "I sent a text to Rey—you know Audrey Anderson at the newspaper."

He nodded. "I know her, yes." Audrey Anderson had been accidentally instrumental in the resuscitation of his wounded career. The remains buried in the basement of her newspaper had set off shock waves from here to Chicago. Not to mention, a highly sought after federal witness had been hiding amid the Mennonite community in Franklin County and Audrey had helped shake him loose.

"I realized that Brennan is about the same age my mother would be if she were still alive," Sasha explained, "so I asked Rey to check her extensive resources to see if the two attended school together. Well, you know Rey—thorough is her middle name. She sent me a very long text this morning. The two went to school together from kindergarten through high school graduation. They were accepted into the same college from which they both graduated, and they were married the same summer—they were each other's maid and matron of honor."

Branch had never been married or even engaged, but even he understood the maid and matron of honor thing was a big deal. "So they were *really* close."

Sasha nodded. "*Really* close. The big difference was

children. Mother and Daddy had me a few years after they were married. Brennan didn't have her first child until the year my parents were murdered. She had a son that fall and then another one two years later. The thing is, I couldn't understand why I didn't really remember her. You would think friends that close would have done more than have the occasional lunch together. I would expect shopping sprees, picnics and barbecues, and maybe even family vacations, but I don't recall anything like that involving Brennan."

"You should ask Arlene," Branch offered. "Maybe there's more to the story that she didn't mention."

"There has to be. It's too strange." She picked up her mug again. "I mentioned to Rey that the murders might have been related to trouble with one or both of my parents' workplaces, so she did a little digging there, too." Sasha touched the screen of her phone, forcing it to light up. "On my mother's side there were several small issues with zoning and site developments, as well as architectural review setbacks, but only a few were noteworthy. The big-box store that opened on the boulevard was one. The drama played out in the courtroom before an agreement was reached. The extension at the auto manufacturer facility created a little commotion in the community. There was some question as to whether the adjoining property was properly zoned. But it was the William Richards Stadium that generated the most buzz. Apparently my mother was embroiled in a major battle over design issues that failed to meet code. According to Rey, it got really ugly in the media and in the city meetings."

"That was the year before, though, right?" Branch remembered his father commenting that the stadium might not happen because of some sort of design flaws.

"It was."

Branch added the stadium to their list. "We can get the developers' names for both the stadium and the big-box store. Anything on your dad's side?"

"There was some issue with the hospital." She shrugged. "The construction company he worked for was contracted to complete some part of the project and then midway into the project they pulled out. Rey said her father did an editorial piece on the disagreement but otherwise there was no mention of the trouble in the papers. Whatever happened, it was settled fairly quietly."

"The hospital would be a Packard project. Brennan works for Packard." Now, there was an interesting connection. "I almost hate to say it out loud, but I can see Packard being involved with murder." Branch surprised himself with the announcement. Maybe it was because his father despised the man, Jarvis Packard. Whatever the case, Branch couldn't help seeing him as a scumbag—a rich one, but a scumbag nonetheless.

"Beyond the connection with Brennan, why would you feel so strongly about Packard? Is there something else I should know?"

"Something my father said on several occasions when I was a kid." He should ask him about it. "He said a man was only as good as his word and Jarvis Packard's word was as worthless as sand in the desert."

Sasha nodded. "That's fairly worthless."

Branch laughed. "In my father's opinion, anyway."

Their gazes caught and for a long moment they looked at each other. It was one of those moments when you didn't know whether to speak or to act. Either one seemed like a risk to what came next, and yet the urge to do the latter was nearly overwhelming. Branch went with the former.

"This is not the time, I get that, but I want to kiss you more than I've wanted to do anything in a very long time."

For another endless second she only stared at him. Then she smiled. "I'm having trouble with that, too. I'm sure we shouldn't—"

Before she could say more, he leaned across the counter and kissed her. She tasted of coffee and felt like silk. He hesitated, their lips still touching, and when she didn't pull away he deepened the kiss. He wanted to walk around this damned island and pull her into his arms. He wanted to carry her to his bed and make love to her. He wanted to do it the right way this time.

A cell rattled against the counter with a lively tune and Sasha drew away. "That's my daughter. I have to take this."

She rushed away, but not before Branch saw her touch her lips and draw in a sharp breath. He wondered if her lips were on fire the way his were or if her heart was pounding as his was. He should have gone after her all those years ago. He'd never wanted anyone the way he did Sasha and he'd kept it to himself all this time. For no other reason than so he could focus on his career, and just maybe there had been a little fear involved.

His dad and his grandmother had warned him often that there were more important things in life than one's career. He'd had to learn that the hard way.

When he'd shaken off the lingering lust, he made a call to Billy and brought him up to speed on what he and Sasha were thinking.

"I can do some checking. See if Packard has had any issues since then. Any lawsuits or code violations. You know," the chief of police pointed out, "it's always easy to finger the bully—the one everybody expects to be bad. But it's not always the bully who does the bad stuff."

Branch shut off the coffee maker and rinsed the carafe as the man spoke. "You've been here all these years and I've been out of the picture until recently. If we're putting the number one pushy developer aside for the moment, who's your runner-up?"

"Keegan and Roark, they built the stadium. They wanted in on the hospital deal—according to my daddy. They intended to make a huge donation and have a wing named after them, but Packard wouldn't have it. He didn't want their money. Some long-ago bad blood, the way I hear it."

Branch had a funny feeling Billy was feeding him all this information for a reason. "Not that I don't appreciate the heads-up," he confessed, "but I have to say, I'm surprised you're sharing all this with me, Chief. Is there something I should be reading between the lines?"

A few seconds of silence elapsed. "This is all speculation, Branch. I don't have a speck of evidence. I can't exactly investigate a problem that doesn't exist. As you well know, that's not the way it works in law enforcement. Someone has to break the law before I can investigate. On the other hand, a guy working off-the-record—on vacation, let's say—can poke around to his heart's desire as long as he doesn't break any laws."

Someone had warned Billy to back off.

"I guess there are folks who don't like to see the city waste resources on a cold case."

"Especially when the fingerprints found in a certain shack lead to a man who went missing twenty-seven years ago and eventually ended up as a long-term resident in a psychiatric facility."

Branch's instincts perked up. Oh, he remembered the case. "Are we talking about Packard's son Devlin?"

"Bingo."

That was one case Branch doubted anyone would forget. Devlin Packard had come home on spring break the same year Sasha's parents died. Before the week's end, he had abruptly disappeared. Months later, when he was found, the guy was strung out on drugs. The word was he never recovered. "Devlin would be what? About forty-seven or -eight now? The last I heard, he was still in an assisted living facility of some sort."

"He was, until he walked out about three days ago. No one has seen him since."

Tension coiled inside Branch. "Was he the one staying in the shack when the Lenoirs were murdered?"

"He's been in there at some point in the past and I'm guessing he was the one in the Lenoir house when Sasha was there. Maybe even in the Simmons house the other night. The timing would fit."

"Is he dangerous?" Worry gnawed at Branch's gut.

"No violent tendencies. Always the ideal patient. Then he just ups and walks out. His daddy has a whole posse of his security minions out looking for him."

Sasha walked back into the kitchen. Branch would have to find a way to convince her to stay close, particularly after this news.

Good luck with that.

"Anything else?" Branch asked. Sasha had her handbag. Obviously she was ready to go. The second intruder had done little to deter her. But then, he couldn't blame her. She had waited a long time for the truth.

"That's it for now. Watch your step, Branch. Something is wrong with this case and I can't quite put my finger on it. I had no idea so much had been swept under the rug. By the way, thanks for the heads-up on Leandra Brennan. She didn't have much to say but she knows plenty. I'll be watching her. I'm hoping when she realizes I'm not pushing this case back into a drawer, she'll come around."

"I'll touch base with you later today." Branch severed the connection and settled his full attention on Sasha. "We may have an ID on the intruder."

"That's great."

He briefed her on the latest from Brannigan. The news only seemed to create more questions rather than provide answers. Branch was feeling the same rising tension.

One step forward, two steps back.

"Why would Packard's son have been staying in the shack?"

Branch mentally ran through a couple of scenarios. "It's possible he was involved with a drug dealer on that side of town and happened upon the shack by accident. It was empty, so he made himself a home. I remember my parents talking about his disappearance. The rumor was he had some kind of breakdown."

"But you said he had shown no violent tendencies, so it's not likely that he committed the murders."

"There's always a first time," Branch countered. "The truth is, if he went over the edge in some sort of psychotic break, he may have done some very violent things and have no recall of the events. This would explain why Packard has kept him locked away all this time."

Even as Branch said the words, he thought of Billy's suggestion that the bad guy was not always the obvious bully. But maybe this time the glaringly obvious bully was the bad guy. Sometimes bad guys liked hiding in plain sight. The boldness of the move gave them a sense of power.

Sasha squared her shoulders. "I intend to track down Dr. Farr today. I want to know why he concluded that I made up the voices. I want to know what else he said in his report. In fact, I believe I have the right to demand a copy of his report."

Branch thought of her daughter and realized that Sasha was the only family the girl had left since her dad was not in the picture. "I'm not sure you going off on your own is such a good idea, Sasha. Your daughter is counting on you to come back home when this is over. Any risk you take is a risk to her."

Sasha held up her hands. "I'm a good mother, Branch. I always consider my daughter's needs first." When he would have tried to explain himself, she added, "I am perfectly capable of driving across town to Dr. Farr's office on my own. I've done pretty well so far."

The woman lived in a major metropolitan area. She was accustomed to taking care of herself in far more risky environments than this one simply due to the nature of her work. She obviously knew how to handle herself. But they were just getting started with this case and a media-binging pop star with a bad attitude was vastly different from a cold-blooded killer. Things could escalate quickly.

"I let you talk me into going our separate ways yesterday and you got into a dicey situation," he reminded her. "I don't think we should go down that same path again today. And for the record, I'm certain you're a fantastic mother and very capable."

"Okay." Sasha exhaled a big breath. "Let's compromise. I'll track down the shrink while you do whatever it is you need to do, and then we'll meet up to see what we have." Before he could utter his protest, she urged, "I will go only to the man's office and to the hospital looking for him. Nowhere else."

"No going back to your old home place or to your grandmother's house without me. Basically no going anywhere you might end up alone and cornered."

"You have my word."

He nodded. "All right, but I want to hear from you every half hour."

She rolled her eyes. "Fine. And what about you? What will you be doing?"

"I'm going to the office where your mother worked and see how difficult it's going to be to get into their archives. Most of the files are public record, so we'll see."

"You think it was Packard, don't you?"

The lady was far too perceptive.

"I think Packard probably has more motive than anyone else simply because of the sheer number of projects he was and is involved with."

"Whoever was responsible," she said, her voice overly quiet, "he had something to hide. Something my mother knew about. But there haven't been any epic fails of structures or roads or anything like that, which seems to negate the entire idea."

"Maybe he's gotten lucky until now. The trouble might be just around the corner or coming in the next decade. But we know there was something. Something big enough to kill for. And if he killed once to keep his secret, he won't hesitate to kill again."

She was backing away from him before he could talk himself out of allowing her out of his sight. "We'll catch up as soon as I've spoken to Dr. Farr."

Branch grabbed his keys and his hat. "I'll follow up with Brennan while I'm at it."

She glanced at him, clearly surprised by that move.

"Now that the chief of police has rattled that cage," he explained, "I'm hoping she'll be a little more cooperative."

Billy's hands had been tied to some degree. Branch didn't have that trouble.

"She has the answers we need," Sasha insisted. "I'm certain of it."

One way or another Branch intended to find out.

Chapter Fourteen

Sasha met Rey at the diner for an early lunch. The toast she'd had with Branch was long gone. A Cobb salad was just the ticket. She decided to forego the dressing and just enjoy the rich ingredients and a glass of sweet iced tea with lemon in honor of her grandmother. Viola Simmons had loved sweet tea.

"I did some additional research on Devlin," Rey said. She stabbed a forkful of her greens. "He's a resident at Mountain View, a private resort-like facility in Sewanee. No hardship there, I can tell you. I did a piece on the services they provide. Only the very best. I'm surprised he walked out of such a posh environment. Mountain View is known for top-notch patient care."

"Do you know his diagnosis?" Rey was good at ferreting out information. However, Sasha wasn't sure if what she was asking with that question was something she could learn without doing so via some illegal avenue. There were some things even the best investigative reporter couldn't uncover. The HIPAA Law was generally a brick wall when it came to protecting the privacy rights of patients.

"A distant cousin who visits him occasionally tells me it's schizophrenia and drug addiction. He can't stay on the prescribed meds and off the nonprescribed ones, so he can't stay healthy, thus the long-term residency. He long ago made the choice to become a permanent resident rather than deal with life outside those insulating walls."

"I guess he changed his mind since he walked out of the place a few days ago."

Rey added a packet of low-calorie sweetener to her tea and gave it a stir. "The family's not talking about his abrupt departure but I hear the father's security team is scouring the countryside for him. You think he's your intruder?"

Sasha nodded. "I do. I think he left the note and that he was the one staying in that old shack when my parents were murdered."

"Wow." Rey's eyes rounded. "That could potentially mean he witnessed what happened that night. It's possible that's what sent him over the edge. The timing is about right."

"Someone knows what happened. Leandra Brennan, Devlin Packard—someone knows." Sasha sighed. "I just have to persuade one of them to talk."

Rey studied her a moment. "How's it going with Branch? I've wanted to ask but…"

Sasha's grandmother and Rey were the only ones who knew who Brianne's father was. Both had sworn never to tell, though her grandmother had warned on numerous occasions that she felt Sasha was making a mistake.

Her grandmother had been a smart lady. Sasha *had* made a mistake.

"It's going well. He's a great guy and…" She shrugged. "I see every day that I'm here how I misjudged him. I should have listened to my grandmother."

"And me," Rey reminded her. "I always believed

Branch would have jumped in with both feet to help with his child."

Sasha shook her head. "I was just so young and I had so many plans. I didn't want to throw away my dreams for married life. I was on fire to make my mark."

"No one said you had to get married." Rey smiled. "Anyway, you certainly made your mark, my friend."

Sasha laughed, the sound weary. "I definitely have." She shook her head. "But you know how it was back then. Branch would have expected us to raise her together. His family would have expected the same, plus a marriage. Certainly my grandmother would have. I can see my shortsightedness now, but at the time I could only see the future I had planned and it wasn't here, Rey. You know that. We both wanted out of this town—the sooner the better."

Rey sank back into the booth. "You're right. After what happened between me and Colt, I couldn't imagine ever coming back, much less ending up with him again under any circumstances."

Sasha felt her lips curl into a real smile. "It's amazing is what it is. You two are great together. I'm glad you came back and ended up a couple again."

"The same could happen for you," Rey suggested.

"I'm afraid my situation is a bit more complicated with a daughter who already believes she owns the world. I can't bring myself to pull the rug from under her." Sasha shook her head. "I can't bear the idea of her hating me for the decision I made."

Rey reached across the table and squeezed Sasha's hand. "You'll know what to do when the time comes."

"Hope so."

Her forearms braced on the table, Rey leaned forward. "As for this investigation, when we figure out what your mom and dad had on Packard, we're going to take him down. I, for one, can't wait. He's always been an arrogant son of a gun."

"What if it's not him?"

"Then it'll be someone like him," Rey argued. "There are some people in this world to whom human life means nothing. To kill someone standing in the way of their ultimate goal is like swatting a fly. Whoever did this, we're going to ensure he pays."

"Branch said he planned to visit my mother's office—her former office—and dig around. Find out who was doing what that year."

"Branch is a smart man," Rey said. "I'm doing a little digging in that area myself. Between the two of us, if there was something going on, we'll find it."

"There were a lot of big projects during that time frame. The stadium, the hospital."

"That decade changed the face of this city," Rey agreed. "At least one of them created a lethal ripple. We just have to figure out which one."

She made it sound so easy.

Sasha checked the time. "I should go. I'm staking out Farr's office. I intend to catch him today. If he doesn't show I'm going to his home."

Rey grinned. "Let me know if you decide to go to the man's house. I've always wanted to see inside that lake mansion of his."

"You're on," Sasha assured her.

They paid their checks and parted ways on the sidewalk. Rey walked back to the newspaper office and Sasha climbed into her rental and headed for Farr's office. It was near the hospital, only a few short miles away from where she was. She made the necessary turns around the downtown square and then drove past the towering Packard building. The hospital was only a couple of miles beyond that iconic structure. Though the hospital was certainly not Packard's biggest development in terms of money, it was the most prestigious. Directly across the street from the hospital stood a row of boutique medical suites, one of which Farr used as an office. Sasha parked in the lot that flanked the cleverly decorated Victorian-style buildings.

To her surprise the entry door for the one on the west end was unlocked. An alarm chimed somewhere beyond the lobby as she walked inside. The interior was elegantly decorated and well-appointed. Four chairs and two Duncan Phyfe tables, along with a magazine rack, made up the tiny lobby. Distinguished-looking artwork adorned the walls. There were two doors, one to the left marked Restroom and one at the rear marked Dr. Bruce Farr. Evidently he did not have a receptionist or secretary. Sasha crossed the room and had just raised her hand to knock on the door carrying his name when it opened.

Dr. Bruce Farr blinked behind the thick lenses of his eyeglasses. "May I help you?"

"Dr. Farr?" She asked the question though she knew it was him. She had done a Google search. Though tall and distinguished in stature, his hair had grayed and thinned to near nonexistence. His skin was mottled, making him look even older in person.

"Yes, I am Dr. Farr, but I'm not taking new patients. I haven't taken new patients in nearly thirty years. I would be happy to recommend others in the area."

"You're retired, I know," Sasha said. "You serve on the board at the hospital and you continue to see a handful of longtime patients but otherwise you're retired."

His brow lined in heavy ruts. "What is it you want?"

"My name is Sasha Lenoir," she said, feeling immensely proud to inform him of this fact. "I'm here to discuss the evaluation you conducted when I was nine after my parents were murdered."

For several long seconds he stared at her. During most of those Sasha was convinced he would refuse to answer. But then he said, "I remember the case."

"Good. I have questions for you, Doctor."

Once more, he stared at her for an extended time. Just when she had decided he would say he didn't have time, he gestured to his office. "Very well. Please join me in my office. I don't have an appointment for a few minutes. I'll answer what I can until then."

He turned and walked deeper into his office, leaving the door open for her to follow. Sasha instinctively glanced over her shoulder before going inside.

"Close the door, please."

She did as he asked and then crossed the room to his desk. He indicated the lone chair waiting on her side of the desk and she sat. What remained of his once dark hair was completely gray. His eyes were a matching shade of pale gray, cold and unforgiving. She had clips of memory related to him, but none that were complete. Most were nothing more than pieces. Snippets of conversation. Him asking questions. Him staring unblinkingly at her.

"What would you like to know, Ms. Lenoir?"

"You concluded that I was making up the voices I heard the night my parents were murdered. I heard those voices, Dr. Farr. According to the county coroner, I spoke of them that very night and I told the chief of police about them a few days later. I know what I heard. Why would you insist they were my imagination at play?"

He held her gaze a long moment. "You were a very frightened and traumatized little girl. You cannot trust your memories from that painful time."

It wasn't necessary to be a shrink to know someone who had in part witnessed the murder of her parents would be traumatized and frightened. "Of course I was, but my memories are very solid from that night. You were wrong, Dr. Farr."

"You are entitled to your opinion, Ms. Lenoir, but my professional opinion hasn't changed. If you've come here to try to change my mind, I'm afraid you've wasted your time."

"Actually, it's irrelevant to me whether I change your mind, Dr. Farr. My question is, who paid you to conclude I was lying? I know it was someone with a large personal stake in the matter of whether or not my story held up in court. Perhaps Jarvis Packard or Seth Keegan. Maybe Hadden Roark."

For a moment he looked stunned, as if he couldn't believe she had voiced her accusations by listing names, or perhaps because she had hit the nail on the head, so to speak.

"You're grasping at straws, Sasha. May I call you Sasha?"

Now he was just patronizing her. "No, you may not." She laughed. "As for my grasping at straws, perhaps when my search for the truth began, that was true. Not anymore. Now I have proof."

The tiniest hint of uncertainty flared in his eyes before he could school the reaction. Oh, yes, he knew plenty about that night, just as she suspected Leandra Brennan did.

"I'm certain if you possessed proof of what you believe, you would be sitting in the chief of police's office rather than mine."

"Actually, Chief Brannigan believes me, too," she countered. "In fact, he has reopened the case. Additionally, Marshal Branch Holloway is looking into the case, as well. Everyone knows my parents were murdered. It's time for you to speak up while you still can. I feel confident there are options for a man in your position, Dr. Farr."

She was overstepping her bounds, she knew, but the words tumbled out.

"Maybe you're simply having trouble letting go of the past, Ms. Lenoir." Dr. Farr nodded as if privy to some knowledge she did not possess. "Your mother had a similar issue, which seems to be why she could not let go of the best friend who caused her husband to stray. Such self-destructive behavior." Farr stood. "I'm afraid that's all the time I have, Ms. Lenoir. I wish you the best of luck in your pursuit."

Scarcely restraining the fury smoldering inside her, Sasha removed a business card from her purse and placed it on the man's desk. "Call me—or Chief Brannigan, if you prefer—when you decide you want to tell the truth, Dr. Farr."

She walked out of the office and climbed into her rental. If she had ever been more angry and frustrated, she had no recall of the event. She drove around for a few minutes, considered going to visit Leandra Brennan again. Branch had said he was following up on her, so Sasha drove on. Besides, she didn't trust herself to speak to the woman right now. Not after what Farr said.

Was it possible the arrogant man was correct? Had her father cheated with her mother's best friend? This didn't make sense and yet it explained why she would keep her ongoing friendship with Brennan away from her family life. This was the reason Sasha didn't recall any outings with Brennan.

"What were you thinking, Mom?"

The idea that she'd forgotten to demand a copy of Farr's report barged to the front and center of her thoughts. Anger roared inside her again. Probably he would insist all records that old had been archived or destroyed. What difference did it make? Whatever he'd said in the report was lies anyway.

She circled the cemetery and then drove to her grandmother's house. She'd fully intended to drive on past but a car parked in the driveway had her turning in. She parked beside the vehicle and rested her attention on the older man standing at the front door of the house. He looked back at her, obviously startled.

Though she had promised Branch she wouldn't come here or go anywhere else she might get trapped alone... she wasn't alone. There was a man standing on the porch. Sasha opened the door and climbed out.

"May I help you?" Since she didn't recognize the man, he likely didn't recognize her.

"Sasha?"

So maybe he did recognize her. "Are you lost?" She closed the car door and started up the walk, taking her time.

He shook his head as she approached, whether in answer to her question or in hopes of making her stop, she couldn't be sure.

"You won't remember me." He adjusted his eyeglasses. "My name is Alfred Nelson. My friends and coworkers called me—"

"Al." Sasha remembered her mother referring to Al. They worked together in the city planning office.

He nodded. "We need to talk, Sasha."

"All right." He looked harmless enough. He was old and frail, his body stooped. There was no telltale bulge in the pockets of his khaki trousers, and that was about the only place he could possibly be concealing a weapon. "Let me unlock the door and we'll go inside."

She reached into her purse and fished for the key. The house was no longer a crime scene, so they could go inside. She unlocked and pushed the door inward, then invited the older man to follow her inside. The house was cool and dark. She flipped on lights as she went. She turned to offer coffee but he had hesitated in the entry hall. He stared at the framed photograph of Sasha with her parents. It was the last one done with her parents before their murder.

"You have to stop digging into the past." His gaze shifted from the photo to her. His look was not menacing. More tired and resigned than anything.

"Why would I do that, Al?" She moved slowly toward where he stood. "I want to know the truth. Do you know what really happened that night?"

"What you're doing..." He stared at the photo again. "What you're doing is dangerous and she would not want you to be in danger. She would have done anything to protect you."

"Who killed my parents, Al?" She stood toe to toe with him now, her gaze insistent on his. He knew something—maybe everything—and she needed to hear the whole truth.

"I tried to convince her to let it go, but she refused." His gaze settled on the photograph once more.

Sasha frowned. Had this man been more than a coworker to her mother? "Were you in love with my mother, Al?"

His gaze clashed with hers, his eyes growing wide behind his glasses. "I loved her, yes, but not like you think. She was like a daughter to me." A smile touched his lips. "She was so young when she first came to the office but she had big plans. She worked harder than anyone else, so no one was surprised when she received promotion after promotion."

"Did you know about her friendship with Leandra Brennan?"

"They were like sisters growing up." He shook his head. "But Lenny took advantage of their friendship. She wanted what your mother had but her marriage was a mess. Their friendship was not a healthy relationship for Alexandra. I warned her about that, too."

"But she wouldn't listen because she loved my father," Sasha guessed. "She loved Lenny, too, so she tried to keep their relationship on some level."

"Lenny was like the snake," the man said. "The snake was cold and hungry and begged for help. Pity and kindness for his plight allowed a young girl to turn a blind eye to the fact that he was a snake. When he bit her, he reminded her that she had known what he was when she picked him up."

"Lenny was the snake," Sasha suggested.

Al nodded.

"Why were my parents murdered?" she asked, unable to breathe for fear he would stop talking.

"Because the snake was too smart. I've said too much."

He turned toward the door. Sasha couldn't allow him to leave without explaining what he meant.

"Wait." She put a hand on his arm. "You say you loved my mother like a daughter. If that's true, then why won't you help me? All I want is the truth."

He stared at Sasha, his eyes filled with regret. "The truth won't change anything."

He reached for the door again. "Don't my parents deserve justice? The truth can give me that if nothing else."

"It's too late. The truth might eventually allow for justice but it won't give you peace, Sasha. It will only bring you pain. There are some evils that are too big to stop."

Sasha followed him out the door. When he had driven away she locked up and climbed back into her rental and drove. She drove until she reached the hospital and then she pulled over and stared at the sprawling compound.

This was the biggest project her mother had been working on. This was a Packard project. Devlin—the man who had most likely left her that message and sneaked in on her twice—was a Packard. And Leandra Brennan—aka the snake—worked for Packard.

It had to be Packard.

He had her mother and father murdered to stop them from exposing something he wanted to hide.

All Sasha had to do was find that something.

Chapter Fifteen

Sasha turned into Branch's driveway right behind him. She had driven around for an hour. Unable to bear the uncertainty, she had gone to Branch's grandmother and asked her about the rumors. Afterward, Sasha had driven around some more before she'd finally stopped and sent Branch a text. He'd called and sent her a couple of texts by then but she hadn't been ready to talk.

She wasn't sure she could now.

Everything felt wrong. She had been so certain the truth would help her to put the past behind her once and for all but that wasn't happening. The more she dug, the more questions and uncertainties she uncovered. Her parents' lives now felt skewed and off-kilter. Where was the happy childhood she had dreamed was real all these years?

Was this why her grandmother had refused to go down this path?

Had she known that hurt and disillusionment were all that waited for Sasha at the end of this journey?

She should have come to Winchester, buried her grandmother, closed up both houses and then walked away without ever looking back.

Branch climbed out of his truck and turned in her direction. A smile spread across his handsome face.

Weakness claimed her and she barely held back the tears. How in the world was she supposed to make any of this right? She had built a career spinning other people's mistakes and she had no idea how to turn her own life around...how to tell her own truth.

How could she be disappointed in the skewed truth of her parents' lives when her own truth was way off-balance?

Did anyone get it all right? Of course not. No life was flawless. There were ups and downs and turnarounds in every life.

It was what you did with those deviations and bumps in the road that mattered.

Sasha climbed out of the rental car and walked straight up to him. "I'm not sure I can handle the truth anymore."

He pulled her into his arms and hugged her. Sasha closed her eyes and lost herself in the scent and feel of the man. He ushered her inside and closed the world out.

"You need a drink." He guided her to the sofa and left her there.

Her entire being felt bereft at the loss of contact with his. He was wrong. She didn't need a drink. She needed his body wrapped around hers so thoroughly that it was impossible to tell where one of them began and the other one ended. She wanted to lose herself in him in that way. She didn't want to think. She only wanted to feel.

He thrust a small glass of amber liquid in front of her. "Drink it. You'll feel better."

She didn't believe him but she drank it anyway. Scotch. She shuddered with the burn of it sliding down her throat. "Thank you."

Branch sat down in the chair across the coffee table from her and knocked back his own shot of Scotch. He placed his glass on the table and then settled his hat next to it. He ran his fingers through his hair and set his attention fully on her. "Tell me what happened."

"The reason I don't remember my mother's best friend is because they never saw each other outside the occasional lunch. Leandra Brennan—Lenny—and my mother grew up together. They went to college together, got married the same summer. They were best friends—like sisters. Until something happened between my father and her. According to Arlene—"

"You talked to her today?"

Sasha nodded. "She said my grandmother never wanted me to know any of this, so they kept my mother's secret. There was a big barbecue when my mother was pregnant with me. Lenny and her husband were fighting and everyone was drinking except my mother. Anyway, at some point that evening my mother caught Lenny and my dad kissing. Arlene said Mother would never elaborate if there was something more going on than just two drunk people doing something stupid. But she and Lenny stopped being friends for a long while. Apparently they had only recently started having the occasional lunch together right before my parents died."

Branch shook his head. "It's easy to forget that our parents are mere humans, too, and they've made mistakes."

Sasha stared at the empty glass in her hands. "I was a child when they died. My every memory is of these perfect people who were above mere human mistakes. I don't even remember ever being scolded. All the memories other than the night they were killed are sweet and cherished and perfect."

"Just because you discovered a painful truth doesn't mean all the happy truths are no longer real or relevant."

She placed her glass on the table and wrung her hands. "I found Dr. Farr. He refuses, of course, to change his opinion of my story. He, apparently, was aware of my father's infidelity, which makes me wonder if it was such common knowledge why I hadn't heard of it before."

"Maybe it came out in the investigation but wasn't necessarily common knowledge."

"Maybe."

"Or," Branch offered, "maybe your grandmother suggested that Luther look into Alexandra's former best friend because of what had happened."

Sasha nodded. "You're probably right. G'ma would likely have considered the possibility. I know I certainly would have." She looked to Branch. "Did you talk to Brennan today?"

"I did." Branch stared at the floor a moment. "She came up with an even crazier story. In fact, she broke down into tears and blubbered her way through most of it. She explained how she and your father had been having an affair and your mother found out and intended to divorce him and take everything. She thinks your father intended to have her killed and things went terribly wrong."

"Are you serious? She said those things?"

He met Sasha's gaze. "She did. She claims she was trying to put her marriage back together but that he wouldn't leave her alone. She and your mother were having secret lunches to discuss how to handle the situation."

Sasha shook her head. "I don't believe it. I would remember that kind of tension."

"At one point you did say they were arguing more during those final weeks."

She had said that. "It was about work. I remember distinctly that he thought she was working too much and she complained that he needed to find a new job."

This—all of this—grew more confusing by the moment.

"Wait." She had almost forgotten to tell him about Alfred Nelson. "I spoke to Mr. Nelson, the man who worked in the office with my mother. He was knocking on the door of my grandmother's house when I drove past, so I stopped and talked to him. He urged me to stop digging around in the past. He said it would only hurt me the way it did my mother. He alluded to how Brennan betrayed my mother."

"At least it sounds like everyone has gotten their story straight."

He was right. Farr, Brennan and Nelson were all suddenly spouting basically the same story. "Seems rather convenient."

Branch nodded. "It does. I think maybe we need to take today's influx of information with a grain of salt."

"Nelson also said something like there are some evils too big to stop. Do you think he was referring to Jarvis Packard?"

"Packard would certainly fit the description."

Sasha shot to her feet. She couldn't sit still any longer. "This is just too much. I don't know why my grandmother didn't simply explain the situation to me once I was an adult. I shouldn't have to be doing this." She crossed the room and stared out the window.

Branch moved up behind her. Her body reacted instantly. How she would love to turn around and fall into his arms.

"You don't have to do this, Sasha. Knowing the truth—whatever it might be—won't bring your parents back. It won't make you feel any better about the fact that your grandmother didn't want to talk about it. It won't change anything unless it helps to put a killer behind bars."

"And clears my father's name," she reminded him.

"If you want to clear your father's name and find justice for your parents, then you have to do this. Otherwise, you don't have to go down this path. No one will fault you if you decide you've had enough."

He made it seem like such an easy decision.

"It's not that simple," she argued.

"It's never that simple," he agreed.

She turned around, her body so close to his she could feel the heat of his skin beneath his clothes. "Why are you helping me?"

It wasn't what she'd intended to ask when she opened her mouth but it was what came out.

He frowned down at her. "Why wouldn't I help you?"

"That's not an answer."

He searched her eyes as if the motive for her demand might show itself, but she couldn't let him see that what she wanted was to push him away. To stop this thing before it was completely out of control. While they could still look back and call what they'd shared the past few days nice, a friend helping a friend.

"I told you I've always wanted a do-over. I've wished more times than I can count for an opportunity to spend time with you again."

Sasha thought of all the lies she had discovered...all the confusing things that didn't add up. Was that the legacy she wanted to leave her daughter? A box of untruths and a trail of uncertainties.

She grabbed Branch and pulled his face down to hers. She kissed him with all the hunger and desire strumming through her. A minute from now he would never look at her the same. A minute from now he would know the one truth that mattered more than all the others.

His arms went around her and he pulled her against him, deepened the kiss, taking control, and she wept with the knowledge that this would be the only time.

When she could bear the sweet tenderness no longer, she pushed him away. When he released her, his eyes glazed with need, she crossed the room, found her bag and pulled out her cell phone.

"What's going on, Sasha?" He watched her, worry in his eyes now. He understood something was very, very wrong.

Something besides her murdered parents and their secrets. Besides her dead grandmother and the truths she chose to take with her to her grave. Besides the urgent need still roaring through her body.

"I've never wanted a do-over of that night, Branch."

He stared at her, confusion clouding his face. "I don't understand."

"That night was amazing." She smiled, swiped at an errant tear that escaped her iron hold. "It was the night I had waited for since I was thirteen years old and first fell madly in love with you."

He smiled, his own eyes suspiciously bright. "I remember thinking that if you would have me I would be the happiest guy in the world, but I always thought you had other plans."

His confession hurt more than she wanted to admit. How could they not have known? Had they been too busy running away from their lives here that they couldn't see each other clearly?

"I did and that was my mistake. I couldn't stop running toward the future long enough to see what was right here in my present. I had all these big plans. I was going to make my mark, make a name for myself. I was never again going to be the orphaned girl who lost her whole world. I was going to be someone who mattered."

"First—" he took a step in her direction "—you were always someone who mattered. To your grandmother. To my family. To *me*."

More of those damned tears flowed down her cheeks. "But I couldn't see that. I allowed the need to prove myself to rule my life and I made a terrible, terrible mistake. One I'm certain you won't be able to forgive me for."

He reached up and tugged a wisp of hair from her damp cheek. "I'm fairly certain you have nothing to worry about on that score. Whatever you did or didn't do when you left, you don't owe me an explanation. I'm here for you now and I'll be here for you tomorrow. I want to be a part of your life—a part of your daughter's life."

Sasha stared at him, her entire being aching. Her fingers tightened around the phone full of pictures of her precious daughter. "She's *your* daughter, too."

The kaleidoscope of evolving emotions on his face took her breath. He went from shock to amazement and then to anger.

"What do you mean?"

"I mean, the one time we were together Brianne was conceived. I didn't know until weeks later and..."

And what?

She made the decision not to tell him. She chose to go on with her life and to not look back.

"Why didn't you call me?"

His voice was hollow. That, too, would change in a moment. "My grandmother said you had accepted a big promotion in Chicago. I had that job offer in New York. The timing was just wrong."

"Timing?"

Now the fire was in his tone. He was angry. She didn't blame him. She deserved whatever he decided to throw her way.

"I should have told you." She took a breath. "I promised myself I would a thousand times, but it never felt like the right time, so I never did."

The entire scene had taken on a dreamlike quality. Sasha felt uncertain of herself and at the same time completely at peace with the decision she had made.

She had told him. At long last. Regardless of what happened next, she had done the right thing.

He looked away, shook his head. "I need some air and to think."

She nodded. "I understand."

He walked out of the room. Moments later she heard the back door close.

She tapped her contacts list and put through a call to Rey. "I need to talk to you."

Five minutes later Sasha had left a note for Branch, telling him that she would spend the night with Rey, and then she left to give him the space he needed to come to terms with her announcement. Her soul ached as if she were driving away from that night all those years ago all over again.

She and Branch had made love and then they'd walked away from each other without ever looking back.

They had both made a mistake, but hers was the far more egregious one.

Rey met her at the Lenoir house.

As much as Sasha would love to lose herself to a bottle of wine, a buzz would not help. She needed to keep her mind busy—to focus on something until she could bear to properly consider what she had done.

Branch knew he had a daughter now.

Now she had to tell Brianne. Maybe it would be better to bring her here and to do the introductions in person.

"What's the plan?" Rey glanced around the dusty old house. "I've got pizza and wine ordered. We have about half an hour before it arrives."

"Pizza and wine?" Since when did the two pizza places in Winchester deliver wine?

"Brian is bringing us dinner. Don't worry—he's not staying. He and his love have plans. He's just dropping off the food and a few other things we might need."

Brian Peterson worked with Rey at the newspaper. He and Rey had been best friends in school and later it had been the three of them. As close as Sasha and Rey always were, there had been a special bond between Rey and Brian.

"I'm afraid to ask what kinds of things."

Rey shrugged. "Nightshirts, sleeping bags, toothbrushes. Just a few necessities."

Sasha was really grateful for good friends like Rey and Brian.

She instantly chastised herself for leaving Branch out. He was a good friend, too. She hoped they would be able to be friends again.

"So." Rey turned to her. "What's the plan?"

Sasha started to say that she had no plan, but then she realized she had a very important plan. "I want to take this place apart."

Rey made a face. "Define *take apart*."

"I want to look inside and under everything. If it's here, I want to find it."

Another of those strange expressions twisted Rey's face. *"It?"*

Sasha nodded. "I have no idea what it is, but we're going to look until we find it—unless you have objections."

Rey shook her head. "None. Except maybe I'll text Brian and add gloves to the needs list."

"Good idea." Sasha smiled. She didn't have to see it to know it was sad; it felt sad. She felt sad. But this was the first step toward moving forward. She did not want to leave this painful black cloud hanging over her daughter's life.

Her daughter deserved happiness.

Her daughter deserved to know her father.

Branch deserved to know his daughter.

And Sasha intended to have the truth—whatever it turned out to be—and justice for her parents.

Chapter Sixteen

Branch knocked on the door of his grandmother's home and waited for her to answer. He usually called before showing up just to make sure she was home, but this time he couldn't bring himself to make the call. He needed to see her in person. He needed to see her face when she answered his question.

Eighty-five-year-old Arlene Holloway opened the door. Branch reminded himself of her age and her station in his family. He reached for calm. Upsetting this woman was the last thing he wanted to do and in his current state he didn't completely trust himself to make good decisions.

"Branch, is something wrong?"

He hadn't called and he always did. "Yes, ma'am. I'm a little upset. May I come in?"

"Well, of course." She drew the door open wide and shuffled back out of his way. "Is Sasha all right? Where is she?"

The sweet little old lady craned her neck to see through the darkness beyond the door.

"She's with Rey Anderson."

Arlene nodded. "Rey's doing a fine job with the newspaper. Far better than her uncle Phillip ever did. He was too busy chasing the widows around town."

Branch smiled in spite of the circumstances. His grandmother always knew how to put a smile on his face, even when she wasn't trying. "I hear he went down to Florida for spring break."

"Spring break?" she grumbled as she locked the door. "He looks like a spring break. The man needs to find a hobby that doesn't involve chasing skirts."

Branch knew better than to encourage her. "I have some questions I need to ask you, Gran."

She stared at him from behind the thick lenses of her glasses. She blinked. "Do we need a stiff drink to make them go down easier?"

"Possibly." No point pretending.

"Have a seat over there." She gestured toward the living room. "I'll round up Walker's bourbon."

His grandfather had been dead for ten years and his grandmother still called the stash of bourbon she kept his. Branch knew for a fact she'd purchased a new fifth of bourbon at least twice in those ten years. Most of the time she had Branch's father pick it up. It wouldn't be proper for her to be seen in the liquor store, much less buying something. She shuffled over to the sofa, two sipping glasses and the fifth of bourbon clasped in her gnarled hands. She poured, passed a glass to him and lifted the other to her lips.

When they'd downed a swallow, she looked him square in the eye and asked, "What happened?"

"Did you know Sasha's daughter was my child?"

Since Sasha left, she had sent him a dozen photos of Brianne via text, some going back to when the girl was a baby in diapers. The younger photos were like looking at candid shots of himself as a kid.

Every time he looked at the photos he felt a punch to his gut. How the hell had this happened? Why would

Sasha have kept a secret like this from him? For a dozen years no less.

He should have gone after her.

"I had my suspicions," Arlene confessed. "But I never knew for sure. Vi never said a word—I imagine because Sasha told her not to. It was like what happened to Sasha's parents. We never discussed it. I tried once and she said no and that was that. We respected each other that way, son. When you get older you realize how important that one thing is. When your loved ones vanish one by one and your health goes by the wayside, you still got your self-respect and the respect of your good friends—if you're lucky."

Branch shook his head. "Part of me wants to raise hell. She kept this child from me for twelve long years."

"Would that fix anything?" she asked. "Make you feel any better?"

He downed his bourbon, winced at the burn. "Not likely on either count."

"Well, there's your answer. If I had my guess, she kept this information from the girl, too. She's going to have herself enough trouble explaining that decision. She won't need any trouble from you on top of that. I think a little patience is in order. And maybe some understanding. She was young and terrified. She's already done all the hard work. Now all you have to do is enjoy. She's a beautiful girl and, from all the things Vi told me about her, smart as a whip to boot."

Branch nodded. "We'll figure this out."

Arlene smiled. "I think you already did."

"I think you're right."

He had a daughter. A beautiful daughter who was smart and who deserved the best dad he could be.

"I guess I should call the folks."

"You might want to have another sip of that bourbon first. Your mama has been pining for a grandchild for years. She will be over the moon."

His cell vibrated and he slid it from his pocket in case it was Sasha. He checked the screen and frowned. Not Sasha. "Hey, Billy, what's going on?"

It was a little late in the evening for the chief of police to be making social calls. Branch braced for trouble. He'd had a text from Sasha not an hour ago, so hopefully all was well with her.

"Hey, Branch, I've got a situation you need to have a look at."

Oh, hell. "What's the location?"

"Alfred Nelson's place. Looks like a suicide but there's a strange note."

"On my way."

When he stood and tucked his phone away, his grandmother frowned up at him. "You have to go?"

"Yes, ma'am. Thank you for the advice and the drink." Though it was a good thing he hadn't taken more than a sip.

"Not to worry, son. I'll finish it off for you." She shot him a wink.

Branch gave her a hug, her body so frail beneath his big arms. "Love you, Gran."

"Love you. Now you be nice to Sasha. She's had enough troubles in her life. She deserves good things and she's just given you a miraculous gift. Enjoy it. Don't fret over how long it took her to get around to giving it."

"Yes, ma'am."

On the porch, he settled his hat into place and headed for his truck. His grandmother was a very smart lady.

ALFRED NELSON LIVED ALONE. His wife had died four years ago. According to Burt Johnston, who knew everyone in the county, Al, as his friends called him, had been instrumental in Alexandra Lenoir being hired in the planning and zoning office. He'd also gone to bat for her big promotion two years later. Though he had worked in that office for a half a dozen years before she came along, he had not possessed the degree he felt the supervisory position deserved. He had insisted that Alexandra was the right person for the job.

It appeared that at some point after lunch today he had decided to end his life. He'd tied a length of clothesline around the ceiling fan and made a noose. Then he'd climbed back up the ladder, put the noose around his neck and stepped off the rung. The ladder had been knocked onto its side by his swaying body.

But before he'd done all that, he'd written a note to Sasha, explaining that her parents' deaths were his fault. He hadn't really meant for everything to turn out the way it had, but he'd made a terrible, terrible mistake. He'd gone to their house with the intention of killing Brandon Lenoir and taking Alexandra far away to be his. He had wanted to have her all to himself for a very long time. But things had gone wrong and a struggle over the gun had taken Alexandra's life. He'd then killed Brandon Lenoir and attempted to make it look like a murder-suicide. His voice was the one Sasha had heard that night. It was all him.

"What do you make of his confession?" Billy asked, his tone heavy with skepticism.

"About the same thing you do, I suspect." Branch shook his head. "This would mean that Alfred was the intruder, and we both know he was in no physical condition to be running through the woods, much less to break into anyone's home. When Sasha spoke to him today, he warned her to stop digging and that some evils were too big to stop."

The strangest part of the entire scene were the empty file drawers in his home office. Any personal or professional papers he had kept were gone.

"Someone is tying up loose ends." Billy watched as the coroner's two assistants removed the body from the scene.

That was the part that worried Branch. "I should talk to Sasha about this before she hears some other way."

"Devlin Packard is still missing," Billy warned. "I don't know if this is his work—frankly, I don't think so—but he's part of this somehow. I've got this feeling that his disappearance and all this are not just coincidence."

Devlin was another of those pieces that simply refused to fit into a slot, like long-missing puzzle parts that were too faded and misshapen to go into place. Yet it was instinctively understood that those pieces belonged in this particular puzzle. There were apparently a whole slew of secrets among the players from twenty-seven years ago and each of those secrets fit together somehow.

"Did you talk to Leandra Brennan again?" Branch wondered if Billy had gotten the same story he did.

"As a matter of fact, she was very forthcoming about her relationship with Sasha's mother and her father. Brennan thinks that during the time she had the affair with Brandon that Alexandra was involved with Alfred." Billy hitched his head toward the body bag. "Perfect timing for her to offer up that previously withheld information. Funny how that keeps happening."

Branch shook his head. "Give me a call if you learn anything new."

Billy gave him a nod. "Will do."

From the Nelson residence, Branch drove to the Lenoir house. Sasha had told him that she and Rey were spending the night there. He wasn't happy about the idea but at least she wasn't alone.

The porch light was on as he climbed out of his truck. He walked past Rey's car. Sasha had left her rental at Rey's. The backyard was completely dark. He wasn't happy about the idea that someone could get all the way to the house from the woods without being seen. For insurance purposes Viola had kept the power and water turned on to the old house, but she hadn't exactly ensured the maintenance was taken care of. Sasha needed to bear that in mind.

He knocked on the door. Half a minute later it opened and Rey beamed a smile at him.

"Branch." She opened the door wide. "Come on in."

He followed her inside and Sasha appeared at the bottom of the stairs. "Hey."

He gave her a nod.

"I'll get back to work." Rey flashed Sasha a smile before bounding up the stairs.

"Is everything okay?" Sasha asked, her expression as uncertain as he felt.

"Billy called. Alfred Nelson is dead."

"What happened?"

"He appears to have committed suicide. He left a note addressed to you."

He repeated the contents of the note and she immediately started to shake her head.

"He insisted that he thought of my mother as a daughter," she argued. "He helped her get the job, pushed for her promotion—both of which sound more like what someone would do for a daughter. I didn't get the impression that he was lying to me or that his feelings were anything other than platonic. This doesn't make sense."

"None at all. And, by the way, in her statement this afternoon to Billy, Leandra Brennan just happened to recall a possible affair between Nelson and your mother."

"We're too close." Sasha's gaze locked with his. "They're worried, so they're attempting to cover all the bases. They hadn't counted on me remembering anything from that night. They thought they'd shut me down."

"They still could."

She looked away. "I'm being careful. Rey is here with me."

"Promise me you won't take any chances, Sasha. I don't like that you're here instead of at my place."

"I'm grateful you feel that way, Branch. I honestly didn't know what to expect after you learned the secret I've kept all these years."

"The decision you made was as much my fault as it was yours," he said. As much as he wanted to be angry, that was the truth of the matter. "If I had behaved differently, you might have felt more inclined to be forthcoming. Either way, what's done is done. We should go from here, not dwell in the past."

She hugged him and for a moment he couldn't move. Maybe it was the shock of her sudden display of affection. Finally, he hugged her back. Whatever else they were, they were friends. They had a daughter. There were a lot of things that needed to be worked out, but this didn't have to be one of those things.

When she drew back she crossed her arms over her

chest in a protective manner. "We're going through everything in the house. If there's anything else to find, we plan on finding it tonight."

"Keep the doors locked and stay on alert. Billy thinks someone is tying up loose ends."

The idea made way too much sense and Branch did not like it one little bit.

She nodded. "We will."

"Call me if you need anything. I'm only eight or nine minutes away."

"I'll call if we need anything. I promise."

As much as he had hoped she would ask him to stay, she didn't. She needed space and time. He understood that. Still, this was not the best time to want distance.

But Rey was here.

That was the only reason he was able to climb into his truck and drive away.

Even then he didn't feel particularly good about it.

Nine minutes later he was in his own house and ready to call it a night, though he doubted he would sleep a wink.

Notification that he had received a text message had him reaching for his cell. The message was from an unknown number. A New York area code. Not Sasha. Her name and number were in his contact list.

He opened the message and read the words.

So, I hear you're my dad.

His heart surged into his throat.

Sasha had told her.

He hadn't anticipated that happening so fast.

Yes. I apologize for the delay in being around. As long as you let me, I plan to make up for it.

Holding his breath, he hit Send.

He didn't breathe again until another text message appeared.

I can handle that.

He smiled and typed a quick response.

Great.

Then he called his parents.

His mother answered on the second ring. "Is everything all right, Branch?"

"Everything's fine," he assured her. "I know it's late, but this couldn't wait."

Chapter Seventeen

Thursday, March 28

It was barely daylight when Sasha awakened the next morning. She and Rey had stayed up far too late going through drawers and boxes and closets. She'd spent a lot of that time talking to Brianne. She'd at first thought she would wait until she was back home to talk to her in person, but considering her grandmother had just died and the rest of what was going on, Sasha had decided a live video chat was the perfect compromise.

Brianne had taken the news in stride. She'd been waiting a long time to learn the identity of her father. Sasha was grateful for her patience and her understanding. One of her first requests was for his cell phone number. Branch had let Sasha know that Brianne had contacted him.

Sasha was particularly thankful that Branch was handling the news so well. For years she had worried about how this would all go down. She should have known her daughter would handle the situation well. Brianne was a very well-adjusted and confident young girl. Sasha was very proud of her.

Branch was a lucky guy to get a daughter as awesome as Brianne.

Sasha ventured into the kitchen. Rey had brought wine and bottled water but she hadn't thought of coffee. Sasha needed coffee badly. She could probably run into town and grab coffee and muffins or something before Rey was up The woman had been like a mini tornado last night. They'd gone through nearly everything in the house. There was nothing else here—nothing that helped with the case, anyway.

So much had happened the past couple of days. There was no question now about whether her parents were murdered or not. They were. Several suspects had come to their attention. Leandra Brennan, Alfred Nelson, Jarvis Packard, Seth Keegan and Hadden Roark. Then there was Devlin Packard. But Sasha had him pegged as a witness rather than a killer.

She grabbed her purse, the keys and her phone and eased out the front door. Locking it behind her, she dropped her phone into her bag.

"You should have listened to me."

Sasha whipped around to face the voice.

She recognized the face from her Google search. Devlin Packard stared at her, his eyes wide with fear or uncertainty—perhaps insanity.

Her first thought was to scream. She resisted the impulse.

"Devlin." She reminded herself to breathe. "I'm glad you came back. I've been trying to find answers. I could use your help."

He stared at her, his expression trapped somewhere between fear and distrust.

"Would you like to come inside? I was going for breakfast. I can bring you back something to eat."

She prayed he was hungry.

He grabbed her by the arm. "You have to come with me now."

Her bag and keys hit the floor.

Fear surged into her throat. Now would be the time to scream. But if she did, any trust she had built with this man would vanish.

Could she trust him not to kill her?

She reminded herself he'd had opportunities before and he hadn't killed her.

He moved faster and faster across the backyard. Dew on the knee-deep grass dampened her jeans. She stumbled in an effort to keep up with his long strides. They hit the tree line and she realized where they were going. The rising sun was abruptly blocked from view by the dark woods.

"You were living in the shack when my parents died."

He yanked her closer as if he feared she might try to take off.

Sasha allowed him to draw her nearer and she didn't fight him. He needed to sense that she trusted him. If he had seen something—if he knew anything about what happened that night—she needed him cooperative.

Her heart was pounding hard by the time they reached the shack. He pushed her through the door and followed her inside, leaving the door standing open, perhaps for the meager light. Still, the interior remained in near-total darkness. She wished she had her phone for the flashlight app.

"You shouldn't have come back asking questions. Big mistake. Big mistake." He was agitated, shifting from foot to foot, shaking his head.

She wrapped her arms around herself and tried to remember what she had seen inside this shack. An old quilt. Some trash.

"I just wanted to know what happened to my mom and dad." She said this softly, quietly, like the child she was when her parents died. Strange, no matter how many years had passed, she still felt like a hurt and lonely child when she allowed herself to be transported back to that time.

"They'll kill you just like they killed them." He leaned close to her. She fought the urge to shudder. "That's why I came back."

"Thank you." *Keep him talking.* Rey would wake up and realize she was gone. She would call Branch.

"I found out you were back and digging around. You should have just buried your grandma and gone back to the big city. You shouldn't have started asking questions. I knew they'd find out and do to you what they did to them."

"Who?" she asked. "Who hurt my parents?"

He shook his head again, moved toward the door, stared outside as if he feared someone might have followed them. "They're dead. Can't bring them back."

Was he talking about her parents?

"We should call the police and tell them what really happened," she urged. The more agitated he grew, the more nervous she felt. But he knew something. She was certain.

He swung around and glared at her. "Are you crazy? The police can't stop them. No one can."

Fear swelled inside her. "You're right. I don't know what I was thinking."

For a few seconds it was so quiet she could hear him breathing, could hear the blood sweeping through her veins.

"Your mother let me stay here because she felt sorry for me. She was nice to me."

"Were you in trouble?"

He glared at her. "I was always in trouble. I couldn't do anything right."

"So my mother was helping you." Sasha mustered up a smile. "She liked helping people."

He shook his head again, so hard it couldn't have been comfortable. "She shouldn't have helped me."

"Do you think they hurt her and my dad because she helped you?" If her heart pounded any faster it would surely burst from her chest.

"They think I don't know but I do." He looked outside again. "They're coming for me. I'm too tired to hide from them anymore. I can't keep running."

Sasha looked outside. "Who's coming?"

"I have to show you before they come. I might not get another chance."

Sasha didn't see or hear anyone. But if he had something to show her it could be important. "Okay."

He went to the farthest corner of the shack and pawed around on the floor.

She had the perfect opportunity to run. His back was to her. She was standing next to the door. He was several feet away. But she needed to stay…to see what he intended to show her.

He stood, turned around and moved toward her. "I kept this. They don't know about it. I wanted you to have it."

He handed her a wad of papers. "If they find them, they'll take them and then you'll never have what you need."

"I'll keep them safe," she promised. Her hands shook as her fingers wrapped around the pages.

The distant sound of a voice jerked their attention to the door.

"They're coming," he murmured.

He shoved the door closed and turned to her. "Stay away from the door. They're here to kill us."

BRANCH WAS JUST about to walk out the door when his cell vibrated with an incoming call. He didn't recognize the number but it was local. "Holloway."

"Branch, this is Rey. Sasha is missing. Her purse and keys were lying on the porch but I can't find her. There are some guys here—they look like SWAT or something. They want to search the property."

Branch was already climbing into his truck. "Do not allow them to search the property. Call Colt and Billy. I'm on my way."

Branch had a feeling the SWAT types Rey meant were some of Packard's security force, and they had no jurisdiction beyond the Packard facility and certainly not on private property. Unfortunately he doubted a little technicality like that had ever stopped them.

It took him six minutes to drive to the Lenoir house, and Franklin County Sheriff Colton "Colt" Tanner's truck was already there.

Rey was on the porch.

"They're in the backyard!" she shouted, pointing around the corner of the house.

As Branch rushed around the corner of the house Billy's truck roared into the driveway. Branch didn't slow down. Rey would send him in the right direction.

Colt had stopped the four-man team dressed in black and armed to the gills at the tree line where the backyard faded into the dark woods.

All four men in black seemed to track Branch's movements as he approached.

"US Marshal Branch Holloway," he called out, identifying himself. "Chief of Police Brannigan is here, as well. You gentlemen are trespassing."

"Morning, Branch." Colt nodded. "I was just explaining to these fine gentlemen that this is private property."

"We have reason to believe our employer's mentally unstable son is in those woods. He may present a danger to himself and to others. We have orders to take him back to the hospital."

If he was here, Branch knew where he had gone. "Sheriff, if you and the chief will babysit these gentlemen, I'll have a look around."

Colt gave him a nod and Branch walked into the forest. He barely restrained the need to run until he was out of sight of the security team. Then he ran like hell. When he spotted the shack, he slowed down, stayed in the cover of the dense foliage.

Quietly and straining to hear any sound, he moved closer.

He couldn't be sure if the man was armed or not. Rather than risk going in, he called out. "Sasha, it's me. You in there?"

"Branch!"

Shuffling and muffled sounds told him that Devlin was with her. He held himself back when he wanted to rush inside and rescue her. He couldn't do anything that might get her hurt...or worse.

"He's my friend," Sasha said.

Branch eased closer.

"I can't protect you," a male voice growled.

Branch wrenched the door open. "I can protect her." He looked from the man who whirled to face him and then to Sasha. She looked unharmed but shaken. "I can protect you both," he said to the man he recognized as Devlin Packard.

Packard shook his head. "They'll kill us if they get the chance."

Branch thought of the assault rifles the men in black had been carrying.

"Stay in the shack and lie down on the floor." He looked to Sasha. "You, too."

Sasha quickly obeyed. She grabbed the man by the hand and pulled him down, too. Branch took a position in front of the door. He called Billy. "I'm at the shack and they're both here. He's terrified of the guys in black. He thinks they've been sent here to kill him and Sasha. We need to get these two out of here and back to city hall."

Thirty-five minutes were required to clear the area. Branch sweat blood every second of every minute. Knowing the kind of powerful man Packard was, he could have several four-man teams combing the woods. Branch kept expecting to be overtaken from one direction or the other.

When Billy and his officers arrived to escort them out of the woods, Branch took his first deep breath.

"The security team has been relocated to city hall via the sheriff's department."

Branch was glad to hear it. He opened the door and held his hand out for Sasha. "It's clear."

As soon as she was out of the shack she went up on tiptoe and whispered in his ear. "Don't treat him like a prisoner."

Branch nodded and offered his hand to the man still lying on the floor of the shack. "It's okay to come out now, Devlin. No one is going to hurt you."

The man took his hand and pulled himself up. He looked around as he stepped out.

"This is Chief of Police Brannigan," Branch explained. "He's going to make sure we get safely out of the woods so we can explain what happened."

Still looking uncertain, the man nodded.

ANOTHER HALF HOUR was required to get everyone transported to city hall. Devlin Packard was settled into an interview room and a court-appointed attorney was on his way. They were trying to move fast, before Jarvis Packard showed up and started to swing his weight around.

Billy, Sasha and Branch stood over the conference table and considered the drawings Devlin had given her. Several of the drawings showed a woman watching through the windows of a house. Sasha presumed it was her childhood home and that the woman was her mother. The other pictures showed men in black looking in those same windows. Sasha thought of the men in black who had shown up to take Devlin. Were these Packard's security thugs in the drawings? Why would they be looking in the windows of her childhood home?

She shook her head. "I'm not sure what any of this means."

"I think I am." Branch picked up his cell phone and tapped on the screen. Then he turned to Billy and said, "Sasha needs to see Devlin. He wouldn't talk to you, but he'll talk to her."

"I think he will," Sasha agreed. "If there's any chance he can explain what this means, it's worth a shot."

"We can try." Billy opened the door. "You and I can watch from the observation room."

"That'll work," Branch agreed.

Billy led the way to the interview room. Branch passed his cell phone and the drawings to Sasha. "Ask him if the woman in the drawings is this woman."

Sasha stared at the image on the screen: Leandra Brennan's face from twenty or so years ago. The photo was from a feature article in the local newspaper. She had noticed it when she'd done an internet search on the woman. Sasha thought of the woman's accusations and renewed fury whipped through her. Then she suddenly understood what Branch was thinking. Their gazes locked and she nodded her understanding of his instructions.

Bracing herself, Sasha entered the interview room and sat down at the table. "Do you need anything to drink or to eat, Devlin?"

He shook his head, the jerkiness of the motion warning her he was still agitated.

"I think we've figured out what you've been trying to tell us, Devlin." She placed the drawings on the table in front of him. He looked from one to the next, the pages faded with time.

"Is this the woman you were watching and drawing?" She showed him the image on the screen of Branch's cell phone.

He nodded, the movement frantic. "She's not a nice person."

"Did she hurt my parents?"

He shrugged. "She only watched. The men—" he tapped another of his drawings "—they are the ones who hurt them."

"You're sure about that?" Sasha reminded herself to breathe.

He nodded. "My father always stopped people who got in his way."

Sasha forced her trembling lips into a smile. "Thank you, Devlin. That helps a lot."

When she had reclaimed the drawings and walked

out of the room, she stared at Branch. "He identified her. Why was she watching my family?"

But she knew the answer. The affair, or whatever it was that had happened between Brennan and Sasha's father.

"Two of my officers are bringing her in now," Billy assured her. "The moment Devlin identified her, I ordered a unit to pick her up."

"What about Packard?" Branch asked.

"I have my best detectives headed to his house now."

Was this really happening? Would Sasha finally know the truth?

TWO HOURS DRAGGED BY. Sasha was keenly aware of every second.

And finally Leandra Brennan confessed. With Branch at her side, Sasha watched from the observation room via the one-way mirror.

"He loved me more than her but she wouldn't let him go. I tried to do the right thing since she was pregnant. But then I saw him again years later—after he lost his job. We ran into each other. He was drinking and I helped him get home. I knew after that day that he was still in love with me. So I decided to make it happen."

"How did you do that?" Billy asked.

"I knew Mr. Packard would never allow anyone to get in the way of his hospital plans. So I set her up. I made her believe that Packard was taking shortcuts. I gave her altered site plans. I made Mr. Packard believe she wanted money." She laughed. "For such a brilliant man he bought the story hook, line and sinker. He ordered his men to take care of her." She frowned. "Brandon wasn't supposed to be home that night. He was supposed to be with me. Only Alexandra and Sasha were supposed to die. But he got in the way and I lost him. If Sasha had died that night, no one would ever have known."

Sasha couldn't listen to any more. She left the observation room.

The idea that her mother had died because her best friend wanted her husband made Sasha sick. She would never know for certain how guilty her father was in the whole mess, if at all. But she did know that her father had tried to protect her mother in the end. That meant something.

Branch stepped into the corridor. "You hanging in there?"

Sasha shrugged then nodded. "I think so. I just need some time to think."

"Rey is waiting to take you home with her. I'm staying here until I'm sure Packard and his minions are all accounted for and arrested."

"Thank you, Branch. I couldn't have done this without you."

He gave her a nod. "We'll talk soon."

He was right. They did need to talk. *Soon.*

Chapter Eighteen

Monday, April 1

Sasha stood in the backyard of her childhood home and stared at the woods. As a child she had loved this place. She had explored every inch of those woods. She turned back to the house. It was a shame for it to continue to fall even further into disrepair. The house could be a home for a family. She would contact a Realtor and a contractor to get started with the cleanout and renovations.

There was a lot of work but it was time to move on from the past.

She had decided to keep her grandmother's house. It felt more like home than this place, or any other, for that matter. Besides, how could she part with the home her grandmother had loved so much? She couldn't. She would pass it down to her daughter when the time came.

Though she had reached a number of decisions, there were more to make.

The breeze shifted, wrapping her in the cool morning air. She hugged her arms around herself. She had taken an extended leave of absence from her firm. Brianne would finish her school year online. Together they would spend the summer exploring their options.

Jarvis Packard had lawyered up and was denying any knowledge of the story Leandra Brennan had told. Not that Sasha had expected him to own his part in the deaths of her parents. Brennan had also insisted that Packard had ordered Alfred Nelson's death, as well. Unless Brennan had proof of her allegations, there was a very good chance Packard would walk away unscathed. Sasha was grateful to know the truth finally and she felt confident Brennan would spend a very long time in prison for her heinous deeds.

Brennan had conspired to end the life of Sasha's mother—her former best friend. Brennan had wanted Sasha's mother's life for her own. The cost had been irrelevant.

Sasha shuddered. She was extremely grateful to Devlin Packard for helping to reveal the persons responsible for the murders of her parents. She might never have known for certain without him. He was headed back to his posh resort-like rehab facility. Sasha wished him well.

More important, Branch had stood with her through this journey into the past. He was the real hero here.

The sound of a vehicle arriving drew her attention to the house. Speak of the devil. That would be Branch. She walked around front and watched as he climbed out of his truck. As he moved toward her, anticipation fizzed in her belly. She would never tire of watching him move or hearing him talk. He smiled. Or seeing him smile.

"Morning."

"Good morning." They met on the front walk. It was actually visible now. Branch had sent the lawn service that took care of his grandmother's property to tame the jungle around this house.

"Billy called," he told her. "Dr. Farr cut a deal with the district attorney. He's going to testify that Jarvis Packard gave him a position on the hospital board of directors in exchange for his expert testimony about you."

Sasha pressed her fingers to her mouth. She had known Farr was lying. When she found her voice again, she asked, "Will his testimony make the difference we need?"

He nodded. "Packard has an entire legal team, but I think Farr's testimony will make the difference."

"This is really good news." Sasha felt immensely relieved. "Thank you."

Silence lingered between them for a moment. When Sasha could bear this new anticipation no longer, she asked, "Did you make your decision?"

He nodded. "I did."

She held her breath. She had no right to expect Branch to alter his life plan for her or for Brianne.

"I'm staying in Winchester."

Relief whooshed through her. "I'm sure your parents and your grandmother are thrilled."

"They are." He grinned. "To be honest, I'm really happy about the decision. It wasn't an easy one to make but it feels right."

"I'm glad."

He held her gaze for a moment. "Good to know."

They were dancing all around this thing between them, but right now neither of them could emotionally afford to go there. They both needed time.

"I've taken a leave of absence to take care of things around here, so I'm not going anywhere for a while either."

"Sounds like a smart plan."

His tone was guarded. Was he worried about where

they went from here? Frankly, she was definitely worried but they had other considerations—like a preteen daughter.

"I think so. I want to stay close—at least for a while. Give you a chance to get to know your daughter."

The anticipation that lit in his eyes made her heart skip a beat.

"I'd like that a lot."

Sasha nodded. "Good, because she can't wait to meet you."

Brianne was giddy with excitement. She couldn't wait to learn all about the other half of her family.

A grin peeked past his guarded facade. "The feeling is definitely mutual."

Branch and Brianne had spoken by phone every day. As soon as the plane landed yesterday she'd wanted to drive straight to his house, but Sasha had insisted on her taking a moment to acclimate herself.

"Would you like to come in and say hello in person?"

He nodded. "I would."

They walked up the front steps together. He reached to open the door and she hesitated. "I wondered if you might like to come to dinner tonight. Brianne and I are cooking."

"Name the place and time."

"Seven, at my grandmother's?"

He gave a nod. "I'll be there."

He opened the door and Sasha walked in ahead of him. Brianne was loping down the stairs.

"Hey, sweetie, this—" she gestured to the man next to her "—is Branch."

Brianne stood on the bottom step for a long moment while she took in the real-life man who was her father.

Branch broke the ice by stepping forward and extending his hand. "It's very nice to meet you in person, Brianne."

She put her hand in his and gave it a shake. "Nice to meet you."

"Brianne and I were about to take a walk. Maybe you'd like to join us."

"Sure."

They walked back outside and wandered across the yard. Sasha hung back to watch the two of them together. It was amazing how much Brianne looked like her father. Sasha had known but it was so much more evident in person. She also understood that this fledgling relationship would not be so easy every day. Right now her daughter was in the honeymoon phase of this new discovery. There would be bumps in the road along the way, but for now they were both committed to building a solid relationship. Sasha was immensely grateful things were progressing so well.

The dark clouds that had hung over her life for so very long were gone.

Moving into the future had never looked brighter.

Even as the thought whispered through her mind, Branch turned back to her and smiled.

If there had been any question in her heart, she now knew with certainty that this really was home.

Whatever the future held, Branch and Winchester would be a part of it.

* * * * *

UNDER THE AGENT'S PROTECTION

JENNIFER D. BOKAL

To John. You are always the one.

Prologue

Wyatt Thornton cocked back his arm as far as he could, then released his grip. The stick somersaulted through the air. Kicking up the remnants of last winter's snow, his dog, Gus, barked happily and gave chase. The land, these miles of foothills in the Rocky Mountains, belonged to Wyatt. It was more than a home, it was a refuge—his place of escape, where the world hardly knew he existed.

A place he could truly be alone.

Gus returned and dropped the slobbery branch at Wyatt's feet. After ruffling the Lab's ears, Wyatt once again picked up the stick. This time, he threw it harder, sending it sailing through the clear blue sky. With another excited bark, Gus raced after it, disappearing into the woods.

Turning his face to the sun, Wyatt closed his eyes and inhaled deeply. He'd never gotten used to the sweet, fresh Wyoming air—not when compared to the miasma of exhaust fumes, cigarettes and sunscreen he had lived with for more than a decade in Las Vegas. The scents of the Strip, everyone used to joke. After exhaling fully, Wyatt again inhaled. A primal wail shot through the silent morning and his breath caught in his chest.

"Gus?"

Heart pounding and legs pumping, Wyatt rushed between the shadows cast by the towering trees.

"Gus," he called. "Where are you, boy?"

He heard a yelp in the distance and his chest contracted. All the dangers that might have befallen his faithful companion came to him in one horrifying rush. A newly awake and hungry bear. An unseen ditch and the dog's broken paw. Poor footing on a slope that ended with Gus maimed at the bottom of a ravine.

He stopped and listened. The silence was total, not even interrupted by the whisper of a breeze.

"Gus? Where are you?"

His call was answered with a bark. The noise ricocheted off the hills, coming from everywhere and nowhere at once. Wyatt stopped and focused.

The first bark was followed by another, this one louder and definitely from his right. Wyatt's pulse spiked, and he followed the sound up a hill. The soft ground crumbled underfoot, and he scrambled on hands and knees to the top of the rise. One hundred yards in the distance stood the old schoolhouse, the farthest point on his land.

Made up of a single room, the century-old stone foundation was still intact. There was a hole in the ceiling where part of the roof had collapsed in the corner. Gus stood on the threshold, whole and healthy. He barked, and his tail was a wagging blur.

Wyatt wiped his hands on the seat of his pants, while his racing heartbeat slowed. "There you are," he said between breaths as he half jogged to the schoolhouse. "Come here."

Gus barked again. With a whine, the dog looked over his shoulder.

"What is it, boy?" Wyatt asked.

Gus darted into the dilapidated building. Wyatt approached and stopped short, recognizing the smell of decay. It was like the rot of a slaughterhouse, but stronger.

Swallowing down his deepest sense of revulsion, he stepped slowly into the structure.

Gus stood near a far corner and pawed at the floor. Behind the dog was the unmistakable form of a corpse.

"Easy, boy," Wyatt said to his dog. With a slap to his thigh, he added, "Come here."

With one last look at the lump on the floor, Gus moved to his master's side.

No matter how long he'd been out of the game, the skills Wyatt had developed over years of training rose to the surface. He began to catalogue all the details—some obvious, others more subtle.

The deceased was male and Caucasian. His age appeared to be between 25 and 40—quite a range, but a wild animal had gotten to his face and throat, making a more exact guess impossible. Wyatt looked around for blood splatter on the walls or floor.

There was nothing.

Wyatt moved in for a closer look, kneeling next to the body.

Dressed in a flannel shirt, down-filled coat and lined denim jeans, John Doe wore the same outfit as three quarters of the state of Wyoming. What made him interesting were the accessories—his hiking boots were high-quality and retailed for over 700 dollars per pair. Wyatt knew that fact as he had a pair himself. The treads were worn, and the tops were scarred with scuff marks. John Doe also wore a top-of-the-line smartwatch. The screen was blank.

But there was no visible sign of trauma. No blackened bullet hole to the chest. No knife wound to the side, crusted over with blood. It was almost as if this man had wandered into the abandoned schoolhouse and died.

No, Wyatt thought, correcting his thinking, there was no *almost* about it.

Cardiac arrest? Perhaps.

Wyatt began to question the scenario before him. Perhaps John Doe—a wealthy tourist, no doubt—had lost his way while hiking in the mountainous terrain. Maybe he'd sought shelter from the frigid temperatures in the old schoolhouse. But in the mountains, it wouldn't have been enough.

The lack of snow was deceptive. The last few nights the temperature had dropped into the low twenties, maybe even high teens. Either way, it was cold enough for someone to die from exposure. It happened all the time, so much so that it was hardly news anymore.

Then again, there were other things that Wyatt would've expected to see and didn't. He touched the flagstone floor. It was smooth, cold and inexplicably spotless. Wyatt inspected the corpse's hands. The fingernails were clean and smooth. It meant that John Doe had hardly struggled in the wild to survive.

No footprints.

No injuries.

No clues.

He pulled a wallet from the man's back pocket and checked for I D. There was an Illinois driver's license in the name of Axl Baker. Conflicting feelings of trepidation and adrenaline dropped into Wyatt's gut. It was the same feeling he had at the beginning of every new case. And even though the scene felt familiar, this time it was different. This time, Wyatt would have nothing more to do with the dead guy on the floor.

Because Wyatt Thornton had left the FBI for a good reason. And nothing, not even an unexplained death, could force him back to work.

Chapter 1

The radio in Sheriff Carl Haak's truck crackled a moment before the 911 dispatcher's voice came through. "You there, Sheriff?" she asked.

Carl looked at the clock on the dashboard. It wasn't even 7:00 in the morning yet. He lifted the radio's handset and pressed the talk button. He continued driving as he said, "Go ahead, Rose."

"A call came in. A body's been found in the old schoolhouse."

Carl's shoulders pinched together with tension and he eased the truck to the side of the road. He only had a couple of weeks left until retirement and looking into another death was not how he wanted to spend his time. Pushing his cowboy hat, emblazoned with a sheriff's tin star on the band, back on his head, he asked, "A body? Whose?"

"A man by the name of Axl Baker. All the way from Chicago, Illinois."

"What happened?"

"Don't know, but the guy who found him didn't think that it was foul play, if that's what worries you."

"What guy?"

"The one who bought the Hampton place a few years back," said Rose. "Wyatt Thornton."

The Hampton family hadn't owned the sprawling piece of land for decades and still Carl knew exactly what property Rose meant. In fact, he passed it every day as he drove to work. "Not foul play? How does Mr. Thornton know?"

"He said there was no sign of injury and that Axl Baker probably died of exposure."

Rose's voice was wistful, and Carl knew why. Ever since Wyatt Thornton had moved to the area several years ago, he'd mostly kept to himself. That didn't mean that his rare appearances in town didn't cause a commotion—amongst the local women, at least. She continued, "He was so sweet on the phone. As nice as he is handsome. He almost reminds me of a movie star."

"What would your husband think of you being sweet on Mr. Thornton?"

"Wyatt," she corrected. "He told me to call him Wyatt, and by the way, Carl, it doesn't do any harm to look. You know, I'm not dead yet."

Carl ignored Rose's comment. Pressing down on

the radio's handset, he asked, "How'd he know it was a natural death? Is he a doctor or something?"

The radio was filled with static, as if Rose was no longer on the other end of the call. The silence stretched. In reality, Carl knew next to nothing about Wyatt Thornton. When the other man first arrived in Pleasant Pines, Sheriff Haak thought about digging into his past.

Yet, Thornton didn't drink, fight, drive too fast or even listen to his music too loud. In short, he was a model citizen. The job of sheriff was a busy one, more important cases arose and Carl never did get around to investigating Thornton.

Now, he wondered if that decision, made long ago, had been for the best.

Finally, Rose answered. "Honestly," she said, "I don't know. He just seemed positive, that's all." Another pause. "He's waiting at the old schoolhouse."

Pressing the talk button, Carl said, "Find out what you can about the victim."

"Sure thing, Carl."

Turning on his lights and siren, Carl swung the truck around on the empty road and dropped his foot on the accelerator. Fifteen minutes later, he was at the turnoff for the old schoolhouse. It was just a wide spot in a dilapidated barbwire fence with low scrub on what used to be a well-worn path.

The ground was covered with frost, and his truck's undercarriage passed well above any dead bushes or brambles. In the distance stood the one-room building. As he got closer, he saw Thornton and his dog standing by the door.

"Just two weeks," he mumbled to himself. Then Carl would be moving to South Carolina, where it was warm all the time and there was a beach two blocks from his tiny condominium. He put the truck in Park and killed the engine. The lights went dim and the siren fell silent.

Stepping into the cold, he shrugged on his jacket. The smell of death permeated the air.

"Morning, Mr. Thornton," he said.

Thornton stepped forward, offering his hand. "Call me Wyatt."

They shook, then the sheriff turned to business. "Well, Wyatt, can you tell me what happened?"

Wyatt gave a succinct rundown of his typical morning walk that today, ended with the dog finding the body. He concluded with, "There's no signs of trauma, so I don't think it's murder."

Carl hefted up his jeans by the belt loops. "How can you know that?"

"Experience," said the other man.

Carl waited for a moment for more information. None was offered. "You a doctor, or something?" he asked, repeating his original assumption.

Wyatt shook his head. "No, I'm not a doctor."

"A movie star?"

Thornton gave a quiet chuckle. "Not a movie star, either." After a beat, he added, "I used to work for the Behavioral Sciences Unit of the FBI."

"You got any identification that says so?" Carl asked.

"What? That says I used to work for the Bureau? I still have my old creds. You can stop by and see them if you want."

"I might do just that. Then again," said Carl, "I'm retiring soon. Two weeks then I'm off to South Carolina."

He waited for Wyatt to say something or offer the expected congratulations. Thornton said nothing. Carl cleared his throat. "One thing I know is that Rose will be excited to hear that we have a real-life G-man in Pleasant Pines."

"If you don't mind," said Wyatt with a lifted palm, "I'd like to keep my former career in the past."

With a nod, Carl said, "I respect a man of discretion."

Wyatt gestured with his chin to the schoolhouse. "Sheriff, you should probably get a look at the scene."

Wyatt walked through the front door and stopped. Carl followed. His gaze was drawn to the corpse at the far side of the room. A dead eye, gone milky white, stared straight at Carl.

Shaking off the skittering sensation that crawled up his spine, he got to work examining the body and the scene. Sure, he'd seen a few deaths in his time on the job—but something about this one just felt *wrong*.

"If you don't mind," said Wyatt. "I want to point out one thing."

"What is it?" asked Carl.

"The floor's clean," Wyatt said.

A beam of sunlight shone from a hole in the roof, illuminating the interior of the structure. Where Carl would've normally seen dirt and debris, there was nothing. "Odd," he agreed. "I would expect at least some dirt collected in a place like this."

"Me, as well," said Wyatt.

"How'd you get a name for the corpse?" Carl asked.

"I found his wallet in his pants pocket. He has a license from Illinois. I left it next to the body."

Carl walked inside and found the wallet. Flipping it open, he found the driver's license, complete with a picture. He looked back at the body. Even with the post-mortem injuries, they were undoubtedly the same man. Legally speaking, it was all he needed to make a positive identification on a John Doe. Standing, Carl dusted his hands on the seat of his pants. "Looks like this is Axl Baker."

"I don't want to disturb anything more than I already have. So, unless you need me," Wyatt said while stepping toward the door, "I'll be on my way."

"I have to get an official statement," said Carl. He followed outside. "Stop by my office tomorrow morning at eleven o'clock."

"I'll see you then," said Wyatt. He called his dog and set off.

Carl watched until they disappeared below the crest of the hill. Returning to his truck, he picked up the radio. "Rose, you there?"

"I am, Sheriff. What d'you need?"

"Call Doc Lambert. I need him to come out and pick up the body."

"Sure thing," she said. "Anything else?"

"Did you get a next of kin for Axl Baker?"

"I did. It's his sister, one Everly Baker, also of Chicago."

Carl scribbled Everly's number on a scrap of paper before signing off. He pulled his cell phone out of his pocket. Even here, there was a strong signal. He entered the number and held his breath. A woman answered the call.

"Yes?"

"Everly Baker?"

"Yes." Her voice rose an octave. "Who is this?"

"Ms. Baker." Carl paused. His temples began to throb, and he held his breath. Calls like this were the worst part of his job. With an exhale, he said, "This is Sheriff Haak in Pleasant Pines, Wyoming. I'm sorry to be bothering you, but I have some awful news…"

The following day

To Everly Baker, it looked as if Pleasant Pines had been carved out of the forest. Pine trees ringed the perimeter, and the center of town was taken up by a village green, complete with a gazebo. Wrought iron lampposts stood on each corner.

There had been a sign, welcoming all visitors and proclaiming that the population was a mere 3,200 people.

The streets were lined with businesses—a grocery store, a diner, a dentist's office and the regional newspaper. People moved about, busy with their own lives. It looked as though not much had changed in the sleepy town for years. A spring snow had started, the flakes swirling across the road. Everly would've found the scene charming, if not for the circumstances.

After receiving the sheriff's call about her brother, she'd caught a flight from Chicago to Cheyenne. From there, Everly rented a car for the last leg of her journey. After almost twenty-four hours of travel, she decided that Pleasant Pines was more than secluded—it was actually cut off from the rest of the world.

Driving down Main Street, Everly shuddered. She still couldn't believe that this nightmare was real. Axl, dead? How could that be? The very idea that her brother was gone forever—and she was all alone in the world—was too overwhelming to handle.

Easing her car into a parking place, Everly turned off the engine. Her throat tightened as a fresh wave of anguish rose from her gut. She drew in a deep breath and waited for the grief to pass.

Using the rearview mirror, she checked her appearance quickly. Her green eyes—puffy. Cheeks—blotchy. Lips—colorless. For the day, she'd swept her hair into a ponytail and a tendril of auburn hair had come loose. Everly was far from put-together. But then again, what did she expect? She'd gotten the call as she was getting ready for work, and still wore the same clothes she'd changed into—black leggings, shearling-lined boots and a long cream-colored sweater.

It was 11:10 a.m. She'd reached her destination with twenty minutes to spare until her meeting with the sheriff.

She hoped that it gave her enough time for a quick detour—even if it wasn't as much as she wanted. Years of experience in public relations had taught Everly to never attend an important meeting without getting all the facts. And as far as Everly was concerned, there was nothing more important than finding out what really happened to her brother.

After draping her purse across her forearm, she hustled through the biting wind to the hospital, situated two blocks from the town square. She followed signs to the morgue, which was located in the basement. The slap of footfalls on the tiled floor kept time with her racing heart as she descended the stairs.

Cold sweat covered her brow as she walked down the white-tiled hallway. A blue plastic sign hung, suspended by chains from the ceiling. Morgue. A metal door was the only thing that separated Everly from the truth. With a deep breath, she pushed open the door and stepped in.

A row of metal tables bisected the large room. There was a figure on the center table, shrouded with a blue sheet.

Sure, the sheriff had told Everly that her brother's body had been found. And yeah, the body had Axl's ID. Yet, she couldn't help but wonder—what if it wasn't Axl under the sheet? What if this had all been a mistake? Because there was one thing Everly knew for sure—her brother didn't die of exposure as the sheriff suggested was the most likely possibility.

She reached out with a shaking hand. Her fingertips inched closer to the sheet, brushing the fabric.

"May I help you?" A man with sparse hair, glasses and a goatee stood next to the sink at the far side of the room.

Everly gasped and pulled her hand away, startled. She took in a deep breath and let it out slowly as her racing heart slowed.

"I hope so," she said. "I'm Everly Baker, Axl Baker's sister. I spoke to Sheriff Haak yesterday and he informed me that I needed to identify my brother's body." Her voice faltered slightly on the last words, and she took another breath to steady her emotions.

"I'm Doc Lambert, ma'am, and very sorry for your loss." The man picked up a clipboard and lifted a sheet of paper. He looked up over the rim of his glasses. "I didn't expect you until after noon, but once the sheriff arrives, we can make the ID."

"Are you the medical examiner?"

"Medical examiner. Pediatrician. General practitioner. Sometimes surgeon."

"If you don't mind, I'd like to see my brother now," she said.

"It's not the way Sheriff Haak likes things done," said Dr. Lambert. "Besides, if the sheriff told you to meet him here, I'm sure he'll be along directly."

"He's not coming right now," said Everly, knowing that the doctor misunderstood her early arrival. Moreover, being direct was the only way to deal with the situation. "But I'm here now."

Still looking over the rims of his glasses, he repeated, "Like I said, Miss Baker, it's not how we do things in Pleasant Pines."

"I have to be honest with you. I think there's been a mistake."

"Mistake? How?"

"I don't think this is my brother." She gestured to the figure on the table.

"We found an ID with the body. He'd checked into the local hotel and used a credit card in his name."

"But aren't I here to see the...corpse and make a positive identification? To me, that means there's a question."

"There is some postmortem gouging to the face." Doc Lambert paused. "Maybe I should call the sheriff."

"Is there a rule in Wyoming that says a law-enforcement officer needs to be present to see a body?"

"Well, no. It's just that Sheriff Haak is particular about his cases."

"No offense," said Everly, knowing full well that she was being persistent—possibly too persistent, "but I'm pretty particular about knowing whether my brother is dead or not."

With a sigh, Doc Lambert set aside his clipboard. "Since it's not against the law, I suppose there's no harm." He moved to the table and pulled the sheet from the body, exposing the head, neck and shoulders.

Everly's chest constricted. A great wave of grief washed over her, threatening to drown her. She reached out to touch her brother's hair then pulled her hand away as the urge to scream flooded through her, pushing its way up into her throat. Yet, she stood without breathing and stared at his lifeless body.

"It's him," she whispered. "That's my brother." It was like a physical blow, acknowledging that he was, indeed, gone for good. "What happened?"

"I won't know until I conduct the autopsy and get some test results back, but it looks as though your brother got caught out in the forest at night and died of exposure. It is fairly common in these parts. Heartbreaking, but natural."

The loss of her brother—her rock for so many years—was unspeakably painful. She didn't know why or how, but Everly was certain of one thing: Doc Lambert was wrong. Her brother's death wasn't natural.

And she was going to find out what really happened to him.

Doc Lambert had given Everly directions to the county office building, only a few short blocks away. It was located on the town square in a three-story granite building, complete with pillars and arched windows. She found the sheriff's office on the second floor and pulled the door open.

A man with dark hair and eyes stood just inside,

his hand outstretched, as if he'd been about to reach for the knob. His abrupt appearance aggravated her already frayed nerves. Her heart slammed into her chest as she jumped back. Her purse wobbled on her arm, and her phone and keys fell onto the floor in the corridor. She bent to get them, and the rest of the contents—lipstick, sunglasses, wallet, receipts, chewing gum—spilled out.

"Damn." She dropped to her knees.

The man let the door to the sheriff's office close and kneeled down next to her. "Let me help you with that," he said.

She reached for her phone in the same instant as the sexy stranger. His fingers grazed the back of her hand. A shiver of awareness traveled up her arm, leaving gooseflesh in its wake.

She jerked her phone away. "Thanks," she grumbled. "I can manage."

"No, really."

He handed her a tube of lipstick. "It was my fault."

With a shake of her head, she said, "It's nobody's fault." She sighed. "I just don't need any help. Okay?"

The man lifted his hands in surrender. "Okay." And yet, he didn't leave.

As Everly scooped the rest of her belongings into her bag, she examined him from beneath her lashes. He was tall, well over six feet. His shoulders were broad and, beneath the fabric of his shirt, she could see the outline of his muscular biceps. Without question, he was more than just attractive—he was achingly handsome. His eyes were a rich and deep brown. He wore a plaid flannel shirt with tones that matched his eyes. He also had on a burnt orange vest—his look was rugged and yet, casually trendy.

Despite everything, Everly's heart gave a flutter.

His outfit was hardly anyone's idea of a uniform. But in an out-of-the-way place like Pleasant Pines, Wyoming, who knew?

"Are you Sheriff Haak?" Her voice trembled as an electric charge danced across her skin.

"Sorry, no." The man smiled and hitched his chin toward the office behind him. "He's in there."

Everly's face flamed red and hot. She had no reason to be embarrassed for the mistake, and yet she was. Immediately, she knew why. She'd been hoping all along that the tall, dark and gorgeous stranger might be the local law in these parts.

What a cliché.

The stranger stood and held out his palm to Everly. She ignored the offered hand and stood as well, taking time to zip her purse closed. Gaze still on the floor, Everly's eyes burned with tears that threatened to fall. How could she feel anything beyond miserable? When she looked up, the man was walking down the hallway.

Exhaling heavily, Everly entered the sheriff's office. Two desks, both empty, sat next to windows that overlooked the town square and gazebo. At the back of the room was an inner office with the sheriff's name stenciled onto the glass panel of the door with black paint.

Sitting behind his desk, Sheriff Haak wore a dark

brown uniform and a khaki-colored tie. A six-sided tin star and gun completed his outfit. In his sixties, balding and with a definite paunch, he looked much more like a grandfather than the Adonis she had just run into. Everly decided it was all for the best that she not let anything distract her from her goal—finding out what really happened to Axl.

"Ms. Baker, I presume," said the sheriff as he rose from his seat. He waved her into his office. "I'm sorry to meet under such terrible circumstances."

Everly approached and tried to speak, but sadness strangled her words and she just nodded.

"Sit, please," said Sheriff Haak as he gestured to a chair opposite his desk. As she sat, he reached for an opened folder. "An autopsy is required in Wyoming to determine cause of death. First, you'll need to see the body and give an identification. I warn you, it may be difficult—"

"I know," said Everly, interrupting what she imagined was a well-worn speech. "I've already been to the morgue."

"Beg your pardon?"

"I met with Doc Lambert and identified the body." She sighed. "It's my brother's."

"That's not how we do things around here," said the sheriff.

"I heard," said Everly, "I'm not interested in procedures. Only in finding out what happened to Axl."

"Doc Lambert is as good a medical man as you'll find anywhere, and will conduct a full examination. After that, you can take your brother's body back to

Illinois. I'd have to say that the ME's findings will be like mine. Sadly, we have several cases like this each year—tourists who don't understand the danger of the mountains. The way I see it, your brother died of exposure and his death was accidental."

"You're wrong," she said.

The sheriff spluttered. "I'm what?"

She had gone through the scenario several times in her mind, but now that she had the chance to plead her case the reasoning seemed thin. No, she reminded herself. It wasn't her case. She was here for Axl. And Everly would be damned if she was going to let a small-town sheriff talk her out of what she knew to be true.

"My brother was an experienced outdoorsman. He worked as a wildlife photographer," she continued. "He was here for his job—and more than that, he'd never wander off alone. He was murdered." There, she'd said it.

"Hold on a second." The sheriff poked the desk with his finger. "With all due respect—this isn't some big city, where folks get shot on every corner. Pleasant Pines is a nice, quiet town with nice people, and I've kept them all safe for decades." The sheriff leaned forward, his tone softening. "I'm sure this is all very hard for you to accept."

"My brother had been a wildlife photographer for more than twelve years. Even if he did end up lost on a cold night, he'd know what to do." Everly knew she had to convince the man. "My brother has photographed Alaska's Denali National Park in winter.

He's also done photo shoots of Death Valley at noon in July." She pressed on. "What about his camera? Did you look at the pictures he'd taken so far? There might be some kind of photographic evidence."

The sheriff leaned forward in his chair. "There wasn't a camera found with the body," he said pointedly.

Everly went numb. She'd given Axl a top-of-the-line camera for his thirtieth birthday two years ago. It cost as much as her last month's rent and he kept it with him always. "Are you sure?"

The sheriff slid a piece of paper across the desk. "This is the list of all his belongings from the scene. I catalogued everything myself. There's no camera."

Her pulse began to hammer, and her breath froze in her chest. She scanned the list, not seeing anything. "This doesn't make any sense. If my brother wasn't taking pictures, why was he outside in the middle of the night?"

"Even a seasoned outdoorsman, like your brother, could've gotten lost," said the sheriff. "I've likely been sheriff longer than you've been alive, Ms. Baker. In my experience, in cases like this, there's alcohol involved. And if your brother'd been drinking…" His voice trailed off, but she heard the implication loud and clear.

She couldn't deny that the sheriff's explanation was plausible. Sure, it had been years since the last time her brother drank. But, more than once, Axl had sworn off drinking, then fallen back into old habits. Was the explanation really so simple? She wasn't sure, but Everly refused to give up on her brother so easily.

"Have you searched for his camera?" she asked.

"Until now, I didn't know to look for one."

"Well, you should see what you can find."

Sheriff Haak gave an exasperated sigh. "Ms. Baker, why don't you let me do my job?"

Biting off what she really wanted to say, Everly clenched her teeth until her jaw ached. This man wasn't going to be any help, she could tell. That meant it was up to Everly to discover the truth. "Then if you can point me in the direction of where my brother's body was found, I'll look myself."

"Can't do that."

The hollow nothingness of grief was slowly replaced with a seething fury. She managed to keep her voice calm and steady. "Why not?"

"First, you could contaminate the scene," he said. "But there's more. Your brother was found on private property. You'd need the owner's permission to go traipsing around his land. He was the one who found Axl Baker, by the way, and called in the report."

Jaw still tight, she asked, "Can you introduce me to the owner of the property?"

"Don't need to. You've met him already."

Before Everly could ask what in the world the sheriff meant, he said. "Wyatt Thornton—he's the man who almost knocked you ass-over-teakettle at the door."

Not bothering with a goodbye, Everly rose to her feet and rushed into the corridor. She knew it was probably a bad idea to blow off the sheriff like this, but she refused to miss a chance at finding Wyatt Thornton and learning everything he knew.

But where had he gone?

She pushed out the front door and stood in the bitter cold. Luckily, Wyatt Thornton was tall, and therefore easy to find. He stood on the opposite side of the square with a large tank of propane in each hand. He began to cross the street and she rushed after him.

"Mr. Thornton," she called. "Mr. Thornton, can I speak to you for a minute!"

His pace increased.

She ran after him, her lungs burning with the thin mountain air.

He stopped next to a blue pickup truck and set the tanks in the rear bed, before strapping them in place. He removed a set of keys from his pocket.

"Mr. Thornton," she said as she advanced, her breath ragged. "That is you, right? I need your help."

Without a word, he opened the door. "I thought you said you didn't want my assistance."

So that's how he was going to act? Childish? Everly swallowed down the sharpest edges of her anger. "Look, I'm sorry if I was rude before. But I need to speak to you. It's important, Mr. Thornton."

"Wyatt," he said.

"What?"

"Call me Wyatt."

"Okay, Wyatt, I just need a few minutes of your time."

He didn't ask what she needed, but neither did he

walk away, so Everly continued. "The sheriff told me that you found my brother's body yesterday. I'd like to ask you a few questions."

Nothing.

Repeating what she'd told the sheriff, she said, "My brother was a wildlife photographer. If he was out in the middle of the night, it was for a reason—likely some assignment or other. Did you find his camera?"

Shaking his head, Wyatt said, "I didn't, but I didn't know to look for one, either."

It was the same thing the sheriff had told her. "If I could just get your permission and some directions, I could take a look. I won't be a bother, I promise."

"Sorry, but no."

"No?" she asked, her voice reedy. "Why not?"

"I told the sheriff everything. The investigation's up to him."

"I just want to see where you found his body. It might help me understand what happened. He was my brother, my only family." She paused, hating that she had shared more than she intended—hating even more that she was about to beg. "I really need answers. Please."

For a long moment, Wyatt said nothing. Everly could sense the war raging in his mind, see the furrows between his brow, his jaw flex.

"Please," she whispered again.

"I'm sorry," he said at last. "I can't get involved, and letting you come out to my place won't bring your brother back."

"What am I supposed to do?"

Wyatt looked at the ground as he scraped his toe on the cracked sidewalk. "The medical examiner's report will be in later today or tomorrow. After that, you'll have the answers you need."

Another thought came to Everly—Wyatt Thornton was hiding something. To hell with being polite—she was done. "What aren't you telling me?"

"The mountains are a hard place to survive, even with training. Accidents happen. The death of your brother is a monumental life event and you want it to have a greater meaning than just…he simply ran into bad luck." He met her gaze. "But sometimes that's all you have—a lousy destiny. I hope the autopsy gives you the answers you need."

"And if it doesn't?"

"Go home, anyway. There's nothing here for you," he said, not without sympathy.

With that, Wyatt Thornton got behind the wheel. She remained rooted to the spot as he started the engine and backed up. She watched as he drove down the main road and out of town.

He wanted her to go home—give up was more like it. Well, if he thought that she was going to be that easy to get rid of, Wyatt Thornton had better think again.

Chapter 2

Everly parked in front of the Pleasant Pines Inn, a sprawling late 19th century building of stone and timber that overlooked the town. It was the only hotel for miles and while it wasn't a five-star property on Michigan Avenue, it had loads of charm and would suit her needs nicely.

Trailing her suitcase behind her, she approached the front desk. A tall and muscular woman, with her blond hair pulled into a tight bun, greeted Everly with a smile. "May I help you?"

"I need a room," said Everly, stating the obvious.

"Reservations?" the woman asked.

In her haste to get out of Chicago, Everly hadn't bothered with the online registration. "No," Everly said. "I hope you have something available." If not, she'd have to make the three hour commute from Cheyenne.

The desk clerk tapped on a computer keyboard. "You're in luck. We have one room available, second floor. There's also a pub on-site along with a restaurant that serves dinner and breakfast. Both open today at five o'clock." She pointed in the direction of the establishments as she spoke. "What brings you to Pleasant Pines?"

Without question, the clerk was the most helpful person she'd met in Pleasant Pines. Everly read her name tag. "Darcy, can you tell me if Axl Baker had a room here?"

The desk clerk looked over her shoulder before answering in a low voice. "He did…but Mr. Baker's room is off-limits by the order of Sheriff Haak."

At least Everly knew for certain that her brother had been at this hotel. The question was, how could she get the sheriff to let her search her brother's room? Or rather, she knew that answer—he wouldn't. What she needed was a way, legal or not, to get inside the room.

She didn't have much time to plan, so her strategy was simple. Yet, it might just work.

Coughing, Everly touched her throat. "Any chance I can get a bottle of water?"

Darcy held up one finger. "Just a second, I can grab you one from the back."

Heart racing, Everly waited until the other woman disappeared through a doorway. On tiptoe, she looked over the edge of the counter. Papers. Pens.

A computer keyboard. She lifted a pile of papers and it fell out. It was the size and shape of a credit card with two stylized pine trees intertwined with the words *Pleasant Pines* in gilt script. Written in marker were four other words, the ones she needed to see: *Front desk. Total access.*

She'd found a passkey. *Score.*

She didn't hesitate and slipped the keycard into the palm of her hand. She put the papers on the desk and stepped back just as Darcy returned.

"Here you go," she said, holding out the water.

Everly took the bottle awkwardly with her left hand. "Thanks," she said, slipping her right hand into her pocket, where she deposited the stolen card.

Reaching for the handle of her suitcase, she turned from the front desk. How many rooms did this inn have and, more important, how would she find out which one had been her brother's?

"Ms. Baker?" Darcy called.

Everly increased her pace, as if she could outrun the awful truth that she had stolen a key to every door in the hotel.

"Ms. Baker? Ms. Baker?"

Damn, she'd been caught. Everly tried to think of an excuse. Nothing came to mind. Her mouth went dry. She stopped and turned around. "Yes?"

"You forgot your key." Darcy held up a keycard, a twin to the one she had in her pocket, save for the note in marker. "Room two twenty-three. Second floor. The elevator is at the end of the hallway."

Everly swayed as her knees went weak. She was

determined to find out what really happened to her brother, a few rules be damned. And yet, she was hardly used to a life of crime. What she was used to—and quite good at—was public relations, which meant knowing her customer. If her read on Darcy was right, the other woman was likely to be helpful and sympathetic.

"Thanks," she said again. Then she asked, "Do you happen to remember Axl Baker? He's my brother. He *was* my brother." Everly's voice cracked on the last word.

Darcy lowered her eyes. "I heard what happened. I'm so sorry, hon." She lifted her gaze to Everly's. "I wasn't at work when he checked in, but he did come through the lobby on his way to and from the pub."

The pub. Had Axl decided to have a beer? Or more? It wouldn't have been the first time he thought that he could handle a little alcohol and been wrong. Hadn't she worried that eventually out-of-control drinking would be the death of him? More than that, the sheriff had all but predicted that drinking was involved in the accidental death.

That was, if Axl's death was an accident. "Any idea what he was doing?"

"I'm not sure," said Darcy with a shake of her head. "He wasn't there long—thirty minutes or so." She paused and bit her bottom lip. "The bartender comes in at four o'clock—she might remember something."

Everly checked her phone for the time. 12:04 p.m. What might Everly discover in the next three and a half hours?

Did it really matter in light of the fact that Axl was gone? Was what Wyatt Thornton had said been true? Did Everly want a monumental explanation for a simple set of facts? No. She owed her brother the truth and she'd never forgive herself if she didn't find out what happened.

"Oh, if you could talk to the bartender and see what she remembers I would so appreciate it," said Everly with a small smile. "You'd be the first person actually trying to help me around here."

Turning, she wheeled her luggage down the main corridor. There were a dozen rooms on the first floor, and she guessed there were twice as many on the second. A deep green runner stretched the entire length of the hallway, with identical doors on each side. Brass numbers were affixed to each door, along with a keycard entry.

Since she had no idea which room had belonged to her brother, Everly decided a room-by-room search was in order. She also decided to start on the second floor, when something caught her eye. A paper tag had been placed over one of the locks. *Do Not Disturb* had been preprinted on the label. But it was the printed memo from the Pleasant Pines sheriff's office on the door that caught her attention:

No entry by order of the Sheriff's Department.

Bingo.

Everly didn't want to wait another minute to get into her brother's room. Looking over her shoulder, she found that the corridor was empty. After fishing the passkey from her pocket, she opened the door. Even before she stepped into the room, she knew she'd found the right place. It smelled like Axl. It was a combination of grass and dirt. No matter the occasion, Axl always smelled like the outdoors. Yet, to smell it now was both cruel and beautiful. She bit the inside of her lip hard enough to staunch a new flood of tears.

To Everly, it looked like the sheriff's deputies had already gone through the place. All the clothes had been taken from the suitcase and were piled haphazardly on one of the beds—something Axl wouldn't do. Likewise, the closet doors were open, his jackets thrown next to the pile.

A fine gray powder covered the dresser. The nightstand. Even the TV remote. It must be fingerprint powder.

For a moment, she wondered about all the crime shows she'd ever watched on TV. Was she contaminating the room, with her fingerprints or hair, just by being here? Then again what she needed were facts about what happened if she wanted to get the sheriff to look into Axl's death.

Setting aside her suitcase, she left the door slightly ajar. The curtains had been drawn and only a sliver of light shone through the place where the seams did not meet. In the dim light, she scanned the nondescript hotel room. A bureau with a TV stood against one wall. A mirror hung just to the left. A desk was next to the bureau. A chair and small table took up a corner.

There were also two beds. Both were made, but one had an opened suitcase and a shaving kit piled on it, but no camera. She riffled through the suitcase and patted down the pile of his clothes. In the pocket of a fleece jacket, she found Axl's cell phone.

Alarm bells began ringing in her mind. Like the camera, Axl was never without his phone. Everly picked it up and pressed the home button. At one time her thumbprint had been programmed into the phone. But was it still?

Holding her breath, she waited.

The home screen appeared. She scrolled through the texts—all from his work. There were no voice mails. She checked his calendar...and found one entry.

9:00 p.m. March 21. Meet at bar.

So, he had gone to the bar to meet someone. But who? More than that, was the sheriff right? Had her brother been drunk and foolish?

Everly heard the whisper of a sound and turned. As her gaze passed over the mirror, she caught a fleeting glimpse of a shadowy form. Blood froze in her veins and she began to scream. The sound died in her throat as a sharp pain filled her skull. Everly stumbled, her legs no longer able to hold her upright.

And then she pitched forward, falling into a pool of blackness.

* * *

The engine revved as it climbed the hill. The wrought iron gate that led to Wyatt's property stood open and inviting. In the distance, he saw the wide porch of his refurbished farmhouse. The newly installed solar panels winked in the early afternoon light. Pressing down on the accelerator, he rocketed past the driveway, cursing himself for what he was about to do.

Three years ago, Wyatt walked away from the FBI, after realizing he could no longer trust his instincts. So why was he now returning to the place where Axl Baker's body had been found? Did he not have any confidence in the sheriff? Had Baker's sister goaded him into looking for something that may not exist?

Or was it what he feared—that the similarities to his final case proved that he was *still* stuck in the past after all this time?

Wyatt didn't like any of the possibilities.

Nothing that happened was really any of Wyatt's business. Yet, he couldn't let it go.

It was almost twelve fifteen when the turnoff for the old schoolhouse came into view. Pulling onto the shoulder, Wyatt turned off the ignition. With a final curse, he leaped from the truck. Wind whipped off the mountains and howled as it danced along the plain. Shoving his hands into the pockets of his vest, he walked slowly to the rutted track.

He kneeled next to a sapling. The little tree was hardly higher than ten inches, and yet it had been snapped in half. Wyatt recalled the sheriff clambering out of his large truck, the undercarriage more than a foot off the ground. There was no way that the big truck had broken the little tree.

If not Haak's vehicle, then what had?

On foot, Wyatt followed the path. It was as if every plant that grew above four inches had been mowed down. Definitely done by the grille of something low—most likely a sedan. Was it a clue to a mystery, or simply an oddity with a reasonable explanation?

Clouds roiled at the peaks of the Rockies, promising to bring cold, wind and more snow. In less than ten minutes, he'd covered the last half of a mile and the little schoolhouse came into view.

The first thing he noticed was that the stench of death was gone—once the body had been taken away, no doubt the structure had been able to air out. Yellow-and-black police tape had been stretched across the door, barring entry. But it was more of a warning than a true obstacle and Wyatt ducked underneath to enter the single room. Without the body, the space seemed bigger and brighter. Less ominous.

Wyatt spent a minute trying to imagine the room in a bygone era, with a score of children sitting obediently behind rows of wooden desks. The image never held, and his mind returned to what he had seen yesterday. The body. Stone and wood. Sunlight and shadow.

A gust of wind shook the walls and sent a leaf

skittering across the floor. Bit by bit, the natural world was laying claim to the structure. He kneeled and picked up the leaf, twisting it between his fingers. Yesterday the floor had been clean, and now not.

There had to be something that he'd missed.

Thinking back to Everly Baker's insistence about her brother's habits, Wyatt stepped back outside, scanning the ground around the cabin for any sign of Axl's missing camera. The glint of metal. Glass, reflecting the light.

There was nothing.

With his back to the door, Wyatt crossed his arms over his chest and looked across the horizon. The mountains. The plains. The sky. And him alone in the world, just like he wanted.

Still, the mystery of Axl Baker's death was now, uncomfortably, a part of him, like dirt tattooed into the creases of his knuckles. The unanswered questions lingered, pinging away at him like popcorn in a hot pan. A body with no evident cause of death. No signs that the deceased had struggled, either. The floor, that yesterday was swept clean. Plants, broken on the trail. The missing camera. The sister, desperate for answers.

Each was a piece to a puzzle. But in reality— together, did they create a picture? Or were they even connected in the first place?

Was the broken vegetation a clue? Not really, especially when Wyatt considered that the medical examiner would've followed the same path when he came to collect the body. The dirt-free floor was harder to explain but wasn't impossible.

But what about Everly Baker? He had the power to help her. What had he offered? Nothing but trite advice. Definitely not his finest hour.

He spoke her name out loud. "Everly Baker." The wind stole the words before he could decide if he liked the way they tasted.

The feeling of their accidental touch lingered on his fingertips. Her skin had been soft, and a sweetly spicy scent surrounded her. It was somehow homey and sexy at the same time. Her eyes, a jade green, had spoken of sadness and strength.

He rubbed his fingers on his jeans.

But it had been there, something he hadn't felt— or wanted to feel—for such a long time. It was a connection with another person.

He'd come to Wyoming three years before to escape. Escape the scrutiny of higher-ups. Escape all of the questions from the media. Escape the stress, and, most important, escape the doubts that constantly nagged him, even in his dreams.

No. He wouldn't get involved in the unexplained death. He'd left the need to hunt down killers in his past life—that was, if Axl Baker hadn't died of natural causes. A few stray snowflakes danced on the wind. He looked at the mountains and the peak was gone—completely obscured by the clouds. Soon enough, the storm would be in the valley and Wyatt didn't want to be caught lingering by the old schoolhouse.

Turning back to the track, Wyatt began the walk to his waiting truck. From there, he'd take the road home and return to the life that kept him safe. Sheltered.

Alone.

Everly was swimming. The water was dark and cold. The surface hovered above her, just out of reach. A voice called to her from the shore.

"Ms. Baker? Ms. Baker? Can you hear me?"

Everly wanted to speak, but her mouth filled with murky water. Gasping, she broke the surface and found that she was lying on a carpeted floor. She could feel a rough mark imprinted on her cheek, yet nothing else seemed real.

"Ms. Baker?" A tall blond woman was kneeling next to Everly.

And then it all came back to her—Axl's death, his missing camera, her stealing the keycard to get into his room. But why was she on the floor?

"Ms. Baker, can you hear me?" It was the woman who worked at the front desk and her name was Darcy; she now remembered that, too.

"What happened?" Everly's mouth was dry, her lip was tender.

"I came down the hall and saw that the door was opened a bit. I thought maybe one of the deputies had come by. I almost closed it without looking, but I peeked in and saw you on the floor."

Everly sat up—the back of her head throbbed. She glanced at the bedside clock. She'd only been out for a few minutes. "I was hit," she said, recalling the single glimpse of the silhouette in the mirror.

"Hit?" echoed Darcy. Her voice was a whisper. "By who?"

"I didn't see a face," said Everly. "Just a shadow."

"Are you sure? There wasn't anyone in the hall. Nobody came through the lobby, either."

"Well, I know what I saw, and I know what happened to me," Everly insisted.

"You wait here," said Darcy as she got to her feet. "I'm going to call Sheriff Haak, and the doctor, too. A hit to the head that's strong enough to knock you out probably gave you a concussion."

The sheriff? So far Darcy hadn't pressed Everly for how she got into the room, even though it was obvious. What would the sheriff say? Certainly, Everly had broken at least one law when she stole the keycard and entered a room that wasn't hers—the official order to stay out notwithstanding.

Then again, Everly would bet anything that the attack hadn't been random. She'd been targeted. That didn't put anyone else at risk, but it left *her* exposed. The bump on the back of her head was a warning—nothing more. If anyone wanted her dead, they could've easily killed her in the minutes that she was unconscious. The thought left her chilled, and she crossed her arms over her chest to staunch a tremble.

"Hold on a second," she called to Darcy. Everly stood slowly, the throbbing at the back of her head increasing in tempo and intensity. "I'm not sure that

I was hit. I mean, I hit the back of my head—but I might have fainted and come down on the edge of the nightstand."

"You were so sure you'd been attacked just a minute ago."

"My brother died unexpectedly, and I flew all night from Chicago to be here. I was standing in his room and it smells like he did, you know. It was overwhelming." Everly sighed and touched the lump on the back of her head. She winced. "To be honest, there's nothing that I'm actually sure of right now."

"Even if you don't know, you should still talk to the sheriff."

"I really don't want him involved."

Darcy shook her head. "You have been through a lot and I don't want to make trouble for you. Just, please, don't make any trouble for yourself. Sheriff Haak is a good man—he'll figure out what happened."

"I hope so," said Everly.

"If you fell, you still need to see a doctor. I can call him for you."

"I've met Doc Lambert already. I'll get in touch once I get to my room," said Everly, even though she had no intention of calling anyone.

"Are you sure?" asked Darcy.

As if to prove that she was fit, Everly grabbed the handle of her suitcase and rolled it from the room. "Positive," she said, then added, "Thanks for everything."

Darcy followed Everly and pulled the door closed.

"Call the front desk if you need anything at all—that's legal at least."

Everly held out the purloined keycard. "Sorry about that," she said.

Darcy took the card. "Just don't do it again, and we'll be even."

After giving the desk clerk a wave, she walked to the elevator. Thank goodness Everly knew how to sell a story. In fact, her bit about fainting had been so convincing that Everly almost believed it herself. Now that she didn't have to deal with the sheriff, she needed to find out who would want to keep her away from Axl's death.

In her estimation, there was only one suspect. It was the same man who wanted her gone and had also found her brother's body.

Everly wheeled the luggage to her room and entered. Despite the fact that her head still throbbed, she sat at the desk. Removing her laptop, she powered it up and entered two words into the search engine. Wyatt Thornton.

There wasn't much on the internet about Wyatt Thornton. A real-estate transaction, along with a local address. She wrote down the address. And a notice that he'd adopted a dog from a county rescue.

There had to be more. In this day and age, nobody lived off the grid. And if they did, it was because they didn't want to be found.

She tried again. W. Thornton.

The search was met with a question. *Did you mean Special Agent W. Thornton?* Thousands of hits followed. She scanned headlines from articles about a notorious serial killer in Las Vegas and the FBI profiler in charge of the case: W. Thornton. She moved the cursor to hover over the *No* icon. Then she stopped. Her eye was drawn to a photograph of several FBI agents, and one of them was unquestionably the same one she met earlier today, Wyatt Thornton.

His hair was longer now, with just a touch of gray that he hadn't had when the photo had been taken years ago. The suit he wore had been replaced with jeans, but it was him.

Immediately she wondered why he'd come to Wyoming and, more important, why not tell Everly if he had a professional opinion about her brother's death?

She clicked on the article, which was four years old. A string of killings—all single men—had stunned the hard-to-shock city of Las Vegas. The FBI, through their behavioral scientist, Thornton, had a suspect. On closer scrutiny, the suspect had an alibi for one of the killings. It was a fact that had been missed, or possibly suppressed, by Thornton.

The media didn't have a killer, but they had an incompetent or possibly dishonest FBI agent. Thornton had been crucified by the press. And the killings? They stopped. One subsequent article wondered if it hadn't been a fabrication of Thornton's all along.

For a moment, she felt sorry for Wyatt. And then she wondered—if he'd have come to her for public-relations help, what would she have said? Probably that he should move someplace where no one knew who he was, or didn't care.

At least she knew what he'd been trying to hide and why he wanted no part of a possible murder investigation.

She hesitated for only a minute before pushing back from the desk. She grabbed the keys to her rental car. As she picked up the hastily copied address, she made a decision. Wyatt Thornton had investigated murders before. He was an expert in unexplained crimes. He would know how to put all the puzzle pieces together and his was an expertise she was determined to use.

Chapter 3

Wyatt sat behind his desk and stared at the computer screen. Nearby, a fire crackled in the hearth. Gus was lying in the middle of the room, soaking up the warmth. Eyes closed, the dog's chest rose and fell with each breath.

Call it a compulsion, but despite vowing that he'd leave the Axl Baker investigation alone, Wyatt had dug an old case file from where he stored his important paperwork in the spare bedroom. He'd also opened an internet search for the deceased. So far, there was nothing of interest. Criminal record: two DUIs along with one violation of the Illinois open-container law. All three incidents had occurred more than seven years ago.

Wyatt also found a testimonial from Axl detailing his time in a Chicago addiction treatment center, along with several of his photographs that were part of an auction held five years back. Since that time, there'd been nothing.

Professionally, Baker was a successful photographer who worked freelance for some of the world's most popular nature magazines. Just as his sister had said, he had plenty of experience to survive a night or two outside in the wilderness. Could it be suicide? It was impossible to really know anyone. Still, taking his own life didn't seem to fit the profile here.

Gus lifted his head and looked toward the window, letting out a bark.

He heard the engine a moment before he saw the car's light cutting through the gathering storm. A car turned from the main road onto his driveway. The promised snow had arrived, and the car's headlights illuminated the flakes as they fell.

Standing at the window, Wyatt peered into the storm. Gus moved to his side and lifted his paws to the sill, barking as the car pulled up to the house.

"I see her, boy." Even from a distance, he could see the driver—Everly Baker. The feeling of her hand beneath his fingertips returned. The memory ran up his arm and traveled down his spine. With a shiver, he threw another log on the fire.

Gus began to bark in earnest and Wyatt saved the internet search for Axl Baker, then powered down his computer. The doorbell chimed, and he paused a moment. Everly Baker was the first visitor to his house and Wyatt's jaw instinctively tightened.

He glanced around the room—sofa, desk, easy chair. TV on the wall. Exposed wooden beams on the ceiling. He'd done all the work to the house himself, knocking down walls to create a single room. More that, Wyatt had kept the original moldings and window seat. Through all his time and effort he had created more than a home—a refuge.

Yet, he hadn't dedicated years to have his house invaded by an uninvited guest.

He opened the door and there she was, on his stoop, hand lifted and ready to knock. The wind whipped through her hair, making it look like she was surrounded by flames. She was more than beautiful, she was fierce—the vengeful goddess of a Celtic clan. Then he reminded himself that her problem was not his and he decided to be as unfriendly as possible. "What do you want?"

Gus nosed past Wyatt, his tail wagging. The dog approached Everly, panting.

She bent down and ran her hands through the dog's coat. "Well, who's a handsome boy?"

The dog licked Everly's chin. So much for being unfriendly. She giggled.

"Gus, come here."

His order went ignored.

"Gus," he said, dropping his voice.

The dog looked over his shoulder and trotted to stand at Wyatt's side.

"Sweet dog," said Everly, rising to her feet.

Wyatt shrugged. "You didn't come here to meet my dog. What do you want?"

"Aren't you going to invite me in?"

"I wasn't planning on it," he said.

"It's freezing out here and I just want to talk to you for a minute." She blew on her hands and rubbed them together. "I bet Gus has a warm belly that he likes to have rubbed."

The dog barked excitedly. Wyatt opened the door. "You can have a minute but leave my dog's belly alone."

After leading her to the den, he gestured to the sofa. "Have a seat."

She sat as he took a chair opposite her. She slipped out of her coat and Wyatt took a moment to admire her outfit and the way it molded to her curves. A long, cream colored sweater accentuated her breasts and a pair of leggings skimmed over her long legs. Despite the simplicity of her outfit, Everly Baker was chic and totally out of place in his modified farmhouse.

"I won't waste your time with small talk," she began. "I need your help."

"Lady," he said. "I'm the wrong person to come to for help."

She ignored his statement and continued to speak. "There's something wrong regarding my brother's death and I don't know what it is. I get the feeling the sheriff wants this all to go away quickly and aside from him, there's no one I can trust." Everly paused, then said, "Except you."

"What makes you think I'm trustworthy?"

Gus wandered to the sofa and placed his head on Everly's lap.

Traitor.

"I did a little Googling." She stroked the top of Gus's head and continued, as if talking to the dog. "It wasn't like the information was hard to find. I know who you are, Special Agent Thornton. More than that, I know that you can help me figure out what happened to my brother."

Wyatt hadn't been called Special Agent for years. Nor did he ever want to hear his old title spoken again. His insides turned cold and hard. "You really should leave."

"The press didn't treat you fairly," Everly continued as if he hadn't just ordered her from his home. "I mean, it's their job to sell papers and get viewers— but I don't think you did anything wrong."

Who was she to decide how he'd been treated? She wasn't there. She didn't know what it was to have his life ruined by innuendo and implications. Rising to his feet, he pointed to the door. "Out," he said.

Everly lifted her palms. "Like I said, I'm trying to figure out what's going on. I need an expert and you're an expert. I need you. I can pay, if that's the problem. Just name your price."

"My past is none of your business and I'm definitely not interested in your money." His pulse raced, pounding in his skull. Clenching his teeth, Wyatt said, "Get the hell out of my house and don't ever come back."

Gus whimpered and slunk to his bed in the corner.

Everly stood. All the color drained from her cheeks, leaving her chalky. She drew in a deep breath. It didn't do much for her complexion. "I didn't mean to invade your privacy."

Snorting, Wyatt said, "You're kidding, right? You look me up on the internet, find out all my dirty secrets, get my address and then come to my house uninvited? The only thing you've done is invade my privacy."

With a nod, Everly turned to go. She picked up her coat from the sofa and slid it over her shoulders. "You're right," she said. "I didn't care anything about your privacy, but I need to know what happened to my brother. I snuck into his hotel room and was attacked. That's why I found you on the internet—"

"Attacked?" Wyatt interrupted. "By whom?"

With a shake of her head, Everly said, "They came up from behind and hit me hard enough to knock me out. When I found out who you are—were—I knew I had to ask for help. I'm sorry to have bothered you."

"What did the sheriff say about the attack?" Wyatt really had to stop acting like he cared. Someone might get the wrong idea.

Everly regarded him for a moment. Her eyes were ringed with dark circles. She didn't just look tired, she looked exhausted. "I imagine Sheriff Haak would be more upset that I broke into Axl's room than that I'd been assaulted."

"I'm sure you know that you shouldn't be driving if you'd lost consciousness."

"I was healthy enough to drive out here, wasn't I?"

"No offense, but you look like crap."

"Gee, thanks."

"You just look like you've had a rough day, that's all."

"The worst of my life," she said. Her eyes shone with tears and she looked away.

Wyatt hesitated. Against his better judgment, he could feel his resolve softening slightly. "If you looked me up on the internet, then you can guess why I don't want to get involved in any suspicious deaths."

"You think there's something to investigate?"

"I didn't say that," Wyatt retorted. "I meant that there's no immediate medical reason for your brother to have died."

"Axl was found on your property, right? You can take me there now and show me where you found him, at least. Maybe we can find his camera. It wasn't in his room, which means it's still out there, somewhere. There's got to be a link or a clue."

Wyatt refused to admit that she was right. He also refused to admit that he'd already looked for the camera but found nothing. He turned to the floor-to-ceiling windows and saw nothing but the whiteness of the swirling snow. "There's no real road out to the old schoolhouse, just a rutted track. With weather like this, it'd be easy to get disoriented or stranded. So, I'm not going out there until the weather clears, and neither are you." He exhaled, realizing that he was about to make the worst decision of his entire life. "I'll give you a ride back to town while the roads are clear, though. You shouldn't be driving with a head injury and in a storm, no less." He held up a hand to stop her protest. "And, I'll agree to review all the facts and evidence that we have so far. If there's something that doesn't seem right about your brother, I'll talk to Sheriff Haak personally."

Back in Pleasant Pines, Everly stood on the sidewalk in front of a restaurant. The wind was turning the snow into projectiles that left the skin on her face raw. The lump at the back of her head thumped with each beat of her heart. "Pie?" she said, echoing Wyatt's last word.

"Yeah, pie. Flaky crust. Filling of choice."

A lock of hair blew across her face and she pulled it away. "Why pie?"

Wyatt lifted one shoulder and let it drop. "I like pie," he said. "It's like a ritual. Helps me think." Pulling open the glass door, he gestured for her to enter. "Come on. Let's get out of the cold."

Everly stepped into Sally's on Main. Half a dozen booths lined the wall by the door. Opposite was a counter with stools and in between sat several small tables. Aside from another couple in the back booth and a woman behind the counter, the restaurant was empty.

Wyatt slid into a booth halfway back and Everly took the opposite seat. The woman from behind the counter approached with a pen and order pad in hand.

"Hey, sugar," the older woman said to Wyatt. "What can I get for you?"

"Got some apple pie, Sally?"

"Sure do," she said. "You want that warmed and served with ice cream?"

"Is there any other way?" asked Wyatt. "And a cup of coffee."

Sally turned to Everly. "What about you, hon?"

"I'd love some apple pie, thanks."

The couple from the back of the restaurant stood and walked forward. The man, tall with a shaved head, nodded a greeting at Everly, then glanced at Wyatt and stopped abruptly. "Wyatt? Wyatt Thornton? I haven't seen you in forever."

"Marcus?" Wyatt got to his feet and shook the other man's hand. "Marcus Jones, it's great to see you. What're you doing in Pleasant Pines?"

"I'm grabbing a late lunch with my friend Chloe Ryder. She's the local district attorney." He whistled through his teeth. "I honestly never thought I'd see you again. You disappeared after leaving the Bureau. What are you doing with yourself these days?"

"I live in Pleasant Pines."

"Well, it's great to see you. Wyatt, this is Chloe. Chloe, Wyatt."

Chloe, a tall brunette with a fringe of bangs, took Wyatt's hand. "It's a pleasure," she said with a smile.

"Nice to meet you, Chloe," Wyatt said. "Ah, this is Everly Baker." He paused, and she wondered how he was going to explain her to the duo. "She's from Chicago."

Pleasantries were exchanged and then Wyatt

asked, "How's work? Are you still the special agent in charge in the Denver office?"

"I left the Bureau, if you can believe that."

"Been there, done that, have the T-shirt."

Marcus laughed. "Anyway, I joined a private security group out of Denver and we've opened an office in Wyoming. What about you? Where are you working now?"

"Me?" Wyatt shook his head. "I quit altogether after what happened in Las Vegas. A quiet life suits me just fine."

"Maybe you should stop by. You could be a great asset to the team."

"I'm not much into being a team player anymore," said Wyatt.

"You never know. Private security might suit you better than a quiet life."

"Private security," Wyatt repeated. "What does that mean? Are you a private investigator? Do you find cheating spouses?"

"We are so much more than that." He took a pad of paper and a pen from his coat pocket and scribbled for a moment. "That's my cell number. Call and I'll give you the tour—tell you a few war stories. Hell, some of them might even be true."

"I'm not interested in work, but thanks." Wyatt waved away the offered paper.

"Take it," said Marcus. "You never know when you might need a friend."

Wyatt folded the sheet of paper placing it in his back pocket.

"Anyway," said Marcus, "Chloe has to get back to work, and I'll let you two get back to your date."

Date. The one word hung in the air, like smoke. It reminded Everly of how handsome Wyatt Thornton was and how very long it had been since she'd actually gone out on a date. "He seems nice," said Everly once they were alone.

"Marcus Jones is as good as they come."

Sally returned with their pie and coffee. The conversation stalled as she set everything on the table. Everly took a bite, chewing slowly. The crust was light and buttery, the apples inside sweet, with just a touch of spice. She sighed. "You're right," she said. "Best pie ever."

Wyatt smiled. "I'm glad you like it, but let's get back to why we're here to begin with. First, do you know what your brother was supposed to photograph?"

"A wolf-pack migration, I think," she said. She bit her lip. "I can't recall the magazine he was on assignment for, but I can find out."

"Do you think he was targeted because of his work?"

She took a sip of coffee, which was surprisingly good for a diner in Nowheresville, USA. "No way. My brother was a good person and could charm the hell out of anyone. And he was good at what he did, the best photographer I've seen. Everyone loved Axl."

Wyatt scooped a bite of pie into his mouth. "What else?"

Everly's mind had been so full of possibilities, but now it was empty. Then she remembered. "The sheriff gave me a list of all Axl's possessions." She dug through her purse and found the folded note.

Flattening the sheet on the table, she read aloud. "Shirt, shoes, socks, wallet, three credit cards in the name of Axl James Baker. One hundred and twenty dollars in twenty-dollar bills and half of a two-dollar bill."

"Wait," said Wyatt. "Go back. Read the last line again, the one about the money."

"One hundred and twenty dollars in twenty-dollar bills and half of a two-dollar bill."

"The last case I worked." He paused.

"The serial killer in Las Vegas," Everly offered.

"He left a calling card of sorts on each of the victims. To avoid copycat killers, we never shared that fact with the media." Wyatt paused and took a drink of coffee. "It was half of a two-dollar bill."

Everly began to tremble. She grasped her hands together and asked with a whisper, "Are you saying...? Did a serial killer murder my brother?"

"It's worse than that," said Wyatt.

Everly couldn't imagine what might be worse. "Really? How is that possible?"

"Not only was your brother murdered, but the killer is on the loose in Pleasant Pines. As that bump on your head proves, he knows exactly who you are—and you could very well be the next victim."

The stench of antiseptic hung in the air and Carl Haak's eyes watered. He leaned against the stainless steel counter and concentrated on the feeling of cold metal against his hip. The corpse of Axl Baker was laid out on a table, a cloth pulled up to his chest.

"My initial finding," said Doctor Lambert, "is that the deceased had a blood-alcohol content of point-one-five."

"That's good and drunk," said the sheriff, "and well above the legal limit, but not enough to cause death."

Doctor Lambert was a slight man with gray hair and a pointy beard. The combination always put Carl in the mind of a billy goat. Doc Lambert stroked the end of his beard for a moment. "I don't think so, either."

"Then why do we have a corpse?"

"My best guess? Our Mr. Baker drank too much, got lost and either laid down to sleep it off or he passed out in the old schoolhouse. The alcohol would've slowed his circulation, making it easier for hypothermia to set in. He simply never woke up."

"Are you willing to put that as the cause on a death certificate?"

Doctor Lambert stroked his beard again. "There's no other explanation. No other trauma. No bruising anywhere. No signs of cardiac arrest. Nothing." With a nod, he moved to the counter next to Carl and a tablet computer. After typing in a few notes, he said, "I'm calling it. Cause of death is accidental exposure. I'll file the paperwork with the county office and the body will be ready for transport first thing in the morning."

Carl quickly thanked the doctor and pushed open the door. He took in deep, gulping breaths as he strode down the basement hallway. A set of stairs led to the hospital's ground floor. He avoided the main entrance and emergency room, sneaking out a side door instead.

A cold wind hit him in the face and blew away the remaining odor from the morgue. He pulled up the collar of his coat and shouldered his way through the gathering snow. Only two weeks, Carl reminded himself, and he'd be done with the bitter cold. Done with this job. Until then, a few things remained to be done.

He needed to meet with Axl Baker's sister. And he was dreading the conversation.

Figuring she'd have checked into the Pleasant Pines Inn—since it was the only lodging in town— he headed in that direction. Walking down Main Street, he glanced in the window of *Sally's* and stumbled. There, in one of the middle booths, sat Everly Baker along with Wyatt Thornton. No time like the present, he thought, so he pushed open the door and entered the restaurant.

Everly looked up and Carl lifted a hand in greeting. As he approached the booth, he said, "I saw you from outside and decided to stop. I hope you don't mind, but I have news."

Wyatt moved over in his seat, making room for Carl. "I'm glad you're here, Sheriff. We have something for you, too."

Carl didn't exactly ignore the comment, but he

didn't want to be distracted. "I just spoke to the medical examiner. It seems your brother had a good bit of alcohol in his system. It decreases circulation and the cold and exposure likely affected his body temperature as well, no matter how good an outdoorsman you tell us he was." He removed his hat, set it on the table and sat. "I'm sorry, Ms. Baker, but your brother's death has been ruled as accidental."

Everly's cheeks reddened. "That's impossible."

"I know this is a shock and not what you'd hoped we'd find." He wasn't sure how to proceed and be delicate at the same time. "I am sorry for your loss."

"It's impossible," she said again. "We have proof that he was murdered."

Carl leaned back in the booth, looking skeptical. "Proof? What kind of proof."

Wyatt spoke then. "When I was with the FBI, I investigated a string of killings. All the victims were white males and each body was left with half of a two-dollar bill in their pocket or wallet."

"So?"

Wyatt pushed a sheet of paper in front of Carl. The sheriff recognized the list of Axl Baker's belongings. Pointing to a line on the page, Wyatt said, "See...here—a two-dollar bill, and only half of it found with the body."

"And this is your proof? That doesn't mean anything. He could've gotten that money anywhere."

"Tell me if I'm wrong but isn't it odd to find only half a bill?" asked Everly.

"You're wrong," said Carl. "All you have is circumstantial evidence. You're playing guessing games."

"All the victims in Las Vegas had very high blood-alcohol content and had been left for dead."

"Let me get this straight—you're telling me that a murderer was killing people with booze? I've been a police officer for a long time. Too much drink will make you sick long before it'll kill you. It'd be a tough way to murder someone."

"Once we made the connection between the two-dollar bills, we also discovered that the victims had high levels of anti-nausea medicine in their bodies. It was enough to knock them out and let the alcohol poison them."

Carl didn't have anything to counter that claim, not yet at least.

He did have another idea, though. "Well, let's just figure that Axl was killed. Who should I suspect, Wyatt? You? The deceased was found by you on your land, after all. Most of the information I have is from you, too."

"Don't be ridiculous," said Wyatt. "If I killed him, why would I link it to my previous case?"

"It's no more ridiculous than you telling me that there's a serial killer in Pleasant Pines."

"That brings up an interesting point," said Everly. "How many accidental deaths are there in the county each year? How many men go missing while hunting or skiing or hiking in the area?"

Carl poked the table with his finger. "This is my

town. How dare you insinuate that I can't keep my own people safe."

She continued, "I didn't mean to suggest anything, it's just that there's a connection that needs to be explored."

"Your brother's death has been ruled as accidental. End of story. His body will be ready for transport back to Illinois first thing tomorrow. When that happens, I want you gone, Ms. Baker. There's nothing for you to suss out here in Pleasant Pines."

Carl stood and shoved his hat onto his head. He stalked out of the restaurant and into the soft afternoon light.

Chapter 4

Everly gaped at the retreating sheriff. Her shock at the thought that her brother might have been the victim of a serial killer mixed with incredulity over how Sheriff Haak acted. Or was it overreacted? She wanted to scream or cry or throw something. Instead, she just stared after him, numb.

"Tell me that didn't just happen," she said, after a moment.

"It happened."

"I can't believe that Sheriff Haak would dismiss our evidence so quickly."

Wyatt took a sip of his coffee and then scraped up the last bit of pie. He lifted the fork to his mouth and stopped. "He's too territorial for his own good," he said, and then took a bite. After chewing and swallowing, he informed her, "He's retiring soon, and he thinks that having a serial killer in his town would say a lot about the job he's done."

"Well, it would," said Everly.

"I'm not saying he's right or that you're wrong. But I've seen this before—for him it's personal. Then again…" He paused. "It's always that way with cops and a homicide."

It didn't take much for Everly to realize that Wyatt was talking about himself and the case from Las Vegas. "So you're saying that even though there's evidence potentially linking Axl's death to a serial killer, there's nothing I can do, because the sheriff might feel bad? That's the most ridiculous thing I've ever heard."

Wyatt's gaze met hers. "Lower your voice," he whispered.

Everly didn't realize that she'd been yelling, and in truth she really didn't care. All the same, she cast a glance toward the counter and found it empty. Most likely, Sally was in the kitchen. "It doesn't matter how loud I am, or what tone I use," she said, matching Wyatt's whisper with a hiss of her own. "My brother is dead, and the sheriff is willing to sweep all the evidence under the rug."

Wyatt looked outside, his reflection trapped in the window. "I'm in." Turning, he met her gaze. "I'll help you figure out what happened to your brother."

"Are you sure?"

"Do you want my help or not?"

"Of course. It's just…until now, you were just so certain that you wanted nothing to do with this case."

Wyatt sighed. "This is my mess that I failed to clean up in Las Vegas."

"I just want justice for Axl."

Wyatt picked up his cup and took a long drink. "You'll get it, but first we have to keep you safe. Since the killer knows you're in town, you can't keep staying at the Pleasant Pines Inn. Especially since someone already attacked you there."

"It's the only hotel in town. What am I supposed to do? Sleep in my rental car?" Everly asked. At the same time, she knew Wyatt was right. She couldn't stay in the hotel—not alone and with a murderer on the loose.

"I was thinking," said Wyatt. He lifted his eyes to hers.

His eyes were more than brown—there was dark gray woven in, as well. It reminded her of the sky as a storm rolled in from Lake Michigan. He had a cleft in his chin that she hadn't noticed before. She reached for her fork and twirled it through her fingers.

"I was thinking," he repeated. "You could stay at my place."

"I could?" Dear God, had she just squeaked? Clearing her throat, she tried again. "It's a nice offer, but I'm not sure I should accept."

"The way I see it, you really don't have a choice. Besides, this is for your own protection."

Everly felt drawn to Wyatt even more. She'd seen how isolated he was—rather than warning her off, there was something almost…alluring, about him. As if he was a puzzle to be solved.

She'd have to be careful not to become too attached. The reclusive ex-agent wasn't her ideal partner, that's for sure. And yet, there was something undeniably intriguing about him.

"So," she said, "what do we do now?"

"We'll need to get your things from the hotel. Then when we get back to my place, I'll look through my old case file. There might be something in there that can help me."

"Us," she said. "You mean *help us*."

Wyatt rose to his feet and withdrew his wallet from the back pocket of his jeans. He threw several bills on the table. "In all honesty, I work better alone. I always have."

Everly got to her feet, as well. "It's too bad then, because this time you have a partner."

Wyatt pulled into a parking space in front of the Pleasant Pines Inn and turned off the ignition. Was he really going to bring Everly to his house? His home was a sanctuary and to allow another person inside would taint the sacredness of his space. Then again, what he said earlier had been true. She couldn't stay at the hotel, not with a serial killer out there, somewhere. She needed protection.

The question was, did it have to be him?

He gave a passing thought to calling his old buddy from the Bureau, Marcus Jones. A private-security outfit might suit Everly's needs better. But Wyatt knew the real reason he had offered up his house.

He wanted Everly with him.

It was extremely simple and monumentally complicated at the same time.

"I'll be right back," said Everly as she opened the door.

Cold air hit Wyatt in the face, sweeping away the regrets and doubts. He took the keys out of the ignition, shoved them into his pocket and opened his own door. "I'll come with you."

"I'm used to doing things on my own and can handle getting a suitcase by myself," she said with a smile. "I am a big girl, you know."

Wyatt knew all too well that Everly was one-hundred-percent woman. From her long legs, to her fiery tresses, to her full lips, Everly was the complete package. He put aside his attraction and said, "Remember what happened last time?"

She touched the back of her head, her fingers prodding the place where she'd been hit, no doubt. The smile faded. "You're right. Thanks."

They approached the front of the hotel and he pushed open the doors. The desk clerk looked up from her post.

"Hi, Darcy," said Everly. "My plans have changed, and I'll be checking out. Can I get my bill?"

"Since you really didn't use the room there won't be a charge."

"Thanks for everything," said Everly with a smile.

"Ms. Baker," the desk clerk said. "I spoke to the

bartender about the night your brother came into the pub. Do you have a moment?"

Everly sucked in a breath. The color drained from her cheeks, leaving her skin the delicate shade of porcelain. "Of course," she said, still breathless.

"Well, Johanna, that's the bartender, said that she overheard your brother arguing with one of the cooks. His name is Larry Walker."

An argument that ended up with one party dead was never good. Did Sheriff Haak know? And if so, why didn't he mention the fight to Everly?

There was also the very real possibility that Haak hadn't bothered to ask too many questions. Maybe he knew nothing about Larry Walker.

Doubt snuck up on Wyatt. Was Haak simply old and tired of doing his job? Had he been sheriff so long that he didn't care? Or was it worse? Could the sheriff somehow be involved in Axl Baker's death— and the others in Las Vegas, besides?

True, Carl Haak didn't fit the typical age range of a serial killer. Most of killers hunted in their mid-twenties to early thirties. But, he was a white male— the hallmark gender and race for most, if not all, serial killers.

It was an interesting theory that deserved to be explored more. Until then, it was up to Wyatt to find out all he could about Axl's last day in Pleasant Pines.

"Do you know what they argued about?" he asked.

The desk clerk shook her head. "Johanna didn't overhear much beyond raised voices and something about immigration."

"Could it have been migration? As in a wolf-pack migration?" Everly asked.

To Wyatt, the question made complete sense. Especially since Axl had come to the area to find a wolf pack migrating.

The desk clerk shrugged. "To be honest, I have no idea. I'm just telling you what Johanna told me. Like I said earlier, Everly, Johanna should be in by four o'clock."

"What about Larry?" asked Wyatt.

Darcy shook her head. "He's not on the schedule. I checked."

"Thanks, Darcy," said Everly.

Wyatt echoed, "Thanks."

"You're welcome, Wyatt," she called after them.

Without comment, Wyatt and Everly walked down the long corridor and stopped at the elevator as they waited for the doors to open. "How well do you know Darcy?" Everly asked.

He shrugged. "I don't know her, not really."

"She seems to know you."

Was Everly jealous? At least she was interested in his life. It had been years since anyone cared and Wyatt wasn't sure how he felt about the intrusion. The elevator doors opened, and he waited for Everly to enter.

"Small town, I guess," he said, following Everly. "Anyone new would cause a stir."

The doors closed and then they were alone. The exotically spicy scent of her perfume filled the tiny space, coating his skin and lingering on his lips. It was an exquisite torture to be alone with Everly and Wyatt's mind was occupied with images that were as sexy as her fragrance. His body reacted, reminding him how long he truly had been without a woman's touch.

"What do you think about what Darcy said?" Everly asked, interrupting Wyatt's thoughts. "Isn't it suspicious that my brother has an argument the night that he also happens to be murdered?"

"It's more than a little suspicious. It's something that Sheriff Haak should've known and investigated."

The elevator doors slid open and they stepped into the hall.

"My room's up here," said Everly. "Two twenty-three." She used a keycard to open the door and crossed the threshold.

From where he stood, Wyatt could clearly see two beds. His mind immediately returned to his sexy musings. From the hallway, he mumbled, "I'll wait here."

She seemed not to notice his reluctance and said, "It'll be one second."

For years, Wyatt had lived with the fact that he'd failed to catch a killer. It was a scab that he picked at every day, never allowing it to heal. Was he really willing to try and catch the serial killer again? And what if all ended badly a second time?

Maybe it was better if he stepped away from the investigation—and Everly—right now.

True, he'd promised to help her. Yet, weren't promises made to be broken?

Underneath it all, there was a magnetic pull toward the case. To ignore that draw went against everything Wyatt was—or at least, everything he used to be.

In less than a minute, Everly wheeled her suitcase from the room. Strapped to the handle was a laptop bag. "Let me get that for you," he said, reaching for the bag.

Everly released her grip on the handle. "Thanks." They walked back down the hallway and she pushed the button for the elevator. The doors opened immediately, and they were once again in the confines of the car. The air was heavy and settled on his flesh.

"What should we do about Larry Walker?" Everly asked as the elevator came to rest on the ground floor.

"Without question we need to look into the cook and the possibility that the argument became deadly."

"How do we do that? I've watched all sorts of cop shows over the years. Do we interrogate him?" she asked as they exited the elevator.

He laughed. "It's not quite that simple, even if you are a sworn law-enforcement officer. But, neither one of us has a badge, so we're on our own and can only learn what people are willing to share. I say we start by talking with the bartender."

"Darcy said that Johanna's shift starts at four." She removed the phone from her purse and brought up the home screen. "Which is now."

At the far side of the lobby stood the in-house

bar. Despite a sign that read, Open 5:00 p.m., the lights were on.

"Looks like she's right on time," said Wyatt.

With Everly's suitcase in tow, they entered the pub. A long mahogany bar filled one wall, shelves full of liquor bottles and several beer taps sat behind. A row of bar stools stood in front and more than a dozen tables filled the rest of the room. A TV hung on the wall. There was a cable news show on, but the sound was muted. A young woman with dark hair pulled into a ponytail stood next to a cash register. She looked up as Wyatt and Everly approached.

"Sorry, folks, we don't open until five o'clock. If you come back in an hour, I can get you a drink then."

"Are you Johanna?" Everly asked.

"I am."

"Mind if we ask you a few questions?" asked Wyatt. "It's about a customer who came in two nights ago. His name was Axl Baker."

Johanna's eyes widened with sudden recognition. "That means you must be Mr. Baker's sister. Darcy told me that you might stop by."

Despite the tears that shone in Everly's eyes, she nodded.

Wyatt saw the sadness in Everly's expression, and wondered what he should do. Take her hand? Squeeze her shoulder? Nothing seemed right, and it only made him want to get the answers she sought. He said, "So, you remember Axl Baker?"

"Of course, I remember him. He was really cute,

kind of hard to forget. Then the next day we all heard what happened. It was just real sad."

"We were told that you overheard an argument between the deceased and the hotel's cook. Do you know what they disagreed about?"

"It was pretty busy that night. But their voices were raised, and I heard a little bit of a quarrel over the other customers' conversations."

"What makes you say it was an argument?" asked Wyatt. He knew enough not to prejudge what had happened without more evidence. "If it was noisy, they might have been talking loud to be heard."

"It was their body language, too," said the bartender. "Larry poked Mr. Baker in the chest and Mr. Baker swiped away his hand."

"What happened next?" asked Everly.

"Then Larry sort of threw up his hands and I told him he couldn't argue with the customers and to go home. He left without causing a scene. Afterward I kind of made a joke that Mr. Baker shouldn't order anything from the menu, you know—because Larry's the cook and all."

"What did Mr. Baker do afterward?"

"He kind of laughed it off, then paid his bill and left."

Everly asked, "Do you remember what he had to drink?"

"Oddly enough, I do. It was a seltzer water and he left a tip that was twice the price of his drink."

Wyatt pictured the room as it would have been, filled with midweek customers. The two men, their discussion becoming heated. Words exchanged. One person had laid hands on the other. But did it end there? Did Larry go home and fume, getting angrier and angrier until he had to exact revenge? And while the scenario might fit a hundred other crimes, how did a serial killer play into the circumstances?

"Today's Larry's day off," said Johanna. "But I can text and let him know you're looking for him."

That was the last thing Wyatt wanted. "No thanks." He paused. "I do have one other question. Is Larry a native of Pleasant Pines?"

Johanna narrowed her eyes and pursed her lips. "I'm not sure where he's from originally. I've only been in town for a little over six years, but I do know he moved here from Las Vegas not much more than two and a half years ago."

Las Vegas? Everly felt herself shaking. There was a hot breath as Wyatt's whisper touched her neck. "Don't react here. Just listen to my voice and let's get to the truck."

Dazed, she let him maneuver her through the lobby. With a hip, he pushed open the door. Cold air and blowing snow hit Everly full in the face, shaking her from her state of shock. Drawing in a deep breath, she said, "I'm fine now."

Wyatt continued to hold her arm. She liked the feel of his strong hand on her flesh. The warmth of his body. The feel of his hot breath on her cool skin.

"Really?" he asked.

She feared that if he let go, she truly would fall.

But she'd die before admitting it. "I'm better, at least."

He opened the door to his truck and held Everly's hand as she climbed into the seat. He stowed her suitcase behind the bench and closed the door, then rounded to the driver's side. Everly concentrated on taking deep, cleansing breaths. She tried to clear her mind, just for a moment. Still, the fact that Larry Walker had moved from Las Vegas couldn't be ignored.

"Are you sure you're okay? You might be in shock, and getting hit in the head won't help anything," Wyatt said. "Maybe we should take you to see Doc Lambert."

"I'm fine," she said again. This time it was closer to the truth. "Las Vegas. That's something that links your old case to Larry Walker. The timing seemed right, too. It can't just be a coincidence."

Wyatt silently put the truck into Reverse and pulled out of the parking lot. He drove, his eyes on the road.

"I'd say Larry Walker is a decent suspect. He's better than the guy we arrested when I was with the Bureau."

"What do *we* do next?" she asked.

"We go back to my place and see what can be found about Larry Walker, formerly of Las Vegas. We check to see if he's got a criminal record. Employment history. Friends and family."

Everly sat back in the seat and stared out the window. The sky was a leaden gray and snow zoomed past like a million tiny stars. Had she really only been in Pleasant Pines for a few hours? It seemed like days. And yet, Wyatt Thornton was giving her the first shred of hope she'd had since she arrived. "I'm not sure that I've thanked you properly," she said.

"I'm not the kind of guy you should count on," he said. "I can run an internet search and ask a few questions."

"Not to be too forward," she said. "But you don't give yourself enough credit."

"Too forward?" he echoed with a laugh. "Everly, you have been nothing but forward since you tripped over me this morning."

She gave a quiet laugh. "Fair enough," she said. "I'm glad you knocked me over. You're a great resource—and someone I can trust."

"That's where you're wrong. You shouldn't trust me. I'm nobody's hero."

Everly glanced at Wyatt before looking back out the window. She wasn't some foolish girl, trying to find a man who needed fixing. If a guy came with a warning, she always listened.

Everly reminded herself, once again, that she didn't need the burden of romance. Especially if she wanted to figure out what happened to her brother.

Wyatt turned on to the long drive and his house came into view. It stood on a rise, with a thick copse of trees nearby. To her, it looked as if the home was part of the landscape, like the Rocky Mountains, the forest, or the sky.

"This house must have a lot of history," she said. "How'd you come to own a place like this?"

"I was given a really good severance package when I left the FBI. It paid for the house and gave me enough to live on for a couple of years."

That answered some of Everly's questions, but not all of them. "Why Wyoming? How'd you pick Pleasant Pines and this house in particular?"

"I was angry when I left the Bureau," he said. The truck slowed as they neared the house and Wyatt parked next to Everly's rental car. "At first, I wanted to get away from everything and everyone. No connections. Nothing. One day, I stumbled on Pleasant Pines and stopped at the diner on Main Street."

"The one you took me to earlier?" she asked, then rolled her eyes. "Please don't tell me you decided to stay because of the apple pie."

He turned off the engine but stayed in his seat. "To be honest, I don't know why I stayed. But I found a Realtor and she brought me here. Nobody had lived in this house for years—a decade almost. You should have seen it then. Peeling paint. Rotted roof. Crumbling porch."

Everly could well imagine the house and Wyatt's labor of love.

He continued, "Because it was in such rough shape, I got a great deal. I adopted Gus from a local shelter. The house needed a lot of work and those renovations occupied my time. Made it harder for me to think about…things I didn't want to think about. There's not much else to tell."

He opened his door and stepped from the truck, and Everly assumed he was done talking. Following suit, Everly hopped down just as Wyatt rounded to the passenger side. He hefted her suitcase from behind the seat and carried her bag to the door.

"I haven't had a guest before, but we can make do," Wyatt said. "The sofa's comfortable enough."

No guests? No job? No more repairs? "What is it that you do out here?"

"I walk my dog."

"That's a lot of walking."

"I go into town once a week for supplies. I stop in at Sally's and get pie and coffee. What else do I need?"

"It sounds about as opposite to my life as you can get. I work for a public relations firm in downtown Chicago and my schedule is nothing but meetings, lunches and dinner parties. And you know what? I love my job. I wouldn't have it any other way."

Wyatt kicked open the door and slapped a switch, turning on an overhead light. "After what happened to me in Vegas, I'd never go back to living at lightning speed."

His words came out with venom. Her face burned. Obviously, she'd said something wrong. "I never meant to suggest that you should. Or to criticize your life here," she began. He stared at her, his eyes as dark and stormy as the sky. Everly's words failed her. "It's just that we're different, that's all."

Wyatt cleared his throat. "I guess we are."

For the first time, Everly understood that she'd

been hoping that somehow, she and Wyatt Thornton were compatible—the wish was so secret that she hadn't even acknowledged it herself—and only felt disappointment once it was gone.

Gus ambled into the room and greeted them with a happy bark and a madly wagging tail.

Cold from the outside had crept into the house and the room held a chill. Wyatt knelt at the hearth and within minutes, flames crackled in the fireplace, filling the room with light and warmth. She sank into the sofa. Tension that she hadn't realized she'd been holding slipped from her neck.

Padding softly across the floor, Gus approached and put his head in Everly's lap. She stroked his ears and the dog closed his eyes, sighing in complete bliss. "If only it were that easy," Everly said.

"Pardon?" Wyatt stood. His body was backlit by the flames and Everly swallowed. He was strong, solid and unyielding—much like the mountains around his home.

Looking back at the dog, Everly said, "If only it were so easy to be at peace. Just a warm lap and someone to scratch you behind the ears."

"It's a whole lot easier to be tranquil when you only focus on what's important." He stoked the logs with a poker. "It's why I left the FBI."

"Have you found it, yet?" she asked. "Peace?"

Wyatt sniffed and Everly lifted her gaze. "Not exactly, but I'm closer than I was." He turned to a desk that sat in the corner and opened a drawer. After pulling out three accordion files, he returned to Everly's side. He let them drop and they hit the sofa with a *thwack*.

"What's all this?" Everly asked.

Wyatt sat down on the opposite side of the pile. "This," he said handing the top file to Everly, "is everything I saved from my final case in Vegas. Some of it is just media reports. Some are my notes. Some is confidential—but nobody asked for anything back when I left, and I sorta kept it all. I also have a flash drive with information on each of the victims' social media accounts and some pictures we took at the time of the murders. I also have copies of every victim's text messages and emails."

"Let's start with all of your hard copies." Peeling back the flap, Everly removed several sheets of paper.

"It's all in chronological order," he said.

Everly read through several police reports and couldn't help but wonder how often Wyatt looked through these files. Had he spent years perusing these same pages as he searched for clues that he'd missed?

She'd never ask, but somehow knew that her suspicion was right.

Everly held a newspaper article, probably one of the final ones written.

It was much like what she'd found on the internet earlier in the day. Over the course of eighteen months, five men had been murdered. It wasn't until corpse number three turned up that the local police involved the FBI.

At the time the article was published, a blackjack dealer was in custody and prime suspect. Yet, Everly knew that eventually, he'd been set free.

"You arrested one man for the crimes," said Everly. "What made him a suspect?"

"Serial killers seek to relive their crimes. They take trophies from the victims. They can also leave calling cards. It was my belief then, as it is now, that the killer keeps the other halves of the two-dollar bills found with the bodies. Another way that the killers relive their kill is to revisit the scene. The blackjack dealer made trips to all the sites where bodies were found. He attended all press conferences and discussed the murders in general with his coworkers. He fit the profile," said Wyatt. "So, we brought him in."

"Aside from Larry is there anyone local you suspect?"

"Until a few hours ago, I didn't have any reason to suspect anyone of any crimes. Give me a bit to see what I can find."

"We," Everly corrected. "What we can find."

"We," said Wyatt with a snort.

The conversation waned and Everly turned her attention back to the stack of papers she held. The next sheet was a letter from the Office of Professional Responsibility for the Federal Bureau of Investigation.

The letter stated that the OPR had opened an investigation into the conduct of Wyatt R. Thornton for suppressing an alibi that cleared the dealer from one of the murders—and therefore exonerating him from all of the crimes.

Due to the egregious violation of Bureau policy, the OPR recommended that Wyatt's position be terminated.

A handwritten note was scrawled across the bottom of the page. It stated simply that, "Thornton has chosen to resign. No further action will be taken."

Everly felt ill and slipped the letter back into the file folder. Had Wyatt's lie ruined his career? Was he really so bent on appearing to solve the case that he was willing to let an innocent man go to jail?

If he was, what did that mean for Everly—and her search for Axl's killer?

Chapter 5

Wyatt's eyes burned. He'd looked at all these documents hundreds of times. Hell, maybe even thousands. There was nothing new to see, and yet, he had sat and shuffled through papers as the snow quietly fell and covered the ground.

He flipped over a piece of paper and set it in the appropriate stack. There were still thousands of documents remaining. "I've looked at all of this before," he said. "Every damned time I go through the file, I think I'll find something that I missed before."

"What about now?" Everly asked as she rolled her shoulders. Reaching her arms above her head, she arched her back.

The thin material of her sweater strained against her breasts and the hollow of her neck was visible.

For a moment, he imagined what it would feel like to slide his lips over the spot, to kiss his way lower, until— "Sorry, what did you say?" *Busted.*

"What about now?" she asked.

What about now, indeed?

"Did you find anything new?"

He shook his head. "Nothing."

"What should we do next?" she asked.

"Let's take a break and eat something. Then we'll get back to reading these documents to see if there's something—anything—that has been overlooked. I've got a pizza in the freezer. It's not fancy but it is edible."

"Edible is my favorite kind of food," Everly joked.

Getting to his feet, Wyatt took the pizza from the freezer to thaw a bit on the counter while he let the oven preheat. "It'll be ready in a bit," he said.

"Isn't there more we can do—about the case, I mean?"

"Unfortunately, most cases are like a puzzle—but we're looking for the piece that doesn't quite fit." He stood. Blood flooded his legs in a hot rush and his feet tingled with pins and needles. It had been too long since he'd studied a case for hours. The aches and pains were minor when compared to the gale of adrenaline that blew threw him.

"Sounds tedious," Everly said in response to his previous comment.

"More than tedious, it can be downright mundane. Until it's not." Wyatt slid the pizza onto a baking sheet, then put it into the oven.

"When does that happen?"

"When you find something important. That's the worst of it," he said. "With an investigation, you can't make something happen—as tempting as it sometimes seems."

"Why did you choose to focus on investigating serial killers anyway?" she asked. "What was the draw?"

Wyatt hadn't meant to start a conversation about his past life. He knew that he could stop it with a brusque reply. Yet, he drew in a lungful of air and exhaled slowly. "Tracking a killer is usually about trying to understand how the killer thinks and predict their next move. Solving a puzzle. Looking for that missing piece is mundane, like I said—but it can also drag you into the darkness."

Even in the firelight, Wyatt could see Everly's cheeks redden. "It sounds like more than a job, but it was a calling."

She was right. But there was so much more to it—the camaraderie of the team, their dependence on each other. Knowing too well that their backup was often the only thing that gave him clarity as he lost himself in the depths of an investigation.

Not for the first time, Wyatt felt a connection to Everly. First it had been physical, now it was emotional. God, he wanted to kiss her, make that connection complete. Then he would finally know if her lips were as soft and full as they looked.

Wyatt forced his libido to chill and moved to the window. Wind buffeted the house as drifts of white snow blew past. He needed to concentrate. He hadn't caught the serial killer in Vegas and he'd had the full support of the FBI behind him. Back then, he didn't have any distractions like Everly Baker, either.

For the first time in years, Wyatt was having company for dinner. Or any meal really. He'd come to Wyoming for seclusion and to turn his back on all of society. But as Everly moved to the kitchen table, making stacks out of his clutter, Wyatt felt a warming in his chest. It was tempting to think that somehow his life had changed with Everly's arrival. But he was smarter than that and this moment of domesticity was fleeting and fragile as a single snowflake.

Wyatt knew if he wanted to find this killer, he needed a focus. One that was so narrow it didn't have room for romance.

Everly stood at the sink and rinsed the final plate.

"You don't have to do that," Wyatt said for what felt like the hundredth time. "I can do my own dishes."

Everly tucked the plate into the dishwasher and dried her hands on a towel. "I was brought up to be a good houseguest," she said, joking slightly. "If someone makes me a delicious dinner, I can at least clean up afterward."

"It was just a frozen pizza," he said.

She threaded the towel through the refrigerator's handle. "It wasn't freshly made, deep-dish-pizza good, but it was tasty." She turned to Wyatt and winked, to show that she was still teasing.

He gave a snort of a laugh.

"Next time I'll let you make me dinner," he said. "Maybe some famous Chicago-style pizza."

Her chest constricted, squeezing her heart. "Will there be a next time? Don't you think that Sheriff Haak is going to kick me out of town? I've definitely become persona non grata."

"You aren't going anywhere until we figure out what happened to your brother. In fact…" He paused and pivoted to face the desk. "Let's do a little internet snooping and see what we can find out about Larry Walker—the cook from the Pleasant Pines Inn who argued with your brother."

Wyatt pulled a kitchen chair up next to his desk for Everly and then sat in his own seat. He powered up the computer and entered a few keystrokes. "I paid a fee for access to a site that finds criminal records."

She scooted closer and examined the screen. A previous search bar was open and filled with three words. Axl James Baker. Her throat felt raw, like she had just swallowed a handful of gravel. When she spoke, the words were filled with flint. "You looked up my brother? Why would you do that?"

He glanced her way and then looked back at the screen. "Your brother's corpse was found on my property. You think I wouldn't be curious?"

Everly admitted he had point, even if she wasn't willing to say so out loud. "I thought you said you didn't want to be involved."

"I might not want to actively investigate a suspicious death—to take responsibility for clearing up a mystery. Tell me who wouldn't want to know more about a dead person found on their property?" He exhaled and turned away. "I didn't mean to upset you by digging into your brother's background. But I'm not going to apologize for looking. Especially since it's the only way to help gather information that might lead us to our suspect." After clearing Axl's name, Wyatt began to type.

She wanted to pursue the conversation, but how? Wyatt Thornton was proving to be an enigma and yet she sensed one thing. Wyatt was more than alone— he was also lonely. She returned her attention to the computer screen.

On a different website, Wyatt spent a few minutes finding Larry Walker's birth date. Then, Larry Walker's details, along with the locations of Las Vegas, Nevada and Pleasant Pines, Wyoming, had been entered into the original search field.

One hundred and twenty-eight hits were found.

Everly pointed at the number. "Seems like Larry has been busy being bad."

"It does," said Wyatt. He clicked on the first link. "Assault. Pleasant Pines, Wyoming. Seven months ago. Looks like Larry got into a bar fight at the Pleasant Pines Inn. He spent the night in jail and was fined five hundred dollars and released."

Wyatt scrolled through the list. "Assault. Larceny. Driving under the influence. Possession of a controlled substance."

"Doesn't sound like a nice guy. In fact, his criminal record makes him look like a total creep."

"It does," said Wyatt. He leaned back in his chair and cradled his head in his hands. "And that is what bothers me. Most serial killers aren't crooks and delinquents. They're methodical. They fit in to society, so nobody suspects them of anything—especially nothing so horrible as murder. They're violent, sure, but it's like the cold precision of a scalpel. This guy is an inferno—out of control and raging hot."

"The way I see it is that this Larry guy is violent and that's all that counts."

"That's just it—I'm not saying that Larry wouldn't hurt someone. He will. He has. In fact, I think he could actually kill someone."

"There you have it," said Everly. "He's capable of murder."

Wyatt held up a hand. "Not so fast. Larry would beat a person to death. Or shoot them in a fury. Not pump alcohol into their system and then leave them outside to freeze to death."

"Is that what you think happened to my brother?"

Wyatt sighed. "I do. There's no other explanation."

"But why?"

"*Why* was the one question I could never figure out. I guess that's how I never caught the guy. As far as the FBI is concerned, there are four things that define a serial killer. First is that the same kind of attack is repeated over time."

"As in a series of murders," said Everly. "Hence, a serial killer."

"Exactly," said Wyatt. "The second is that the methodology is the same. They might get more efficient, but the mode of killing never varies."

"So, all of these men were given too much alcohol and, once incapacitated, left for dead."

"That's how we know all the deaths are connected, and it was unquestionable once the link was made with half of a two-dollar bill found in their wallet."

"Did you ever try to get fingerprints from the money?"

"During the investigation, we got fingerprints from everything. Nothing turned up on the money—aside from thousands of other partial prints—and no two were the same. We figured our doer wore gloves. Still, we can ask the sheriff to run prints on the bill found in your brother's wallet."

Just thinking about the stubborn cop left Everly frustrated. "Do you think he'll do that for us?"

Wyatt sighed. "I have no idea."

"What about finding other fingerprints? The killer couldn't have worn gloves all the time. They had to have made a mistake once."

"The problem with the killer in Vegas, and here, is that the deaths all looked natural. After the victim's been buried—or worse, cremated—there's very little or no evidence to be collected."

"Too bad it hadn't been that easy." She hated to hear about the perverse mind of a serial killer, but if she was going to find justice for Axl, she needed to understand everything. "What else do serial killers have in common? You said there were four hallmarks."

"Third is that the victims are similar. Same gender. Same build. Same race. Same hair and eye color. In other words, they have a preference in the type of victims and the killings aren't random."

Everly stomach roiled. "It's all too twisted."

Wyatt nodded. "Then the last factor isn't going to make you feel any better."

"Which is?"

"There's usually a sexual nature to the crime. And that's one thing in this case that had me stumped. There was no sign of sexual contact between the victims and the killer—consensual or otherwise."

"Then why do you assume there was a sexual element?"

"It could have been one-sided. Perhaps the killer masturbated into a condom at the scene. Or maybe he took pictures and used them for gratification later. Or maybe there was another motive entirely."

"If everything you said is true, and the serial killer is active in Wyoming, then there have to be more victims here."

Wyatt leaned forward and brought up another website.

"The *Pleasant Pines Gazette*," she said, reading the masthead.

"The sheriff mentioned that he sees deaths like your brother's all the time."

"He did," said Everly. "He even brought up the fact that Axl might've had too much to drink and that's how he got lost. Funny that it turned out just like he predicted." Everly shivered. "Do you think he's involved?"

"Sheriff Haak?" Wyatt shook his head. "No way."

Everly wasn't willing to let go of her theory so easily. "Isn't Haak the one investigating all the killings? Who better to be the killer than the man who determined the deaths to be accidental?"

"For one thing," said Wyatt. "He doesn't have a connection to Las Vegas. You heard him. He's lived in Pleasant Pines his entire life."

"He could have traveled back and forth between Wyoming and Nevada," she said, realizing even as she said it that Wyatt was right. Haak wasn't guilty of anything beyond overlooking some pretty subtle clues.

Wyatt spoke. "What I do think is that this has happened before enough times that Haak recognizes the situation. Yet it hasn't happened so much that he's gotten suspicious. He's not wrong, Everly, when he says that people die of exposure out here all the time. Which is why it could be especially tough to catch whoever did this."

Wyatt navigated the newspaper's site, pulling up the police blotter. He entered several phrases. *Death from exposure. Blood-alcohol content. Male.*

"Try searching 'out of town,' too," suggested Everly.

Wyatt did as she advised and then hit the magnifying glass icon. The search lasted only a few seconds and a list of five men appeared. The first death had happened a little less than three years ago. The last was from the day before yesterday. Axl James Baker. Wyatt hit the print icon and a sleeping printer sprang to life and whirred as it reproduced the police reports for each of the men.

Wyatt retrieved the sheets and stood reading by the firelight. Everly approached and peered over his shoulder. "The circumstances are all the same," said Everly. "I can't believe that nobody put all of this evidence together until now."

"Pleasant Pines doesn't have a large police force and the technology they use is pretty dated. All the killings are months apart and each one has a natural cause of death."

"Are you saying that they aren't connected?"

"No, I think they're probably connected, all right. It's just that I can see how the sheriff missed all the links."

"Look at this." She pointed to one page. "They all stayed at the Pleasant Pines Inn. It's where Larry works." Excitement coursed through Everly's veins. "In the morning, we can take this information to the sheriff and force him to open an investigation."

Wyatt shook his head.

"Why not?"

"We need something more substantial than five bodies who happened to stay at the only hotel in town. Until we have concrete evidence that connects the cases *and* a solid suspect, I don't want to make accusations," Wyatt said.

Everly knew that past accusations had cost Wyatt his job. He was obviously reluctant to make the same mistake. Yet, without Wyatt she'd have a hard time convincing the sheriff to even consider that Axl had been murdered.

"What more do you need besides all these deaths and Larry's connection to Las Vegas?" Everly asked.

"I want to see if any of the other victims were found with half of a two-dollar bill."

"And do you have a website that can tell you that?"

"I don't."

Wyatt turned to her. Firelight danced on his face, his shoulders, his torso. An inner fire sprang to life in her middle, consuming her until she was nothing but ash blowing in the storm. She looked away.

"What do we do now?" How many times had she asked that same question of Wyatt? And yet, he always had an answer.

"We need to look at the list of personal belongings for all the men. Sheriff Haak has those in his files, I'm sure. I'm just as certain that he won't share them with us." He paused and slipped a hand into his back pocket. He withdrew a slip of paper and held it up to the light. "I think I know what we can do, though."

Everly looked at the phone number. Underneath it was three words: Rocky Mountain Justice.

Snow swirled, rising and falling on currents of air. The night was vast and endless—an ocean of darkness. And then the Darkness took form. Snow crunched underfoot. The cold, biting and burning, was nothing compared to the heat of hatred that filled the Darkness to the very core.

"'And when he had opened the fourth seal, I heard the voice of the fourth beast say, "Come and see." And I looked, and behold, a pale horse.'" The words hovered, a mist in the cold, only to be swept away by the wind.

The old farmhouse sat alone. The windows were ablaze with light and the scene within was visible, even at a distance. The two of them stood next to the table, shoulders close but not touching.

The woman's hair fell forward, and she tucked a lock behind her ear. Wyatt watched her, as if he could drink in the woman and her gesture. The woman didn't interest the Darkness. She wasn't its to claim. And yet, here she was—with Wyatt.

Dense and heavy loathing filled the Darkness until it could crush the world.

Continuing, the Darkness said, "'And his name that sat on him was Death, and Hell followed with him.'"

In the distance, Wyatt lifted his head and looked to the window. Had he heard the words? Did he see the Darkness? Sense its presence?

Sometimes the Darkness thought Wyatt knew and was still playing the game. But he never made a move, not even when the bodies began to turn up in Wyoming. It was if he had forgotten who he was and what he needed to do. They were the opposite sides of the same coin, Wyatt and the Darkness. That's why the latest body had to be brought to his property. It was a trap to draw in Wyatt. And draw him in it had.

But the woman was in Wyatt's home. At his table. Smiling at him, as if she understood. She wasn't part of the game and her presence could ruin everything.

Well, that wasn't going to happen. And sadly, there was no helping her now. She had to be devoured by the Darkness.

Wyatt folded the pillow over and adjusted it under his neck. He flipped to his back and stared at the ceiling. Even though it was the middle of the night, moonlight seeped in around the curtain's edge. He'd been asleep, yet something had awakened him. What? He didn't know. The air crackled with static, as if lightning had struck in the room.

On the floor, in his dog bed, Gus growled in his sleep.

Rolling to his side, Wyatt spied the dog. Head up, ears alert, Gus looked at the door.

"What is it, boy?" he whispered.

Another growl, this one deeper.

Wyatt sat up. The covers slid down his torso and pooled in his lap. He strained to hear. The silence was complete, not even interrupted by the occasional creak of the settling foundation or the wind in the eaves. It was as if the house was holding its breath.

He exhaled.

Wyatt reached for the bedside light. His fingers

brushed the cold metal at the lamp's base. He hesitated, not bothering with the switch. Blindly, he opened the drawer of the bedside table instead. Hidden in the back, behind a book, was a SIG Sauer. It was empty, but a full magazine was tucked in next to the gun.

He shoved the clip home and pulled back on the slide, chambering a round.

Wyatt set his feet on the floor and stood. The old boards creaked in protest.

"Gus," he said in a harsh whisper. "Stay."

Treading lightly, he moved to the door and into the corridor. A small, circular window at the end of the hallway let in silvery light. Wyatt glanced outside. The storm had stopped, and a full moon hung in the sky. He peered down at the snow-covered ground. There, clear in the lunar glow, was a set of footprints.

He froze. Blinked. Looked again.

No doubt there was a single set of footprints leading to his back door. None going away. But he'd locked the back door. Hadn't he? He tried to recall those awkward moments as he'd left Everly and checked all the points of entry while she settled on the sofa and couldn't remember if he had.

Had he really been so careless, tonight of all nights?

Without question, someone had come to his home. Were they inside right now? If they were—well, then it was a game of cat and mouse.

Rushing to the stairs, Wyatt pressed his back into the wall and glanced into the yawning abyss of the stairwell. Moving as quietly as possible, he descended to the landing. From there, he glanced down again. The entire living room was visible from where he hid.

The fire was low in the grate. Cold seeped up the stairs, icy tendrils snaking around his bare feet and ankles.

Everly stood in the middle of the living room. The unmistakable glint of a metal blade was at her neck. The perpetrator was hidden behind her, face obscured. His heart raced. His palms grew damp and a bead of sweat trickled down his back.

The knife flashed, nicking Everly's skin. Like a seam had opened, a bead of red blood gathered on her throat. She shrieked. A shadow took form and rushed from the room. The back door shut with a crack.

Wyatt sprinted through the living room and pushed against the door. It didn't budge. He fumbled with the doorknob and leaned his shoulder into the door, knowing it was a smart move on the intruder's part. Barricade the door. Wyatt was trapped—a prisoner in his own home.

He kicked the wood. The door gave. Gun drawn and at the ready, Wyatt ran into the night. His bare feet sank in fresh snow. The cold left his bones brittle and seared his flesh. He ignored the discomfort and pressed on. But to go where? A gust of wind blew, erasing the footprints and leaving Wyatt alone in the darkness.

Chapter 6

In the distance, taillights appeared near the end of his drive as a car sped away. Wyatt leveled his gun at the retreating auto, took aim and pulled the trigger twice. He felt the recoil in his shoulder. The boom expanded to the edges of the horizon, as the stench of cordite was swept away by the wind. The car fishtailed as it rocketed away, disappearing into the night.

Wyatt cursed and returned to the house. He examined the door on the way in. Scratches had been gouged into the wood, where the door had been pried open. He slammed the door shut.

Every light on the ground floor was illuminated and Everly stood inside the threshold. A wound on her neck trickled blood. "I heard gunshots. Did you get him?"

His galloping pulse slowed as he shook his head. "I don't think I hit anything." Then he asked, "How are you? You're cut. Is anything else hurt?"

She touched the wound. Her fingers trembled. "I think I'm okay. This is just a little scratch. I should get cleaned up, though."

He recalled the metal blade pressed into her flesh and went cold with dread for what might've been. He pulled out a kitchen chair. "Sit," he said. "Let me help you."

Everly dropped to the seat. Wyatt set his firearm aside and wet a kitchen towel before dabbing at the cut on Everly's throat. The slash was short, only two inches long, and thankfully shallow. The bleeding was already slowing. "I don't think you'll need stitches," he said. "But you might end up with a little bit of a scar."

"Who cares about a scar?" she asked, her voice cracked. "What just happened?"

It was exactly what Wyatt wanted to know. As far as he knew, she was the only person to meet this killer twice and survive. "What do you remember?"

"I was asleep," she said, "and I woke up with a knife at my throat." She shut her eyes as a shudder wracked her body and tears threatened to leak from her eyes.

Wyatt waited while she gave in to the terror she'd been holding back. She needed only a moment to let it out and pull herself back together.

Everly swallowed and wiped her eyes with the back of her hand. Taking a deep breath to steady herself, she continued her story. "I was pulled to my feet. I was so frightened I couldn't even speak. I heard Gus upstairs. He was growling, and then..."

"I showed up a moment later," Wyatt offered.

"Yeah," she said with a nod.

Wyatt pulled open a couple of drawers, shuffling around until he found a tube of antiseptic ointment, gauze and medical tape. He tended to her neck without speaking. Wyatt thought of a million questions he wanted answered and yet, there was only one that really mattered. "Why are you alive?"

"Excuse me?"

Wyatt had lived alone for more than three years. Yet he hadn't been on his own long enough to mistake the tone of Everly's question as anything other than being insulted.

Yet this wasn't the time to worry about being polite. If he was going to catch this killer once and for all, he had to understand everything.

"Why didn't the killer cut your neck while you slept? Or why weren't you smothered after you'd been knocked unconscious at the hotel? Why are you still alive?"

Everly pressed the heels of her hands into her eye sockets. "I've asked myself that same question again and again."

"Do you have an answer?" There was one thing that Wyatt was certain of now. The killer's reluctance to murder Everly was the key to discovering his identity.

She exhaled and let her arms drop to her sides. "No," she said. "Not really."

God, she was beautiful. He wanted to take her into his arms and offer her comfort and solace. He wanted more. "You look tired," he said instead. "Why don't you go up to my room and get some rest?"

She shook her head. "There's no way I can sleep now."

"You might be surprised." Wyatt stood in front of Everly and held out his hand.

Everly stared at his outstretched fingers for a moment before placing her hand in his. It was there again. The warmth. The tingle. The connection. He pulled Everly to her feet and she stood slowly. "Thanks," she said.

"I'll even let you keep Gus in the room with you," Wyatt said, trying to lighten the mood, and at the same time knowing that Gus was a vigilant protector. "He'll keep you safe."

"And what will you do?" Everly asked.

"Me? I'll be fine down here."

Everly pressed her lips together, an argument ready to break free, no doubt.

Before she could argue or demur, Wyatt pointed to the stairs. "I insist."

"Thanks," Everly said, with a yawn. Even after everything that had happened to her, she'd be asleep within minutes. Or maybe she'd be asleep because of everything that had happened.

He watched as she walked to the stairs and disappeared past the landing. When he was alone, Wyatt moved to the front window and looked out at the night. He saw nothing but felt as if there were eyes everywhere.

"Come and get me, you bastard," he muttered. He aimed the gun at his own reflection in the glass. Sliding his finger onto the trigger, he continued, "This time, I'll be ready."

Everly sighed and rolled over. Her wound touched the pillow and she grimaced. She flipped to her back and the throbbing in her head began anew. "Wyoming sucks," she said out loud.

On the floor next to her, Gus whined.

"Sorry for waking you," she said to the dog.

Funny, but Gus was easier to talk to than most humans. He was definitely easier to converse with than his owner. Wyatt Thornton had built such an impenetrable wall around himself that Everly imagined she could see the concrete and rebar. Not that she blamed Wyatt and yet, she couldn't help but think he would be well-served to get out of the house more. Heck, maybe he should make a friend or two.

Then again, his problems weren't hers and she had plenty of troubles of her own. Rolling to the other side, she finally found a position without discomfort. Her eyelids felt heavy and sleep began to claim her...

An icy shard of pain stabbed her chest and Everly sat up, breathing hard. Had she heard something downstairs? She strained to listen, hearing only her racing heart and labored breathing.

There it was, a howl. The wind? A wolf? The

killer, returned? Everly reached for the bedside lamp and turned it on. The room blazed with light. She glanced at Gus. He was lying in his bed, blinking.

Sure, the dog seemed nonplussed, yet Everly knew that she had heard something...

Moreover, there was no way that Everly was going to lie in bed and allow herself to be attacked a second time.

Wyatt stretched out as much as the sofa would allow. His feet dangled over the edge and he figured that this was as comfortable as he could get. A creaking came from upstairs. Wyatt sat up, reaching for the gun.

It had to be Everly. Unless it wasn't.

She appeared on the landing. His fingers twitched with the need to touch her.

"I thought I heard something," she said. "It was like a howl."

Wyatt exhaled. "It's the wind in the eaves," he said. He set aside the gun. "I should've warned you. It can seem pretty loud upstairs, especially during a storm."

"Okay," she said, pivoting to go back up the stairs. "Thanks for letting me know. Good night."

Wyatt wasn't good at dealing with people, not anymore at least. And being helpful? Forget about it. All the same, he said, "I can check upstairs, make sure that it's only the wind. It might help you sleep better."

She gazed up the stairs, and Wyatt was certain she

was going to decline his offer. After a moment, she turned back to him. "Sure, that'd be nice."

She wore a pair of loose pajama pants in a blush rose. They hung low at her waist. A cream-colored tank top skimmed her body like a second skin. She ascended the stairs and Wyatt followed, mesmerized by the sway of her hips and the perfect form of her butt.

He forced his gaze to move and he looked over her shoulder, at once seeing Gus's smiling face at the top of the stairs.

"Hey, boy," he said, scratching the dog's head as he passed. "You keeping Everly safe for me?"

The second floor of Wyatt's home consisted of a master suite with its own bathroom. At one time, the suite had been two separate rooms and a closet. Before Wyatt moved in, he'd modernized the space. The rest of the second floor, not so much. There was a hall bath that had last been remodeled at the end of World War II and two small bedrooms filled with stuff that Wyatt no longer used but lacked the motivation to discard.

He pushed open the first door. Downhill skis. Cross-country skis. Snowshoes. A mountain bike with a broken chain and flat tire. "Everything looks in order," he said.

"Are you sure?" asked Everly. "I mean, how can you tell?"

"I can tell," Wyatt snapped. Who was she to question how he lived? True, he hadn't gone skiing the whole time he'd been living in Wyoming. And the mountain bike? It had sat, in need of repair, for over eighteen months.

Everly lifted her hands in surrender. "There's just a lot to keep track of, that's all."

"Chaos is the natural order," he said. "Did you know that?"

Everly shook her head. "I did not, and I didn't mean to offend you, either. I guess I shouldn't be speaking my mind so freely," she said.

"Apology accepted," said Wyatt. He moved to the second room and paused at the door. "This is where I kept all the notes from all the cases I've ever worked. It's a lot and I'm warning you now."

She inhaled and noisily exhaled. Shaking out arms and legs, she said, "I'm ready."

He was beginning to appreciate her frankness and her sense of humor, especially after the horror of earlier that night. He couldn't help but smile. "Smart-ass," he said, teasing.

Turning to the room, he flipped the light switch. It was just as he expected. Towering from floor to ceiling, dozens of boxes were stacked on top of each other. They ringed the wall and created a corridor through the middle of the room.

Everly came up behind him, so close he felt the heat from her body. The hairs on the back of his neck stood on end. "Wow," she said. "That is a lot of cases."

"I was the top behavioral scientist for the Bureau," he said. "I used to travel all over the world and consult on cases of all kinds."

"You should write a book," said Everly. "It'd be a blockbuster."

"The thought has crossed my mind before," he said. "But I put that part of my life behind me and I intend to leave it in the past," he said.

She didn't say anything, only nodded. It left Wyatt wondering her thoughts on the matter. Then again, why should he care? He continued, changing the subject completely, "Anyway, nothing's been moved in this room. It's exactly like I left it after coming up for the old case file this morning."

He turned to leave and came face-to-face with Everly. Her breasts pressed against his chest. The shadow of her nipples was unmistakable under the thin fabric of her tank top. He could see her pulse flutter at the base of her neck. His skin tingled, and his own heart began to race. "I'll just..." he began. His eyes were drawn to her lips and he forgot his next words. Pointing to the bathroom, he said, "I need to look in there."

"Oh, sure," she said.

He stepped to the side. She mirrored his movement. "Sorry, I'll go this way."

He stepped back. She did, too.

Wyatt placed his hands on her shoulders. God, she was so soft. A spicy sweetness still surrounded her like a halo. He looked at her mouth and licked his lips, hungry to kiss her. Yet, he knew that he had to remain professional. Not that being professional wasn't a good idea, it's just that Wyatt wasn't in the mood to make respectable decisions right now.

Hands still on her shoulders, Wyatt said, "You stay here."

He stepped past her and turned on the bathroom light. White and black tiles. Claw-foot tub. Shower curtain on a circular rod. Pedestal sink. It was just as it should be, down to the sliver of soap sitting in an indent on the back of the sink.

"There's no one else in this house," he said, "except you and me."

Gus whimpered from his place on the threshold.

"You, and me, and Gus," Wyatt amended.

She nodded. "Well, then." Hitching her chin toward the master bedroom, she continued, "I guess I better…"

"Sure," he said. He gestured to the stairs. "I should go."

"G'night, then."

Gus came to stand at Everly's side, and she stroked his ears. Gus sighed contentedly.

Lucky dog.

Wyatt felt the void in his own chest. Funny, he thought he'd gotten used to the solitude and now Wyatt wished that Everly would stay up a little more and talk. When had he last craved company? Turning, he moved to the stairs.

"Wyatt." She'd spoken his name softly, musically.

He froze with one of his feet hovering above the abyss.

"Wyatt," she said again.

This time he looked toward her.

"Do you mind?" she asked. Using her thumb, she

pointed to the bedroom. "I hate to be so forward, but…" She swallowed.

Wyatt's jaw tensed.

"Will you sleep with me?"

Everly could tell by Wyatt's widened eyes that he'd misunderstood her request. Then again, she'd been naive in the extreme not to realize the sexual implication. Her cheeks flamed red and hot. She cleared her throat and tried again.

"I've been attacked twice today. My brother was murdered. I don't know when I'll ever feel safe again, but I definitely won't be able to sleep by myself. I don't snore too much," she said, making light of the awkward moment.

Wyatt climbed the stairs that separated them and came to stand on the landing until he was only inches away from her. Heat radiated off his body, igniting something deep inside her.

"How do you know you can trust me?" he asked. His voice was dark as midnight and smooth as velvet.

For a moment, she was breathless with longing.

After realizing that she'd stood mute for a moment too long, she began speaking. "Well, obviously you aren't the person who gave me this." She touched the cut on her throat. "Which means you didn't give me this, either." Her fingers grazed the goose egg at the back of her skull. "Which means you aren't a threat and so…" She shrugged. "You're the one guy I can trust."

She raked her fingers through her hair and let out

all the air from her lungs. "Never mind. This has been a horrible day and I can see from the look on your face that I'm asking too much."

"I think wanting someone with you for protection and comfort makes sense, Everly."

"But I'm asking too much from *you*," she said.

"I'm not used to sharing anything," he said. "Especially, these days, my bed."

Her face felt as if it was on fire. Thank goodness the lights were off, and he couldn't see her blushing. "You'll be downstairs for protection, right? And I have Gus here for company." The dog ambled to Everly's side and leaned into her. She ran her fingers through the downy fur on the top of his head.

She waited a minute for Wyatt to say something. But what else needed to be said? With a nod of resignation, she stepped into the room.

"Everly," he said. His voice was smoke—dusky and dangerous. "Wait."

She paused but didn't turn around. The floorboard behind her creaked with his approach. Wyatt's breath warmed her shoulder.

"You're wrong," he whispered. "You can't trust me, and I don't think you need a man as shattered as I am right now." His fingertips brushed against her collarbone and his hand trailed from her shoulder to her arm. "And if you and I get in that bed, I promise you that sleeping is the last thing I'd want to do."

His whispered words washed over her. A shiver traveled through Everly. It wasn't from fear...but desire.

Holding her breath, Everly stood in the middle of

the room. She waited a minute…and a minute more. When she turned, he had gone. Padding softly across the floor, she slipped under the covers. She called softly to Gus. The dog approached. After lifting his paws to the mattress, he hesitated.

"Not you, too," she said. "I'm not sure I can handle being turned down twice in one night."

Gus cocked his head as if considering and then leaped onto the bed. He nosed the quilt for a moment before settling near the foot of the mattress.

Like a small, frightened animal, Everly burrowed under the covers. The blankets smelled of crisp pine and sunshine and the biting cold. They smelled like Wyatt. She inhaled deeply, and Gus began to snore softly. Relaxing into the pillow, Everly stretched out on the bed and her eyes began to feel heavy with sleep.

Wyatt had been right—and he had been wrong. Having Gus in the bed with her made a difference. Wasn't that what she'd wanted from Wyatt—another living and breathing soul to remind Everly that she wasn't alone?

But he'd also been wrong when he said that she didn't want a man as shattered as he was. In fact, Everly imagined that Wyatt wasn't really shattered, not like a broken mirror that was fractured into thousands of pieces. Rather he was an antique-looking glass, veined and faded with disuse. She dropped into a deep well of sleep, floating endlessly until she came upon a mirror. There was something familiar about it. Large. Rectangular. Mounted to a wall. Then she remembered—it was in the hotel, in Axl's room.

Behind Everly stood a figure. She looked at the face in the reflection. The eyes. The nose. The mouth. All the features were clear as crystal.

She sat up, her pulse racing. She gripped the sheets, her fingers winding in and out of the fabric. The dream had been terrifying for sure, but what bothered Everly the most was the realization that she'd seen the killer. And as she'd awakened, the face disappeared into the shadowy corners of her memory.

Chapter 7

In the morning, Wyatt was anxious to get started. He'd showered early and eaten a bowl of cereal—pretty much all he had around resembling breakfast. Everly was also up before the dawn and had showered and eaten early, as well. They knew that today would be monumental for them both. Despite the restless energy that coursed through his veins, he had to get Gus out of the house for a long walk. Besides, there was something else that Wyatt needed to do for Everly.

He was glad to see that she'd dressed for the weather. Jeans. Sweater. Shearling-lined boots. Coat. Hat. Gloves. They strolled through the woods. Dappled sunlight illuminated the blanket of sparkling snow, disturbed only by Gus's paw prints.

Wyatt cast a sideways glance at Everly. Despite her casual clothes, she was still the warrior goddess, but today she was serene—and sad.

Perhaps he could help.

"In town yesterday," he began, "you asked me for help. Asked me to show you where your brother was found. I turned you down on both counts."

"You're helping now. That's all the matters."

Was it? "I can help in other ways, if you want."

She quirked up one eyebrow. "Oh?"

"If you want, I can show you the old schoolhouse. That's where I found your brother."

Everly's pace never faltered. "Okay."

Ever since he'd met her, Everly could be fast, furious, passionate—like a force of nature. But today, she seemed fragile—breakable. Or maybe she was already broken.

Was she offended the he didn't stay in the room last night? It wasn't that Wyatt was an animal, unable to control his basest needs. It's just that where Everly was concerned, he'd have a hell of a time reining himself in.

"Maybe we should talk about last night," he said.

"I had a dream," she began. She kept walking, head down, arms folded. "It was about the killer. I looked in a mirror and I saw their reflection. More than that, I don't think it was simply a dream but actually a memory."

Wyatt stopped in his tracks. Despite the cold, he began to perspire. So, Everly had seen the killer. It just took a bit of sleep to bring that important detail to the surface. He'd seen it happen before in other cases, it's just that he hadn't dared to hope that Everly's memory would resurface.

Wyatt's mind was working out the problem of how to identify someone from sleep. It'd take a good bit of doing. He began to think out loud. "I can find a sketch artist and then we can enter the likeness into a national database of violent offenders."

She shook her head. "Sorry," she said. "I can't…"

"What do you mean?" he asked interrupting.

"I can't remember what they look like, that's the problem," she said, sounding frustrated. "I keep replaying the dream in my mind, but when I look in the mirror, there's nothing there—only a shadow."

Damn. They were so close. "Memories are tricky things," he said. "The harder you try to force the recall, the more it slips through your fingers."

"You seem very calm for someone who's been chasing the same killer for the better part of a decade."

Wyatt placed his hand on his chest. "I'm glad I look serene, but I'm not. My heart is racing and the killer's so close I can almost smell him in the air."

Everly drew in a deep breath, as if trying to catch the scent.

"That memory's in your mind," he said. "Something will trigger it. It'll come back."

"What if it doesn't?" she asked.

"It will," said Wyatt. "Until then, we have other ways to investigate your brother's death." The trail wound around a hill and ascended to a field in the middle of the forest. Mist, rising from the melting snow, surrounded a single dwelling. "We're here," he said, pointing to the old schoolhouse. "That's where I discovered Axl's body."

For a single agonizing moment, the call about Axl's death was more real than the biting air and the distant mountains. Everly had walking out of her apartment, barely on time for a staff meeting. She'd only taken the call because of the Wyoming area code and knowing that her brother was working in the state for the next few weeks. She had expected to hear his voice. Never before had she been more wrong.

"Everly Baker? This is Sheriff Carl Haak of Pleasant Pines, Wyoming. I'm afraid I have some terrible news. It seems there's been an accident."

At that moment, her life had been irrevocably altered. Less than two days later and she had only the haziest recollection of the hours that followed. Somehow, she had the wherewithal to fly to Cheyenne and rent a car—deciding along the way that Axl's death hadn't been accidental and she was determined to find justice for her brother.

Now, she was here—bruised and battered. All the same, she no closer to discovering the truth.

Her throat burned. Her chest ached. A sob bubbled up in her middle and she bit her lip to keep it from breaking free.

"Tell me," she said, her voice hoarse. A single tear rolled down her cheek and she swiped it away with the back of her hand. "Tell me everything you remember about that morning."

Wyatt scratched the side of his face. It was a gesture she'd seen before—his way of buying time while he decided what to do or say next. "It was Gus. We were out on our morning walk. He went after a stick, then ran off and started barking. I just followed."

Walking toward the building, Wyatt left tracks in the snow. Everly followed. Two strands of plastic police tape blocked the doorway. Wyatt stopped at the threshold and Everly stood by his side. "The body, I mean your brother, was in the back corner. There were gouges on his face, but that was postmortem. In fact, I'd say your brother was fed the alcohol and anti-nausea medicine somewhere else and then was dumped here to die."

"Dumped." The word made her sick. "Like garbage." One day soon, she'd cry and curse life for being unfair, but not now. Losing herself in grief wouldn't accomplish anything for Axl. Everly had to stay focused.

Wyatt ducked under the police tape, entering the old building. Everly was right behind. Even after a century of wind, and snow, and rain, all the walls were intact. As if in a dream, she moved to the corner, the place her brother had been found. Tracing her fingers over the cold floor, she tried to find something of Axl—his soul, his energy, or whatever remained after someone died.

There was nothing and Everly knew that she was truly alone in the world. After a moment, she asked,

"What do you think happened? I know he got drunk one way or another and was left here to die, but do you think he suffered?"

"I doubt he felt anything beyond intoxicated," said Wyatt. "In fact, I'd be surprised if he ever knew that he'd been left in this building."

"Axl was a recovering alcoholic," said Everly. "I wonder why he decided to drink again."

"Maybe the taste was somehow masked," Wyatt suggested. "And he was tricked into drinking too much."

"It's subtle," said Everly.

"It's evil," corrected Wyatt. "And calculating as hell."

"I guess what I want to say is that there's no violence to these deaths. The killer didn't shoot anyone or stab anyone or strangle a single person. It's almost like, 'Oops, you got too drunk. Now, I'm going to leave you outside until you die.' You know?"

Wyatt shook his head. "I think that the cut on your neck paints a different picture."

Picture. "We need to look for Axl's camera," she said, interrupting what else Wyatt was about to say. Maybe her brother had taken a picture of his killer. She rushed to the doorway and stepped into the snow. Spinning in a tight circle, Everly scanned the horizon. There was nothing to see beyond snow and trees.

"I doubt we'll find anything now. Let's come back after the snow melts."

"Unless I'm no longer in Pleasant Pines. Didn't

Sheriff Haak tell me I had to leave town as soon as Axl's body was ready to go back to Chicago?"

"Damn. He did. That means we have a lot to do and not as much time as we need." Wyatt consulted a smartwatch on his wrist. "It's a quarter after eight. We can be in town by nine o'clock and go straight to the Rocky Mountain Justice offices."

It wasn't much of a plan, but it was more than Everly could ever do on her own. "Thanks for bringing me out here," she said as they turned back to Wyatt's house. "In a sad way, I think Axl would've appreciated being left in that old schoolhouse. He loved the outdoors—hated the city." She glanced back once more at the ramshackle building then fell into step next to Wyatt, heading toward a future she could barely comprehend.

It was darkest in the shadows cast by the trees. Beyond, the fresh snow sparkled in the morning sun, like a carpet of diamonds. From this distance, the Darkness could see Wyatt and the woman, but not hear what they said.

From the tree line, the Darkness had watched as they trekked to the final resting place. Or one of them, at least. The Darkness made sure that each spot was sacred. Serene. Wyatt had brought the woman, showing the power of the Darkness.

Hatred bubbled up from deep inside. It was almost as if the woman would defile the inviolability of the place. Still, she was the one who had goaded Wyatt and once again, he was playing the game.

And what a game it was!

The Darkness had dared to enter Wyatt's house and trembled with ecstasy for the risk of it all. It was too damn bad that the plan hadn't worked. But if it had? Ah, just to think of Wyatt's terror when he discovered the woman's corpse.

How many years had it been since the Darkness had first seen Wyatt? He'd been interviewed on television in Las Vegas after the third body had been found. It was then that the Darkness knew that finally a worthy opponent had been found. Handsome. Brave. Smart.

When the public turned on the white knight the Darkness knew it had won. Yet, it wasn't enough for the Darkness to win. It wanted to be known. It wanted to look Wyatt in the eyes and see adulation, admiration and love.

The Darkness watched from the shadows and seethed. There—a flicker of emotion passed across Wyatt's face. What had it been? Tenderness? For who—for the woman? What if Wyatt had started to play the game again and it wasn't to defeat the Darkness, but to provide comfort for the woman?

Had the Darkness been wrong to try and harm her? Had that moment allowed Wyatt to protect her—and become the woman's champion? What if she lured him away and Wyatt stopped playing the game?

That would never do. Never. Never. Never.

"'Thou shalt beat him with the rod, and shalt deliver his soul from hell,'" said the Darkness.

Could Wyatt still be saved? Perhaps. But that would require another sacrifice...

Wyatt parked the truck next to the corner and consulted the piece of paper he had thrown on to the dashboard. Glancing at the two-story Victorian mansion on the edge of the Pleasant Pines business district, he admitted it was hardly what he expected from an outfit that slyly referred to itself as providing "private security." Then again, this inconspicuous home might just provide the perfect camouflage.

He scanned the front stoop for a placard or any kind of sign. There was nothing beyond the house number. Everly sat in the passenger seat and he glanced her way.

"Everything okay?" she asked.

Wyatt turned off the ignition and pocketed his keys. "Let's find out."

They walked up the sidewalk and rang the bell. A sleek, silver intercom had been set into the wall. It squawked with a burst of static for a single second before a woman's voice asked, "May I help you?"

Wyatt looked for a call button, but there was none. He leaned forward. "I'm here to see Marcus Jones."

"Name?"

"Wyatt Thornton," he said. "From the Bureau."

"And?" asked the woman.

Wyatt looked around for a camera and saw none. Obviously, appearances were deceiving. "Everly Baker," he said, leaning toward the intercom and raising his voice. "Marcus met her yesterday at the diner."

Wyatt's first impression that this was nothing more than a home—renovated to office space—was quickly replaced. The high-tech and thorough security employed by Rocky Mountain Justice was impressive.

The woman's disembodied voice came through the intercom. "Look at the camera."

The what? Wyatt didn't see anything.

The lock clicked, leaving the door ajar. "Marcus can see you now," said the woman.

Wyatt pulled open the door and stepped into a foyer. The walls were covered in white paper with a golden paisley pattern, so understated that it was only visible in direct light. There was a chair rail of deep mahogany and a striped paper of maroon completed the walls. The floor was covered in hexagonal tiles of black and white—all a typical look for a Victorian mansion, except for one unmistakable difference. The door leading to the house was reinforced steel, controlled by a keypad lock and screen for facial recognition.

Everly moved close behind Wyatt, her mouth close to his ear. "It looks like something out of a James Bond movie."

Before Wyatt could agree, the door opened with a *whoosh*. Marcus Jones stood on the threshold. He wore jeans, a button-up shirt with light blue stripes and a navy blazer. The classic outfit was at odds with the innovative surroundings. "Hey, Wyatt," said

Jones. He offered his palm. "I didn't think I'd see you again so soon."

Taking the other man's hand to shake, Wyatt said, "I—we—need your help."

"Sure," said Marcus. "What can I do for you?"

"Is there someplace we can talk?" asked Wyatt. "Someplace that's a little more private."

Jones nodded. "Follow me."

They stepped through the metal entrance. A similar keypad and monitor for facial recognition were also attached to the inner door. Marcus tapped out a six-digit code, then stepped up to the scanner. Marcus's likeness appeared on the screen. Twenty identification points were checked. A green light atop the scanner flashed and the door slid open.

There was a curving staircase in front of them and another door at the back of the hall. There were also two wooden doors—one on the left and the other on the right. All of them were shut, the lock controlled with a keypad and scanner.

"That's quite the security setup you have," said Wyatt, half conversationally, half in awe. "What is that you do here again?"

"We do a little bit of everything. Anti-industrial espionage. Security for businesses. Sometimes we help out when local law enforcement needs a hand."

Wyatt was starting to get a picture of the work done by Rocky Mountain Justice. "The government hires you because you don't have to play by the rules and can push boundaries they can't," said Wyatt.

Jones didn't bother answering the question, which was an answer in itself.

"Right now, we're a small crew. Elite, I like to call it," said Jones as he led them up a winding staircase. "RMJ's headquarters are in Denver. We have three operatives in the Wyoming office, myself included, as well as a communications specialist. I'm looking to expand with the right people."

The offer to join the crew was definite. "I appreciate you hearing me out and offering to help," said Wyatt. "But I'm retired."

"Retired?" Jones chuckled. "You sound so old when you say that. How old are you?"

"I'll be thirty-seven in August."

"You've got plenty of years left to work."

"Still not interested," said Wyatt with a shake of his head. Everly had been silent during the exchange and he wondered what she thought about him leaving the work force at such a young age. She had an opinion—he'd bet money on it—if only because she had an opinion on everything.

Then again, why did he care what she thought? He was helping her find justice for her brother—and in turn, he was tying up the biggest loose end of his life. When he thought about it that way, Everly's opinion didn't matter as much.

The staircase ended in the middle of a hallway. Seven doors stretched out along the corridor—three to the right and four to the left.

"This way," Marcus said, pointing to the right. At the second door, Marcus entered yet another code and waited while the facial-identification software ran. The latch automatically released with a click and Marcus turned the handle and opened the door.

It was a computer lab, as sophisticated as any Wyatt had seen in the secure rooms at the Hoover Building or the in bowels of the NSA. Several monitors hung on the wall and even more sat on a semi-circular group of tables. There were four keyboards, and a private server hummed at the back of the room.

So, while this incredibly high-tech operation wasn't uncommon at the highest level of the government, it sure as hell was uncommon for a private agency. He doubted that Marcus Jones would give him more information about RMJ than he'd already gotten, but Wyatt was certain he would now have access to any database he needed.

"Have a seat," said Marcus. There were four chairs on wheels and Everly selected one. Wyatt took a seat next to her and Marcus sat near the door. He rested his elbow on the table. "Downstairs you said you wanted to speak privately," he said.

Marcus was like that. He didn't exactly ask questions, just gave openings for information to be given. Yet, what did Wyatt want to say? Marcus had been a special agent in Charge of the Bureau's Denver field office. Even though he'd been part of management, he hadn't worked on the Las Vegas case. He didn't know everything Wyatt did—it was time to bring Jones up to speed.

"This is about the last case I worked," said Wyatt.

"Las Vegas." This was from Marcus. Again, not a question, not a statement.

Wyatt nodded. "The serial killer I was hunting there has resurfaced here in Pleasant Pines."

Jones sucked in a breath and his eyes widened. It was a quick reaction, yet unmistakable. "You have my attention."

"My brother was one of the killer's victims. We think there might be others, but we need access to information in some law enforcement databases." Everly said. "We're hoping you can help us with that search."

"What do you need?" asked Marcus.

Focusing on the important details, Wyatt said, "The killer in Vegas left a calling card of sorts—it was half of a two-dollar bill that was placed in the wallet of all his victims. It's how we first knew all the killings were connected."

"I never heard about that link between the victims."

"It was kept classified. We didn't want any of it leaking to the media and then having to deal with copycat killers."

"I'm guessing that there's a link with this newest death?"

Everly rolled her chair forward an inch. "Half of a two-dollar bill was found in my brother's wallet."

"And the circumstances around the death were similar." Wyatt added, "In Nevada, all the victims had a very high blood-alcohol content and were found in the middle of the desert."

"Several men died of exposure in Pleasant Pines over the past couple of years, just like my brother," Everly continued. "They all had a similarly high blood-alcohol level and had happened to wander into the woods where they died."

"You want to see if those men have half of a two-dollar bill among their possessions?" Marcus asked.

"Exactly," said Wyatt.

"I have to ask—did you take this information to the sheriff?"

"We told him about the two-dollar bill and the connection to Wyatt's old case," said Everly. "But the medical examiner ruled accidental exposure as the cause of death and Sheriff Haak didn't want to listen to what we had to say."

"I know the sheriff kept a record of all the personal belongings found with each body. I also assume a copy's been kept in the database, but without the sheriff giving us access to his computer, we're stuck..." Wyatt let the statement dangle like a hook in the water, and he hoped like hell that Marcus would take a bite.

"Which is why you came here," said Marcus.

"Pretty much," Wyatt said.

Marcus swiveled toward the table and began tapping on a keyboard. The RMJ site filled one of the monitors on the wall. "Let's see what we can find out about these recent deaths." The sheriff's office site came up and within seconds, they had accessed a private page.

"Is this legal?" Everly whispered.

Marcus held up his hand, tilting it from side to side. *So-so.*

Wyatt's gaze was drawn to the computer's cursor. His pulse grew stronger with each beat until the steady *thump, thump* echoed in his skull. "See if you can find a master list for property located on recently deceased."

Marcus typed, and another field appeared.

"Try *half of a two-dollar bill*," he said.

Marcus didn't hesitate and entered the phrase into the search engine. A colorful ball spun for a minute and stopped. *Your query has four matches.* There were four names listed, as well. Wyatt picked up a notepad and pen from the table and scribbled them down. "Robert Barnes. Jeffery Stone. Brian Green. Seth Carlson."

"So, what do we do now?" Everly asked. "Go to the sheriff?"

She looked from Wyatt to Marcus and back again.

It was Marcus who answered. "There's at least some proof that four other men were found with half of a two-dollar bill on their person. It's a lot more than a coincidence if you ask me. More than that, it should warrant some kind of investigation."

Wyatt folded his arms across his chest. With a shake of his head, he said, "It's still thin. We need to know as much as we can about the other guys—see if there are connections beside the obvious."

"Gender. Place of death. The torn-up money." Marcus counted out the facts as he spoke. "That's more than a little thin."

"If this is a serial killer—" Wyatt began.

"If?" Marcus interrupted. "If? I thought you were sure, that's why you came here. Why the sudden change of heart?"

"I keep coming back to the same question—why? What's his motivation? Why does he need to kill these men?"

"Plain and simple," said Everly. "He has his own agenda, even if nothing he does makes sense to us."

"That's where you're wrong. Serial killers are highly intelligent and very methodical. There's always a reason for everything they do. More than that, every case that I'd worked before this one had another common theme. All the killers fed off the terror of their victims."

He continued. "They liked knowing the other person was in pain and feared for their life. This morning, Everly pointed out that there's no viciousness to any of these killings. Aside from the calling card, each death looks natural."

"Maybe he's a new breed of serial killer," Marcus suggested.

Wyatt lifted one shoulder and let it drop. The scenario didn't fit. Or rather, it was too perfect of a fit. So why the hesitation? Was there something wrong with his theory? Or was he paralyzed by the past, afraid to make another mistake that might ruin him once and for all?

Chapter 8

Everly and Wyatt had spent the better part of two hours tracing the life of each of the victims. Marcus Jones stayed with them for the first hour but left when he received a phone call from RMJ's headquarters in Denver.

While consulting the notepad in front of her, Everly said, "The similarities in all these men are eerie."

"They were all from out of state, visiting for work or waiting for friends—and therefore by themselves." Wyatt shifted in his seat. "The fact that they were alone made them easy targets. No one to miss them when they first disappeared."

Had Axl been an easy target? Everly hated to think that somehow her brother had been exploited.

A shard of grief stabbed her in the chest. She bit her lip. The pain was cleansing.

"I'm sorry if what I said sounds callous. I guess sometimes I can come across a little academic," he said.

How was it that Wyatt could read her so well? Oh, yeah—he was a behavioral scientist and she'd be wise not to see something special about his attentiveness.

"I'm okay," she said with a shake of her head. "You're right. Axl was alone and he was an alcoholic years ago. He went to treatment, and maybe thinking he could control his addiction left him more susceptible to being..." Everly couldn't bring herself to finish the thought, much less the sentence.

"Do you want to take a break?" Wyatt asked. "This has been tough on you."

"A break from what?" She laughed, and her voice cracked. "Finding out who killed my brother is the only thing that matters to me right now. Or might ever matter again."

"Let's wrap this up then," said Wyatt as he let go of her wrist. "Let's go over everything we've found so far."

She paused. "Each man in this list is almost exactly the same. Sure, their hometowns were different, as were the reasons they were in Pleasant Pines—but they were all the same, down to their approximate height, weight and coloring. It's as if the killer has a type."

Wyatt leaned back in his chair and cradled his

head in his hands. "Like I said earlier, a serial killer is obsessed with having the same kind of victim. Basically, the killer is recreating an event from their past. What they need is new people, similar looking people, to replay the same role again and again."

"Unfortunately," said Everly, "my brother was a perfect fit." She waited a beat. "How have these deaths not been connected? How is it that no one ever figured out that four men have been murdered by the same person?"

"Look at the dates," he said. "While it's becoming obvious to us now, those dots are pretty far apart for anyone who's not looking to create a picture. Still, years ago, I had a team of two dozen agents and more than twice that number of police officers dedicated to finding the killer. Even with all those resources, we never figured out who was responsible."

Before Wyatt could say more, Everly's phone began to ring. She fished it from her bag. "It's Sheriff Haak," she said. "Axl's body is probably ready to be taken back to Chicago, which means I need to get out of town."

"Put the call on speakerphone and tell him I'm here. He may not agree to open an investigation now, but I think we can get him to meet with us."

Everly swiped the speaker icon before setting the phone on the table. "Sheriff Haak," she said. "I'm here with Wyatt Thornton." How many business meetings had Everly taken in the same manner? So many that the words felt comfortable and yet, this phone call wasn't about anything as mundane as an advertising campaign or a client's public-relations problem.

"Oh, really?" the sheriff said, his tone brittle.

Wyatt leaned toward the phone and spoke. "I'm sure you remember that I found a link between the death of Axl Baker and an old case of mine."

"I do remember," said the sheriff, "and I'm sure you can recall that I told you there was no way in hell that a serial killer was loose in Pleasant Pines."

"I know you've been in law enforcement for years," said Wyatt. "I trust your instincts, but we've done a little digging of our own and have a total of five men who've died over the past three years—all of them died due to a combination of alcohol poisoning and exposure."

"I'd say you went digging in the wrong place. The number of those types of accidental deaths is likely three times as high. This is Wyoming. People go hunting and twist an ankle, making it impossible to get back. They go skiing and lose the trail. Hell, sometimes they just go outside, and a blizzard catches them unawares. Do you want me to continue?" asked the sheriff. Everly could imagine the older man sitting in his office, finger stabbing the desk as his face grew redder and redder with rage and frustration.

Wyatt continued, the pulse at the base of his neck thrummed with the urgency of his words. "Each man was in his early to mid-thirties, from out of town, visiting alone—or waiting for his group to arrive. The cause of death was exactly the same."

"Anything else?" asked Sheriff Haak, his voice small.

"And," Wyatt continued, "each man was found with half of a two-dollar bill in his wallet."

Sheriff Haak didn't respond, yet the seconds of the call ticked by.

"I know how much you care about this town," Everly said. It was time for her to contribute and do her job. "I know you've dedicated your life to keeping everyone in Pleasant Pines safe, but there's too much evidence to ignore." She paused, waiting for the sheriff, or even Wyatt, to add something to the conversation. Neither did, so she continued. "I've been attacked twice since arriving in Pleasant Pines and started asking questions about Axl. It's hard to believe that those are random events and not meant to scare me into leaving town."

"Why's this the first time I'm hearing about you being attacked?" the sheriff asked.

"You haven't been interested in seeing Axl Baker's death from another angle," said Wyatt. "We needed more information before speaking to you again."

"Can we meet with you? We can be at your office in a few minutes," said Everly.

"I'll hear you out," said the sheriff, "but not at my office. The county building is a busy place with folks coming and going all day. I don't want any of your theories being overheard and needlessly frightening anyone." He sighed.

"Obviously," said Wyatt, "we'd be discreet."

"I can't use my place," said the sheriff. "We have contractors working in the office. It's too chaotic."

"Where then?" Everly asked.

"There is no discretion in my office, trust me."

The line was filled with a moment of silence. Finally, the sheriff said, "There's a conference room we sometimes use at the Pleasant Pines Inn for training and such. At this hour it'll be empty and private. Meet me there in twenty minutes."

Everly exchanged a glance with Wyatt. A conference room at a hotel? How secure could that be? All the same, she wasn't well-versed in small-town American law enforcement. *Maybe this is just how it's done here*, she thought. Scooping up her notepad, Everly said, "We'll be there."

"Before you go," said the sheriff, "I have one question. How'd you know that the men were found with half of a two-dollar bill?"

Wyatt answered. "An old friend of mine works for Rocky Mountain Justice. He let me access databases from his office."

"I don't know what Rocky Mountain Justice is, so you need to bring him, too," said the sheriff. "I have lots of questions and if I don't like the answers I get, there's going to be hell to pay."

The conference room was located on the first floor of the inn, just a space tucked off of the now closed restaurant. Darcy, the desk clerk, had been overly helpful when they arrived. She arranged the room for the meeting, bringing water bottles, a tray of sandwiches, and pads of paper emblazoned with the Pleasant Pines Inn logo. By the time Sheriff Haak appeared, Everly, Wyatt and Marcus were fully prepared to brief the local lawman.

Since then, more than an hour had passed. The water bottles were empty, and the tray only held crumbs.

Everly sat at the circular table with Wyatt on her left and Marcus on her right. Sheriff Haak sat directly across from her. His sheriff's hat, with the tin star on the band, rested on the table in front of him.

Wyatt had just finished going through all the connections between the local deaths, Axl Baker and his former case from Las Vegas, painting a grisly picture. Wyatt concluded with "That's why I'm convinced that Pleasant Pines has become the hunting grounds for this murderer."

Running his fingers over the brim of his hat, Sheriff Haak asked, "This is your professional opinion, Mister G-man?"

Wyatt ignored the comment and tapped a pen on the table. "It is."

Sheriff Haak turned to Marcus Jones. "What about you? What do you think?"

"I think that Wyatt Thornton is as fine an agent as there is," he said. "This information is real—and you need to open a full investigation into these killings."

The sheriff's cheeks turned a blotchy red. He obviously took a great deal of pride in his community. Moreover, Everly guessed that he didn't welcome anyone telling him how to do his job. Nor did he want to be accused of having missed something so important as a serial killer in his town. If pushed too hard, she knew that the sheriff would push back.

"Sheriff Haak," she said. "I don't have experience in this kind of thing, like the three of you. But I do want to know what happened to my brother. Believe me, I wish his death was a simple accident, as you originally told me. But that's not the case. No one is accusing you of being a second-rate sheriff. If you don't look into these cases now and find out what's really going on, the whole town will be at risk. You're too good of a man to do that," she said.

With a grunt, the sheriff asked, "What do you know about the killer?"

"Typically, the profile for most serial killers is similar," said Wyatt, nonplussed, as usual. "They tend to be Caucasian, highly intelligent and in their late twenties to early thirties."

"Is that always true?" asked Sheriff Haak.

Wyatt said, "No, not always. Maybe eighty-five percent of serial killers are Caucasian men. Some can be people of color. Even fewer serial killers are female. During the initial investigation in Vegas we assumed that the killer fit the most basic profile. There was never any evidence to prove otherwise."

Wyatt continued. "Because of the simple mode of killing, we doubt that the killer has much more than a high-school education but is intelligent. He is most likely manipulative or, at the very least, charming. Leaving half of a two-dollar bill with each victim, I believe, represents a broken promise. In Vegas, we suspected a hospitality worker."

"Any old hospitality worker, or a specific one?" the sheriff asked.

Everly knew the answer to this question. In Las Vegas, Wyatt had accused a blackjack dealer and the man had been arrested. Later, an alibi was established for the suspect, and Wyatt's career had been left in tatters. It wasn't a fact he'd confessed to her and it left Everly wondering what Wyatt would say.

"We arrested a man who worked in a hotel casino on the Strip. Not all the facts fit, and he was let go," said Wyatt. "After that, the killings stopped, and then local law enforcement took over. There were never any other arrests and to this day, case is cold."

"What you're telling me is that you don't have a clue," said the sheriff.

"I still believe the killer worked in the service industry. We just had the wrong guy in Vegas."

"That makes sense. There's a connection to this inn," said Marcus. "All the victims have been guests here."

"This is the only place in town," said the sheriff. "It's not like visitors have much of a choice."

"But they were here," said Marcus, his fingers splayed across the table. "It's also the last place any of them were seen alive."

"That has to be a clue worth something," Everly said.

"It's worth a lot more than something," said Wyatt.

"Especially since we found a link. Axl Baker had an argument with a cook at the hotel—Larry Walker."

"I know Larry," said the sheriff. "What'd they argue about?"

"I'm not sure," said Everly. "The bartender overheard them having a heated discussion. From what she said, it had to do with what my brother was here to photograph."

"It might do for us to have a chat with Larry and see what he remembers about Axl," said Marcus.

"Larry fits your profile from the Nevada case," the sheriff said to Wyatt. "Down to the age, educational level and employment. He was even a troubled kid—fights at school, running away when he got mad at his mother and the like. He's no charmer, though. Larry was born and raised here, but he left five or six years ago to find work. Came back less than three years past."

"Not too many months before the first victim was killed," said Wyatt.

"It might do to ask Larry more than what he remembers about Axl Baker, but what he knows about all of these men," Marcus suggested.

"I agree," said Sheriff Haak. "I'll bring him in and officially question him about all of these deaths..."

His statement was followed by a clattering in the hallway. Metal clanged against metal and the sound of shattering glass screeched. Everly's heartbeat hammered against her chest and she swiveled in her chair toward the sound. A lanky man with sparse dark hair and a high forehead stood in the doorway, with an oval tray in his hands. A coffeepot, broken cups, spoons and saucers littered the floor at his feet.

He stared into the room with a wide-eyed gaze. The tray wobbled on his hand before toppling from his precarious grasp with a clang. With a final, wild-eyed look the man turned and sprinted from view.

On their feet in the same instant, Wyatt and Marcus rushed from the room. Their footfalls were thunder in the small space.

Then they were gone, and silence followed.

Everly turned to the sheriff. "Who was that?" she asked.

Haak shook his head. "That was Larry Walker. Your prime suspect."

Wyatt's heart hammered against his chest, his breath resonating in his skull. His footsteps slapped on the floor of the cramped hallway. Marcus was just a step behind. But Wyatt wasn't concerned about who followed. Rather, he was focused on who was in front.

He'd never met Larry Walker, yet Wyatt would bet good money that he was the man they now chased. Wyatt reached out and his fingers touched the fabric of a sleeve. He tried to grab hold, but the man slipped from his grasp.

Daylight erupted into the dark corridor, the glare blinding, as the man pushed the side door and exited. Wyatt's speed carried him forward a pace or two, then he skidded to a stop. He pivoted and burst through the same door.

He was in a parking lot, half-full and covered in gravel. Larry was a full ten yards away. The lights on a small pickup truck flashed and the engine revved as Larry used a key fob to engage the remote starter. Larry was already halfway to the truck. And if he got there before Wyatt got to him, he knew the suspect would disappear—and it would be hell to find him.

Wyatt had only one chance. He caught up and dove forward, grabbing the other man around the middle. They tumbled to the ground, coming to a stop with Wyatt pinning Larry facedown. Gravel gouged his flesh and scraped his skin raw. Wyatt cared nothing for the pain.

Larry clawed at him, trying to escape, but Wyatt grabbed the other man's arm and tore the key fob from his grasp. He stood slowly and turned off the truck. The motor fell silent. Wyatt's labored breathing was the only thing he heard.

Marcus approached. He'd drawn a sidearm and was pointing it directly at Larry. "Hold your hands where I can see them," Marcus ordered.

Larry lifted his palms. A tremor shook his arms. "Come on, what'd you want, man?"

"We need to talk," said Wyatt.

"Talk if you want, but you don't need to point that gun at me. I didn't do nothing wrong."

"If you didn't do anything wrong, why did you run?"

"Because a room full of cops was talking about me in connection with the dead guy," said Larry.

"If you were in my place and had any sense, you'd run, too."

"On your feet," Marcus ordered. "I think we need to have a little chat with the sheriff."

Hands still lifted, Larry walked back to the conference room. Marcus was directly behind Larry, with Wyatt bringing up the rear. Once in the conference room, Marcus gestured to a chair with the barrel of his gun. "Sit," he said.

Larry took a seat and turned to the sheriff. "What the hell's going on? Those two chased me down. That one—" he pointed to Wyatt "—took the keys to my truck. And the other one pulled a piece on me. I can sue for this. I have rights, you know."

"Shut up, Larry," said the sheriff.

Larry fell silent.

Marcus slid his gun into a holster on his ankle and sat. Wyatt took a seat as well, choosing one directly across from Larry.

"We need to ask you a few questions," said Wyatt.

"I don't have to answer anything," said Larry. "I know my rights."

"You don't have to say anything here," said the sheriff. "Even more than that, you aren't under arrest. This is a friendly conversation, but if you don't want to talk, I can take you to my office and things will work out different."

Larry rolled his hand. "Fine. We can talk."

"What do you know about Axl Baker?" Wyatt asked.

Larry pulled his eyebrows together. "Who?"

"Axl Baker," said Everly. "My brother. You argued with him at the bar and then his body was found the next morning."

"That's bad luck, man," said Larry.

For the first time, Wyatt saw yellow sweat stains on Larry's shirt at the underarms and neck. He also noticed how they'd become damp again as the other man perspired. He nervously folded his hands together and unfolded them, moving constantly. Signs of discomfort were uncommon for sociopaths, the likes of which had been killing people for years.

"Whose bad luck?" asked Wyatt. "Axl's or yours?"

"Both, I guess," said Larry.

"Tell me what happened the other night," said Wyatt.

"Nothing," said Larry.

From years of training, Wyatt knew that the best way to get information was to wait. A subject with ample time and too much silence would eventually fill both with what they assumed an investigator wanted to hear. Eventually, it would lead to the truth. Too bad Wyatt didn't have the patience to wait for Larry to talk in circles. "Don't screw with me," he said. "I'm not in the mood."

Larry looked at the sheriff and then back at Wyatt. "We argued a little, it's no big deal."

"What'd you argue about?"

"Nothing."

Wyatt slapped the table, the sound causing everyone to jump. Larry leaned back, his eyes went wide. "Let's assume it's not nothing."

"It really wasn't anything important. The Baker guy wanted to track wolf migration. I told him that the wolves weren't for his amusement. He said that he was on an assignment, trying to do a job to educate people. I didn't care. Things got a little heated and voices were raised. That's all."

Sheriff Haak asked, "Why were you listening at the door?"

"Darcy told me to bring some coffee to this meeting. I was about to knock but heard my name." Larry shrugged. "I eavesdropped a little, I guess."

It explained the shattered coffeepot and broken cups.

"Where were you the night before last?"

"Come on, Sheriff," said Larry, his tone wheedling. "You aren't going to let them question me like this, are you? I have the right to my privacy."

"If you have nothing to hide, then answer the questions," said Sheriff Haak.

Larry cursed under his breath and wiped a hand across the back of his neck. "The kitchen closed around nine o'clock. I cleaned up and came out for a drink. That Baker guy started chatting me up. Had I always lived in Pleasant Pines? What did I know about the wolves? I just wanted my drink and to relax. His constant questions were annoying, and I said something. Johanna said I couldn't fight with the customers and told me to go home. I did, and it was quarter after ten when I walked out of the inn."

"Wife? Family? Roommates?" asked Marcus. "Anyone who could corroborate your story?"

Larry shook his head. "I live alone in an apartment two blocks away."

"What about last night?" Wyatt asked. He had a hard time imagining Larry Walker breaking into his home much less thinking to barricade the door and then getting away. But, if Larry was the killer, then he'd done just that. "Where were you?"

"Home by ten thirty. No arguments in the bar, so I got to finish my drink."

"I have one more question," said Wyatt.

"No." Larry held up his hands and waved away the probe. "No more questions. I haven't done anything wrong and I'm not going to be treated like a criminal. I don't have an alibi for the night that Baker was killed, but unless you're going to arrest me, Sheriff, I'm leaving."

"Consider yourself a person of interest in this case, Larry," said Sheriff Haak. "Don't leave town or I'll issue a warrant for your arrest and throw you in jail."

"For what?" Larry asked.

"For killing Axl Baker," the sheriff said.

After cursing under his breath, Larry said, "I need the keys to my truck." He pointed to Wyatt. "That guy took them."

"Go ahead, Mr. Thornton. Give them back," said the sheriff.

Wyatt uttered a curse of his own as he fished them from his jeans and slid them across the table. Larry scooped up the keys and shoved them into his pocket.

"This is total crap," said Larry as he stood. His

chair teetered back before toppling and clattering to the ground. Larry kicked it out of the way, then stalked to the door and disappeared into the hallway.

"Let me handle this," said Marcus Jones as he got to his feet. "I'll keep an eye on Larry for now."

"I'll be in touch," said Wyatt before the other man left.

Everly folded her arms tightly across her chest. She glared at the sheriff, her green eyes flashing with incredulity. "Are you kidding me? You're just going to let Larry go? You heard him—he doesn't have an alibi for the night my brother was killed. Or last night, when I was attacked. He works in the hotel, which means he might've attacked me yesterday morning, as well."

"Now might be a good time to tell me about the attacks you just mentioned."

Everly caught the sheriff up to speed on everything that had happened, not leaving out any details. As she finished, she said, "You can't just let Larry go."

"Unfortunately, we don't throw people in to jail without a reason," said Haak. "He was voluntarily answering the questions we asked, and his answers make enough sense that I'm not placing him in custody. But, I am putting him under twenty-four/seven surveillance. If he tries to leave town, we'll know."

"Is that it?" asked Everly. Her tone dripped with the same skepticism that Wyatt felt.

Wyatt clenched his jaw. To Haak, he said, "I want a murder investigation opened. We need a search warrant to get into Larry's apartment *now*, before he disposes of any evidence. Or worse, skips town and we never see him again."

"Why don't you give me all of the evidence you've collected?" suggested the sheriff. "I'll review everything again."

With only two weeks left on the job, Wyatt wondered how diligent the sheriff would be with any new investigation. That meant it was up to Wyatt, and hell would freeze over before he gave Haak any information he collected. "That's not good enough," he said.

"I've said this before, and I'll say it again—I've kept this town safe for decades. I'm not going to get everyone into a panic for no reason, especially since I only have a few weeks on the job."

"I get it," Wyatt said. "You don't want to sully your reputation with an at-large serial killer, not when you're retiring in a few days."

"That's a harsh criticism and I won't have it," said the sheriff. "This town has been my life and I won't have you two show up and cause an upheaval for a lot of people."

Wyatt wasn't certain if he should believe the sheriff or not. Either way, he decided that that lawman was irrelevant. Besides, wasn't it working with a team that had ruined Wyatt's career all those years ago?

"Tell you what," said Wyatt. "I'm going to keep looking into this case. Because I know we're on the right track."

"Do what you have to do," the sheriff said. "I will

get a deputy to follow Larry around like I promised."
Haak stood slowly and picked up his hat. "In fact,
I'll see to it now."

The sheriff left the room and it was Wyatt's turn
to be pinned by Everly's fiery stare. "What was that
all about?" she asked. "Are you just going to let the
sheriff ignore the facts? I thought you wanted the
serial killer brought to justice."

Wyatt sighed. "Haak is a decent man, but he's old
and has some misguided notion of needing a legacy."
He continued, "Or maybe he's just tired. Either way,
it's obvious that he's not going to give this investigation the attention it needs."

"And you will?" asked Everly, finishing Wyatt's
sentence for him.

It was exactly what he'd planned. In fact, this was
a perfect scenario—Wyatt's continued investigation
had been given the blessing of a disinterested sheriff.
Along with his expertise and the resources of RMJ,
Wyatt would have the chance to rewrite history. To
catch the killer and erase the stain on his career. Hell,
on his life. Like an electric current under his skin,
Wyatt itched to begin the hunt.

"Will you give the investigation all the attention it
needs?" Everly asked, repeating her question.

Giving a noncommittal shrug, Wyatt asked, "Why
is that a problem?"

"It depends," she said.

The room was silent, save for the beating of
Wyatt's heart and the whisper of Everly's breath. His
skin suddenly felt too tight. "It depends on what?"

"On whether you plan on having me help—or not. Because you aren't getting rid of me, Wyatt Thornton. I won't rest until my brother gets justice."

Wyatt didn't hate the idea of Everly staying around for a few more days. And the fact that Wyatt wanted Everly to stay with him was the biggest danger of all.

Chapter 9

Everly sat at the computer desk in Wyatt's living room. A fire burned in the hearth and the late-afternoon sun shone through the windows. They had once again found a copy of Larry Walker's criminal history and the computer glowed with a litany of misdeeds.

"Here's what we know," said Wyatt. "Larry Walker doesn't fit the textbook definition of a serial killer. Serial killers are sly and cunning. Larry Walker is the human equivalent of a bullhorn."

"But he is a violent man, who happened to fight with Axl the night he died. He also had access to all of the other victims," she said. "Besides, he fits your initial profile—age, gender, ethnicity."

"True, but there are a lot of crimes on his rap sheet and none of them are close to murder."

"There's a progression of violence. Troubled kid. Drugs. Larceny. Assault. Jumping to murder isn't a big leap."

Wyatt paused and she knew that she'd scored a point.

After a moment, he spoke. "If Larry were to kill someone, it'd be in a fit of rage. A shot to the head over a woman or a fistfight gone awry."

Everly sucked in a breath. "What is it that you're trying to do, Wyatt? Prove that Larry isn't guilty?"

He shook his head. "Look, I'm covering my tracks. I was wrong about a suspect before. I'm not going to be wrong again." He sighed. "More even than the profile not matching perfectly, is that fact that there's no direct link between Larry and any of the victims—here or in Las Vegas—other than your brother. Without that, we'll have a hell of a time proving that he's guilty."

"So, what do we do? Go back to RMJ and use their equipment?"

"We could," said Wyatt. "Sometimes all a case needs is some old-school investigating. I have a buddy with the Las Vegas Police Department. He owes me a favor. Now might be the time to cash in."

He placed a call on his cell. Turning on the speaker, Wyatt set the phone on the desk. After the third ring, a man's voice came over the line. "This is Davis."

"Davis, this is Wyatt Thornton," he said.

"*Wyatt?* Where the hell have you been, man? I

never thought that I'd hear from you again, not after how it ended here."

"I'm...not with the Bureau anymore. Actually, because of how things went down, but that's why I'm calling. Some information has come my way about that case, and I was hoping I could call in a favor."

"You know I owe you, man. Ask away."

"Can you run a name for me? Lawrence or Larry Walker." Wyatt added in Larry's birthdate. "I need residences. Places of employment. Anything you got."

"That might be too big of a favor," said Davis. He paused a beat and added, "Without a reason, at least."

"A body turned up in Pleasant Pines, Wyoming. The circumstances are similar to Las Vegas."

"Similar how?" Davis asked.

Wyatt paused. Could he trust Davis? All the same, there was a more important question he knew that he should be asking. What was the likelihood that Davis would help without the facts?

"Two-dollar bill, ripped in half, in the victim's wallet. High BAC. No other trauma. Good looking Caucasian male," said Wyatt, running down the list.

Davis cursed. "Same thing we had here."

"That's exactly what I thought."

"Without a warrant this would have to be on the down-low," said Davis. "But you knew that already. Is this the best number to call?"

"It is," said Wyatt. "And thanks."

"Don't thank me yet," said Davis. "I haven't given you any information."

The line beeped and went dead.

"Now what do we do?" she asked. "Wait?"

"There's not much more we can do now."

"This sucks," she said.

His palm rested on the desk, and he inched closer, his fingers grazed hers. Everly's breath caught.

It was such a simple gesture, barely a touch, but it made her pulse race, and her body throb with heat. It was futile to lie—even to herself. The small caress of his fingers held the promise of much, much more.

Was that really what Everly wanted? To lose herself in Wyatt's arms…? To feel his lips on her mouth? To burn with desire as his touch scorched her skin? To savor the breathless moment when he entered her fully?

Then again, could she really get tangled up with her emotions when the only thing she should be focusing on was finding her brother's killer?

Like ice had been poured into her veins, Everly froze. She pulled her hand away and moved to the window seat. Placing her palms on the sill, she stared at the jagged Rocky Mountains in the distance. The sky had turned to rose and violet. The distant peaks were black in the waning light.

Everly longed to fall into Wyatt's arms and let him take away all of her worries, even if it was for a single night. But that would be a terrible mistake. He was helping her find Axl's killer. How would they navigate their tenuous partnership if they slept together?

A sob escaped her throat. She couldn't believe

she'd let herself be distracted by thoughts of something like sex. Tears streamed down her cheeks. She scrubbed her face. "I'm sorry," she said. "I don't know why I'm crying."

"Because," said Wyatt, "you've been through a lot of trauma in a few short days. Your brother's been killed. You were attacked. This is a lot to take on."

Sad didn't seem a large enough word for Everly's emotions. She was filled with rage and hatred and despair and loneliness and anguish and, yes, sadness. "Axl was a real wanderer. He traveled all over the country—he'd go anywhere for work, really loved his job. Just going from one assignment to the next. But I always knew that eventually he'd come home. Now? That'll never happen again."

"Do you have other family?"

She shook her head. "Our parents died when I was a junior in college in a car crash. Axl was in art school and moved back to Chicago just so I could come home over breaks. He always looked out for me."

Wyatt took a seat next to Everly and wrapped an arm around her shoulder. He pulled her to him, and she leaned into the embrace. The tears seemed endless, but eventually the crying stopped. Everly let Wyatt hold her.

Originally, Everly had sought out Wyatt for his expertise. It was a decision that had been driven by desperation and fear.

What would happen if she stayed—enveloped in Wyatt's embrace?

"Do you think it's safe for me to go back into town and try staying at the inn tonight?"

"No," he said simply. "I don't. Not while the killer is still at large. In fact, I don't really think it's safe for you anywhere."

A trace of his breath tickled her cheek. Everly knew she should move away, and yet, she was rooted to the spot. "I mean, since our prime suspect is being watched by the police, he can't exactly attack me again."

"I hate to say it, but having him under surveillance isn't foolproof. You hope that the subject doesn't sneak away," said Wyatt. He shook his head. "More than that, what if Larry isn't guilty? That means someone else is the killer. Someone outside our surveillance."

"I don't want to die," she said. Everly was exhausted. She turned to the window, pressing her palms onto the glass.

"Then stay," he offered. Wyatt moved closer, shoulder-to-shoulder, and placed his hand next to hers.

"Stay, and then what?" she asked.

"Stay with me. I'll keep you safe."

Yes, that's what she wanted—needed. In Wyatt's arms, Everly could pretend that the world was safe and beautiful. It would be a lie, but it was her lie—and certainly no one would get hurt by her small fib.

Everly studied Wyatt in the reflective glass. His image looked worn, faded—like a ghost. Yet she knew all too well that he was flesh and blood. A steady pulse rose and fell in the hollow of his throat. She reached out again, surer this time, and placed her palm over Wyatt's hand.

His gaze dropped to where they were connected. She slid her fingers between his and closed the space between them. She pressed her breasts into his hard chest and rose up on tiptoe to lick the seam of his lips. He wrapped an arm around her waist and pulled her hard, drawing Everly in closer still. She gave a gasp of surprise and Wyatt placed his lips on hers.

Wyatt slipped his tongue into her mouth. Everly opened herself as he explored, tasted, conquered. And she was in the mood to be taken captive.

He sat her on the window seat and tilted her back. Cold from the glass seeped through her sweater and chilled her flesh. The heat from Wyatt's body was scalding. Ice and fire. Wyatt lifted the fabric of Everly's sweater up inch by inch, and she shivered with anticipation. Her nipples were already hard, and he stroked them through the silky fabric of her bra.

"Wyatt," she breathed, unable to think of anything beyond the man who claimed her with his touch and kisses.

He broke away, his eyes searching her face. His eyebrows were drawn together. "Are you okay?" he asked.

She was trembling. "I'm fine."

"These past few days have been a lot for you," he said. "I doubt that you're fine."

"What are you saying?"

"I'm saying that we won't do anything you don't want to. I don't want to take advantage because of this situation you're in."

She raked her fingers through his hair and jerked his head back, exposing his throat. Everly ran her tongue over his flesh, tasting the salt of his skin. "I'm no china doll," she said. "I won't break."

Wyatt gave a low growl of desire. "I can see that."

"I want you, Wyatt."

Wyatt's hand traveled to Everly's rear. He squeezed. "Is this what you want?" he asked. His grip tightened. The front of his jeans pressed against her. He was hard.

"Yes," she said.

His hand moved back to her breast. He rubbed his thumb over her hard nipple. The sensation was delicious. "This?" he asked as his lips brushed hers. "Do you want this?"

Gooseflesh covered Everly's skin, yet she wanted a more intimate touch. "Yes," she gasped.

Wyatt's fingers trailed from her chest to her waist. He opened a button on her pants and pulled down the zipper, exposing the lace at the top of her panties. His hand slipped inside the fabric. She was already wet. He applied the slightest pressure to the top of her sex, rubbing in a slow circle.

"Do you want me to do this?" he asked.

"I want *you*, Wyatt," she said.

Already, Everly could feel that she was being taken away by the current of yearning. In answer to his question, she rocked her hips forward and opened her thighs, offering herself to Wyatt. He buried his finger inside of her and her muscles clenched around him. He began to use long, slow strokes. She reached for Wyatt, pulling his mouth to hers. She kissed him deeply, hungrily, as if she might never be sated.

He pulled away from the kiss. His thumb stroked the top of her sex and his fingers still moved inside of her. "Look at me," he said.

Slowly, she met his gaze.

"You are so beautiful, Everly Baker. I want to watch you. Your eyes. Your mouth. The flush of your cheeks. I want you to see me."

He thrust inside her again, harder this time. Everly gasped. Her skin was too close-fitting, and she feared that she might burst with unfulfilled longing. Wyatt continued to bring her pleasure with his hand and her eyes never left his. His jaw tensed, and his dark gaze held yearning, barely restrained. Yet, there was more to his look. He saw Everly—truly saw her. He saw her loss and fear and determination. He understood her need for more than justice, but vengeance.

And he didn't find her lacking for the flaws.

A haze filled her vision as Wyatt brought her closer to the brink of passion. She tried to focus on him, his deep brown eyes, the stubble on his chin. It was no use. She was too close to the edge. Her eyelids fluttered closed. Resting her head back on the cold glass, Everly cried out as she finally let go.

Wyatt's mouth was on hers, smothering her cries of delight with his hot kisses.

"I'm not done with you," he said. "Not by a long shot."

The echoes of her pleasure still resonated through her body, and her knees were weak. "You aren't done with me," she teased lightly. "My legs won't even hold me upright."

"No need," said Wyatt, as he held himself above her. An amber glow from the fire shone from behind, casting him in shadow. Nothing seemed real and yet, this was no dream.

Wyatt slipped off one of Everly's boots. He pressed his strong fingers into the pad of her foot, easing away tension she never knew she held.

"That feels good," she purred.

"You like?" he asked.

She bit her bottom lip and nodded.

He removed her other boot. He massaged the second foot, his eyes never leaving hers. He tugged on her pants and she lifted her hips. He slid off her slacks and dropped them in a heap. Sitting up, she pulled off her sweater, adding it to the pile. She shivered, despite the fire that blazed in the hearth.

"You can't be cold."

"Lace and satin don't keep in much heat," she said, referring to her bra and panties.

"Let's see what we can do about warming you up," said Wyatt. He backed off the window seat and kneeled on the floor. "Open your knees for me."

She did as he ordered. He moved to her, lifting her thighs over his shoulders. He pulled aside the stride of her underwear and placed his mouth on her sex.

Everly bucked against him. The pleasure was so intense that she wanted to run, escape to a place where she was in control.

Wyatt pleasured Everly with his mouth and his hands. Caressing. Tasting. Exploring. Worshipping. The ecstasy was too much. She climaxed for a second time, crying out his name.

"Still not done," said Wyatt.

He stripped out of his shirt and jeans. He was hard, as she knew he would be. But it was more than that—he was truly a work of art. His pecs were chiseled, his stomach was flat. A dark sprinkling of hair covered his chest and narrowed to a strip that dove to his groin. He stood and turned, giving her a full view of his tight rear and long legs.

While she was admiring Wyatt Thornton in all his male power, he'd taken a moment to retrieve a condom from his wallet. Everly was happy that he was prepared to be safe for both of them.

"Can I help with that?" she asked.

He handed her the foil packet. "Sure," he said.

Everly removed the condom and unrolled it down his length.

He moved to her, his lips on hers. She held tight to his shoulders as he spread her open, and then he was inside her. She wrapped her legs around his waist, taking him in deeper, needing him more.

She ran her hands through his hair. Down his back. She cupped his buttocks as they tightened and flexed with each thrust. She felt his strong arms and broad shoulders. His skin was hot and dampened with sweat. He was all muscle and sinew. Solid. Powerful. Unbreakable. His strokes increased. Faster. Harder. Wyatt threw back his head and gave a guttural howl.

He kissed Everly deeply, pressing his chest into hers. Their hearts shared a rhythm. The sky had turned from violet to indigo and the Rocky Mountains were now lost in the darkness.

Leaving a kiss on her shoulder, Wyatt rolled off Everly and strode to the half bath, closing the door behind him.

Taking advantage of the moment, Everly donned her panties and sweater. When Wyatt returned, she was sitting on the sofa, with a table lamp aglow.

"Hey, there," he said as he approached. He was still gloriously naked.

"Hey there, yourself," she said back.

"About what just happened..." He scratched the back of his head, lengthening the muscles of his torso and arms. "We should talk."

Everly wasn't in the mood to parse through feelings, not when her toes still tingled with pleasure. "We had mind-blowing sex," she said.

Wyatt pulled on his pants. "Mind-blowing, eh?"

"Yeah," she said. "Mind-blowing."

He chuckled and sat down beside her. She tried not to gawk at his bare chest, to recall the feel of his hard muscles. It was a wasted effort. Even though Everly didn't want to chat about their escapades—or any ensuing feelings—the silence left her fidgety.

"It's so quiet out here," she said, blurting out the first lame thing that came to mind.

He harrumphed and slipped a T-shirt over his head.

Everly should take the clue and keep her mouth shut but was compelled to fill the silence with something—anything. "Doesn't it bother you?"

Wyatt shrugged. "At first, sure. Las Vegas is a noisy place, and everyone gets used to their environment. It's the same with the quiet and slower pace."

"Do you ever miss it?" she asked. "Having a job, working, being social."

"Who says I'm not social?"

"I kind of figured it out," she teased. "But you're still hiding. Will you ever come out?"

Wyatt leaned back on the sofa and pinched the bridge of his nose. "Do I miss the real world?" he asked. "Honestly, sometimes."

"Let's say that Larry is the killer and you catch him," said Everly. "What would you do? Would you stay here, or would you go back to work for the FBI?"

"You're assuming a lot. First, that Larry's the killer and second, that the Bureau wants me back."

Everly tucked her legs beneath her. "Humor me."

"Maybe," he said. "Assuming that everything you said was true. Larry's the killer. I build a case. The FBI wants me. I might go back."

A little thrill of excitement ran up Everly's spine. Would Wyatt want to go to Chicago? They would make a fabulous couple... But she quickly pushed the notion from her mind. Really, it was ridiculous to even consider and yet, she could hardly think of anything else.

Before Everly could say anything, Wyatt's cell phone buzzed from where he'd left it on the desk. Everly's heart stilled, and she was taken back to the moment when she got the call—the one from Sheriff Haak, telling her that Axl was dead.

Her pulse began again as Wyatt crossed the room. He lifted the phone from the desk and glanced at the screen. "It's Davis, my contact with the LVPD," he announced before answering the call. "Hello?" he said, and then after a beat, added, "Let me put you on speaker so I can write all this down."

Everly rose to her feet as Wyatt sat at the desk and pulled a pad and paper from a drawer. "Go ahead," he said.

Davis cleared his throat. "I've got an employment history for Lawrence Walker." Davis then listed the names of three different casinos and a corresponding set of dates. Larry hadn't held any one job for longer than a few months. "I only have his name on a single lease. He lived in the same apartment for nineteen months. Grand Canyon Gardens. Small. Inexpensive. Not too far from the Strip."

As far as Everly could tell, they were getting information but nothing useful.

"Any roommates?" Wyatt asked.

"The lease doesn't say, but he had a two-bedroom unit."

Wyatt scribbled some notes, then said, "Thanks for the information. Anything else?"

"I was thinking about taking a ride by the Grand Canyon Gardens on my way home, see if any neighbors remember anything helpful," said Davis.

"Let me know what you find out, will you?"

"If it finally helps catch that monster, I'm willing to do anything." Then Davis ended the call.

"What do we do now?" Everly asked, suddenly aware of the fact that she was only in her top and panties.

"I'm going to cross-reference the victims in Las Vegas to Larry's employment history and see if anyone was a guest at a hotel where he worked."

Everly scooped up her discarded clothing from the floor. "I'll get dressed and be right back to help you," she said.

Wyatt had already powered up his computer and had the case's flash drive in hand. He turned in his seat and pinned her with his dark eyes. "If Larry's the killer, we'll prove it."

Everly nodded and slipped into the half bath. She dressed and turned on the tap. Holding her hands under the running water, she let it sluice through her fingers. She needed to find Axl's killer, but what if it wasn't Larry? Or worse, what if it was but they couldn't prove it?

It was obvious that Wyatt had his doubts about Larry Walker's guilt. Now that same worry gnawed at her middle. What if Wyatt was right and Larry wasn't involved at all? Still, Everly wouldn't accomplish anything by hiding in the bathroom. She splashed water on her face and turned off the tap.

Somewhat refreshed, Everly dried her face and opened the door.

Wyatt sat in front of the computer. After running a hand through his hair, he cursed.

"What is it?" Everly asked.

"None of the victims stayed at a hotel where Larry worked." He pressed the heels of hands into his eyes. With a mirthless laugh, he said. "It was really stupid to think that we'd bumble around and find a killer who's eluded law enforcement for years."

"There has to be more," said Everly. Her pulse raced and the metallic taste of fear and desperation filled her mouth. "I went to Reno a few years back for work. It's not Vegas, but the setup is similar. You stay at one hotel, but you might gamble at another, eat at the next and see a show at a fourth."

Wyatt waved his hand at the screen. "See for yourself. I have credit-card receipts for all activities. None of them are at the hotels where Larry worked."

"He might have gone to a different casino," Everly offered. "And if he paid with cash, there wouldn't be a credit-card record."

"He might have, but we need proof—not guesses."

Everly's cheek stung as if she'd been slapped. Biting her bottom lip, she counted to ten. It wouldn't do to say exactly what she was thinking. Instead, she pulled up a chair and sat next to Wyatt. "Let's start from the beginning. What do we know about the first victim?"

Wyatt moved the mouse and opened up a file. It was all there—the victim's name, age, occupation.

Hometown. Reason for his visit. Everly read the information again and again. Nothing. She pointed to the last line—reason for visit. "It says that the victim was in Las Vegas for a family wedding."

"So? Lots of people get married in Las Vegas."

"That's true, but was it a destination wedding, where everyone traveled to the ceremony? Or did the wedding take place in Las Vegas because that's where the bride and groom lived?"

Wyatt sat back in the chair and cupped his chin in his hand. "I think it was a cousin who got married. She was a graduate student at UNLV."

"Do you have her address?"

Wyatt jiggled the mouse. "I do."

He opened another document. Everly leaned forward, every muscle tense.

They both silently scanned the page. Wyatt pointed to a line in the text. "She lived in graduate-student housing," he said. "But it was a good thought."

Everly tried to tell herself that there was much more information to sift through. Yet, she'd been so sure. "What about the fiancé?" she asked.

"I get that you're disappointed," said Wyatt. "There are some connections, but we need something a little more substantial than Larry living in both places at the time of the killings."

Everly wasn't ready to give up. "It seems like a lot to me," she said.

"It's mostly circumstantial," he said.

"So that's it? You're quitting?"

"You have to understand, sometimes you follow a set of clues and they lead nowhere."

"What do we do now?"

Wyatt shook his head. "There is nothing more to do."

Rising to her feet, Everly paced around the room. "You're afraid of making another mistake." She paused. "I saw the OPR's report."

The minute she spoke, Everly knew she'd made a mistake.

Wyatt's eyes flashed with rage and for the first time, she understood that he might be as dangerous as the killers he hunted. When he spoke, his words were measured but his voice was filled with steel. "You had no right to go pawing through my things..."

"Paw through your things?" she asked, interrupting. "The report was in the file *you* handed to me." Working her jaw back and forth, Everly continued, "You arrested a man, but knew he was innocent. Why would you hide the alibi?"

"That's not what happened," he said.

"Oh really? Illuminate me with the truth."

"Nah," he said with the shake of his head. "It's not worth it."

Everly wanted to leave—to get away from him. But where would she go? Glancing over her shoulder, she looked at Wyatt. He was typing on the computer, oblivious to her, or her anger.

She started to walk away.

"Wait," he said. "You need to see this."

"What is it?"

Wyatt didn't bother looking her way. "I found a concrete link that connects Larry Walker to the first victim."

Everly went numb. "What is it?"

"Neither the bride nor the groom lived at Canyon Gardens Apartments," said Wyatt. "But a member of the wedding party did."

"Is that enough to arrest Walker?" Everly asked, her heart racing.

He shook his head. "Arresting him is up to the sheriff," said Wyatt. "But it's enough to bring Larry in for a serious conversation."

Chapter 10

Wyatt itched with the need to act, yet he knew that a certain amount of preparation was necessary if they were going to track Larry Walker down and speak to him. There was more that he knew—and hadn't been willing to say before. Now, Wyatt knew what Larry had been hiding. Yet, before speaking to the cook, he wanted to make two calls. The first was to Sheriff Haak.

He finally reached the sheriff at home. When Haak answered on the fifth ring, Wyatt activated the phone's speaker feature. Haak's voice was thick with sleep. "This better be good," he said.

Wyatt glanced at the clock on his computer screen—11:00 p.m. already? Not that the time mattered. "This is Wyatt Thornton. You needed a connection between Larry Walker and the victims from Las Vegas," said Wyatt. "And I have one."

The sheriff took in a quick breath. "I'm awake."

"The first victim was in Las Vegas for a cousin's wedding. The bride—his cousin—was a student at UNLV and she lived on campus."

"You woke me up for that?"

Wyatt bit back a curse and continued. "It's not the cousin, but one of the people in the wedding party. He and Larry Walker lived in the same apartment complex."

The line went silent. Everly stood near Wyatt. He did his best to not look in her direction. After the words exchanged about the OPR's report...well, Wyatt wasn't sure what he thought about her now.

If he was honest with himself, he was more concerned about what she thought of him.

"You sure about that?" Haak asked.

The question drew Wyatt from his reverie. "Positive," he said. "Do you know where Larry is now?"

"Give me a minute," the sheriff said. "I'll call the deputy I assigned to watch Larry from my cell phone."

The sound of voices was unmistakable in the background. Too bad Wyatt couldn't make out a word of what was being said.

"You there?" Sheriff Haak asked.

As if Wyatt would hang up. "I'm here."

"My deputy says that Larry's still at the Pleasant Pines Inn."

"Is the pub crowded tonight?" Wyatt needed all

the information he could get in order for a successful apprehension.

"Closed," said the sheriff.

"Closed? It's only eleven o'clock. That's kind of early, isn't it?" Everly asked.

The sheriff said, "Sometimes they shut down if there isn't much of a crowd."

"But Larry's still there," said Wyatt. He hated that their prime suspect hadn't been placed into custody. Yet, it was the sheriff's call who got arrested and when. Then again, maybe the Sheriff Haak was smarter than Wyatt. Hadn't it been a mishandled arrest that cost Wyatt his career?

"He hasn't been seen leaving the building and his truck is in the lot," said the sheriff. "The deputy thinks that he's having an after-work drink by himself."

The late-night cocktail followed what they knew of Larry's behavior. Yet, it wasn't the absolute answer Wyatt wanted. Still, it was the best they were going to get. "We're on our way, Sheriff."

"I figured as much," said Haak. "I'll meet you there."

Wyatt ended the call and entered another number.

"This is Marcus Jones."

"Marcus," said Wyatt. "We have a connection between Larry and one of the victims. Larry's still at the pub." He hesitated. "Feel like a beer?"

"I thought you'd never ask."

As promised by Sheriff Haak, Larry's truck was in the employee parking lot of the Pleasant Pines Inn.

A single light was attached to the back wall and illuminated the rear door.

The plan was straight forward. Marcus Jones and Sheriff Haak would go in to the hotel through the lobby. The sheriff had jurisdiction, since the supposed crimes had occurred in his county. He'd be the one to arrest Walker. Marcus Jones was with the sheriff for added reinforcement, if needed.

Wyatt was to come in from the back and go directly to the pub. The deputy, Travis Cooper, was to remain in the parking lot, covering the rear egress and Larry's truck—the most likely means of escape.

Wyatt was ready. It was moments like this where Wyatt felt as he truly understood what it was to be alive—to have a purpose.

With his SIG Saur tucked into his waistband at the small of his back he turned to Everly. "I want you to stay in my truck. If anything happens, leave."

"And go where?" she asked, her tone as cold and hard as the metal of the firearm tucked into the small of his back.

"Go to the RMJ offices," he said. Belatedly, he realized that he should have left Everly there in the first place. It was too late now to correct his mistake and he continued, "That'll be the safest place for you."

"How many times do I have to tell you that I'm not worried about my own safety? I only care about catching my brother's murderer."

Wyatt was desperate to catch the killer, as well. It's just that he cared far more about keeping Everly from harm's way than anything else. The thought struck him like a fist to the chin. Sure, they'd become lovers, but Wyatt didn't love Everly, right?

"I'd argue with you," he said to Everly, "but it won't help. I know it."

"No," she said. "It won't."

"You can come, but you have to do exactly as I say. One wrong move and you could get shot."

"I understand," said Everly.

Wyatt used a crowbar, provided by the sheriff's office, and pried the door open. It led to the same hallway he'd chased Larry down that morning. His pulse raced like he was still running, his breath echoed in his ears. He drew his gun and stepped lightly, listening for sounds beyond those of his footfalls on the floor. Ahead was the pocket door to the conference room where they'd held the meeting. The hallway continued, ending at the back of the main pub, where they'd hopefully find an unsuspecting Larry.

Wyatt held Everly's hand as he pushed open the door. It gave a whisper of sound.

"Stay with me," he whispered to Everly.

She gripped his hand tighter. "I'm not going anywhere."

A recessed light illuminated a long, mahogany bar. A mirror hung on the wall and showed a reflection of the room. Tables, with chairs placed on top. An empty dance floor, with parquet tiles. A forgotten mop and bucket. No Larry.

Marcus Jones and Sheriff Haak came through the doors adjacent to the lobby.

"Anything?" Marcus asked.

"Nada," said Wyatt.

"Which means he's somewhere," said Everly.

"Unless he snuck away," said Wyatt. "And left his truck as a decoy."

All eyes turned to the sheriff. If Larry had escaped, his office would be to blame. "I'll see if the front desk has video of the last two hours," said Haak.

"I'll do a floor-by-floor search," said Marcus.

"Everly and I will check through the kitchen and restaurant."

With a nod, Marcus and the sheriff left to do their tasks. Another door was tucked into the back corner.

"That's got to be the kitchen," said Everly.

"Stay behind me," said Wyatt. He pulled his weapon again as he slowly pushed open the door. The room was black as pitch. A faint light from the pub seeped in and spread across the threshold. There was a faint creaking. The room stank of ammonia... and blood. Wyatt immediately recognized the stench. He ran his hand along the wall, searching for a light switch. Using the flat of his hand, he flipped all the switches upward.

The room filled with blinding light.

A piercing scream filled the small kitchen, and the noise ricocheted off the steel appliances. Wyatt spun to the sound. Everly stood on the threshold, her face chalky white. She lifted a trembling hand and pointed to an alcove at the back of the room.

Hanging from a noose was the body of Larry Walker.

* * *

Larry hung by his neck, the rope slowly swinging. His complexion was gray, and a trickle of blood leaked from his mouth. His eyes were open, even in death. A chair was lying on the ground, toppled to the side, from where he'd kicked it away.

Everly began to shiver. Wyatt was at her side. He placed a hand on her shoulder.

"It's okay," he said.

"No," she said, her voice shrill. "It's not."

"Don't look. Look at me," Wyatt insisted.

She moved her gaze to his face. His dark brown gaze anchored her. Slowly, she stopped shivering.

"Wyatt! Everly!" Sheriff Haak stood on the threshold, breathing heavily. "I heard screaming." His color faded as he took in the scene. With a gasp, he asked, "Dear God, what happened?"

"It's a suicide," said Everly, surprised that she'd found her voice and even happier to use it. "Larry knew that we suspected him of all the murders. Then he killed himself before being caught."

"It doesn't make sense," said Wyatt. "Serial killers typically don't commit suicide."

"There's a piece of paper on that table," said the sheriff. He pointed to the stainless steel workspace in the middle of the room. He ambled over to investigate.

Placing his palms on either side of the page, he began to read out loud. "'I'm not going to apologize for what I've done. Those men deserved to die—every last one of them. I'm not going to tell you why

I did what I did. You wouldn't understand. I'm tired of hiding and running and being afraid of getting caught. Today was the closest I've ever come to being apprehended and I'm not going to jail.'

"It's not addressed to anyone in particular," said Sheriff Haak.

Everly remained mute, but she suspected that Larry had written the note for Wyatt's sake.

The sheriff continued, "Nor is it signed."

"How can we tell if the note really came from Larry?" Everly asked.

"Who else would write this?" the sheriff asked.

He had a point. Everly shrugged.

"It'll be easy to prove whether it is his or not. All we need is a confirmed writing sample from Larry Walker and a handwriting expert," said Wyatt. He continued, "Even if Larry wrote this note, I still don't like this. Serial killers aren't afraid. They don't feel remorse. None of this is typical."

Pulling the phone from his pocket, Wyatt placed a call. "Marcus," he said. "Come into the kitchen, we found Larry." He paused, listening to the answer, and hung up.

"I need to call Doc Lambert and have him collect the body," said the sheriff. He exited the kitchen, leaving Everly and Wyatt alone.

"If you want to go and wait in the pub," he said, "you can."

The offer was tempting. In fact, Everly wanted to get away from Larry's unrelenting stare. Yet, this man had taken her brother's life. She owed it to Axl to see the investigation through to the end. She shook her head. "I'll stay," she said.

"Suit yourself," said Wyatt. He approached the body.

"What are you doing?" Everly asked, her pulse racing. "This is a crime scene. You can't tamper with evidence."

"Technically," said Wyatt. He spotted a box of plastic gloves on one of the counters, used for food prep, grabbed a pair and slipped them on, then patted down the corpse. "It hasn't officially been labeled a crime scene yet, although you are right about the evidence tampering."

She cast a quick glance over her shoulder. "Then what are you doing?"

"Looking for something to connect Larry to the killings."

Using two fingers, Wyatt withdrew a wallet from Larry's back pocket. He brought the wallet to the island and set it down. It was nylon with Velcro closures. Wyatt opened the main compartment. There was fifty dollars in cash and a driver's license, along with two credit cards. Inside was another compartment, hidden behind the first. The material bulged.

"There's definitely something in here," said Wyatt as he opened the second section.

Everly moved closer to get a better view. Larry had hidden away dozens of bills. "More money?" she asked.

Wyatt pulled them out. "Not just money. He has a stack of two-dollar bills—all of them have been ripped in half. My guess, each of these bills matches the other halves found on each of the victims."

Carl Haak hated that his department was so small they needed Rocky Mountain Justice—an organization new to Pleasant Pines and he knew next to nothing about—to process the scene, taking photos, dusting for fingerprints, collecting evidence. He hated that his deputy, Travis Cooper, was looking to Marcus Jones for leadership. He hated that, even though there were only three RMJ operatives—Julia McCloud, Luis Martinez, and Marcus Jones, the trio were top-notch at their jobs. But what he hated the most was that Larry Walker never should've gotten away with so many killings in Pleasant Pines, and that responsibility belonged to Carl.

He'd failed the town in more ways than he cared to count. With his retirement in a couple weeks, he'd never make amends. His gut was filled with painful acid. He'd called in Dr. Lambert to collect the body. With the spate of serial killings, Doc Lambert didn't want to be too hasty this time around and he refused to name a cause of death or call it a suicide. All the same, it seemed obvious to Carl Haak—Larry Walker knew he was about to get arrested. To avoid spending the rest of his life in jail, he had taken his own life.

At the scene, Carl had catalogued the stack of two-dollar bills, torn in half, found in Larry's wallet. The way Carl saw it, Larry had placed one half of a bill with each victim and then he'd kept the other for himself—a macabre souvenir from a kill. Since more than twenty bills—all ripped in half—had been found, it meant that Larry had taken more lives than anyone had ever guessed.

It also meant that people other than Carl had missed the obvious. Still, it was the most singularly humiliating moment in his long life.

"Sheriff?" someone asked. It was one of the guys from RMJ—Martinez. He was an ex-cop from Denver, and even though he was thirty years Haak's junior, he knew his way around the scene better than the sheriff ever would. "Did you want to organize a team to search Larry's home?"

That was another thing that grated on Carl's nerves—all these impressive operatives running a search while trying to make Carl, the failure, feel like he was in charge.

After a moment's pause, he said, "Why don't you do it?"

The big guy held a camera that cost more than Carl's monthly mortgage payment and looked over his shoulder. It was obvious that he was taking pictures for evidence and didn't want to leave before the task was done.

"I'll do it," Wyatt Thornton offered. "I want to get into that bastard's house and see what else he has from previous victims. You should probably come with me, Sheriff."

It was a measly bone thrown to an old dog.

"Yeah," said Carl as he pushed himself to stand.

His knees creaked with the effort. "Sure. Travis," he called to the deputy.

The young man was working with the female operative, Julia, a tall blonde with her long hair pulled into a ponytail.

Travis said, "Yeah, Sheriff?"

"You stay here and..." He paused, not sure what to say. "I'm going to Walker's house and see what's what."

Wyatt turned to Everly Baker. "I'm going with the sheriff to look at Larry Walker's house. You should stay here. Maybe get a room and try to rest."

"No way," said Everly. "I still haven't found my brother's camera. What if Larry had it?"

"You can come along if you want," Wyatt offered.

Everly accepted a little too quickly for it to only be about her brother's camera—something that could be brought to her if found.

Carl studied Wyatt and Everly as they walked from the pub and into the lobby.

Despite her tenacity, Sheriff Haak had come to like Everly. If it hadn't been for her urging, nobody would have ever looked into her brother's death, or any of the others. He hoped that once she went home, she'd rebuild her life and maybe find peace.

They headed through the lobby. The front door opened and Darcy Owens, the desk clerk, stepped in from the night. Her blond hair fell loose around her shoulders. Wrapped up in a heavy coat, she wore sweatpants and sneakers.

"Is it true, Sheriff?" she asked in a breathless whisper. "The owner called me and said that Larry committed suicide." Her voice cracked on the last word.

"He did." Carl hitched his pants by the belt loops. "Hanged himself in the kitchen."

Darcy went pale. "Why?"

Wyatt stepped forward and answered her question with one of his own. "How well did you know Larry?"

Darcy appeared to be taken aback by Wyatt's question. "How well do I know him?" she said. "Well enough, I guess."

"Did you socialize with Larry?"

"Occasionally, the employees would have drinks in the pub after it closed. The inn holds parties for employees a couple of times a year. I've hosted game night at my house. Larry was always invited." She chewed on her bottom lip. "What's all of this about?"

"It seems that none of us knew Larry as well as we thought we did," said Carl.

Twin dots of red appeared on Darcy's cheeks. "What's all this about?" she asked again. This time there was an edge to her question.

Carl shifted from one foot to the next. He wasn't ready to tell folks what was happening; or admit that he'd failed at his singular task of keeping the town safe.

"It seems as if your tip paid off," Wyatt said for him. "Larry was involved in Axl Baker's death."

Darcy's jaw dropped.

Everly stepped forward. "I'm going to miss my

brother every day for the rest of my life. Now I know what happened—or, at least who was to blame."

Darcy wiped tears from her eyes. "I'm just so sorry."

"It's not your fault," said Everly. "Besides, if you hadn't pointed us in Larry's direction, we never would've figured any of this out."

"Wyatt," Darcy breathed. "You caught the killer."

Yep, Carl had been right about Wyatt Thornton from the get-go. The man had the kind of looks that made the ladies go gaga. "Well, Darcy, if you think of anything, you let me know," said Carl.

"There is one thing," said Darcy. "One night, when we were all having an after-hours drink, Larry became really sad. Like, really, really sad. I asked him what was wrong, and, told me that he'd... done things in Vegas."

Carl's shoulder blades pinched together. "What kind of things?"

Darcy chewed on her lip.

"You have to tell us," said Wyatt. "Larry's gone and you don't need to protect him anymore."

"And besides," added Everly, "there are other family members, like me, who want to know what happened to their loved ones."

"I'm not sure that it's much. I mean, at first, he told me that he'd had legal troubles with some girlfriends. Fights that got out of hand, that kind of thing."

"And then?" Everly persisted, when Darcy didn't seem to know what to say.

"Well, I told him that we all have issues and exes who've treated us badly. He said it was more than that. He told me that he thought he was evil."

A chill ran down Carl's spine. "He actually told you that?"

"At the time, I thought that it was the whiskey and he was just depressed. But it seems like he might've been right. If Larry did kill Axl Baker, and those other men, then maybe he was right. Maybe Larry really was evil."

"You might have to talk to Chloe Ryder," said the sheriff. "She's the new district attorney."

"Chloe Ryder," Darcy repeated. "There was a social work intern at my high school named Chloe Ryder. I wonder if it's the same person."

Before Haak could respond, Marcus Jones approached at a trot. "I was examining the body and I think there's something you need to see." He held a fancy camera, with an illuminated screen.

"Can you give us a moment," the sheriff said to Darcy.

"Sure thing," she replied, before heading over to the reception desk.

Marcus paused for a moment, no doubt waiting for Darcy to be out of earshot, before holding up the camera. Everly and Wyatt moved in close.

"See this," Marcus said, showing a picture of hands, mottled and purple.

Carl said, "I see the fingers of a dead person, but I assume there's more."

Marcus made the picture bigger. "Look here. The fingertips are scratched."

Sure enough, the pads of the thumb and two fingers were scraped raw. "Do you think he struggled? And was forcibly hanged?" Carl wasn't going to miss any obvious signs of foul play a second time.

"I think we need to consider every angle," said Marcus.

"Or his hands might've gotten scraped when I tackled him in the parking lot," said Wyatt. "Or he might've struggled during strangulation. Even if Larry was determined to kill himself, his instinct would've been to claw at the rope."

"And he worked in the kitchen," added Everly. "As a cook I imagine that he was always getting burned or cut."

For Carl, the simplest explanations were usually true. But that belief had caused a heap of grief and he wasn't about to make the same mistake again.

Chapter 11

Larry Walker had lived in a small apartment at the back of a run-down house. It consisted of a kitchen/living room combination, a single bedroom in the rear and small bathroom between the two. From the Spartan furnishings to the lack of acquired junk, it was obvious that Larry didn't have much use for material possessions.

"How long has Larry been in Pleasant Pines?" Everly asked. "Two years? Three? Doesn't it seem odd that he has next to nothing?"

There were other things about Larry's apartment that bothered Wyatt more. "Here's what gets me the most," said Wyatt. "There's absolutely nothing to connect Larry to any of the killings—not even Axl's missing camera." He continued, "You saw that stack of money. If each bill represents a killing, then Larry is responsible for over twenty murders. Keeping personal belongings from the victims illustrates the power of the killer. In short, I'd expect to see trophies from each of the victims—and we haven't found any yet."

"Or maybe that's just it," said Everly. "Larry hasn't been a typical serial killer, if there is such a thing, from the beginning. Maybe that's why he'd gotten away with his crimes for so long."

Maybe Everly was right. Could Larry be a new breed of serial killer? One that could seamlessly blend in to society? Or had Larry just gotten lucky, been smart enough to kill without arousing suspicion? Even that idea was hardly satisfactory. It brought back the original question. "Then where is the camera? We already know from the initial discovery of your brother that it's not near the old schoolhouse."

"Easy," said the sheriff. "Wyoming is a big state. Larry could've dumped it almost anywhere."

Wyatt knew, deep in his bones, that Larry hadn't committed suicide. Like a magician's sleight of hand, all eyes had been directed to what the real killer wanted them to see—leaving the actual crimes hidden.

The real question was, what next?

"There's not much more we can do here tonight," he said. Wyatt glanced at his phone for the time— 3:15 a.m. "This morning," he corrected.

"You folks go on ahead," said the sheriff. "I'm

going to close off the crime-scene, then head back to the inn and see how everything is progressing. I need to check in with Deputy Cooper and send him home. I imagine that we can release your brother's body in the morning, Everly. Then you can take him home and give him a proper burial."

Everly gave a wan smile. "Thanks for everything, Sheriff," she said.

"Don't thank me," he said. "If it wasn't for you, we never would've looked into any of these deaths. Without you, Larry would've kept getting away with murder." Hooking his fingers through his belt loops, the sheriff hefted up his pants. "I reckon that it's me who should be thanking you."

She flashed him a grateful smile, then turned to the door.

"One last thing," said the sheriff. "Don't talk to the media right away. I need to contact the next of kin for all the other victims. That'll take some time. Don't want them to hear it on the news."

Wyatt said, "You don't have to worry about me. I'm not exactly a big fan of reporters."

Sheriff Haak nodded. "I can't exactly blame you for that." The older man turned to Everly. "I hope you'll come and visit us now and again—when the circumstances of your stay are more pleasant."

"I'd like that, Sheriff," she said. She opened her arms. The sheriff leaned in for a hug and patted her back.

"Although, I'm retiring in a couple of weeks and

moving to South Carolina. You might need to come and visit me at the beach."

"It's a date," said Everly with a small wave. She walked to the door. Wyatt was right at her heels and used the remote starter to unlock the auto. Everly slid into the seat next to Wyatt's.

"You look tired," he said, getting behind the wheel of his truck. He reached across her and placed his gun into the glove box.

"Then I must look phenomenal, because I feel exhausted."

Wyatt chuckled and backed down the short drive. He wasn't in the mood for conversation. He had too many thoughts—feelings—to deconstruct and was thankful for the silence.

The sky unfurled above him, an inky swath of velvet. "Must be cloudy."

"How do you know?"

Damn. He'd spoken out loud without meaning to. Over the years, he'd gotten so comfortable with his own company he forgot what it was like to have someone around who listened.

"No stars," he said.

Everly leaned forward in her seat and looked to the sky. "That's too bad. We never see the stars in Chicago." She was quiet for a moment. "There's a certain appeal to seeing stars."

Wyatt worked his jaw back and forth. "I was ordered to lie," he said. He'd never spoken about his ordeal to anyone—and he wasn't completely sure why he was speaking now. Maybe it was the darkness or the quiet or maybe it was because Wyatt was telling his secret to Everly.

Continuing, Wyatt said, "My higher-ups wanted a suspect in custody. The blackjack dealer had been on our radar, but we knew he had an alibi for one of the killings. I was told to arrest him anyway. The guy was smart. He hired a lawyer. The lawyer brought his alibi to the press and then we had to let him go. The whole case fell apart and I was the one who took all the blame."

She placed her hand on his thigh. "Wyatt, I'm so sorry."

"I don't want your sympathy," he said. "I just wanted you to know the truth." He paused. "The truth about what I did."

"I don't know what to say," she said.

"There's nothing to say." Wyatt turned his attention back to the road and the night.

The earlier silence, which had been soothing, was replaced by a chasm that separated Wyatt from Everly. At the same time, the quiet was filled with a single question. Now that Everly had forced Wyatt out of his sanctuary, would he ever be able to live a solitary life?

Everly stared out the window of the truck, seeing nothing of the surroundings. Fragments of memory flashed in and out of her mind. Larry's body, dangling from a noose. A faceless form reflected in the mirror. The old schoolhouse surrounded by mist.

Wyatt's driveway came into view and he eased

off the paved road. In the distance, the ancient farm-house rose out of the barren landscape. She exhaled, relaxing farther into the seat. They were home.

Everly's spine stiffened at the word: home. With-out her brother, would she ever feel like she belonged in Chicago again? True, Axl's job always took him to the far corners of the earth, but he came back be-tween gigs. And now? Well, Everly had her job and friends.

What she lacked in Chicago was a family, people who loved her most of all.

Wyatt parked his truck next to her rental car, and she turned to face him. "Why don't you come back with me?"

"What?"

"Come to Chicago. You've solved the unsolvable case. The FBI must have a field office downtown. If you don't want to go back to the Bureau, there are tons of other places that would hire you." Everly was in her element, her heart rate creeping upward with excitement. "I can handle your comeback. I have contacts with all the major networks and can craft a press release that'll have you on every cable news channel by dinnertime tonight."

"What?" he asked again.

She hadn't stuttered. Maybe she'd spoken too fast for him to fully appreciate her plan. "You're a hero, Wyatt, and it's time that the world knows."

"You want me to move to Chicago?"

"You have to admit, it checks a lot of boxes for you—for us, really."

"Gus would hate living in a city. He's used to being able to run around."

"There are dog parks," said Everly.

"It's about freedom to roam. You don't have that in Chicago, do you?"

"Well, no," she admitted.

Before she could say anything else, Wyatt turned off the ignition and opened his door. The interior light filled the cabin with its unnatural glare. "And speaking of Gus, I need to let him out before he makes a mess in the house."

Jumping down from the truck, Wyatt slammed the door shut. Everly was surrounded in darkness once more. Yet, she didn't need the light to be able to see what was happening. She and Wyatt were different people, with different wants and different lives. And those differences were too much for a compromise.

Everly opened her own door and hopped from the big truck to the ground. She exhaled, her breath instantly freezing into a cloud. Everly's arms ached. Her back was sore. Her legs throbbed. She was exhausted and wanted nothing more than to sleep and sleep and sleep.

Yet for one glorious moment, Everly had seen the possibility of a future with Wyatt. What she envisioned had been perfect. Like most dreams, it faded with the coming dawn.

Reaching her arms above her head, she stretched and rotated, easing away some of her physical discomfort. Tilting her head back, she caught a glimpse of the sky. There, just above the horizon, was a brilliant light. A star, which had been hidden by the clouds, emerged.

Wyatt had gone into the house and returned with Gus. The dog whipped his tail back and forth so hard it was nothing more than a cream-colored blur. Gus nudged Everly's leg and she scratched the scruff of his neck. "Hey, boy," she said.

"You're right," she said to Wyatt. "I can't expect your dog to adjust to living in a city."

Gus trotted off, as if to give them privacy.

"So where does that leave us?" Wyatt asked.

"I can visit," she said. "You can come to Chicago now and then."

"You want to try to make something work out between us long-distance?"

From the dubious tone of his voice, she knew that he didn't like the idea.

"I don't think that would work," she said.

Wyatt sighed. "You're probably right."

Everly looked back to the sky, to the star. It was as if her brother was watching. The notion gave Everly a sense of calm, and yet she couldn't help but wonder what would Axl, the free spirit, recommend?

She didn't need to think about it for long. Axl would tell Everly to embrace life, and not look back. Without adventure, he would say, she wasn't living—she was just existing.

Gus ambled back from the darkness and sat on his haunches, waiting.

"You're welcome to stay for now." Wyatt opened

the front door. "It's late and you don't want to fall asleep while driving back to town."

"Sure," she said. "And thanks."

Everly crossed the threshold and stepped into the house. The building had to be over one hundred and fifty years old, built when things were made to last. More than being able to see the stars, Everly appreciated the connection to the land and to history.

Behind her, Wyatt kicked the door closed, making the darkened room even darker. He moved, a shadow in the blackness, and her pulse began to pound in her skull. She didn't fear for her own safety, but Wyatt was dangerous, nonetheless. Without question, Everly's heart would certainly break as soon as she left him.

"Where do you want to sleep?" His voice came from the gloom, swirling around her, becoming the air that she breathed.

"Upstairs," she said, "in the bed." Everly stopped, taking only a moment more to think before she spoke. "With you."

"You don't have to do that," he said. He moved toward her, the shadow becoming flesh.

"I know," she said. "But I want you. If all we have left between us is tonight, I want to take this memory home with me. Make love to me, Wyatt."

Wyatt took her hand in his. He pressed it to his chest. Beneath her palm, his heartbeat was strong and steady. "I'll miss you once you're gone."

She stepped closer. "Shut up," she said, "and kiss me."

His lips were on hers. The kiss was hungry and

possessive. She wrapped her arms around his neck. Sensations washed over her, cleansing Everly of every thought beyond Wyatt and the embrace.

Her fingers grazed the back of his neck. His lips moved to the hollow of her throat and the fire of passion began to burn, warming Everly with desire. Wyatt's hands were at the small of her back, drawing her to him. He was already hard and the memory of being filled by Wyatt came on so strong that Everly moaned.

She needed him closer, needed the heat of his flesh warming her, needed to become one with Wyatt again. She loosened his belt and Wyatt gripped both her wrists in one hand.

"This time it isn't going to be a mad rush," he said.

She was drawn into his banter. "Oh, yeah?" she asked. "What do you plan to do, then?"

"Enjoy myself," he said. He pressed his lips to her ear. "I'm going to enjoy myself as I explore every inch of your body and make you come again and again and again." His whispered words blazed down her shoulder, and Everly shivered with anticipation.

Everly was much more accustomed to action than delay and she wanted to explore Wyatt everywhere and all at once. Yet, there was an unmistakable attraction to being touched by an unhurried hand.

He held the back of her head, tilting Everly so she could only look at Wyatt. In truth, she didn't want to see anything beyond his face. His gaze was filled with the same heat of longing she felt building, sweltering, within.

Her wrists were still in his grasp. He gently lifted her arms above her head. She was stretched out long, her breasts lifted.

"Don't move," he said as he stepped away. From the darkness, he studied her form. "You are so beautiful."

She felt beautiful. And desirable. And unrestrained.

"Kiss me," she said.

"Beautiful and pushy," he teased.

"You want someone meek and timid?"

"Never," he said. "But I told you to stand there."

"Is this all about power? Control? Are you only teasing me, Wyatt?"

"Would you mind if I was?" he asked.

She dropped her arms and reached for Wyatt's hand. "Come with me," she said, pulling him toward the stairs. "Game time is over."

Wyatt let Everly lead him up the stairs. He liked that she took the initiative, even though he wanted to slowly strip Everly out of every piece of clothing she wore. For him, taking his time wasn't simply about power, as she had suggested. Wyatt wanted the moment to last. Because there was one thing he knew—in the morning, all he would have were memories.

It was dark at the top of the stairs and he was blind with need. He reached for Everly and claimed her with his mouth. She let out a noise, a little mew of surprise, and he grew harder—if that was even possible.

Wyatt pulled Everly into the bedroom. He lifted her sweater over her head. Her bra was black, all lace and silk—a testament to Everly's wicked and sexy nature.

Pulling the front of her bra down, he exposed her breasts. Each nipple was a perfect bud. Wyatt bent his head and took one nipple into his mouth. She gave a little cry of delight. God, he was going to explode if she didn't stop. She clung to his shoulders, her nails biting through the fabric of his shirt and gouging his flesh. The pain didn't bother him. It was another sign that Everly was as lost in passion as he was, and it gave Wyatt a sense of power.

Everly had been right when she accused Wyatt of playing games. He didn't mind teasing her a little. Maybe he did want control. He applied pressure with his teeth. This time, she hissed and thrust her chest forward.

"Wyatt," she breathed. "I want you. Now."

"I'm taking my time," he said. He unhooked the back of her bra and let the straps slide from her shoulders. The bra fell to the floor.

She grabbed the hem of his shirt and tugged it over his head. She pressed her palm to his chest, burning his flesh with her touch. "I want to feel your skin next to mine. I want you inside of me."

Wyatt was no longer able to ignore the primal draw of Everly. But it was more than sex—even more than the mind-blowing sex from earlier. It was the fact that when they were together, Wyatt wanted to be a better man—the kind of man she deserved.

Was it really possible to fall for a person so quickly and so hard?

He lifted her from the ground and carried her to the bed. He removed her boots, taking a moment to rub the instep of each foot. Wyatt tugged on each leg of her pants. Everly lifted her nicely shaped rear from the bed as he finished removing her slacks.

And there she was. His goddess in a pair of black lace panties.

Wyatt wanted to bury himself so deep inside of her that he could taste it.

"What?" she asked, a small smile pulling up at the corner of one lip. "What are you thinking?"

It was his opportunity to say something suave. Instead, he told her the truth. "I want you, Everly Baker. It's a need. A hunger. A thirst."

She reached for his belt and unfastened the buckle. Wyatt took over from there and stripped in seconds. From a bedside drawer, he found a condom and rolled it down his shaft.

"I love looking at you in your sexy little panties; but those have to go."

Everly pulled them off slowly. Hip. Thighs. Calves. Feet. Then she let them slip from her fingertips to the floor. Like a lion of the Serengeti, Wyatt pounced on Everly, his quarry. He entered her in one hard thrust. Everly fitted him perfectly. Wyatt felt a tingling at the back of his neck, as if a warning from his brain told him that he might be overcome with passion too soon. He eased back his hips, until just the tip remained inside. He used languid, full strokes to set the rhythm.

Yet, he was always balanced on the precipice, ready to tumble into oblivion. He focused on the sweat that dampened his brow. He tried not to think about Everly's full breasts, which pressed into his chest. Yet he reached for her, rolling a taut nipple between his finger and thumb.

"Wyatt," she gasped, her hips lifting, bucking against him.

His control wavered, but he needed to make sure she was satisfied. He reached between their sweat-slicked bodies and found the top of Everly's sex. She was swollen with want and he applied pressure as he rotated this thumb. She moaned, and her inner muscles tightened around him. She was close to a climax, he knew it. Funny, it was only his second time with Everly and already, he could read her like a book.

He hooked one of her legs over his shoulder, diving in deeper. He loved the way her lips parted and how her eyelashes gently fluttered on her cheeks. Her breath came in short gasps as she called out his name. "Wyatt. Wyatt. Wyatt."

She placed her lips on his, the little whimpers becoming part of the kiss. His strokes were fast and hard, and Wyatt wasn't sure how much longer he could hold off. Then she cried out one last time and her grip on his shoulders loosened as her inner muscles contracted and released.

Wyatt couldn't contain himself any longer. With his pulse racing, he gave a low growl and let go. The bass of his heartbeat resonated throughout his body and Wyatt collapsed with Everly beneath him. She was soft and sweetly scented and perfect in every way.

He searched for the right words to let her know... But, let her know what? That he'd changed in the last day and half. Yes, that was exactly it. Somehow, he was a better man for having known her. Even though their paths crossed briefly, he would miss her once she was gone. But the words escaped him, so instead he whispered, "I'll be right back. Gotta take care of the condom."

In the dim bathroom, Wyatt cleaned up as quickly as he could. He didn't need a light to see that Everly was important. What was keeping him in Pleasant Pines? He loved his old farmhouse, but he'd never completely unpacked. He didn't have a job. Or friends. Or any other connection to the community.

He'd used Gus as his first excuse, but Gus was a good dog. He could adjust to living somewhere new. Maybe a change was just what Wyatt needed—and it made sense that Everly was the catalyst for his new beginning. Barefoot, he padded back to his bedroom. Everly was lying on her side, one arm tucked beneath her head. Her eyes were closed, and her breathing was deep. He reached for her shoulder, ready to give a slight shake and tell her that perhaps he could give Chicago a try.

Yet, after losing her brother, being attacked, helping him discover Larry's identity and then finding the killer dead, well, Wyatt knew she was exhausted.

He got in the bed beside her. Settling in, with her back nestled into his chest, Wyatt draped his arm around her waist. Everly stirred in her sleep, reaching for his hand.

There was something about lying next to Everly, with her in his arms and their hands joined. It was an emotion—not happiness, it wasn't anything as sentimental or simple as joy or even bliss. It was like the calm that followed a storm. Then, Wyatt knew. With Everly, he'd become content. In the morning, he'd tell her he wanted to talk about a future together.

Chapter 12

Wyatt quickly fell into a deep sleep. In a haze-filled dream, he stood before a closed door. Pushing it open, Wyatt found Larry's corpse hanging from the ceiling of an industrial kitchen. The body gently swayed, as if in a light breeze. The piss stain on Larry's jeans was still damp. The eyes were closed. The room was silent, save for the slow and steady creak of the rope as it rubbed against the rafters.

He approached the body. Reaching out, his fingers inched closer and closer to the dead man's mottled and swollen hand. Like a viper, the hand struck, closing Wyatt's wrist in an unbreakable grip. He tried to pull away, but the icy hand was too strong.

Wyatt looked at the corpse. The eyes that had been shut were now open. "It was all right there for you to find," admonished the corpse. "How could you have missed everything? Will you even bother to look now?"

Wyatt was frantic to escape death's grip. He twisted and pulled. Nothing. He pried one finger up and then another, until he finally burst free and stumbled, slamming into a set of metal shelves. Pots and pans rained down, before clattering to the floor. The clanging morphed into a ringing and Wyatt woke in his own bed. He pulled a shaking hand down his face and realized it was slick with cold sweat.

Everly was still in bed beside him. Her hands were tucked under her cheek and he stroked the side of her arm, wanting nothing more than to wake her with a kiss.

The ringing came again. But this was no dream. He cursed as he threw back the covers, letting in the cold.

Everly stirred in her sleep. Wyatt grabbed his pants off the floor and fished the phone from a pocket. He swiped the call open and stepped onto the landing at the top of the stairs.

"Hello?" He held the phone up with his shoulder as he put on his jeans.

"Wyatt, this is Davis. I'm sorry to be calling so early, but I turned up some information and I thought you'd want to know right away."

"Sure," said Wyatt. He descended the stairs and turned on a light over his desk. He pulled a pad of paper and a pen toward him. "Go ahead."

"I went to the apartment complex and there was a

long-time resident who remembered Larry. The man said that his cat disappeared not long after Larry moved in. He always suspected Larry of doing something to the cat—that's why he remembered the name and photo I showed him."

Wyatt said, "Is he sure that it didn't get hit by a car or wander off and become a coyote's dinner?"

"Even though he suspected Larry, he knew that something else might've happened to his cat. He got another kitty. One day he sees Larry trying to coax the cat from beneath a bush, and then that cat disappeared, too."

"Cruelty to animals is a hallmark of a serial killer's progression," Wyatt said.

"That's exactly what I thought. So, I went to the manager of the complex and asked if I could search the place."

Obviously, Davis had been given permission and found something interesting, otherwise he wouldn't be calling before dawn. The line had gone silent. Wyatt waited a beat. "You still there?"

"I work homicide in Las Vegas. I've seen stuff. Weird stuff. Stuff I can't unsee."

"I can well imagine," said Wyatt. And honestly, he could. He used to be a profiler for the FBI, after all. "What's got you so shaken?"

"There was a compartment hidden behind the wall. It was full of dead cats—there were a dozen of them, at least."

"Cats? Even boarded up, they'd stink while decomposing. Wouldn't someone notice the smell?"

"That's just it, they'd been mummified. As in full-blown Pharaohs-of-Egypt-in-the-Pyramids kind of mummified. But there was more. We found a trophy from each of the Las Vegas victims with the cats."

Davis kept talking, detailing all the items he'd found. Wyatt was hardly paying attention. He'd stopped breathing, and his pulse echoed in his ears. How many lives had Larry taken? And Wyatt, the supposed expert, had never suspected him of a thing.

"There's something I need to tell you," Wyatt said, interrupting Davis. "Larry Walker is dead. We went to arrest him, and he'd hanged himself. He left a note confessing to some killings, although he wasn't specific. More than the confession, he had half of several two-dollar bills in his wallet. Five of them match those found with the men who died in Pleasant Pines."

"Dead?" said Davis. "I hadn't seen anything on the news or heard about it from my superiors."

"The local sheriff wants to keep the whole case under wraps until he contacts all the families. I imagine that the feds will get involved eventually and take over the case."

"Then have whoever ends up in charge call me. I still don't have an ID on Larry Walker's roommate."

Most serial killers were loners, needing privacy to carry out their murderous activities. That fact struck Wyatt as more than a little odd. Then again, it was another peculiarity to add to a long list of things that didn't make sense.

"He had a roommate?" Wyatt scribbled the word on the pad of paper and circled it several times.

"He did," Davis said. "He lived with a female."

"Are you sure?"

"The neighbor with the cat remembers a woman living with Larry."

"What about the complex manager?"

"She's new to the job, so Larry's time as a resident was before her arrival."

"What's your sense about the roommate? Was the woman an accomplice? A victim?"

"Your guess is as good as mine," said Davis.

"Can you do me two favors? First, don't mention what I told you about Larry being dead—or what we suspect about his serial killings."

"Suspect?" scoffed Davis. "I'd say the kitty tomb adorned with victims' trophies makes him a little more than a suspect."

Wyatt ignored the detective's comment and continued with his next request. "Second, get the neighbor to talk to a sketch artist. See if he can come up with a composite of the roommate."

"I'm one step ahead of you," said Davis. "The neighbor already talked to our artist, but they didn't come up with anything useful."

Wyatt cursed. "Even without the roommate's ID, you found a lot. Thanks again for everything. I owe you."

"I'll put it on your tab," said Davis before ending the call.

Wyatt set aside the phone and scrubbed his face

with his hands. His eyes burned from lack of sleep. His back ached from tackling Larry in the parking lot. For the first time, he noticed a scrape on his knuckles and another on his forearm.

A floorboard behind Wyatt creaked and he turned in his seat. Everly stood at the bottom of the stairs. She'd donned his discarded shirt. Her long legs were bare, and her hair cascaded around her shoulders and down her back.

"I woke up and you were gone," she said.

"Sorry about that. I got a call from Davis. He'd been to Larry's old apartment. He found a compartment hidden in the wall."

"That's odd," said Everly.

"It was full of mummified cats."

A horrified expression crossed her face. "I take that back. A concealed compartment full of dead pets is pretty twisted."

"And personal effects from the Las Vegas victims," Wyatt added.

"I know you had some reservations about Larry. Especially since he doesn't seem like a textbook serial killer. But doesn't the evidence seem to be pretty overwhelming?" she said.

Wyatt looked at the notes he'd scribbled. He recalled the cold fear that had awakened him from the dream about Larry. Something wasn't coming together.

He looked at Everly. "You're right. I mean, everything does seem to point to him as the doer. So why can't I shake the feeling that there's something more? Something that we've been missing all along?"

Everly watched Wyatt from across the room. He wore only a pair of pants and, even at a distance, she could see the cords of tension that ran from his shoulders to his neck. She longed to massage away whatever bothered him. But now, in the cold light of morning, this was a problem she had no idea how to solve.

"What's wrong?" she asked.

"There's more to this case," he said. "I can feel it."

"You keep saying that, but what other evidence could there be?" As she spoke, her pulse spiked, and her hands began to shake. "Someone with a criminal record or who is cruel to animals? Check. Evidence that connects Larry to the victims? Check. Or maybe you'd be happy with a confession? Got that, too. Sincerely Wyatt, I don't get you. You finally tracked down a notorious serial killer, why can't you be satisfied?"

Wyatt's eyes flashed with anger. He turned to the desk. The muscles in his back, neck and shoulders were tighter than before. "I'm plenty satisfied."

"You don't look it," she said.

"Just drop it, Everly. You might be good at manipulating the media, but you're hardly an expert on me."

"You think that's all I do? Influence news reports?"

"Am I wrong?"

"Completely," she said. "But this isn't about me— it's about you and your inability to let go of this case, even though it's over."

Wyatt got to his feet and began to pace. "What do you want me to say? That I lost everything because I couldn't find a serial killer? Now that he's been caught I should be able to snap my fingers and get back to normal? I've been messed up for so long that I don't remember what ordinary feels like."

"I don't believe that for a second," said Everly.

"Why not? Because you've fallen in love with the idea that you'll rehabilitate me and my career, and then we'll become some power couple in Chicago? Did it occur to you that is your dream and has nothing to do with me?"

He stopped pacing and turned to face her. "No serial killer has ever been caught because of dumb luck. This guy was methodical and careful. We just happened to stumble on our prime suspect, Larry. There was no 'solving—'" he made air quotes "—of this case. Everything that points us to Larry is circumstantial and convenient as hell."

Everly's throat burned with the need to scream. But she wouldn't allow herself to be goaded into a rage. She bit the inside of her lip until the moment passed. Inhaling deeply, she tried again. "I was the one who saw Axl's death as more than an accident. I forced you back into this case and you figured out what happened. What's so wrong with that?"

"Nobody forces me to do anything," he said.

A look flashed across his face, and then it was

gone. Had it been anger? Or was it hurt? What Everly wouldn't give to be a mind reader.

A whimpering came from the corner. Gus, his eyes downcast, stood near the front door. He lifted a paw and scratched at the jamb.

Everly dropped to the bottom step. She was exhausted by it all—her brother's death, the murder, the investigation. "I think your dog needs to go out," she said.

The sun was just starting to peek over the distant Rocky Mountains, turning the sky crimson and orange. Everly studied Wyatt from her perch on the steps. She wanted to go to him and fall into his muscled arms; to tell him she was sorry for being difficult. Yet, why?

Everly had stumbled into Wyatt's life. While she believed that luck had brought them together, in a few days, she'd realized that he was so much more than just a specialist to use for her own advantage.

He was smart, brave, careful, but still passionate. He was definitely not like any other man she'd ever met.

His toned chest rose and fell with each breath and she remembered the warmth of his flesh. The salty taste of his sweat. The musky scent of their shared passion.

Gus scratched the door a second time.

Wyatt said, "Let me get dressed, boy, and I'll take you for a walk."

He approached the stairs and held tight to the newel post. Their eyes met.

"I'll be gone for about fifteen minutes," he said. "Will you be here when I get back?"

Was that an invitation to stay? Or worse, a not-so-subtle suggestion to leave? In the end it didn't matter. Everly had come to Pleasant Pines with one goal— to discover what really happened to her brother, not to fall in love. She shook her head. "I think it's best if I get back to town. I don't know how complicated it is to transport a body, but I'm sure there are arrangements to be made."

"If you wait," said Wyatt, "I can come with you."

Yes, said Everly's heart. *Say, yes.*

She dropped her gaze from his. "You've already helped enough." Then she added quickly, lest he mistake her sincerity for sarcasm, "Honestly, without you I never would have found out what happened to my brother."

"Maybe that's what is bothering me," said Wyatt. "We still really don't know what happened, or why. All we have is a suspect."

She wasn't sure if Wyatt was admitting he thought that Larry was guilty or not. Yet, she decided to question him no further. "I guess knowing who is guilty is enough for me."

Gus pawed the door again, this time with more force.

"You know," he said. "This isn't over. Larry Walker was set up to look guilty, but he's not."

Everly was defeated. "If not Larry," she asked, "then who?"

Wyatt shoved his hand into his pockets and shook

his head. "I'm not sure," said Wyatt. His voice was filled with gravel. Gus whimpered. "I'm sorry for snapping at you. Obviously, we aren't going to agree on any of this."

Everly wasn't sure what to say. She was unable to hold his gaze any longer and looked away.

Gus pawed at the door again.

"I have to take my dog out."

"Go," she said.

"Will you be here when I get back?" he asked.

Everly shook her head.

Wyatt snorted. "Probably for the best."

Then he was gone.

Standing alone in the middle of Wyatt's house, Everly's chest ached. Her throat was raw. Her eyes burned. She recognized the feeling and had come to know it well. It was grief, only this time the loss was Everly's choice.

She had to wonder: What if she chased after Wyatt now? What if she told him that coming to care for him was unexpected and scary? Yet through this whole intense episode, she'd learned you were only guaranteed the day you had and the next one may never come. There was something between Wyatt and Everly, they both knew it. Shouldn't they cling to whatever happiness they could find? Shouldn't they hold on to each other?

Then again, they couldn't even talk about who murdered her brother, the single thing they had in common, without arguing.

Leaning against the wall, Everly knew that her chance with Wyatt had vanished.

Wyatt assumed that Everly would be gone when he got back with Gus. She'd told him as much, and still he hoped that she changed her mind. The house came in to view. Her car was gone, and an emptiness filled his gut.

Why did he care? Everly had burst into his life only a few days before, disrupting his carefully cultivated world. Once again, he had all the solitude he wanted. Funny thing, though—Wyatt now hated the idea of entering a house where nobody was home.

Gus sniffed the ground where Everly's rental car had been parked. He looked to Wyatt and whimpered.

"I know, boy," said Wyatt. "It's just the two of us again."

The dog whined.

Wyatt agreed.

He opened the door and stepped into his house. His one-time refuge felt like a prison. He wandered to the window seat where they'd made love and sat down looking out at the mountains. For the first time in years, Wyatt was left without a direction, or a purpose, for his life.

"Now what?" he asked.

Gus sat in the middle of the kitchen, staring at the counter.

"Breakfast?" asked Wyatt.

The dog barked and thumped his tail in agreement.

Wyatt poured food in Gus's dish and set it on the floor. He should eat something—he hadn't grabbed a bite since lunch yesterday—but his appetite was gone. Leaning against the counter, Wyatt knew that he needed to pass the information he'd gotten from Davis onto Sheriff Haak.

Maybe everyone else was right, and Larry Walker really was guilty. After all, it wouldn't have been the first time Wyatt had made a mistake.

After moving to the desk, he powered up his computer and typed out an email. After hitting Send, he leaned back in his seat. His eye was drawn to the flash drive that held all of the information about the victims.

Assuming that Larry Walker really was the prime suspect, there had to be something that he'd missed. Why had Larry Walker never turned up during the investigation? He knew Everly's prime focus was to find out who'd killed her brother—not examine Larry's psyche, uncover what had driven him to commit all the crimes—but Wyatt wanted to know.

Wyatt inserted the flash drive into his computer and began opening all his files.

He recalled the initial reason they'd suspected the blackjack dealer all those years ago. It was the man's intense interest in the case. In fact, they'd found his face in several photos that had been taken of crowds at a press conference.

Could Larry Walker have been in those crowds as well?

There were a dozen photos, taken at various times

during the investigation, and Wyatt printed them all. Next, he scanned each picture for Larry Walker. Without question, the assumed killer wasn't among those in the crowd.

Wyatt changed tactics and began with the first Las Vegas victim—the one with the connection to Larry via the apartment complex.

Just as a seemingly inconsequential argument had led to Axl Baker's murder, had this man argued with Larry, as well? Was there some insult that had triggered Larry into a murderous rage? And if so, how would Wyatt figure it out all these years later?

He had transcripts of the victim's voice messages sent and received. There were text messages, too. He read them again, even though every message had been scrutinized, and any mention of an altercation would have been flagged as suspicious.

After half an hour, he had nothing to show for his time.

Sitting back in the desk, Wyatt squeezed the bridge of his nose.

Gus was lying in the middle of the room. He lifted his head and looked at Wyatt before flopping back down.

Turning back to the computer, Wyatt opened the saved social-media account for Victim #1. He knew all the pictures before he saw them. There were smiling faces of happy people, oftentimes with drinks in hand. The identities of those in the photos had been tagged.

He moved on to the next picture—this one was

a close-up selfie of the victim in a dark blue shirt. Wyatt expanded the picture, so that it filled the whole screen. In the lower left corner was a detail he hadn't noticed before. What appeared to be the victim's shoulder was actually the top of a head with dark brown hair. On closer inspection, Wyatt found the beginning of a forehead, just a sliver of flesh, at the very bottom of the picture.

A woman? For the moment, he'd assume so.

The photo had been taken at night, as evidenced by the dark surroundings. The backdrop was an adobe wall with an out-of-focus sign. Wyatt expanded the picture, focusing the screen on the sign. He increased the resolution. Only a few words were visible, but they were enough: No Swimming After Midnight. By Order of Grand Canyon Gardens Management.

Wyatt's pulse increased. He had evidence that the photo had been taken at the same place Larry lived. It proved that the victim had been in proximity to the suspected killer.

His next question focused on the woman in the picture. Had she just been passing by and been caught in the photo? Or was the mystery woman supposed to be in the picture and later been edited out?

The sheet of paper Wyatt had scribbled on while talking to Davis had been shoved to the back of the desk, all but forgotten. One word was circled. *Roommate.* Beneath that he'd scribbled two more words: *1 Female.*

Could this woman in the photo with Victim #1

be Larry's roommate? It was a long shot, sure. But sometimes a long shot was the only one you got. Wyatt immediately formed a possible scenario—one that fit all the facts he knew. Larry had a history of violence against women. In Las Vegas, Larry had lived with a woman.

What if the victims weren't connected directly with Larry, but his female roommate? Larry could very easily be a jealous boyfriend or, worse yet, a spurned lover. He knew it was a leap. Yet, Wyatt was ready to make that final jump.

He stared at the picture of Victim #1. Light brown hair. Blue eyes. Bright white smile. He opened another window on his computer and searched for Axl Baker. His professional website topped the search list. A picture of Axl checking his camera was on the first page of his site.

Light brown hair. Blue eyes. Bright white smile. Both men had similar looks and, moreover, they were the kind of guy that women found handsome. Wyatt knew that all the other victims were similarly good-looking, same age, race and gender, and therefore fit the victimology.

But then he remembered the cats. And the trophies from past killings, along with a list of everything that Davis had found.

Wyatt pressed down on the pen. Ink seeped from the tip, leaving a black stain.

Serial killers were ritualistic, he knew. They did things for a reason—and those reasons never change. If Larry had kept personal belongings from his victims in Las Vegas, why hadn't he done the same in Pleasant Pines? Why change?

His house had been thoroughly searched last night. There were no hidden compartments. Nothing linked Larry to victims from Pleasant Pines, or elsewhere.

Then again, that really wasn't the question Wyatt should be asking. Larry Walker didn't fit the typical profile of a serial killer because he wasn't one. He'd been set up, but by who?

If Wyatt's instinct was right, it meant that the real killer was still at large in Pleasant Pines. It also meant that nobody—especially Everly—was safe.

Chapter 13

The sun began creeping upward, changing the sky from red and orange to a light blue. Shadows stretched across the mountainous roads as Everly drove into town. She felt emotionally drained, but she had more to do—namely, get her brother's body home.

Using her cell phone, she contacted the airline and worked out the details for the transport of Axl's body. Next, she contacted a funeral home in Cheyenne that advertised early morning hours. She hired them to take Axl to the airport. By the time she finished both calls it was 7:15 a.m. Even though it was early, Everly had several things to accomplish before leaving Pleasant Pines.

Finally, she needed to contact the sheriff and file

the official paperwork that would release Axl's body. She doubted that Haak would be in the office yet and it left her with some time to kill. Everly hadn't been worried about food at Wyatt's house and now, she needed some breakfast. Turning her car onto Main Street, she found the diner Wyatt had taken her to the other day, Sally's on Main.

She tried not to think about Wyatt, or the pie he'd sworn by. The thought came to her, anyway, and she smiled.

Everly pulled into a parking space and walked to the front door. Taking a booth at the back of the room, she picked up a menu.

Sally, the waitress, approached with a coffeepot in hand. "Care for some high-test?" she asked.

Everly flipped over her cup. "Please."

"What can I get for you?"

"Two eggs over-easy, wheat toast and a side of fruit," she said.

Sally wrote down the order. "There was a lot happening at the inn last night. Do you know anything about that?"

"Too much," said Everly.

"Will Wyatt be meeting you? It's good to see him out and about. He's alone too much," she added.

Everly wasn't sure if she should be offended that the server assumed they were a couple. Or if she should be sad that they weren't. "It's just me for breakfast. I'm heading back to Chicago this morning," Everly said.

"Well, we hope you'll come back soon."

Everly smiled. "Thanks."

Sure, Pleasant Pines didn't have the busy lifestyle or attractions that could be found in Chicago. But what it lacked in museums and shopping, it made up for in kindness.

That sense of community was rare. Beyond caring for Wyatt, had Everly fallen in love with Wyoming?

Maybe there was a middle ground for them after all. Perhaps they didn't have to be either recluses in the boonies or live a fast-paced life in the big city. She pulled her phone from her purse and brought up Wyatt's contact info. She'd slunk away without saying goodbye or even thank you. She owed him a call.

Without another thought, she hit the phone icon. The call went straight to voice mail. Damn. Everly sat up taller, refusing to lose her nerve again.

"Wyatt, it's me." She paused. "I hate how things ended between us. I wanted to apologize for leaving while you were out. I have a flight back to Chicago this afternoon but will be in town until Axl's body is released." Everly knew she was rambling. She let out a deep breath and tried again. "If you get this message...well, I'd like to see you. I'm at the diner now."

Everly ended the call, just as Sally delivered breakfast. "Here you go, hon."

She ate quickly, and when done with her meal, Everly checked her phone. Wyatt hadn't called. He hadn't texted. She didn't know if he'd even heard her message. Or maybe he had heard the message but decided not to call her back. Maybe he didn't really want her to stay in Wyoming. If that was the case, then it was best if she left town.

The waitress approached with the coffeepot. "Need a warm-up?"

"No thanks," said Everly.

Meeting with the sheriff was the final thing that Everly needed to do. Once her brother's body was released, she could take him back to Chicago. She was leaving Pleasant Pines, yet Everly knew that memories of the town—and Wyatt in particular—would stay with her long after she'd gone.

"You wouldn't happen to know what time Sheriff Haak gets to the office?" Everly asked.

"He usually doesn't show up until half past eight," said Sally.

Everly glanced at the clock. She had almost another hour to wait.

"Anything else?" the waitress asked.

Sally seemed to know everything about everyone. "Any idea what time Darcy Owens goes into work at the inn?"

"Her shift usually begins at ten o'clock." Sally shrugged. "I only know because she sometimes stops in to get coffee and a bear claw first."

Maybe the cordiality of life in a small town was beginning to rub off on Everly. She felt compelled to thank Darcy personally before leaving town.

A quick internet search gave Everly an address for Darcy's home. Sure, it was early, but without Darcy's initial lead, she'd never know what had happened to Axl—despite Wyatt's misgivings. After a quick visit, Everly would be done with Pleasant Pines and she wouldn't look back.

Pleasant Pines wasn't a large town, but Everly needed her GPS to find Darcy Owens's house. The street was filled with small homes and neatly kept yards. Parking at the curb, Everly hoped that an uninvited visit wasn't considered rude. After turning off her engine, Everly walked up the path and rang the bell.

A sheer curtain was drawn over the front window and lights were on in the room beyond. She waited. There was no answer. A carport was off to the side of the small house and a sedan was parked in the drive. Someone was home, she knew.

She knocked on the door. Her knuckles grazed the wood and the door creaked open slightly. Everly realized that the handle hadn't been latched, and now, the door was ajar.

"Sorry," she said loudly. "I didn't realize."

She heard a woman's voice—it was faint, but distinct. Had she been told to come in?

"It's Everly Baker," she called out, "from the hotel. I wanted to thank you. Mind if I come in?"

There it was again—the woman's voice, with a quick laugh. What had she said?

Everly pushed the door open farther. There was a small entryway, covered in linoleum tile. It was connected to a living room, decorated in light blue and sunny yellow. "Darcy?" she said. "I hate to intrude, but I'm leaving for Chicago in a little while and I wanted to thank you for all your help."

Beyond the living room was another room. From where she stood, Everly could see a ceiling light ablaze and the edge of a counter. The kitchen?

Everly stepped into the house and shut the door. "Hello?"

She followed the voice. Like she had guessed from the entryway, the person was in a kitchen. The counters were pristine and white. The wooden cabinets gleamed in the overhead light. The only thing that seemed out of place was the cluttered kitchen table, and the TV that sat atop the refrigerator.

A morning newscast played, and two female anchors discussed the day's weather. Everly immediately recognized the voice she assumed had belonged to Darcy.

No matter how friendly people seemed in Pleasant Pines, coming in to someone's home without permission was rude—or worse, criminal. It probably didn't really matter, though, as long as she could sneak away.

Then she saw it and froze.

The metallic taste of panic coated her tongue. She reached for it, but her hand was unsteady. Her finger grazed the cold, metal casing, and she lifted it from the table. Everly turned the camera around and looked at the bottom—there, just as she knew it would be, was an inscription.

To Axl on your 30th B-day
Capture the best of life
Love, Everly

For a moment, Everly was back in Axl's hotel room at the Pleasant Pines Inn. This time, the memory was complete. In that moment, there had been a whisper of sound behind her and she had turned. In the mirror, she caught the glimpse of a figure. Without question, it was Darcy Owens.

"Everly?" Darcy Owens stood on the threshold of the kitchen. She wore a robe. Her hair was wet, and she held a towel. She looked stunned. "What are you doing here?"

Darcy's gaze dropped from Everly's face to her hands and the camera she held. The smile faltered, and Darcy narrowed her eyes.

"You," Everly growled. Her face was hot, and she began to sweat. "It was you all along. You killed my brother. You killed them *all*."

Wide-eyed, Darcy gaped. "I don't know what you're talking about."

"You don't? Well, I imagine that Sheriff Haak will be interested in why you have my brother's camera in your house." Everly stepped forward, ready to brush past Darcy.

The other woman blocked the way, trapping Everly in the kitchen. "I wish you hadn't come here, Everly. Because you aren't going to leave alive."

After running the social-media picture of Victim #1 through several programs, Wyatt discovered a few important points. First, the photo had been cropped before being posted to social media. With his equipment, he couldn't return the picture to its original form.

What he needed was a more advanced computer, like the one at Rocky Mountain Justice.

He opened his phone's contact app. After finding Marcus Jones's info, he placed the call.

Jones answered on the second ring. "Wyatt? What's up?"

Wyatt paused. He knew they all assumed that Larry Walker was the killer. He knew that he'd followed all the clues, leading them to a perfect suspect. Yet, he also knew he'd been wrong.

His heart stilled.

Wyatt refused to hide anymore while terrified of making another mistake.

"Wyatt?" Jones asked. "You there?"

"It wasn't Larry. He was set up."

"If this is your idea of a joke," said Marcus, "it's a bad one."

"I wish I was kidding, but Larry isn't our doer." Wyatt gave a quick rundown of the Las Vegas find, the hidden compartment with the mummified cats and the trophies from previous victims. He pointed out that nothing of that nature had been found in Larry's Pleasant Pines residence.

"People change," said Marcus. "Even sickos."

"More than most people, serial killers are consistent. True, sometime circumstances vary from one kill to the next, but that has more to do with opportunity and the victims than it does the killer. Their modus operandi is pretty reliable. That's been true of this killer, as well."

"But he lived in that apartment," said Marcus. "You can't deny that the trophies were found in his home."

"According to a neighbor in Las Vegas, Larry had a roommate," said Wyatt. "No other tenants were listed on the lease, so we don't have a name. We do know that the roommate was a female."

"Tell me you have more on this case. Maybe another suspect?"

"I have a picture from the first Las Vegas victim. I think Larry's roommate might be in the photo."

"Can we get an identity?"

"Not with the way it is now. It's just a little bit of a woman's scalp. But I can tell that the photo's been edited."

"And you're wondering if you can use RMJ's equipment again?"

"Exactly," said Wyatt.

"How long before you can get to the office?"

"I'll see you in fifteen minutes," he said and ended the call.

Wyatt saved what he had on the flash drive and shoved it into his pocket. He placed all the printed photos into a file folder and grabbed those, as well. He reached for his phone before slipping on his vest. He jogged to his truck and started the engine. The tires kicked up gravel as Wyatt raced down the driveway. He turned hard to the right as he hit the pavement. The big engine revved and the truck fishtailed as he sped down the road.

Everly was trapped. Darcy stood on the threshold, blocking the only exit. Everly's heartbeat slammed into her chest and bile rose in the back of her throat.

Clutching Axl's camera, she dropped her shoulder and ran straight at Darcy, crashing into the other woman. Darcy toppled back, slamming into the floor. Everly rushed forward, focusing on nothing other than the door and freedom.

Darcy reached for her, catching her ankle. Her foot twisted, a bolt of pain shot up her leg and she stumbled. Darcy wrenched Everly's leg upward, and she fell to the floor.

Her chin slammed into the carpet and her teeth cracked together. She crawled forward, determined to escape.

Darcy pounced, scrambling on top of Everly and pinning her down. From behind, she gripped Everly's throat. Still clutching the camera, Everly swung out. The metal-and-plastic casing connected hard. Everly felt the satisfying reverberations travel from her hand to her shoulder.

Darcy's grip faltered and Everly inched forward, freeing herself. She flipped to her back, just as Darcy lunged again. On instinct alone, Everly lifted her foot and drove her heel forward. The sole of her boot connected with Darcy's mouth.

The other woman's blond head snapped back and Everly was on her feet. She reached for the door handle, her fingers brushing the cold metal. Pain erupted in her scalp as Darcy grabbed a handful of Everly's hair and twisted.

Holding tight to the camera, Everly swung out, catching the killer in the cheek. Darcy gave a feral wail and fell over, her hand full of Everly's hair.

Everly ignored her throbbing head and her burning throat, focusing only on freedom. She lunged forward. A hard shove came from behind, slamming Everly into the door. The handle gouged her side, and she cried out with pain.

She drove her elbow back. It connected with Darcy's middle and the other woman let out a wheeze.

Everly gripped the handle and turned.

Darcy chopped Everly's wrist with her fist. "You aren't going anywhere, bitch," she snarled.

Everly whirled around. Darcy looked wild. Her eyes were glassy. Her teeth were stained red, and a trickle of blood ran from her lip.

Everly had to get out of the house, now. She pressed her back to the door for leverage and kicked out, hitting Darcy square in the chest. The other woman flew back, crashing into a coffee table, her head slamming into the glass top.

Darcy didn't get up.

Everly opened the door and she drew in a lungful of fresh air. She took a step across the threshold, her car in sight. She'd call Wyatt and the sheriff for help, tell them what she'd discovered. And she'd tell Wyatt that he'd been right all along—that the real killer had been hiding in plain sight.

Then pain exploded in Everly's skull. For a moment, her stomach reeled, and she only saw red. Then her knees gave out and she dropped to the ground.

Then there was only blackness.

Wyatt drove and wondered if he was pursuing yet another dead end. Even if they could return his copy of the picture to its original form, what would it get them? A face without a name? After pulling up in front of the RMJ safe house, Wyatt killed the engine. He stepped onto the curb and the front door opened. Marcus stood on the threshold.

"The camera down the street picked you up as soon as you rounded the corner," Marcus said.

"That's impressive tech you have," Wyatt said as he strode up the walkway. "Hopefully, it can help us with this." He removed the flash drive from his pocket and held it up.

"I have confidence in my team," said Marcus. "Come on in."

Wyatt followed Marcus into the house. Even with its state-of-the-art recognition software and impenetrable accesses getting inside took only seconds.

"This way." Marcus opened a door to Wyatt's right.

They were back in the conference room. Three people sat around the table. Wyatt recognized two of them from last night at the Pleasant Pines Inn, when the kitchen had been teeming with law-enforcement officers of all kinds.

After shaking hands with RMJ operatives Luis

Martinez and Julia McCloud, Wyatt dropped into a chair at the end of the table.

Martinez gestured to a dark haired woman in her fifties and said, "Wyatt, this is Katarina." She lifted a hand in acknowledgment.

Marcus continued, "She's our communications expert and hopefully the person who can recover your photograph." Then to Katarina, he said, "This is Wyatt Thornton. He used to work the FBI's behavioral-science unit. He thinks there might be a problem with designating Larry Walker as the Las Vegas and Pleasant Pines killer."

How many years had passed since Wyatt gave his last briefing? It was in Las Vegas and they were hunting the same killer he now faced. Filled with confidence, he'd stood at the head of a conference table and laid out all the facts knew. They had a suspect—but a single problem. The man had an alibi for one of the murders.

Perhaps, one colleague had surmised, the suspect had committed most of the crimes—just not all of them. A copycat killer, he had suggested.

Wyatt had assured everyone in the room that there was no copycat killer in their case, and their serial killer was responsible for all the killings. Besides, each victim had been found with the same calling card, that half of a two-dollar bill. It meant that each man had been killed by a single person.

It was then that Wyatt's supervisor had spoken up. People in Las Vegas were afraid. The task force needed to show progress. The suspect would be arrested, and, moreover, investigative resources would be turned to disproving the alibi.

At the time, Wyatt had balked at the plan. To him, it was wrong to let an innocent man languish in jail—plain and simple.

In the end, Wyatt was overruled.

The next day, a local reporter had discovered the alibi and Wyatt was thrown under the bus. Some days, he could still feel the tread marks on his back.

All those years ago, Wyatt placed his faith in his colleagues, and in the end, he'd been betrayed.

The operatives from RMJ were basically strangers. Was it prudent to trust anyone, especially people he didn't know?

Then Everly came to mind. If he could trust her, he could take a chance now. Besides, he'd asked them for help. If he wasn't willing to share what he knew, Wyatt should just go back to his house and never leave again.

"I have a picture of the first victim in Las Vegas taken at the apartment complex where Larry Walker lived. It was cropped before being posted on social media, but another person was in the photo. I want to know who she is."

"Do you think she's an accomplice?" Martinez asked.

"Or a victim?" It was Julia who spoke.

"To be honest, I don't know if she's either—or neither. But if this is Larry's roommate, she can tell us something about what happened."

"If you have the photo on a drive, I can get to work," Katarina said.

"Sure do." Wyatt placed the flash drive on the table and slid it toward the woman.

She opened a black leather portfolio that held a wireless keyboard. After hitting a few keys, a screen lowered from the ceiling. She inserted the flash drive into a USB port in the table. A list of all the files appeared on the screen, the letters more than a foot high.

"It's under social-media photo number one," Wyatt said.

Katarina opened the picture.

"Can you get it back to the original file?"

Katarina tapped on the keyboard. "It'll take a while," she said, "but I can get something."

Julia scooted next to Katarina and the women began to talk in hushed tones. Wyatt only caught a few words, but it was enough to know that they were working on a strategy to get a complete picture.

He turned to Marcus. "What's next?"

"I think that we should investigate in-house and see what turns up. There's a substantial case that makes Larry Walker our killer. I have to wonder, what if you're wrong now?"

Acid roiled in Wyatt's gut. It was just like last time. His phone vibrated, saving Wyatt from saying something he'd later regret—or worse, saying nothing, and regretting it now.

He pulled the phone from his pocket and looked

at the screen. Everly had left a voice message more than an hour ago. "Damn," he cursed.

"Everything okay?" Marcus asked.

"I got a call, but it didn't show up until now," he said.

"Take it in the hall if you want," said Marcus.

Wyatt left the room and opened his voice-mail app. "Wyatt, it's me," Everly said. "I hate how things ended between us. I wanted to apologize for leaving while you were out. I have a flight back to Chicago later this morning but will be in town for a few hours." She let out a deep breath. "If you get this message...well, I'd like to see you again. Give me a call. Maybe we can meet up. I'm at the diner now."

Everly was at the diner—and more important, she wanted to see him. Yet, he couldn't leave RMJ, not until he found out who was in the picture. Hours could pass before they had an image. By then, Everly would be gone.

Was he really willing to miss his last chance to see her—even if she only wanted to say goodbye?

Chapter 14

Wyatt stood in the hall, just outside of the conference room. He listened to Everly's message a second time, trying to determine her feelings from the tone of her voice. There was nothing.

The conference-room door opened, and Wyatt turned at the sound.

Marcus stood on the threshold. "Katarina just told me that this is going to take a while. She's not even sure if there's much more of the picture to recover."

Disappointment rose in Wyatt's throat. He swallowed it down. Then again, the delay allowed him to leave RMJ and deal with more important things, like Everly. "I need to be somewhere," he said. "Text me if you get anything."

Wyatt could've walked the four blocks to Main Street and the diner, but he took his truck, parking right by the front door.

He peered through the window and saw several patrons. No sign of Everly, though. She was gone. The instinct to hunt, to find her, kicked in and he opened the front door. The salty scent of bacon frying mixed with the deep, dark smell of coffee.

"Morning, hon," said Sally. "Take a seat and I'll be right with you."

"Actually, I'm looking for someone. The woman I was here with the other day—"

She interrupted. "You mean Everly?"

He should have known. Word traveled fast in a small town. "Yes. Have you seen her?"

"She was here about an hour ago, had breakfast and left."

"Did she say anything about where she was going? Was she leaving town straight away?"

"She didn't say anything about leaving just yet, but she did ask when Sheriff Haak got in to his office."

"So, she's with the sheriff," said Wyatt. "Thanks."

Wyatt pivoted and pulled the door open. Cold mountain air rushed in to the small diner.

"Wait," called Sally. "Sheriff Haak hasn't come in for his morning coffee yet, so he's not gotten to work. Everly did mention something else," Sally said.

Wyatt's curiosity was piqued. "She did? What?"

"Everly wanted to thank Darcy Owens for being so kind."

"Darcy? The desk clerk from the inn?"

"That's the one."

Finding Darcy's address would be simple enough, he'd just look it up when he got back to RMJ.

"Thanks, Sally," said Wyatt. "You're the best."

After stepping onto the street, he opted not to wait that long, and opened his phone's internet browser and found an address for Darcy Owens. It was only a few blocks away.

While walking to his truck, his phone began to ring. He glanced at the screen before answering the call. "Marcus," he asked. "Anything new?"

"We have a photo, but the resolution isn't great. I'm not even sure that we can enter the picture into recognition software. I'm sending it to you right now, anyway."

"I'll take a look and get back to you," said Wyatt as he backed onto the street.

The phone buzzed with an incoming text. Wyatt ignored it until he pulled up at a stop sign. He glanced at the phone—and froze. The photo was blurry, as if the subject had been moving while the picture was being taken, but he could just make out the resemblance.

Marcus was wrong. There was definitely something familiar about the photo. "Damn," he cursed.

He'd been so sure that there was a connection—and he was right.

Dropping his foot on the accelerator, the truck

shot forward. The file of photos dropped from the seat and scattered across the floorboard. Pulling to the side of the road, Wyatt bent down to retrieve the pictures.

There it was—one face out of hundreds. Sure, the hair color was different, but the face was the same.

In the crowd of onlookers was Darcy Owens.

He flipped through each picture in rapid succession. Despite the fact the she'd donned a disguise—glasses, hats, once a green wig—he found her face in each one.

For Wyatt, suddenly all the questions, and all the foggy and dissatisfying answers, became clear. The serial killer's hesitation to take Everly's life made sense—if the killer was female. The fact that the male victims were easily lured from the hotel also made sense—if the killer was female.

In fact, poisoning had been the preferred method of female killers for centuries. And in reality, isn't that what she had done? Poisoned her victims before leaving them for dead?

It was Darcy who enlightened them all about Larry Walker's fight with Axl Baker—thus providing a suspect. It was also Darcy who sent Larry to the meeting with a tray full of coffee, just as his guilt was being discussed. No doubt, Darcy predicted that Larry would run, making him look guilty.

Then again, if he was innocent, why would Larry commit suicide?

What if he was deeply in her thrall? Wyatt could easily imagine Darcy convincing Larry to stage a hanging. Perhaps promises were made to find Larry in time to save his life. Perhaps she convinced Larry to kill himself—telling him it was the only way she'd avoid jail time—and he had agreed.

Time began again. And Wyatt knew one thing for sure. He needed to get to Everly, now—or she was as good as dead.

Accelerating around the corner, Wyatt pulled onto the narrow street filled with small houses. Like the beam shining from a lighthouse on a stormy sea, sun glinted off the windshield of Everly's rental car. Yet, he didn't relax—he wouldn't relax, not even for a second, until Everly was safe.

He parked across the street. After opening the glove box, he removed his SIG Sauer and slid it into the back of his pants. Wyatt considered contacting Marcus or Sheriff Haak. Then again, he wasn't going to wait for backup to arrive, much less take the minutes needed to make a call.

He hustled up the walkway. The door was ajar, and he pushed it open. The hinges creaked, as the door swung inward. Wyatt stepped into the room and his heart dropped.

Shattered glass was scattered all over the floor, several shards covered in blood. Wyatt kneeled next to the table. The blood was viscous—not wet, not dry. He'd guess that the whole episode had taken place an hour ago, no more.

Standing, he surveyed the rest of the room. A snarl of red hair was stark against the white carpet. There was a tiny piece of scalp attached.

A venomous rage burned in his veins. He would make Darcy Owens pay for the pain she'd caused Everly. That emotion was quickly replaced with icy fear. What if Darcy really had killed her this time?

He wiped a shaking hand down his face. He wouldn't do Everly any good if he let his imagination rule his intellect. He needed to assess the situation—and then act.

Obviously, there had been a struggle. Had Everly somehow figured out that Darcy was involved in Axl's death and confronted the other woman? Or was Darcy—knowing her own guilt—suspicious of Everly's unannounced visit? In the end, the answer to those questions didn't matter. For Wyatt, all that counted was who had won.

Removing his gun, Wyatt stayed low as he moved down the hall. There was a door to the left. Gripping his gun, he pushed open the door and slid into the room. It was a bedroom with an adjacent bathroom.

The bed was unmade, the closet door closed. At first glance, there was nothing amiss. He opened the closet and pulled all the clothes from the rack. Nothing. Nothing under the bed or hidden between the mattress and box spring. The bathroom was likewise empty.

There was another room across the hall.

Wyatt stood on the threshold, his heartbeat hammering. He wanted to find her, needed to see Everly—unharmed. He knew that his hope was foolishness and yet, he felt as if by sheer will alone, he could make it a reality.

He pushed open the door. It was a second bedroom. Bed. Table. Desk. He conducted a quick, systematic, but fruitless search. None of the rooms bore the scars from an attack. No overturned tables or broken lamps. It looked as if the fight had been contained to the living room, as if it happened when someone tried to enter—or maybe it was leave.

How could he have left Everly alone? He cursed his pride and moved to the last room to be searched. A shattered camera sat near the doorway separating the living room from the kitchen. Taking a knee, Wyatt examined the rubble. Engraved into the bottom was a note:

> To Axl on your 30th B-day
> Capture the best of life
> Love, Everly

The final puzzle piece snapped into place. Wyatt didn't take time to either congratulate or berate himself. This was proof that Everly was in the hands of a killer. He had to act quickly. Wyatt's instinct was to rush out, but go where?

Standing in the middle of Darcy's living room, he tried to get a sense of what everything meant. It was a cozy house. Yet, Wyatt knew that Darcy was far from being the homey type. That meant it was an act and this place was a stage, but for whom?

There had to be a connection between Las Vegas and Pleasant Pines.

Like a sun cresting the horizon, he understood

that there was only one thing that would bring Darcy Owens to Wyoming—it was him. It had been Wyatt all along.

Darcy was playing a sick game, and he was her unwitting opponent.

It was why the killings stopped when he left Las Vegas.

It was why a body was dumped at the old schoolhouse, where he would be the one to find it.

It was also how he knew exactly where she'd taken Everly.

Knowing where to look was a good thing, but he'd never be able to catch Darcy unaware. What Wyatt needed was help. Taking the phone from his pocket, he placed a call.

"Wyatt," said Sheriff Haak as he answered. "I was just reading your email. It looks like you finally caught your man."

"Larry Walker's not the serial killer—and I need your help," said Wyatt. He felt the seconds ticking by with each beat of his heart. He rushed from the empty house to his truck and started the engine. "I don't have time to explain everything right now, but it was Darcy Owens all along. She was Larry's roommate in Las Vegas, so she'd have access to the apartment."

"His roommate? I don't get it? Last night, it sounded like she barely knew him."

"It was a lie," he said. Tires squealing, he pulled away from the curb. "We need to act now. She's got Everly."

"Whoa there," said the sheriff. "Hold your horses one second and tell me what's happening. How's Everly involved, exactly?"

Wyatt took a deep breath to steel himself. "I went looking for Everly at Darcy's house. There's evidence of a confrontation and there's blood on the floor. And...her brother's missing camera. It's here."

Wyatt felt desperation threaten to choke him, but he tamped it down. He had one goal—and he wouldn't be distracted by emotion. "Everly's car is still in front of Darcy's house but both of the women are gone."

"Tell me what you need," said Sheriff Haak. "And I'll do it."

"I think I know where Darcy's taken Everly. They're at the old schoolhouse. I'm going there now and need backup. Can you meet me?"

"I'll do you one better," said Haak. "My house is less than five minutes away from your property, so I'll get there first."

Wyatt ended the call and placed another. Marcus Jones answered. "Hello?"

Not wasting any time on pleasantries, Wyatt began, "Darcy Owens is the killer and she's kidnapped Everly. I think she's taken her to the old schoolhouse."

For his part, Marcus asked few questions while Wyatt briefed him as he drove.

"The sheriff should be there soon. I'll call you

once I hear something, but it's going to take all of us if we're going to catch Darcy Owens."

"I'll round up the team from RMJ and we'll have your back ASAP." He hesitated. "Good luck, Wyatt."

"Thanks," said Wyatt. "But I don't need luck. For me, this is personal."

Everly's head was throbbing. She swallowed, but her throat was tight, as if a weight pressed down on her neck. Her eyes burned, yet she pried her lids open. A bright light shone in her face. With a curse, she screwed her eyes shut again. She tried to rub her neck, but her hands didn't—or more accurately, couldn't—move.

Suddenly awake, Everly remembered finding Axl's camera at Darcy's house. And then, the fight to escape—a fight Everly had lost. She pulled at her arms again. They were pinned behind her back and her wrists were bound. Fighting the pain in her head, she studied her surroundings. In an instant, Everly knew exactly where she was—in the old schoolhouse on Wyatt's property.

A thick rope was wound around her neck, tightening each time she drew a breath.

"Careful..." A woman's voice came from the shadows. "You are perched on top of a wobbly stool, and you've got a noose around your neck. A very precarious place. If you struggle too much, if you try to get down, if you budge that stool at all, you'll end up hanged."

Darcy stepped into the light. A trickle of blood

had dried on her cheek. Her bottom lip was swollen and split. The white of one eye had turned bright red.

Everly grew cold as she listened to Darcy. Her knees shook and the stool beneath her began to sway. The rope tightened further, cutting off all her breath. Everly's hands and feet went numb. Her heart raced as panic began to claim her.

No. She couldn't lose it. Not now.

Everly forced herself to stand still and focus on one thing: survival. She held her breath as the stool gradually steadied and she slowly exhaled. "What have you done?"

"Me?" Darcy placed a hand on her chest. "What have *I* done? The question you should be asking is what have *you* done? Why are you here?"

Everly swallowed. The stool teetered, tightening the rope. "Okay. Why am I here?"

"First, it's because you are really stupid. You can't take a clue, can you?"

Everly didn't think Darcy expected an answer, and she didn't give one.

"I could have killed you twice. First, at the hotel while you explored your brother's room. Then the other night at Wyatt's house. I didn't, because I don't kill women. You aren't the problem. Still, if you slip from this stool and die, well, it's your own fault, isn't it?"

Everly's eyes burned with angry tears. Darcy had constructed the perfect trap and there was no way Everly could escape, much less survive. No matter what scenario she turned over in her mind, she just couldn't figure a way out of this. Her only hope was to connect with Darcy, maybe talk to her—woman-to-woman. "Cut me loose, Darcy. We both know you really don't want to see anything happen to me. Like you said, you could have killed me before, but you didn't."

"Don't presume to know what's in my heart," said Darcy. Her lips twisted into a snarl and spittle flew from her mouth. Rushing to Everly's side, she knocked over the stool.

For a moment, Everly hung in the air. Then all her weight was on her neck. Her throat collapsed. Her eyes bulged. Her legs thrashed. She couldn't breathe. Her heart felt as if it would explode in her chest.

"You should have left when you had the chance," said Darcy. "You had your killer—Larry, that idiot—and you and Wyatt would have lived the rest of your days thinking that you'd solved the crime of the century. But no." Darcy retrieved the stool and slid it under Everly's feet. She loosened the noose just a little. "You couldn't leave well enough alone, could you?"

Everly settled her tiptoes on the stool and drew in deep breaths. "Why kill me? You said that I wasn't the problem."

"Not at first," said Darcy. "Did you know that when Wyoming was a territory, thievery was a capital offense? When this building was used, a person could be hanged for stealing something of value."

The question made no sense. Obviously, Darcy

had a point to make. What Everly needed was a way to escape. Her only plan—her only option—was to play along. "I didn't know that."

"I think it's a just punishment. Don't you?"

"No," said Everly. She had to fight to keep her voice steady. "I don't. Property isn't the same as a life."

"A thief denies a person of their possessions. They take from someone what's rightfully theirs."

"I haven't taken anything from you," said Everly.

"Haven't you?"

"The camera? That belonged to my brother. Why did he have to die? What did he steal from you?"

"Him," Darcy growled. "You stole him from me."

"Axl? I didn't take my brother from you," Everly said. Even as she spoke, Everly knew her guess was wrong.

"Your brother?" Darcy snorted. "He was nothing to me, only a means to an end. You stole Wyatt Thornton. And now, you have to pay for your crime."

Carl Haak dropped his foot onto the accelerator. The truck shot forward, pressing him back into the seat. The tires kicked up gravel as he raced down the dirt road to the old schoolhouse. His siren's scream filled the silent morning and his lights cast shadows of red and blue across the landscape.

Over forty years of law-enforcement experience had taught Carl a thing or two. The number one lesson was that sometimes a big show of force—

lights, sirens, guns—ended many violent situations peaceably.

He pulled up next to the schoolhouse. A small, gray sedan was parked nearby, and he immediately recognized it as belonging to Darcy Owens.

She was there and if Wyatt's report was right... so was Everly. His heartbeat spiked and sweat began to drip from his brow. He didn't have time to think of a plan. Slamming on the breaks, the sheriff skidded to a stop next to Darcy's car. He turned off the ignition and pocketed the keys before opening the door. While jumping down, he drew his sidearm and held it at the ready.

Carl's breath came in short, ragged gasps and he rushed toward the little building. He pressed his back to the wall and glanced into the single room. He withdrew just as quickly and tried to make sense of what he'd seen.

Everly Baker had been hanging by her neck. A rope was tied to a thick, wooden beam in the ceiling. Was he too late? No. She stood on a stool. Her eyes had been opened wide. What else had been in the room? Or rather, had he caught a glimpse of Darcy Owens?

Sheriff Haak exhaled. Aside from Everly, the room had been empty. No doubt, Darcy Owens had heard his approach and fled the scene. Gun drawn, he stepped into the old schoolhouse.

"Sheriff," said Everly. Her voice was raspy. "Be careful."

He ignored her warning. Holstering his gun,

Carl rushed to Everly's side. The noose was growing tight around her neck as she grew agitated, and she stood on a stool that wobbled, one leg shorter than the others.

Carl circled Everly and stopped at her back. "Your hands are tied together," he said. "Let me at least get you loose." He didn't bother to add that with free hands she could grab the rope and save herself from strangulation if things went from bad to worse. After removing a utility knife from his pants pocket, he sliced into the rope.

The stool wobbled with each swipe of the blade.

Everly screamed in pain as the noose tightened, digging deeper into her neck. Carl grabbed her legs, supporting her weight and keeping her still. The stool remained steady and he released Everly's legs. Sweat dripped down Carl's back and his pulse pounded. "I got to get you down from there somehow, but this isn't working."

"Darcy heard your truck approaching and left. She might be watching us even now. You need to leave me here," she said, "and go."

"I'm not going anywhere," said Carl. "Not until I get you down and take you with me."

He glanced over his shoulder. There was nothing—and no one—in the room. "I have a ladder in my truck. Once we get you on something solid, I can get that rope from your neck. Hold tight and I'll be right back."

He turned for the door, stopping to peer outside. Aside from his truck and Darcy's car, there was nothing beyond mountains and blue sky.

He knew that Everly was right about Darcy—she couldn't have gotten far, not without her own car at least. Wily as she was, Carl figured that Darcy was a smart woman and wouldn't risk a standoff with an armed man. Still, Carl kept low as he ran to his truck. He jerked open the door and reached behind the driver's seat. He grasped the folding ladder he had stored there and pulled it from his truck. Not bothering to shut the door, Carl turned back to the old schoolhouse.

Carl kept low and moved at a brisk pace. He crossed the threshold and held up the folding ladder. "I got it," he said. "You'll be down in a jiff."

Everly's expression changed from wide-eyed worry to white-faced horror. She opened her mouth, but there was no sound.

Carl heard a sharp crack, like the snap of a whip. The sound was followed by a whiff of cordite carried on the breeze. A hot pain shot through his bicep. Carl's arm went numb and the little ladder slipped from his grasp, tumbling to the hard ground with a clatter. Carl's gaze moved to his hand. Blood dripped from his fingertips. The front of his shirt was wet and sticky. A black stain spread across his chest.

There was another pop. Another whiff of cordite and pain hit him again from behind, striking his shoulder and spinning him around.

Darcy held the shotgun Carl had left in his truck. She pulled back on the stock, chambering another round. A blaze erupted from the barrel and Carl was knocked backward by the force of the slug. He fell, and as the ground rushed up to meet him, he could only think that he'd set his retirement date two weeks too late.

Chapter 15

Wyatt stopped his truck half a mile from the old schoolhouse. He didn't know what he'd find and needed more intel before rushing ahead. Peering through a set of binoculars, he surveyed the scene. From his vantage point, Wyatt couldn't see the front door, only the back wall and a corner. Yet, Sheriff Haak's truck and a gray sedan—most likely belonging to Darcy—were visible from where he stood.

He pulled out his phone and placed a call.

"Marcus," he said. "I'm here. Where are you?"

"We're on our way. Less than ten minutes out. Do you have Everly? Or Darcy?"

"Not yet, but I know where they are." He then gave a brief description of what he'd seen. "I'm going in on foot, but I'm going to need cleanup."

"Don't you mean backup?"

"I'm not waiting another second to save Everly," he said and ended the call. Wyatt pocketed the phone and returned to his truck. Removing his AR-15 from the rack, he loaded a clip of twenty-eight bullets.

If Darcy was nearby—and he assumed that she was—he needed the element of surprise. Still, he wanted to make good time and veered from the road, using the surrounding brush as cover. He'd gone less than a hundred yards when he heard it and drew up short.

A gunshot. Once. Twice.

No. Three bullets had been fired in quick succession.

His heart ceased to beat as a vision of Everly's lifeless body came to mind. Once he'd gone down that dark road in his imagination, he could conceive of nothing else. He had to get to her, to save her, to protect her. To convince Everly that he did want to be with her, whether that meant here in Wyoming or joining her back in Chicago. Nothing mattered more than being by her side.

But first, he had to keep her alive.

The hell with being sneaky—Wyatt held tight to the assault rifle and sprinted toward the old schoolhouse. He rounded the building as Darcy Owens came out of the front door.

For a moment, they only stared at each other, neither of them daring to move or speak.

"You're too late," said Darcy. She held a shotgun, the barrel pointed down.

"Drop the gun," he said.

"I'd never hurt you," she said, placing the gun on the ground. Standing, she said, "They're both dead—the sheriff and your girlfriend. I shot him and hanged her. You can shoot me, too. But it won't bring them back—any of them."

He'd heard the gunfire. Why shouldn't he believe Darcy? A burning rage filled Wyatt's chest. Leveling the assault rifle at Darcy, he asked, "Give me one reason why I shouldn't kill you now?"

"Because I did this for *you*," she said. "I killed them *all* for you."

Of all the things that Wyatt expected to hear, that wasn't it. The complete nonsensicalness of her statement stole his breath and left him nauseated.

"This has nothing to do with me."

"Oh, really?" She laughed. "Let me ask you this, Wyatt? Does anything make you feel more alive than hunting a killer? I gave all of that to you. The adrenaline. The danger. The focus. Admit it—it's better than sex."

"I'm not admitting anything to you, Darcy."

"Aren't you proud of me? Don't you think I was clever for fooling them all for so long?"

"I think you're sick," he said. "You've hurt a lot of people. You need to be in prison."

A look of hurt crossed Darcy's face, only to be quickly replaced by a placid expression. "You don't mean that. I know you."

"I don't know you. You definitely don't know me."

"Oh, don't I?"

It was a taunt, nothing more—and yet, Wyatt couldn't help but feel a disturbing stab of accuracy to her statement. She had found him, after all. More than that, she knew exactly how to orchestrate her killings to get him involved in the investigation. He hated to think that Darcy had studied him with the same vigor he'd used to analyze her.

She spoke again. "I watched you in Las Vegas and even knew when you'd arrested the wrong man. I gave you the tip exonerating him. I knew you'd let him go. But you didn't. That was a mistake. I wasn't going to let a man take credit for all my hard work. So, I went to the newspaper instead."

"But why'd you do it, Darcy? Why'd you kill all those people? The victims, those men, were innocent."

"Innocent?" She laughed. "They were dirty. They wanted to make me dirty. I had to clean up the filth."

"Dirty, how? What did they do to you?"

"Smiled. Talked. Touched me. They wanted me to touch them, too. You never, never touch a man. You can never, never want his touch. If you do, the hand has to be made lifeless."

Obviously, this was the missing piece. Darcy had been attracted to her victims and for her, a sexual attraction was akin to a sin so black that death was the only remedy.

"What about Larry Walker? You lived with him in Las Vegas. You followed him to Pleasant Pines."

"Me? Follow him? Wyatt, I took you for a smarter man. I'd never follow the likes of Larry Walker anywhere. He followed me. He never wanted to come to Pleasant Pines. I don't blame him, either. It's too claustrophobic here. But I heard that you'd moved to Wyoming and I knew that you needed me, so I came."

"I don't need you, Darcy. I never have."

"That's the biggest lie I've ever heard."

"Why'd you kill Larry? Was he dirty, too?"

Darcy waved the question away. "Sometimes sacrifices have to be made. The Darkness told me to do it."

"What's the Darkness?" Wyatt asked. All he had to do was keep her talking until the RMJ team could get here.

And where in the hell are they? Goddammit, they should have been here by now!

Darcy smiled and flipped her hair over her shoulder. Was she flirting with Wyatt?

"You know the Darkness."

Maybe she was right. Maybe he did know the darkness. Gripping the rifle's stock tighter, Wyatt's finger caressed the trigger. A single shot and Darcy Owens would be no more. The case would be solved. Wyatt would have the truth and his vengeance with a single bullet.

The wind whipped around the schoolhouse, bringing with it a faint noise. A groan. A creaking. A cry.

"Everly!" Was she still alive? His gaze darted toward the doorway.

In that split instant, Darcy dipped low. The shotgun was in her grasp. Wyatt didn't think. By instinct alone he pulled the trigger. His aim wasn't as true as he hoped. The bullet struck Darcy in the shoulder. The power of the impact knocked her into the wall of the old schoolhouse, painting the worn wood red with her blood. The gun slipped from her grasp. She gripped the wound. Blood filled her hand and cascaded down her arm.

He aimed once more and fired. This time, the bullet tore through the hood of her car, destroying the engine.

Running past Darcy, he retrieved her gun. Coming to the threshold, Wyatt stopped short. The body of Carl Haak was sprawled on the floor, surrounded by a pool of blood, black as tar.

Just beyond hung Everly Baker. A rope was tight around her neck. Her eyelids fluttered. Was it a reflex in death or was Everly still alive?

After setting both weapons aside, Wyatt rushed forward. He grabbed Everly's torso and he took all her weight on his shoulder. He loosened the noose and felt the whisper of Everly's breath on his skin. In the distance, the sound of an approaching vehicle was unmistakable.

RMJ. *Finally.*

Withdrawing a knife from his pocket, he sawed through the rope that held Everly. Once she was free, he laid her on the floor. At the same moment, Marcus Jones, Julia McCloud, and Luis Martinez entered the old schoolhouse.

Sure, they were Marcus's crew, but Wyatt began to bark orders. "We need an ambulance," he said.

"Someone needs to provide first aid to Haak. And someone else has to take Darcy Owens into custody."

Four things happened at once. Julia kneeled next to the sheriff. Martinez removed a cell phone and placed a call. Marcus rushed from the room, apparently ready to apprehend Darcy. In the same instant, Wyatt searched for Everly's pulse. He felt a faint fluttering under his fingertips.

Thank God, she was alive.

Julia dropped back to her heels. The body of Sheriff Haak was unnaturally still. Looking at Wyatt, Julia shook her head. "He's gone," she said.

"We have an ambulance on the way," Martinez said. "How is she?" He meant Everly.

"Alive," said Wyatt. He studied Everly and watched her chest rise and fall. Tracing the angry, red welt around her throat he tried not to think of what would have happened if he'd been distracted by Darcy for a few minutes more.

The wail of a siren filled the quiet morning. "That's the ambulance," said Martinez. "I'll direct them in here."

Martinez passed Marcus at the door. Jones approached Wyatt. The other man's breathing was shallow and sweat coated his brow.

"What is it?" Julia asked.

"She's gone," said Marcus. "Darcy's escaped."

Wyatt was on his feet. "Escaped? That's impossible. She was wounded. I left her by the door."

"It's what I'm telling you, man. She's gone."

"And she wasn't by the door when we arrived," said Julia.

"Damn," Wyatt cursed. "We need to find her."

"We will," said Marcus.

His words were interrupted by two sets of paramedics who passed by with medical bags and stretchers. One group began to check for signs of life with the sheriff while the other tended to Everly.

"We will find Darcy…" said Marcus again.

"There is no *we*. She's *my* mess to clean up," said Wyatt. He moved to the door but couldn't help but look over his shoulder at Everly. She was alive now, but gravely wounded. What were the chances that she could survive a hanging?

"Finding the killer is *our* responsibility," said Marcus.

"Our?"

"Wyatt, you're on a team now. We are all taking a part in this investigation," said Marcus. "You stay here, and I'll take Julia and Martinez with me. If Darcy's as wounded as you say, then we should find her quickly."

Wyatt loathed the idea of leaving the capture to someone else. He wanted more than to see justice served—but also vengeance. All the same, maybe what Wyatt needed right now was a team.

Everly moaned and Wyatt turned to the sound.

"Go," he said to Marcus. "And good luck."

"Yeah," said Marcus, looking at Everly. Then he put a hand on Wyatt's shoulder. "You, too."

Without another word, the other man was gone.

The paramedics had placed Everly on a stretcher that was still flush to the ground. Two IVs were threaded into her hand.

"How is she?" Wyatt asked.

One of the paramedics answered. "We've gotten her stabilized—started both a saline drip and morphine for the pain. But we won't know anything conclusive until we can get her to the hospital and run some tests." The stretcher was lifted. Two sets of legs sprang out from the bottom and they began wheeling her toward the door.

Wyatt stayed at Everly's side as she was moved. He reached for her hand and wondered if she could feel his touch. He hoped like hell that she could. "I'm here," he said as they reached the rear doors to the ambulance. "And I'm not leaving."

Blind with pain, Darcy Owens stumbled through the woods. With each step her strength ebbed away, leaving her in a whirlpool of confusion and despair. Her foot caught, and she tripped, sprawling to the ground. She cried out in pain as her shoulder filled with fire.

Her lips were coated with dirt. She spat. Her spittle was brown with earth and red with blood.

"Get up," a voice snarled at her from behind.

Darcy used the last of her strength to flop to her back. The sun shone at him from behind, yet she recognized him even in shadow.

"Get up," he said again.

She began to quiver. Her father had been dead

for years. He couldn't be here, not now—not unless she was dead…and he had come to drag her to Hell.

"You aren't real," she said. Yes, that was it. She'd lost too much blood and was hallucinating. "You're a figment of my imagination."

He moved out of the shadows and kneeled next to Darcy. She clearly saw the golden flecks in the irises of his eyes. "Am I?" he asked. His stale breath washed over her cheek. It still smelled of whiskey and cigarette smoke.

She recalled other nights when she smelled the stench of the same breath. Darcy's stomach revolted, and she retched on the forest floor.

"Go away," she said. She swatted at him, using the last of her strength.

He grabbed her wrist, his fingers digging painfully into her flesh. "Does this feel like your imagination?"

She jerked her hand away. "What do you want?"

"Now you listen to me, girlie. You need to get up and move."

"I can't," she said. "I'm just so tired."

"If you stay here, they're going to catch you."

"I don't care," she said. Her eyelids were heavy, so heavy. Too heavy.

And then her father disappeared with the mist.

Darcy floated, as if above her body. The woods melted away and for a moment, she was in Las Vegas. As a child, Darcy sought shelter in the Darkness. As an adult, she thought it was no longer needed and hoped the desert sun would chase it all away. What she hadn't understood was that night in the desert was black as pitch. It was then that the Darkness would envelop her. The first time had been an accident. She hadn't meant to hurt him—much less let the Darkness take control.

She'd been lying out by the pool, the noonday sun warming her and filling her with light. Darcy had almost felt normal, whole and human.

A shadow passed over her face.

"Hey," a deep voice had said.

She shielded her eyes and looked up. He stood there, looking down at her, and gave a slow smile.

Her stomach summersaulted, and despite the desert heat, gooseflesh covered her arms.

"Hey," she said.

"You look lonely," he said. "Mind if I join you?"

Darcy felt a smile pull up one corner of her mouth. She ran a hand over her mouth, smothering the ridiculous expression.

"It's a free country."

"Ouch." The man placed his hand on his heart, as if mortally wounded.

This time, Darcy laughed.

"I'll take that as a *yes*," he said, sprawling out on a chaise beside her.

"So, you live here? In Vegas?" he asked.

She nodded, unable to think of something to say.

"It must be great," he said.

Darcy shrugged.

"Listen, I don't want to be a creep. If you want me

to leave—just say so. It's just that you're so pretty, I couldn't help myself."

Darcy stared forward. She'd heard the words before and felt sick with the familiarity. "You're so pretty," her father had said. "I can't help myself."

After, Darcy's mother told her that what happened was all Darcy's fault. She was dirty, and wholly to blame.

It was then that Darkness had come to protect her and keep her safe.

That day, by the pool, the sun had glinted off the water. It was so bright that tears streamed from her eyes, even now.

"Maybe we should hang out this evening," Darcy had said, in a voice that wasn't hers. It had been the Darkness that had invited the man to stay.

The Darkness waited for the nighttime sky to unfold—a chasm of nothing. He drank too much, touched her, kissed her. She couldn't let herself be violated—not again. That's when the Darkness took over. It told her to ply him with more drinks, even after he asked for water. It told her to tear a two-dollar bill in half and put part of the bill in his wallet, using the same money her father used when paying for her silence. The Darkness told her to take the man to the desert, leave him and never look back.

Darcy's shoulder throbbed. She longed to close her eyes and never open them again. There was a rustle in the brush. Using the last of her strength, she turned her head. It was a hulking figure, covered in thick black fur. It growled, the rumbling sound low and menacing.

It took a step toward her and then another. Its eyes were dark brown, almost black, and in them...she saw her own distorted reflection. She was beaten, bruised and certainly no match for the beast. Darcy turned away, no longer caring what happened.

Julia McCloud had spent years in the Army. She was one of the few women accepted to Ranger School. She'd served in combat, hunting the Taliban in the Hindukush mountain range. Most recently, she'd assisted in the apprehension of a Russian Drug Lord in Denver. Yet, after four hours of hunting through the woods, Julia had to wonder how hard was it to find a lone and injured woman?

More than that, she had to admit that she'd lost the trail as soon as they started. "This is a total goat-rope," she said, using the euphemism for what she really wanted to say. "She's gone. Yet, there's no such thing as magic. People don't disappear."

"Is that it?" asked Martinez. "Are we giving up and going back?"

"Rangers don't quit," she said.

Martinez removed a water bottle from his backpack. After taking a drink, he shrugged. Julia read the gesture as *have it your way*.

"By now," said Marcus, "other teams have to be looking for Darcy Owens."

In their haste to find the killer, the RMJ operatives had set out before any other law enforcement officials had arrived. It meant that RMJ led the chase, but it also put them at a disadvantage. They lacked communication and coordination with the other teams. For all they knew, Darcy Owens had been found already.

"One more mile," she said, while scanning the surroundings. There, less than a quarter of a click to the east, was a flash of red. "What's that?" Julia asked before doubling-timing it toward what she had seen.

Martinez and Marcus were on her heels.

Snarled in a tree branch was a small scrap of fabric. At one time, it had been white, but was now covered in blood.

"You think that belongs to Darcy?" Marcus asked.

"The fabric is still tacky, so the blood is fresh," said Martinez. "It hasn't been here long. Maybe a few hours, so I'd say it was a possibility."

Julia examined a nearby snapped twig. The break was still wet with sap. She concurred with Martinez's assessment. "Two hours at the most."

"That means she's close," said Marcus.

Once again, Julia scanned the woods. There were no other broken branches. No underbrush was disturbed. There weren't even drops of blood on the ground. Sure, Darcy was close, but where? There were a million different directions she could have gone.

Even though she'd been honest in saying that Rangers never quit, she also knew something else to be true. It took an Army to win a war.

"Can you get in touch with the state police?" Julia

asked Martinez. She already knew the answer. He was the one carrying the satellite phone.

"Sure can," he said.

"Maybe it's time we bring in some air power," suggested Julia. "With heat sensing radar, they should be able to see everything we can't."

"In finding a trail to follow," said Marcus, "we've done good work. But we aren't done with this case. Until Darcy Owens is found, dead or alive, RMJ will be on the hunt."

Chapter 16

For almost twenty-two hours, Wyatt sat in the hospital, next to Everly's bedside. He drank stale coffee, ate take-out food from Sally's and waited for two things.

First was for Everly to wake up. The second was for news that the team had captured Darcy Owens. It seemed as though the killer, wounded though she was, had walked away from the old schoolhouse and simply vanished.

Of course, there were rumors and theories, supplied by the operatives from RMJ. They ran from the absurd—she'd been hauled off by the same wolves Axl Baker had been sent to photograph—to the probable—she died of her wounds and the harsh Wyoming wilderness had claimed her body.

Then there was the single theory that Wyatt thought was most likely.

Darcy Owens had help during her escape.

That brought up a new question—who would help her? Finding the answer was the next mystery to be solved.

Marcus had also briefed Wyatt on Darcy's background. As it turns out, the Pleasant Pines district attorney, Chloe Ryder, had been a college intern in Darcy's high school. The DA had provided a treasure trove of information about the killer as an adolescent.

More than providing updates, RMJ had proved to be stalwart teammates, bringing Wyatt all those takeout meals. In fact, Marcus had even offered to stay at Wyatt's place and take care of Gus.

The news about Everly was equally vague and unsatisfying. Since Everly's heart beat on its own, and she didn't need any respiratory intervention, Doc Lambert felt that she'd eventually wake.

When?

That was a question he couldn't answer.

Despite the fact that Wyatt wanted Everly taken to a larger hospital in Cheyenne, she didn't have a next-of-kin to contact regarding her care.

It left her medical insurance reviewing treatment options for Everly. The first day came and went and they hadn't contacted Doc Lambert with a plan.

For hours on end, Wyatt watched. Each time Everly drew breath, he held his own, fearful that it might be her last. But Everly stayed alive and it left Wyatt with nothing to do, beyond wait and hope.

At the end of the first day, Everly stirred in her sleep. Wyatt rushed to her side on legs that were fatigued and cramped from the rigid little hospital chairs.

Clasping her hand, he said, "Everly. It's Wyatt. Can you hear me?"

She turned to him and blinked, before closing her eyes and letting out a deep breath. As quickly as he had moved to her side, he was on his feet again and at the door to her hospital room.

"Nurse," he called, both hopeful and alarmed. "Get the doctor. Everly opened her eyes."

The nurse didn't have to do anything. Doc Lambert must've heard Wyatt and the older man came running from a side corridor.

Everly was given a complete physical and within an hour, she was proclaimed to be on the mend—physically, at least. "I don't want you traveling for more than a week," said Doc Lambert. "And for the next few days I need you to stay in the hospital for observation."

"Thanks, Doc," said Wyatt. He had no doubt that he would care for Everly until she recovered.

"Call the nurse if you need anything," he said.

"Will do."

Once the doctor left, Everly swallowed. The red welt around her neck had turned to a purple bruise that was slowly fading to yellow and green. "Darcy Owens?" she asked, her voice a hoarse whisper.

Wyatt shook his head. "She got away. But she won't get far. Everyone in the state is looking for her. Hell, she's the lead story on every newscast. She can't stay hidden long."

Biting her bottom lip, Everly nodded. "Sheriff Haak?"

"Sorry," he said, his voice thick with regret. "He didn't make it."

"How is it that I'm alive, then?" Each time she spoke, her voice became stronger and louder. "I remember the moment that Darcy kicked away the stool. Everything went black and I knew I was dead." Swallowing, she asked, "Who saved me? You?"

Wyatt shrugged. "I wish I would've gotten there earlier…" There was so much more that Wyatt wanted to say, but even now, he couldn't find the words.

"How long have I been in the hospital?" she asked.

"Almost a whole day."

Everly's eyes went wide. "You have to tell me everything."

Wyatt began to speak, ready to use the old cliché—*there's not much to tell*. But that would've been a lie.

Because of the information brought to him by Marcus Jones, Wyatt finally felt as if he understood everything that had motivated Darcy Owens' murderous acts.

"Do you remember Chloe Ryder?"

"The DA we met at Sally's?" asked Everly. "Sure."

He then spent the next several minutes outlining the story he had been given. As a college student studying social work, Chloe had been an intern at Darcy's school. A conversation between the young women had left Chloe uneasy and she suspected abuse at home. As per legal requirements, she reported her suspicions to her supervisor. They questioned Darcy, who denied everything and said that Chloe had been mistaken. Since there was no evidence, no action was taken.

A few weeks later, Darcy's father was found dead.

"Let me guess," said Everly. "He drank too much and got lost outside."

"Your guess would be right. But there's more. A few weeks following, her mother committed suicide. Death by hanging. Everyone assumed that her mother was broken-hearted over losing her husband. After that, Darcy dropped out of school and wasn't heard from again."

Everly shuddered. "Is she recreating the accidental deaths of both her parents?"

"Could be," said Wyatt. "Or perhaps, those two were Darcy's original victims and she's just been repeating the same crimes again and again."

"I don't know what to say." Everly's voice was weak again.

"Just rest," he said. "I'll be here when you wake up."

Everly smiled. "Thanks."

Her eyes drifted closed. After a moment, she opened them again. "What do we do now?"

"We focus on you," Wyatt said. He reached for her palm. "You are going to rest and get better."

She stroked the back of his hand. "And after that? What then?"

That was the exact question Wyatt had been asking himself for almost an entire day. "It's not safe for you to travel yet, with Darcy still at large. As far as we know, you're the only person she's tried to kill who survived. Until she's caught, I'm not leaving your side. Once you can travel, I'll go back to Chicago. And after she's captured…" Pausing, he looked at his hands. Was he really ready to commit to Everly? He knew damn well that he wasn't going to be able to let her walk out of his life again. He spoke. "After she's captured, I'll stay, that is, if you'll have me."

"What about the search for Darcy? Don't you want to get back out there and find her?"

"Sure," said Wyatt. "But sometimes priorities change."

Everly shook her head. "I don't believe for a minute that you want to be in Chicago with me while the search for Darcy is happening in Wyoming."

"What I want doesn't matter anymore," he said. "I need to keep you safe. Dammit, Everly. You've become everything to me. I thought I lost you once." His mind was filled with an image of her seemingly lifeless body as it hung from the rafters. Closing his eyes, he waited for the picture and ensuing feeling of loss and loneliness to pass. "I never want to lose you again."

Everly reached for his arm. "I'm not going anywhere," she said. "You and I, we're a team—a family. It doesn't matter whether we're in Chicago or here. There's a lot to love about Pleasant Pines—like you."

Wyatt's chest expanded until it ached. He took a knee beside her bed. Brushing the hair from her forehead, Wyatt placed a kiss on her brow. "I love you so much that it hurts."

"Oh, Wyatt," she said, tracing his jaw with a light touch. "I love you, too."

"So that's it?" he asked. "You'll stay?"

"There's no place else I'd rather be than here, with you." She paused and smiled. "Well, maybe not in the hospital, but you get my point."

He did indeed.

He drew her into an embrace and his mouth laid claim to hers. And there, in the small and stuffy hospital room, their life could start fresh.

The hunt could wait.

Epilogue

Two weeks later

Wyatt sat behind the desk and looked to the window. There was nothing beyond opaque glass for him to see. He missed the view from his house of the Rocky Mountains and the clear blue sky. At the same time, he reveled in his newfound purpose.

Before Everly was released from the hospital, Marcus had again asked Wyatt to join RMJ. Without hesitation, he accepted.

Chloe Ryder had hired RMJ to serve as the investigative body for the district attorney's office and Wyatt's first job would be to lead the hunt for the still at-large killer.

"Knock, knock."

He recognized the voice without having to look.

"Everly." Wyatt sat at his desk, set within a cubicle in a large and open work space. Aside from Wyatt, the room was empty. All other operatives were out.

"I know that you are still getting settled at work, but I wanted to bring a little something for your office." She held out a white box with a big red bow. "I told Marcus I would be stopping by and he let me in," she continued, explaining how she had circumvented RMJ's extreme security.

"Thanks," he said as he lifted the lid. Inside was a framed photo of Everly and Gus, with the Rocky Mountains serving as the backdrop. His family. His home. Wyatt's throat tightened a little.

"Just a little reminder of what's waiting for you at the end of the workday," she said. "And speaking of workdays, I have my first Pleasant Pines client."

In the weeks since she decided to stay, she'd joined a public relations firm in Laramie, forty-five minutes south of town. It was a hefty commute and she planned to work from home as much as possible. Still, he was impressed that she'd already landed a local client.

"Already? Who?"

"The sheriff's department," she said. "The media coverage they've been getting has been awful. I have a meeting in a little bit with Chloe Ryder. Once we present our side of the events, the story will become more balanced."

Everly paused and Wyatt knew what she was thinking. He answered the question before she had a chance to ask. "There's nothing new in the search for Darcy or her body," he said.

Everly gave a quick nod. "I wish we knew something," she said. "That's all."

He did as well, yet he said nothing. He set the photo on his desk. "I like the space better already."

"See you tonight?" she said.

He wrapped his arms around Everly's waist and pulled her onto his lap. Pressing his lips to hers, he gave her a languid kiss. "See you tonight."

He wanted to hold her forever, not just because she felt so damned nice in his arms, but because Darcy Owens was still out there—somewhere. Until they found the killer and put her in prison, nobody would be safe.

The hunt had begun again.

This time it was more than about public safety and justice. For Wyatt, catching Darcy Owens was a personal fight. And he didn't intend to lose.

Darcy awoke with a start. Her throat was parched. Her eyes were swollen. Her shoulder throbbed, and the stench of rot surrounded her. She sat up. Blinding pain split her skull and she leaned back with a groan.

"You up?" a deep male voice asked.

She opened her eyes the slightest bit. A hulking figure stood at the end of her bed. His face was covered in wiry, black hair. His eyes were just tiny dots and his mouth nothing more than a slash.

"You up?" he asked again.

"Yes," she croaked.

"Drink this," he said. A large and powerful arm snaked behind Darcy's back and lifted her. A cup was pressed to her lips and water trickled down her throat.

The man stepped away and she sank into the pillow.

"What happened?" she asked, her mind foggy.

"You were shot," said the man. "I found you in the woods and brought you here."

It all became clear and Darcy's pulse began to race. Her shoulder pounded with each beat of her heart. "Where am I? How long have I been here?"

"You're in my bunker," the man said. "I saw the news. It looks like you're in a heap of trouble, so I haven't said nothing to the police."

Darcy's pulse slowed, more confused than thankful. "Why are you hiding me?"

The hulking man said, "I've been in trouble with the law before. I won't ever help those bastards."

Her eyes began to drift closed. She was still so tired.

Wake up, the Darkness whispered in Darcy's ear. She pried her lids open and her hand went to her throat. Cold and hard, a chain was bolted to her neck. Icy terror dropped into her middle.

The large man grinned as her eyes went wide.

"Who are you?" she asked. "What have you done?"

"As far as who I am," said the man. "I'm Billy Dawson. And what have I done?" He scratched his wiry beard. "Since I saved you, you owe me."

Darcy's breath was trapped in her chest. She wasn't sure she'd ever be able to breathe again.

Look, the Darkness whispered in Darcy's ear. There, in the corner, was an ax. The blade glinted in the firelight.

If she wanted to survive, she'd have to do more than embrace the Darkness, but allow it to take over completely.

"You're right," she said to the man. "You did rescue me. Without you, I'd either be dead or in jail."

He smiled, thinking that he'd somehow won.

Flicking her gaze quickly to the ax, Darcy smiled, as well. Just as Billy had been her savior, she was certain to be his damnation.

* * * * *

LET'S TALK

Romance

For exclusive extracts, competitions
and special offers, find us online:

 facebook.com/millsandboon

 @MillsandBoon

 @MillsandBoonUK

Get in touch on 01413 063232

For all the latest titles coming soon, visit
millsandboon.co.uk/nextmonth